# The Western Passage

## Part 2: Arrival

# G. DiCarlo

Black Rose Writing | Texas

ISBN: 978-1-68433-603-6
PUBLISHED BY BLACK ROSE WRITING
www.blackrosewriting.com

Printed in the United States of America
Suggested Retail Price (SRP) $20.95

*The Western Passage: Arrival* is printed in Palatino Linotype

*As a planet-friendly publisher, Black Rose Writing does its best to eliminate unnecessary waste to reduce paper usage and energy costs, while never compromising the reading experience. As a result, the final word count vs. page count may not meet common expectations.

*For my mom –*
*Thanks for being the Lorelai to my Rory*
*(and for always letting me borrow your clothes)*

# The Western Passage

## Part 2: Arrival

# Far and Away

*Come to me, last love of mine*
*Come to me,*
*As the seas of the world run dry*
*Leaving a story of scars along their empty ocean floors*
*And beds of seaweed that can sway no more in their currents*
*As the fish and birds and animals disappear one by one.*
*Come to me, last love of mine*
*Come to me,*
*As the dying begins, as the dying ends*
*As the whole world sighs its final breath and goes dark*
*As the stars go out and the air grows cold*
*And all things exhale in final expiration.*
*Come to me, last love of mine*
*Come to me.*
*Come to me ...Before I too am gone*

- Final stanzas of 'The Dying', a poem transcribed from the oral
tradition of Clan Ayume

·   ·   ·   ·   ·

The river at the edge of the valley was unusually calm, its current no
more than a gentle susurrus, quieter even than the breeze rustling the

trees in the distance. Soft morning sunlight glinted off the river's surface as the water moved, interrupted only by the orange hue of a passing fish.

On any other morning, Ilona would have found it a welcome sight. On this morning, however, the rustic beauty was lost on her. In a few hours, nothing would ever be the same again, and no matter how idyllic the morning seemed, it could not banish that truth.

"You should be coming with us, Vale," she repeated for what felt like the hundredth time that day.

Her companion responded with a half-hearted shrug of his broad shoulders. "It's not my decision to make, Ilona. You know that."

"I know. It was our Guardian's decision, and her word on the matter was final. Clan Kiernan is to go east, to join the conclave."

Vale's brow creased. "I know," he said. "But my father has come to his own decision and I must abide by it." His blue eyes met her brown ones, and Ilona could see regret there, among other things. "I don't have a choice in the matter."

Ilona could feel her anger building. "Yes, you do, Vale," she countered. She reached out and took his hand—a familiar gesture after so many years. "Your father is making a mistake. It's not right to break from the rest of the clan. Come with us, Vale. Come with me."

A pained smile crossed her friend's face. "Trust me, I wish I could." He put his hand on top of her own and squeezed once before pressing her away. "But I've got my brother to think about," he said. "And my mother. I need to stay for them."

"But what if our Guardian is right?" Ilona asked, her voice dropping. "What if something *is* coming? Something bad? You'll be all alone here. Vulnerable."

"If something comes, I'll fight it."

*Idiot.* "Really, Vale? That's your plan?" She crossed her arms over her chest. "That's a lot of bravado for someone who hasn't so much as bared his fangs before."

Vale's chest puffed out in indignation. "Just because I choose not to get fired up every time someone tries to get a rise out of me doesn't mean I can't bare my fangs. If I have to, I will."

"Vale—"

"Just leave it alone, Ilona. Please. It's decided. Nothing you say is going to change that."

Ilona pursed her lips but said nothing else. What could she do? She understood where Vale was coming from, even if she hated it. Putting family before clan was frowned upon, but she knew how much Vale loved his gangly kid brother. If their situations were reversed, she wasn't sure she would be able to abandon her family.

Still…

"What am I going to do without you?" She asked at last, finally voicing the question closest to her heart. "I can't remember a day I didn't see you, didn't talk to you. You and I…we've always been together. I don't want to lose you."

Before she could protest, Vale pulled her into a tight hug. "Same," he said as he held her. "You're my best friend in the world, Ilona. I'm going to miss you terribly."

Ilona hugged him back, taking comfort in the feeling of his arms around her. "Will you at least try and persuade your father to reconsider?" She asked into his chest.

She felt him nod against her. "Yeah. I promise. Maybe a few weeks without the clan will soften his stubbornness, make him realize community is more important than a piece of land."

The sound of the horn startled both of them, and they broke apart.

Ilona tucked a lock of dark hair behind her ear. "It's time," she said. "I have to go."

Vale gave her a smile that made her want to cry. "Come on, then," he said, trying to be strong for both of them. "I'll walk you back."

．　．　．　．　．

The first few days following the clan's departure were the hardest, and Vale found himself feeling lonelier than he ever had before. The once-bustling streets were deserted, and his home had become a ghost town. No bells rang, no doors opened, no children ran by, no old women clucked at him as he went about his chores. Instead of voices, all he heard were his own footfalls.

Worst of all was the absence of Ilona. She had been his best friend since before he could remember, all the way back to infancy when their mothers had sat beside each other and held them against their breasts. Losing her was like losing a part of himself, and Vale found it hard to do anything but be depressed.

He tried, though, because his little brother needed him to. Liam was only four, and he was scared. He didn't understand why they had stayed when everyone else had gone away, and he cried from the time he woke up to the time their mother shushed him to sleep each night. So Vale steeled himself against his own sense of loss and tried to make things a little easier for his brother.

A week passed, then two, and slowly, the emptiness of the town began to seem normal. Liam stopped crying all the time, and Vale started to spend more time away from home once he'd completed his daily chores.

At first, he just wandered aimlessly, but then he started to actively canvass Clan Kiernan's territory.

One night, long past dusk, he even made it as far as the neighboring valley. There was a herd of large game animals sprawled across it, the likes of which he'd never seen before. He hid on the slope of a hill and observed them quietly for a time, awed by their number. Unaware of his presence, the animals grazed as the moon rose in the sky.

*Liam would love this*, Vale thought as he watched them. Maybe he could convince his father to let him bring Liam here to see them. Maybe all of them could go.

For the first time since Clan Kiernan's departure, Vale felt lighthearted as he made his way back home. The novelty of the animals had given him something to look forward to, and he was grateful for it.

It was a nice distraction from the fact that his father hadn't budged on the issue of their remaining on clan land. Still, Vale hadn't forgotten his promise to Ilona; he would continue to chip away at his father's resolve. He would make headway eventually—he was sure of it.

His thoughts occupied him all the way home, and Vale was so wrapped up in his own head that he didn't realize what he was hearing until it was too late.

There were voices in the town—voices that did not belong to his family members.

Vale was upon them before he realized, and then he stopped dead in his tracks, his eyes going wide at the sight before him.

There was a gathering in the town's main thoroughfare, a mass of strange figures.

The creatures were not vampires—they had distorted bodies and horrible faces, humanoid but grotesque, with teeth and claws that were completely alien to Vale.

The strange beings seemed to notice Vale at the same moment he noticed them, dozens of dead, black eyes homing in on him in an instant that seemed to last an eternity. Then they began to cluck and screech, the sound like metal on metal, and – to Vale's horror – they started to move towards him. Their movements were slow at first, as if they were confused by his presence, but the speed didn't lessen Vale's sense of dread.

He stepped back instinctively. "What the hell...?"

The sound of his voice stirred the foreign mass, and all at once the bizarre calm was shaken. They answered his vocalization in a cacophony of snarls and then gained speed, racing towards him.

"Shit!" Vale cursed as he stumbled backwards, and then he began to run, terror and panic overtaking him. He turned off the main street and raced out into the valley, trying to put distance between himself and the creatures. He had no idea where he was running to, or how he would get away from so many, but it didn't matter.

He glanced over his shoulder to see how far back they were, and then he tripped, falling over his own feet and slamming into the ground.

"Shit!" He cursed again. He rolled over, looking wildly at his pursuers.

Ten yards, five yards, two...

A howl pierced the night, and suddenly the creatures stopped.

Vale froze, not even daring to breathe.

The creatures parted, carving a path in their midst.

A lone figure emerged in the parted space and walked forward, drawing towards Vale. Unlike the mindless stupor the horde had seemed earlier to possess, the figure's slow gait was calm—almost leisurely. Vale stayed where he was, squinting as he watched the thing approach him.

It didn't look like the rest. In fact, it almost looked like a vampire.

Vale swallowed. "Hello?" He asked. "Are you a friend of Clan Kiernan?"

Finally, the moonlight shone upon the mysterious figure, and Vale's hope was crushed in an instant.

Whatever it was, it was not a vampire.

The figure was female, and had fangs, but she was not one of his own kind.

Her light brown skin was beautiful but looked somehow wrong, like flesh that had been stretched and fitted over steel. What he had mistaken at first for armor was actually part of her person, thorn-like projections that rose off of her arms and spine and glinted sharply in the moonlight. In one clawed hand she grasped a sword. In the other, she was holding his mother's head.

Without ceremony, she threw it at Vale's feet.

Vale flinched away from it, horrified beyond words.

Unable to do anything else, he looked up and met the creature's eyes.

They were a shining silver, as mesmerizing as they were cold. As their eyes met, the creature smiled at him, displaying a row of serrated fangs covered in blood.

"You must be Vale," she said. Her voice was a jarring contrast to her person, mellifluous and smooth. Blood dripped from her teeth as she spoke, running down her chin and falling onto the breastplate she wore and down to the grass below.

Vale stared back at her in silence, too shocked to react.

"Your father sends his regards too," she continued, "but alas—I could only carry one trophy for you."

*Run*, his mind urged. *Kill her. Kill them. Get away. Do something. Anything.*

"Why?" The word was a choked cry.

The creature raised a graceful eyebrow at him. "They didn't supply me with the answers I needed."

"What answers?" He screamed at her. "Where is my brother?"

The silver eyes never changed. "Tell me where your clan has run off to."

Vale shook his head. "No."

The smile widened. "No?" He saw her clawed fingers flex. "Do you really think it wise to say no to me, boy?"

"You killed my family!" He cried. "I don't care what you think!"

"Not all of them," she responded without remorse. She motioned to one of the creatures behind her, and Vale cowered as he saw the hideous thing pull a small, terrified figure out of the mass.

"Vale!" Liam cried. There were tears pouring down his brother's small cheeks.

The sight of his brother broke Vale's stupor. He scrambled to his feet. "Let him go!" He screamed, baring his fangs and letting his claws descend.

The female held up a hand. "Answer my question," she said.

Vale looked around at the silver-eyed creature's entourage. They were twitching, itching to move, looking like they wanted to rip him limb from limb. Vale had experienced bloodlust of his own before, had gone on a blood fast once just to know what true hunger would feel like, but never—*never* had he experienced the kind of mad thirst he saw reflected in the creatures surrounding him.

*I can't tell them,* he knew. *I can't. These things…they'll kill Ilona. They'll kill everyone. They'll massacre my people.*

But they had Liam.

Vale took a breath, hating himself to the core of his very being. "They headed east two weeks ago," he confessed. "They are following the interior forest trail."

The female cocked her head at him, as if assessing his words. Finally, she nodded. "Very well."

She lifted her sword and moved with catlike agility and speed, her purpose clear.

Vale cried out *"stop!"*, reflexively stretching out his hands even though he was too far away to do anything but witness her brutality.

Liam's scream was brief.

Vale's was unending. He fell to his knees, sobbing, his clawed fingers digging into the grass.

Suddenly, the sharp edge of a long talon was below his chin, forcing his head up.

The silver eyes were right there, as cold as diamonds.

"I told you the truth," he sobbed. "Why would you...?" He couldn't finish the sentence.

Once more, the woman's mouth opened into a vicious, bloody smile. "Because I wanted to," she said simply. She leaned towards him, pressing her fangs against his skin. He felt her inhale, and then she hummed, as if relishing the scent of his blood, of his fear.

Vale shoved her, hard, and then he lunged at her, fangs snapping. She evaded his jaws with ease.

"I will kill you for what you've done," he hissed at her, hating her more than he'd ever hated anything before.

The female straightened and laughed at him. It was a deep, awful sound. "No, you won't." Then she turned to her minions and barked out a single word. "Feed."

The horde descended on Vale.

He screamed and fought, but it made no difference. There were too many of them, and everywhere he turned, every strike he made, was met with teeth and pain and horror.

The last thing he saw were silver eyes, watching without emotion as he was eaten alive.

. . . . .

The night was anything but quiet. A chorus of laughter and boisterous conversations filled the air, mixed together with the mellifluous sounds of voices raised in song and the vibrato-rich timbre, somewhere farther off, of a lone violin.

From her perch on the wooded ridge, Aya could see and hear it all, and while she took comfort in the sounds, she was content to be a silent observer.

It wasn't that she didn't share her companions' excitement. She did. The group had had its first morph encounter since Aya had joined them four days earlier, and the Moravec warriors had decimated them. Not a single vampire had perished, and everyone was basking in the residual highs of victory. They were set to cross the border into the northern territories two days hence, they'd had a successful hunt, and the storm that had darkened the sky had passed them over, the foreboding clouds moving south.

Aya hoped it wasn't headed for Marcus and the others, but she had no way of knowing.

"I take it you're not one for festivities?"

Aya turned, surprised to realize that she was no longer alone. An old vampire had joined her on the ridge, a man she vaguely recognized. He was tall and impossibly thin, his clothes hanging on his bony frame, and his face was lined with wrinkles. And yet despite his age and his gauntness he was handsome, his features sharp and intelligent, his bearing proud and dignified.

He came to stand beside her, offering her a sympathetic smile. "I don't blame you," he said. "In my younger years I appreciated nights like this, but now I favor rest." He inclined his head. "I know you've seen a great many new faces over the past few days, so in case you've forgotten this old one, I'm Solomon."

Aya returned his smile with a bit of effort. "Aya."

He chuckled. "Oh, I know who you are, child. Everyone in our party knows who you are. It's not often we come across sisters or brothers with such a…unique backstory." He gave her a knowing glance. "I'm guessing that's why you're hiding out up here. You don't strike me as someone who enjoys being the center of attention."

He wasn't wrong. Ever since Esfir had escorted her to the camp, Aya had felt like something of a celebrity. Everyone wanted to meet her and hear her story. She hadn't minded answering questions at first, but after a few days of it, she was feeling drained.

Still, their curiosity was understandable, and leaving during the midst of a celebration had probably been viewed as a slight. Aya felt a blush rising to her cheeks. "I apologize if I seem ungracious," she said. "I've enjoyed meeting and talking with everyone. I just needed some time to…process everything."

"No need to apologize," Solomon said. "I understand. Everything must still be so new to you."

Aya nodded. "It is." It was somewhat embarrassing to admit that, after being alone for so long and then being in the company of humans, she'd forgotten what it was like to be with her own people.

"Well, if you have any questions, please ask. I've been traveling with this group for nearly two years and I've spent countless years with other tribes before that. I'm not so far off from being a walking history book. Or a walking gossip column, for that matter. I've seen and heard it all."

Aya smiled, genuinely this time. Solomon had a relaxed, good-natured demeanor that was infectious, and there was something honest about him that made Aya feel comfortable in his presence.

"I am curious about a few things," she admitted.

Below them, the violin stopped playing and there was a chorus of applause. Then the player began another tune. It was slower and reflective, eschewing the earlier virtuosity in favor of a somber, minor melody.

Solomon closed his eyes for a moment, listening. Then he sighed. "My father used to sing that song to me when I was a child," he said as he eased himself down onto the ground. "It still reminds me of home." He rested his back against a tree and patted the ground beside him. "Have a seat, Aya. I'm happy to answer your questions, but my legs aren't what they used to be."

Aya joined him on the ground, folding her legs beneath her. "Where is home?" She asked once she was settled.

Solomon's eyes clouded over. "Far, far away," he answered quietly, his age suddenly showing on the planes of his face. "Nothing more than a memory now, like so many other places."

Aya recognized the gravel in his voice for what it was. After all, she knew what loss was, intimately. "I'm sorry," she said, meaning it.

"No need to be, child. If you live to be as old as I am, change and loss are inevitable companions." His gaze turned perceptive as he looked at her. "What pains me is when I see someone so young who understands those companions as well as I do."

The sympathy in his expression was so genuine that Aya had to look away to keep her emotions in check. It would be easy to yield her strength, to fall to pieces and grieve in front of someone who would understand, but she didn't want to. She wasn't sure she would be able to put herself back together again if she did. The only reason she'd survived her last breakdown was because Marcus had been there to hold her together.

*Marcus...*

She looked out into the distance, her fingers ghosting over the leather strings tied around her neck.

"So," Solomon said at length, breaking their silence. "What are you curious about?"

Aya refocused her attention on the old vampire. *Everything*, she thought. Their customs were different from what she remembered of her time growing up in her own clan, and there were a great many things she was curious about, including some of the people. General Crow immediately came to mind—the dark-skinned, charismatic vampire leader was as intriguing as he was handsome, but Aya decided against asking about him. Her father had always said that the best way to judge someone's character was to discover it for yourself, not to inherit a second-hand opinion. So instead of speaking of General Crow, Aya asked about something she'd observed that was completely foreign to her.

"I was approached yesterday by a young vampire who offered me her blood. I didn't accept, and she seemed almost offended when I turned her away."

"Do you remember the girl's name?"

"Irina."

"Ah. Irina is a donor."

The term was not one that Aya was familiar with. "A donor?"

Instead of clarifying, Solomon responded with a question. "Tell me, Aya, are you of Clan Ayume?"

"Yes," Aya said, surprised. "How did you know?"

"Well, aside from the whispers spreading through camp in regard to your lineage, I spent time with members of your clan a number of years ago. You look like them. Also, Clan Ayume is one of the only clans that does not use donors. Putting all that together, I made an educated guess."

"What are donors?"

"Vampires that dedicate their blood to their clan. They allow others to feed on them during dry times when other blood sources are scarce—it is their primary function. Now, anyway. In the old days, it was also traditional for the mightiest warriors to drain a donor before a battle to increase their strength, though that practice is extinct."

"That's barbaric," Aya said, affronted.

"It was also purely voluntary. Donors were never forced into service, then or now. They choose that life."

"But why?"

"Because each of us has our place, our role to play. Donors may not have the fortitude of warriors or the wisdom of Guardians, but they have selfless hearts and wish to contribute to society in the best way they can." Solomon paused. "That's not to say that I haven't seen donors abused over the years, because I have, but in every instance the abuser was dealt with very severely. Most of the time, though, donors are treated with profound respect."

Aya considered Irina's wounded reaction the previous day. "I should make amends to Irina, then," she mused.

Solomon nodded. "Yes. Irina most likely approached you as a sign of good will and welcome. You should apologize and accept her offer. I know Irina, and she is not one to hold grudges. If you correct your mistake, she will not hold it against you." His expression turned curious. "Besides, I imagine you must be hungry. I haven't seen you feed since you joined us."

"I haven't," Aya admitted. "But I also haven't had hunger pains. I'm used to blood rationing."

Solomon was quiet for a moment. "If you don't mind my asking, where did you get blood when you were with the humans?" He said at length.

Aya felt a pang of longing. She looked away. "One of the humans gave me his blood when I needed it."

She felt Solomon shift beside her. "More than once?"

Aya nodded. "Yes."

He was silent for so long that Aya looked back at him, her brow furrowing. "Is that something I should keep to myself?" She asked.

Solomon's expression was strange. "That's not the right question," he answered cryptically, mystifying her further. His gaze became inquisitive. "Do you know why this human let you drink from him multiple times?"

Of course she did. Marcus had told her why, plainly, on more than one occasion. "He needed me to be at my strongest so I could help protect our group," she answered, but as soon as the words left her mouth, she realized that Marcus hadn't ever actually said that.

*I owe you.*

*You don't look well.*

*Do you need blood?*

*Take what you need.*

Every time, even when she'd refused, it had been about her. *She'd* been the focus. Not the group. Her.

And now, suddenly, she was as curious to know the answer to Solomon's question as the old vampire was.

*Why, Marcus? Why did you let me feed from you?*

It had to have been for the group's benefit. Nothing else made sense.

Solomon was watching her pensively. "So, it wasn't quite that simple, was it?" He asked finally, clearly aware that she was experiencing some kind of inner tumult.

Aya swallowed. "Maybe not." She cleared her throat and looked down to where the rest of the group was still actively celebrating.

"Do you miss them?" Solomon asked, his voice quieter than before.

Aya frowned. "I shouldn't," she murmured, fingering idly at the leather strings tied around her neck. *I shouldn't, but I do.*

Solomon exhaled slowly and stood up. "Never let fear of someone else's opinion dictate how you feel, Aya," he said, gazing down at her. There was gentleness in his eyes, and a weariness she couldn't quite define. "The world needs new feelings—better feelings. It needs people to come together. So if you miss the humans you were traveling with, good. I for one see that as a sign that change is possible, even in this age of hatred." He smiled. "I know I'm as old as the dirt you're sitting on, but I like to think I still have my wits about me, so if you ever have questions or need help, ask." He reached down and gently patted her shoulder. "And remember, child: it's not a crime to be different."

Before Aya could formulate a response, Solomon straightened and made his way back down the ridge, and Aya watched him, lost in thought.

· · · · ·

"We lost another one."

Clio's words were one more knife in Marcus's gut. "Fuck," he cursed. "Who?"

"Annette—Colleen's younger sister."

"She wasn't even sick yesterday."

The concerned frown marring Clio's face deepened. "I know. She fell ill late last night and by this morning…" He shook his head. "If the illness continues spreading at this rate, we're going to lose more than half our group in a matter of days. The prognosis is not good."

*That* was the understatement of the fucking month. Ever since the snowstorm had hit a few days earlier, conditions had been steadily getting more hazardous. The worst of the snowdrifts along their path were almost waist deep, and between that and the biting winds, the group's progress had slowed considerably. And then, two days earlier, sickness had broken out in their numbers and they'd been forced to stop completely, taking shelter in a series of cramped caves on the leeward side of a small mountain. It was better than being exposed to the elements, but not by much. They didn't have proper shelter, provisions, or medicine, and no one that had taken ill was getting better. And now, counting Annette, three people had died.

Marcus gazed out into the white bleakness ahead of him. Yesterday, he'd tried to navigate ahead to the nearest bunker, which was, at most, two miles away. He'd taken Sloane and Enwezor with him, but they'd been forced to turn back when the storm had picked up. Two stupid miles and they hadn't made it. Two stupid fucking miles.

Marcus's frustration was at its boiling point. "Screw it," he spat. "I'm going to try for the bunker again. We need food and medicine." A chill shot through him, making him shiver. "And warmer clothes."

Clio sighed. "As suicidal an idea as that is, I can't argue with you. There's no telling when this storm will abate, and we can't risk waiting."

He cinched the belt of his heavy cloak more tightly about his waist. "I'll go find us two empty packs."

Marcus glanced up at the hybrid. "You're not coming. I need you here."

"With all due respect, Captain, I *am* coming. You can't take Sloane and Enwezor again—they've barely recovered from yesterday and temperatures are lower today. You need someone who will be less affected by the cold, and right now, I am your only option. I'm coming with you."

Jones was right, Marcus knew, but he was still reluctant to agree. With Aya gone, he and Clio were the strongest fighters left. If they both headed for the bunker, that would mean leaving the civilians alone in the care of Enwezor and Sloane. They were capable kids, but they wouldn't be able to defend everyone if there was an attack, and neither of them would be able to lead the group safely to Ashland, for the simple reason that neither of them knew the route.

"We can't both go," he decided. "We are the only two people who know how to get to Ashland from here. If something happened to us, everyone else would be stranded."

"Then you know what the solution is."

Marcus did know, but he still didn't answer right away. He assessed Jones quietly, weighing the options. The hybrid was a formidable fighter—he'd proven that time and again, and he was also intelligent and resilient and knew how to handle himself on solo missions. Still, Marcus didn't trust anyone more than he trusted in his own abilities. By letting Clio go in his place, he would be effectively putting the group's survival in the hybrid's hands.

*There are still people you can rely on.*

The words came to him in the echo of Aya's voice, and as asinine as it was, it gave him a sense of reassurance.

"All right," he relented. "You can go. If you're not back by the time the storm abates, I'll have the group press forward." *If they're able to*, he added to himself.

Clio nodded. "I won't come back without medicine," he said, and then he paused. "Thank you," he added softly, "for trusting me with this. It is a trust I will not break."

Marcus didn't reply. He watched Jones gather supplies and head out into the white swirling snow beyond the cave, and then he trudged outside and walked the twenty feet or so to the nearest cave, where many of the civilians were holed up.

He found Jillian furthest from the cave entrance, tending to Colleen—the remaining Renault sister. Cody was standing beside her.

The ill girl was lying on a makeshift pallet of cloaks and coats, and she was coughing violently. There was a sickly sheen of fever on her brow, and her thick brown hair was damp with sweat.

Jillian mopped the moisture away from the girl's face with a piece of fabric she was using as a rag and glanced up. "How is it looking out there?"

Marcus shook his head, feeling helpless. "Not good, but Jones went out to try for the bunker. I'll let you know when he gets back."

Jillian nodded and turned back to her patient.

Marcus began to walk away when Cody Reade ran up and tapped his arm. He stopped and turned, looking down into a pair of amber eyes that looked so much like Maggie's that it was painful.

"Sloane and Zor were looking for you," she said quietly. "They don't know what to do with the bodies. I think they moved them to one of the other caves for now because people were getting upset."

There was no emotion in her voice, just a somber frankness that was unsettling to see in a six-year-old, but understandable. The rosiness of her short childhood was over, blotted out by an adult understanding of the world that had stained whatever ignorant innocence she'd once had.

It struck Marcus that looking at Cody Reade now was like looking into a childhood mirror of himself.

He crouched down, feeling a painful wave of empathy for Maggie's orphaned daughter. "I'll find Sloane and Enwezor and sort it out," he said, trying to sound reassuring. "You stay here and keep Jillian safe, all right?"

The little girl nodded gravely. "Yes, Captain."

Marcus rose to his feet. He felt like he needed to say something else, but he wasn't sure what to add and Cody didn't seem to be waiting for some kind of parting remark, so he just nodded lamely and headed out into the snow.

It was blowing down in white, swirling sheets, limiting his visibility considerably and drenching his clothes. Marcus gritted his teeth and pressed forward, keeping his head down as much as possible.

*Only twenty paces to the next cave, shit stain,* Stan's voice taunted in his head. *Just muscle through it.*

And he would have done just that, if it hadn't been for the morph.

It attacked so quickly that Marcus didn't even have time to draw a weapon.

·   ·   ·   ·   ·

The battle – such that it was – was over quickly, but the fact that they'd won and that the handful of morphs were lying dead in the snow did little to ease Enwezor's anxiety. For starters, he'd never seen Cap look this bad after a fight before. A few unlucky others had sustained bites and scratches during the chaos of the attack, but no one had been injured as grievously as Marcus. The Reaper was bleeding from multiple wounds, and the fresh claw marks running down the left side of his chin and neck were glistening brightly against his skin, a very visible reminder that, even though he'd eventually overcome his opponent, some morph had at least momentarily gotten the better of him.

And if Cap wasn't faring well, that couldn't possibly bode well for the rest of them.

For probably the fourth time in as many minutes, Enwezor sidled closer to where Savannah Wix was bandaging Cap.

"How are you feeling?" He asked. "Can I do anything?"

Marcus glared at him. "Balogun, I know you mean well, but if you ask me either of those questions again, I'm going to rip these bandages off and stuff them in your mouth. Please save me the hassle and shut the hell up."

*Typical.*

Well, at least he knew the wounds weren't affecting the Reaper's sense of humor.

Enwezor held his hands up. "Fine, I'll quit asking. I'm just worried, is all. This is the second time we've run into morphs this week. Where the hell could they possibly be coming from in weather like this?"

Marcus shook his head. "Hell if I know, but as soon as this storm passes—" He cut off mid-sentence, reaching out as Savannah suddenly collapsed into him. "Hey!" He exclaimed as she fell.

Enwezor only noticed then how pale the girl was. "Shit, Savannah, are you okay?" He asked as Marcus steadied her.

She shivered. "I'll be—" she started to say, before she dissolved into a fit of coughs.

Marcus waited until she was done before gently helping her to her feet. "I'll go get Jillian," he said grimly, but Savannah shook her head.

"No. I need Clio."

"He's not back yet."

The look of panic in her eyes was bright. "But I…I…" she sputtered, and then her eyes rolled back and she crumpled where she stood. Marcus caught her again, preventing her from falling, fresh blood seeping from the bandages on his neck because of the strain.

Enwezor strode forward. "Let me," he said, reaching for the unconscious girl.

Marcus started to protest but Enwezor took her from his arms anyway. "You're dead on your feet, Cap. Just let me help. You don't have to do everything yourself."

A strange, complicated expression appeared in Marcus's eyes, but he stepped back and nodded. "All right." He sighed. "Put her down in the corner and prop her head up with one of the packs. Then go get Jillian. I know she's tending to other people, but they'll have to wait. We can't lose Wix—the girl's invaluable."

Enwezor nodded and got to it. Out of respect, he pretended not to notice the way Marcus collapsed back down onto the rock he'd been sitting on before, but he couldn't stem the worry in his gut.

So many people were sick and dying, and Cap was more injured than he was letting on. The storm outside was still raging, and there were probably more morphs nearby. Their situation, much like the world around them, looked pretty fucking bleak.

They may have been more than halfway done their journey, but Ashland had never seemed so far away.

. . . . .

The wind was still howling when Savannah came to, and she could see thick swirls of snow moving past the cave entrance. She blinked in pain at the brightness and turned her head away, shivering.

A second later she felt a cold compress being pressed to her forehead. She groaned.

"Savannah, can you hear me?"

She nodded weakly at the sound of Jillian's voice.

"Good. You and I need to have a little chat."

Savannah forced her eyes open and gazed up at the elderly woman, shrinking a little at the obvious disapproval she saw in Jillian's expression.

"You're with child," Jillian stated. "Why on earth would you keep that a secret on a trip like this one?"

"I..." Savannah faltered, swallowed. "It's not a secret. Clio knows, and so does Adam."

"Well then, shame on them, too," Jillian huffed. "They should have said something. Letting you carry on and work the way you have been is incredibly stupid. You're only putting yourself and your unborn child in danger." She sighed. "Of course, I suppose they're not entirely to blame. Men are men. They don't exactly understand pregnancy and motherhood." She pursed her lips, intensifying her look of disapproval. "Which is why you should have come to me."

"I'm sorry," Savannah mumbled. "I just...I didn't want to be a burden to the group, and I thought that if everyone knew..."

"Everyone is going to know soon enough, Savannah. Even the loosest clothing you have won't be able to hide your belly in a month or two. What was your plan then?"

She hadn't ever thought that far ahead. "I don't know," she answered honestly.

Jillian sighed, and it was the type of sigh that seemed to be reserved exclusively for frustrated old women. "Honestly, child," she said.

"You're lucky you've made it this long, just like you're lucky that this fever seems to be breaking." She removed the cold compress from Savannah's forehead. "But luck isn't enough. Changes need to be made, so here's what's going to happen: first, I'm going to tell Captain Marcus about your condition. Then, I am going to find that boyfriend of yours and give him a piece of my mind. He needs to be by your side at all times, and he'll also need to start pulling your weight because I am removing you from the duty roster. You will also need to start doubling your rations. If you are malnourished it means your child is too, and the weaker you are, the more likely it will be that both of you will die before getting to Ashland. Also, from here on out, you will be completely honest with me about this pregnancy. If that baby of yours so much as kicks, I want to know about it."

Savannah nodded even as arguments began to form on her lips. "Adam and I aren't really in a good place right now, so—"

"Hush. You can have all the lovers' spats you want once you get to Ashland, but while we're out here there is no place for them. Put your disagreements behind you, grow up, and work together." She reached behind her and fished around in her bag until she found a ration of dried jerky. "Here," she said, handing it to Savannah. "As soon as you feel strong enough, eat this. I'm going to go find your boyfriend."

Again, Savannah felt a burning desire to argue, but she held her tongue. Jillian might be a slight old lady, but she could certainly be intimidating when she wanted to be, so Savannah kept quiet and simply watched as Jillian gathered her things and headed out into the snow.

She didn't leave Savannah alone for long.

Not two minutes after she'd left, Enwezor came trudging into the cave. "Hey," he called in greeting as he dusted the snow off of his jacket and out of his mohawk. "How're you feeling?"

"A little better." Savannah propped herself up into a seated position against the wall of the cave, but a wave of exhaustion came crashing over her and she instantly regretted trying to move. "Did Jillian tell you to come here and keep an eye on me?" She asked weakly.

Enwezor nodded. "Yeah." He walked over and sat down across from her. "I'll tell you what: in some ways, that lady is just as scary as Cap. When she barks an order, you listen."

Savannah smiled wanly. *Now there's something I can't argue with,* she thought, and then she closed her eyes and went back to sleep.

. . . . .

When Savannah next woke, it was because of the heat. Her skin was damp with a layer of sticky sweat and every inch of her body felt like it was baking. She tossed and turned and groaned, and then, unable to dispel the heat, grudgingly opened her eyes.

And saw a familiar face staring down at her. "Hey," Adam said. He was sitting next to her, looking concerned.

Savannah groaned again and struggled into a seated position, kicking off the pile of blankets and clothing weighing her down. "I think I'm partially cooked," she said, wiping the sweat off of her forehead with a swipe of her hand.

Adam frowned. "Jillian said I should keep you warm—you were shivering after your fever broke so she said to get you covered up."

Savannah snorted. "I don't think she meant for you to suffocate me under fifty pounds of blankets, though." She kicked at the remaining fabric, freeing her legs. "Seriously, where did you even *find* this many blankets?"

The tips of Adam's ears started to turn red. "Well," he said, staring at his lap, "Jillian gave me two but that didn't seem like enough, so I may have, um, borrowed a few more, along with a coat or two."

Savannah raised an eyebrow. "Borrowed?"

His ears were now the color of ripe tomatoes. "I'll give them back."

Savannah sighed. *Adam the blanket thief. Go figure.*

But even though part of her wanted to roll her eyes at his ridiculousness, another part of her was touched. Here he was, once again, caring for her, sincere and helpful to the point of stupidity, and here *she* was, silently judging him.

"I'm sorry," she said, feeling a tinge of color creep onto her own face.

Adam blinked at her in confusion. "What for?"

"Everything." She bit her lip. "I've treated you so badly and I don't know why. You deserve a lot better."

His lips twitched downward into a frown. "Don't worry about it, Savannah. You don't have to apologize."

She leaned forward, propping herself up as tall as she could sit. "Yes, I do. You're the best person I know, Adam, and I pushed you away." She felt tears beginning to surface in the corners of her eyes and she blinked them away. "I miss you," she admitted. "So much. I want to be close again like we were before I messed things up. I want to talk to you about stupid stuff. I want to hear you laugh again. I just...I want to be with you."

"You've got me, Savannah." Adam reached for her hands and squeezed them gently. "I'm not going anywhere. I promise. And we are okay—really."

She searched his eyes. "But you still don't believe that *you* are what I want. I can tell."

Adam looked away, but it didn't matter; she'd already seen the hurt hiding in his eyes. "You don't have to prove anything to me," he murmured. "It's fine."

But it wasn't fine. It was miles from fine.

And regardless of what he said, she did have something to prove to him. She had to prove that she loved him.

But how? *How?* Nothing she'd said so far had made any difference. She kept telling him she wanted to be with him, that she wanted to be a real couple, but he didn't believe her. And she had no idea how to...

And then it came to her.

"Hey," she blurted. "Will you marry me?"

"*Wha...?*" Adam stammered. He looked like she'd just told him that their baby was going to be born with three heads and a tail.

Utter shock was not exactly the reaction she'd been hoping for. She pouted. "Well?"

Adam gaped at her. "Did you seriously just ask me to *marry* you?"

"Yeah, I did." Savannah crossed her arms over her chest, feeling defensive. "Why is that so damn hard to believe?"

"Well—" He started to say, but she cut him off.

"Shut up!" She screeched in frustration. "Don't you get it? I love you! I want to be with you, and I've been trying to prove it to you but you just don't get it, and I understand—I mean, I never asked for a relationship and I guess you thought that meant that what I feel for you is some casual thing, but it's not!" She sucked in a breath. "I've loved you since the first time you made me snort milk all over myself in the mess hall at Easthaven, I love you now, and I'll still love you when I'm old and fat and this baby in my belly is older than we are now!"

Adam's look of bewilderment was slowly transforming into something else. "Really?" He breathed. "You feel that way about me? Not Clio?"

Savannah groaned in exasperation and chucked the nearest blanket at him, feeling a moment of satisfaction when it hit him in the face. "No, you dolt! How many times do I have to tell you? Clio is my friend! *You're* the one I made a baby with, the one who makes me laugh, the one I just proposed to!"

Adam's shoulders were trembling, and for an awful second, Savannah thought he was crying, but then he moved the blanket. "You're insane," he said, grinning, his body still shaking with laughter. "And yes, by the way."

"Yes what?" Savannah barked, still fuming.

"Yes, I'll marry you," Adam said, and then he closed the distance between them and kissed her gently on the lips.

Savannah's anger went up in smoke. "Really?" She said as he pulled back.

"Yeah. Although..." He raised his eyebrows.

Savannah's stomach clenched. "What?"

Adam smirked. "You're gonna have to propose to me again. Properly. That means no yelling the question at me and no name-calling."

Savannah chucked another blanket at him, but this time she couldn't suppress her own smirk. "Not a chance. You said yes, so my job is done."

"Figures." Adam pushed the blanket away and looked at her, and then his humorous smile turned sentimental. "I missed you too, by the way."

Savannah smiled, and for the first time since the fall of Easthaven, she felt like everything might just work out okay in the end.

•  •  •  •  •

The wind stirred the hair around her face, making stray black tendrils sway back and forth where they brushed her shoulders. The wind was colder here in the northern territories than even the most bitter wind she'd experienced when she was still with the Easthaven group, carrying enough bite to easily raise goosebumps on the skin of warm-blooded creatures. As she walked towards the center of camp, she wondered how Marcus and the others would have adjusted to the colder climate. Probably not well.

There were a fair number of tents strung up in the clearing, but it was still easy to find General Crow's. It was larger than all of the others and made of a light blue fabric that stood out in bright contrast to the earth-toned tents around it. Also unlike the rest, there was a guard posted outside of the entry flap.

The man nodded as she approached. "He's expecting you," he said as he reached out and pulled aside one of the flaps so she could enter.

Aya stepped inside, her eyes instantly adjusting to the dimness of the candlelit interior.

It was surprisingly well furnished for a mobile tent. There was a grand desk in the center of the space, flanked by two large candelabras that illuminated the plethora of maps and books spread out on the desk's surface, and a smaller table in one corner, laden with various jars and bottles of liquids. There was also a comfortably sized pallet resting on a fur rug in the other corner. Nearby it was a pile of sketches in differing states of completion, each canvas showing a different vignette of nature. Some were done in black and white, but many had been enhanced with color, imbuing the sketches with a sense of realness that was breathtaking. One in particular – a rainstorm captured by deep blues and blacks – caught Aya's eye. Within its swirling clouds and turbulent sky, it was like the artist had managed to capture not only the accuracy of the storm but its might as well.

"I like that one too. The beauty, the power, the darkness…it is captivating. Much like you."

The voice, like dark silk, was one Aya now recognized well. She turned and inclined her head as the tall, dark-skinned vampire came to stand beside her, trying to ignore the way her stomach somersaulted at the sight of him. Crow was a proud specimen of masculinity: tall and chiseled, with a confident gait and an expressive face—one that exuded lustful slyness as readily as intelligence, and a mane of black hair braided into dozens of tiny, perfect cornrows that he kept secured in a leather knot at the nape of his neck.

"Good evening, General Crow," Aya said, tearing her eyes from him. She gestured to the sketches they'd been admiring. "Are these yours?"

He smiled, a brief tilt of his generous lips, and bowed his head in return. "Ever the polite one," he said. "As I've mentioned before, you are welcome to call me Atticus."

Aya gave him a small smile but didn't acquiesce.

"And no," he continued when she gave no reply. "They are not mine. These sketches were all done by Daria of Clan Moravec—I believe you've met her. Her artistic talent far surpasses mine." He lifted a brow. "Do you draw, Aya?"

"Not well. My father gave me some rudimentary lessons before he…when I was very young, but no. Nothing like this," she added, glancing back at Daria's masterpieces.

Crow lifted his broad shoulders in a casual shrug. "No matter," he said, managing to look completely comfortable despite the way his voice dropped. "You are better suited to be on a canvas than sitting behind one anyway."

Aya felt a blush rising to her cheeks—a somewhat common occurrence whenever she was speaking with the imposing general, and she was suddenly hyperaware of just how near he was standing.

She stepped away in what she hoped was an imperceptible move. "What did you want to speak with me about?" She asked, trying to steer the conversation in a new direction.

Crow smiled. "You are my guest," he replied. He walked over to the small desk in the far corner and uncorked one of the bottles. "I wanted to see how you were getting along and ask if there was anything you needed." He poured a generous helping of a light brown liquid Aya couldn't identify into a glass and held it out to her. "Would you like a drink? It's blood-infused mead—not too strong but satisfying nonetheless."

Aya's first instinct was to decline, but she didn't want him to think her ungracious, so she walked over and accepted the proffered glass, jerking slightly as his large fingers brushed hers in the exchange. "Thank you," she murmured, stepping back once more and courteously taking a sip.

He smiled at her reaction but didn't say anything, electing instead to pour himself a glass of mead as well. "So. How *are* you adjusting here?"

Aya stared down at the drink in her hand before answering, swirling it gently. "Everyone is very welcoming and generous, and I appreciate the gracious hospitality you have been showing me."

"But...?"

Aya glanced up, meeting his eyes. "But?" She repeated.

Crow laughed, the sound a rich, deep chuckle. "You are polite and cautious to a fault, Aya, but I've been playing this game for a very long time. I can tell when someone is holding back." He cocked his head, assessing her intently as he raised his glass to his mouth and took a slow drink. "So, what is bothering you?"

"I'm not bothered, just...somewhat confused," she admitted. "Ever since I joined you, I've noticed that most of the people in your camp treat me with a certain amount of—of deference, and I don't understand why. I am not of noble blood, nor am I one of their leaders."

Crow chuckled again and shook his head. "Forgive me, Aya," he said. "I sometimes forget that you've been surviving on your own for so long." He took another drink. "When the once-hunters decimated our numbers, we lost a great many of our people. Out of the two hundred or so clans formed after the Second War, eighty were wiped out entirely, and almost all of the Guardians were killed. Fewer than twenty – a mere handful – survived."

Aya nearly dropped her drink. "So few?" She asked, aghast.

Crow nodded solemnly. "It makes sense, when you take into account the nature of what Guardians are. A Guardian's job is to protect their clan, so in the event of an attack, they are usually leading the charge. Fighting on the front lines comes with a high fatality rate." He drained his drink and put the empty glass down on the table. "That is why you've noticed people treating you differently than everyone else: because you *are* different. You are the last of an endangered species, a keeper of your clan's history and customs, one of the only surviving vampires trained in the old ways and by far one of the youngest." His eyes darkened. "And easily one of the most beautiful."

"But I am not even officially a Guardian," Aya answered, ignoring his last comment. "My father never passed his leadership on to me."

"But you were trained as a Guardian, and your father would have passed on his position, had he lived until you came of age. Is that not correct?"

"Yes, that is correct," Aya admitted. She took another sip of her drink.

"So," Crow said, as if that settled it. "You are a Guardian in all but name, as well as the last surviving member of Clan Ayume. That makes you a rare and important individual, Aya. You don't realize it now, but when we reach our destination and meet with the leaders of the remaining clans, your voice will carry a great deal of weight. The remaining Guardians have almost as much authority as the generals, and because of your unique backstory, I have a feeling that you will accrue a great amount of respect from the other Guardians once you are presented at the conclave."

Aya was speechless. She'd been alone for years and then in the company of humans, treated like somewhat of an outcast, and now, if Crow was right in his assertions, she was going to go from that to having an influential status among clans of vampires she'd never even met. It was a lot to take in.

And the revelations didn't end there. "You will also have many romantic prospects, I suspect," Crow added softly.

Aya's grip tightened on her glass. "Romantic prospects?" She echoed warily.

Crow stepped closer, closing the distance between them. "That can't come as a shock, not to someone so beautiful." Before she could say a word, he dipped his head down, running his nose along her neck. "Or someone who smells so intriguing," he breathed against her skin.

Aya jolted in shock at the sudden shiver that ran down her spine and the glass fell from hand.

Crow caught it before it could hit the ground and straightened up, his dark eyes gleaming in obvious pleasure at her reaction. "Careful," he whispered with a smile as he set the half-full glass down on the table.

Aya swallowed. "You flatter me, but I am certain you are exaggerating." She paused to collect herself, but then she noticed that Crow looked like he wanted to argue to the contrary. "Nevertheless," she hurried on before he could interject, "I do not think I will be accepting romantic offers anytime soon. I wouldn't want personal attachments to cloud my judgment, especially not when everything and everyone will be so new to me. I will need a clear head." Which is exactly what she was wishing for now, but the combination of alcohol and Atticus Crow was making her head feel anything but clear.

"Spoken like a Guardian," Crow said, mirth audible in his voice. "And also like someone who has not felt the touch of another in a long time." He stepped in close again and cupped her chin, gently brushing her bottom lip with his thumb. "Share my tent tonight, Aya," he said, his blazing eyes full of dark promises. "Let me remind you what you are missing."

It wasn't until he said it that Aya realized just how much she wanted to feel the touch of another, how much she ached for it. Loneliness had been her lover for too long, a cold and empty presence. It was beyond tempting to exchange that for the real, solid presence of the vampire in front of her.

Almost unconsciously, she reached out and spread her palm over his chest. He hummed at the contact, a sound that went straight from his throat to her nerve endings, and he covered her hand with one of his larger ones, brushing his thumb in small circles on her skin.

But Aya barely noticed his ministrations. What she noticed instead was the silence.

There was no heartbeat beneath her palm, no warmth. It wasn't surprising; Crow was a vampire just as she was, so of course he would have no heartbeat. And yet for some reason, that realization *did* affect her. It made her feel a different kind of ache, one that instantly cooled her desire for the imposing man.

She pulled away. "I'm sorry," she murmured. "I can't stay."

Crow covered the look of surprise on his face with commendable swiftness. After a second, he smiled. "A loss for both of us," he said quietly, and then he shrugged, letting her rejection roll off his shoulders. "But perhaps you'll change your mind on a luckier night," he said. His eyes swept over her. "For now, I'll say goodnight." He reached out and captured her hand in his, bringing it up until it hovered just out of contact with his lips. "Rest well, Aya."

"Goodnight, General Crow," Aya said as he released her hand.

"Atticus," he reminded her.

She supposed she could at least give him that. "Atticus," she conceded, and then she slipped out of his tent and into the windy night.

• • • • •

She didn't stop walking until she was in the woods surrounding their camp, and she only stopped then because of the blood. The scent was heavy and fresh, and Aya turned towards it out of habit, her fangs descending involuntarily.

She followed the scent trail for less than a quarter mile when she found its source.

The feasting vampire was bent over the wolf's carcass, and Aya could hear the telltale sounds of feeding. She began to back away, not wanting to interrupt, but the vampire suddenly sat up and turned towards her, offering a bloody smile.

"Hello, Aya," Daria said as she wiped a hand across her mouth and stood up. There was blood on her shirt, but the willowy vampire didn't seem to mind. "I didn't expect to see you sneaking about."

"I'm not sneaking about. I'm just walking."

"Well, *I'm* sneaking about," Daria said with a smirk. "I love nighttime kills...they give me such a rush." She retracted her fangs as the veins beneath her eyes slowly lightened from black to grey. "I am surprised to see you. I thought you would be with General Crow tonight."

Aya colored for the second time that night. "You knew about our meeting?"

Daria tossed her impressive head of hair over her shoulder and raised a coquettish eyebrow. "I know he's wanted you for a lover since your first day traveling with us," she said, voice full of mischief. "Though it looks like he didn't get his way. There is no way he'd finish with you quite so quickly. The man does know how to take his time." Her black eyes twinkled wickedly.

"Yes, I declined his offer," Aya admitted, staring at the ground.

Daria sighed. "Oh well. Atticus Crow is a great many things, but he is not what you are looking for."

It was a statement, not a question, and the absolute certainty in Daria's voice made Aya pause. She looked up. "Why would you say that?" She questioned.

Daria stepped closer to her. "Because you have feelings for another," she murmured.

Aya blanched. "You are mistaken."

An unsettling amount of slyness crept into Daria's smile. "It's no use lying to me, Aya; I see things as they are. I know your heart belongs to another the same way I know you can see without eyes."

"How could you possibly...?" Aya began, but then she put the pieces together. Her eyes widened. "You're a seer?" She guessed. She had never met someone with the sight before. She wasn't even entirely sure she had believed that it was a real gift—until now.

"I am," Daria confirmed. "The sight runs in my family just as your own ability runs in yours. It's in the blood and blood never lies." Daria pursed her lips, thinking. "You know that old saying? It's something like: loyalty and love may be proven false..."

"But blood always runs red," Aya finished. "Yes, I've heard it."

"Well, it's true." Daria smiled again, showing the bloodstains still visible on her teeth. "So even if I didn't have the sight, your blood would still reveal your true feelings."

The more confidence Daria exuded, the less comfortable Aya felt, and yet she had to ask. She had to know. "And what does my blood reveal?"

"I can glean a great deal from scent alone, but to be certain..." Daria held out a dainty hand.

Aya placed her own hand, palm-up, in Daria's outstretched one. "Go ahead," she said, granting permission.

Faster than a striking snake, Daria slashed a talon across Aya's wrist, just deeply enough to draw a bead of blood. Then she raised Aya's wounded wrist to her mouth and lapped the dot of red up with her tongue, swishing it around pensively in her mouth before swallowing it.

She was silent for a moment, and then she licked her lips clean and smiled. "Exactly as I thought, you naughty fox," she trilled. "You taste like exquisite controversy."

Aya drew her arm back. "Excuse me?"

But Daria seemed to be too absorbed in her own thoughts to hear anything else. "No wonder you've only fed once since you joined us," she said, musing aloud. "Ordinary blood doesn't sate your hunger. Of course, I would be the same way if I had my own personal blood bag to feed from. Then again...maybe not. I do love variety. Unlike you, apparently." Suddenly, she caught Aya's eye, snapping back to the present. "You had better keep that to yourself, dear," she whispered conspiratorially, leaning in until her lips brushed Aya's ear. "There wouldn't be much acceptance if people found out you were in love with one of *them*."

"One of 'them'?"

Daria lowered her voice even further. "*A human.*"

Aya jerked away as if burned, but Daria only laughed. "Don't worry, Aya. It doesn't bother me. *My* feelings are rather progressive; I'm just telling you that not everyone here would feel the same way. So be careful." Her voice took on a serious, contemplative tone. "The safest secrets are the ones not shared," she said. "Keep your aura of mystery and be careful who you trust."

There was an edge to Daria's voice that made it difficult to decipher whether she was offering advice or making a threat, but then the moment passed, and her expression softened once more. She gestured to her kill. "Please take the rest," she said. "There's plenty. I was more interested in the kill than the meal and you should eat something. A little variety will help mask that secret of yours."

She didn't wait for a response, just wiggled her fingers in a dainty parting wave and walked away, leaving Aya alone with the dead wolf and her inner turmoil.

And the ghost of a question she'd been pondering since the night she'd left the humans.

*Marcus...*

It wasn't true. It couldn't be true. She was Aya of Clan Ayume, daughter of a Guardian and soon to be a Guardian herself, a *vampire*. She was not in love with a human—especially not a Reaper that was responsible for butchering so many of her own people. No. She wasn't. What she felt now was just a loss of companionship, the loss of a strange friendship formed through weeks of trials and survival. Nothing more. Yes, she trusted him. Yes, she thought about him more than she would like to admit. Yes, she missed him. But love? No. It couldn't be. It would *never* be. What she felt for him – that deep, complicated, confusing, unnamable thing – couldn't be love. It wasn't. That depth of feeling could never and would never exist between them. It was an impossibility.

*Just like the blood bond doesn't exist?* A small voice inside questioned. *Just like that?*

And suddenly Aya realized that she wasn't sure of anything at all.

# Revelations

*14 April, in the field: Woke up with a pounding headache and a strange pain in my stomach. Also feeling on edge and I am ravenous. Tried to eat earlier but food is a total turn-off. The docs told me to mention any side effects that linger longer than forty-eight hours, but these only cropped up yesterday. Will monitor behavior and stop by the clinic when my expedition gets back two days from now if things get worse. Probably nothing to worry about.*
- Final diary excerpt of Cole Fraser, one of the initial recipients of the *Metamorphosis* Vaccine

. . . . .

By the time Marcus made it back to the caves, the sun had already dipped below the mountain line and the moon was visible in the sky. He deposited the foodstuffs he'd scavenged from the bunker, gestured at Sloane and Enwezor to handle their distribution, and walked back outside.

When he was far enough away not to be heard, he leaned back against one of the rock walls and let out a pained groan, clutching at his side. He hadn't told anyone, but he was certain that two of his ribs had been broken in the morph attack the prior week. His side hurt every time he moved (hell—it hurt every time he took a fucking breath), but there was nothing for it. He would just have to muscle through it and hope the pain subsided with time.

His other wounds were healing more readily, though Marcus had a feeling that the claw marks running along his chin and neck were going to scar. It pissed him off—not because he cared about the physical marks but because it would be lasting proof that a morph had nearly killed him. If any wounds were going to scar, he would much rather have preferred that it be the two small fang marks hidden just beneath his shirt.

But those had faded and disappeared, just like the vampire who'd made them.

Like always, Marcus pushed the thoughts of *her* to the back of his mind and focused instead on the present situation.

After seven days of whiteout conditions, the snow had finally stopped three days earlier, a full day after Clio had returned with medicine from the bunker. His success had been everyone's success, and because of the life-saving antibiotics, no one else had died. Even Colleen, who'd been a few hours at most from following her sister into an early grave, had recovered.

In addition to bringing back the medicine, Clio had also marked the trail by tagging trees with brightly colored ribbons on his way back, making it possible for them to navigate back and forth between the caves and the bunker in spite of the snow. Where he'd gotten the ribbons and how he'd managed to accomplish stringing up the markers in the midst of a blizzard remained a mystery, but Marcus was grateful anyway.

He was also grateful for the change it had caused within their group. Since Easthaven, many people had come to accept the hybrid, but many people had retained reservations that had affected group morale. After this, though, the remaining skeptics had come around pretty dramatically, and now Clio was treated – almost down to a person – with newfound respect and awe. It was a shift in attitude that Marcus was extremely pleased with, mostly because it was so long overdue. The hybrid had proven his loyalty time and again, but for some reason, he'd been even less accepted than Aya.

Aya—the loyal, unusual, resilient vampire that – for some baffling reason – Marcus couldn't seem to get out of his head, no matter how hard he tried to forget about her.

*I promised to help you get to Ashland. Let me honor my promise.*

Marcus closed his eyes and sighed, then grimaced as his ribs throbbed anew. *It's just pain,* he told himself. *It'll pass.*

"Captain?"

Marcus opened his eyes, meeting the mismatched gaze of the hybrid. "What is it?"

Clio clasped his hands behind his back. "If we're still planning to push forward tomorrow, I was going to make an announcement to the group, but I wanted to check in with you first."

Marcus pushed himself off the wall and straightened, trying not to let his pain show. "Yes, we're leaving tomorrow," he managed, though he couldn't quite keep the strain from his voice. "The weather is clear, and the snow isn't nearly as deep as it was. We'd be foolish to linger here longer than we already have." He didn't add the reason why it would be foolish because he didn't have to; the threat of morphs was an all too constant presence in their lives. Sheltering anywhere that didn't have walls and doors posed a monumental risk.

"All right." Clio's eyes dropped to Marcus's side, as if he knew what Marcus was hiding. Which he probably did, judging by his follow-up question. "Do you want me to take point tomorrow? You could hang back, act as a sweeper."

Marcus scowled, but he didn't shoot the idea down. Frankly, he was glad Clio had suggested it. He'd only gone to the bunker today to test his strength, and while he'd managed to bring back fresh supplies for the group, the short trip had left him exhausted.

"Fine," he conceded. He gave Clio a pointed look. "I'm not as bad as you think, Jones," he lied, "so quit with the concern. It's written all over your face."

Clio's lips pressed into a line. "Yes, because there are no civilians around and you are every bit as bad as I think you are." He paused. "Have you taken anything for the pain?"

"I took a dose of painkillers yesterday, but I don't want to take any more. I'm not the only person recovering from injuries."

"No, but you are the leader of the group. If you're not strong, we aren't either."

Marcus's scowl soured. "Has anyone ever told you that you have a knack for saying exactly what no one wants to hear?"

To his surprise, Clio chuckled, lines of amusement crinkling on the human side of his face. "More than once, actually, but no one has ever disagreed with me." He arched a brow. "Are you about to be the exception?"

Damn the hybrid and his logic. "No," Marcus admitted. He exhaled, cringed. "Fuck. Fine. I'll help myself to a few more doses of pills, so long as you shut up about my condition. Fair enough?"

Clio nodded. "Fair enough." He gave a brief salute. "I'll go tell the others about our departure plan," he said, and then he turned and walked away.

As soon as Clio was out of sight, Marcus collapsed back against the solid surface of the rock wall once more, his waning energy completely enervated from his bluff of stamina during their conversation.

*Rally, you piece of shit,* Stan's voice taunted him. *Get up and fake it 'til you make it.*

Instead, Marcus's legs went out from under him and he sank down into the snow.

· · · · ·

It was early in the morning and most people were still asleep in the bunker, so Cody decided to go outside and practice her knife throwing. She carved out a target on a tree with a wide trunk and had just managed to land her third knife in a row when she saw Willie watching her from the trees to her left. He bolted as soon as their eyes met, and after a second of deliberation, Cody ran after him.

"Hey!" She called. "Wait up!"

He didn't, but Willie was slower than she was; she caught up to him in no time. She blocked his path, thrusting her arms out wide. "Stop," she said. "I just want to talk to you."

Willie flinched but did as she asked, eyeing her warily.

Cody stared back, letting her arms drop to her sides. She hadn't spoken to Willie – or even seen him, really – since the day her mom had...since the day it had happened, and she was angry. Willie had no right to avoid her—if anything, *she* should be the one avoiding him. After all, he hadn't lost anything that day. His family was still alive.

"Why have you been avoiding me?" She asked bluntly.

Willie kicked at a lump of melting snow. "I'm sorry," he mumbled.

Cody bristled. "That's not an answer. Tell me why."

He looked up at her. His eyes were watery and slightly discolored, and his skin had a clammy sheen to it. Cody wondered if he was sick, but she pushed the thought away. Right now, she didn't want to be anything other than mad at him; if he really was sick, there would be time to feel bad for him later.

She crossed her arms across her chest. "Answer me," she demanded hotly.

Willie caved in the face of her anger. "I didn't mean to avoid you," he whined. "I just didn't know what to do." His bottom lip trembled. "It was so horrible, what happened to your mom, and I felt like it was my fault." He dropped his gaze to his feet. "I kept thinking that if I'd just been fast, like you, none of that would have happened. You wouldn't have had to save me, and your mom wouldn't have had to save you."

Cody stared at him in shock. Did he really think that she blamed him?

"Willie," she said, her voice much gentler than before, "what happened wasn't your fault. A morph killed my mom. Not you."

He sniffled. "Yeah, but I was the one who asked if you wanted to play by the river. We wouldn't have even been there if it wasn't for me."

Cody felt a familiar knot of pain start to tug at the pit of her tummy, but she ignored it. "Hey." She waited until he looked up to continue. "It wasn't your fault, okay? It really wasn't."

"Then why are you mad at me?"

Cody's shoulders slumped. "Because you're supposed to be my friend, and I feel like you're not anymore." It was her turn to sniffle. "I'm so sad all the time, Willie," she said, her voice breaking. "I miss my mom so much, and it would have…it just would have been nice to have a friend."

"I…I am your friend," Willie said, but despite his words Cody could hear the uneasiness in his voice. She blinked back her tears and looked at him, confused, but the expression on his face made all the pieces fall into place. Suddenly, she understood why he'd been avoiding her, why he couldn't look her in the eye for longer than a second. She even understood why right this minute he was fidgeting like he was a split second away from bolting.

Willie couldn't deal with what had happened, and she was a walking, talking reminder of it. He was staying away from her because he couldn't cope. The fear, the attack, the tragedy…it had just been too much for him to handle.

He might say that he was still her friend, but he wasn't. He couldn't be, not anymore.

Cody swallowed, steeling herself against how unfair it all was. "Thanks for talking with me, Willie," she said, her voice sounding hollow to her own ears. "It means a lot."

"Sure," he said. He tried to give her a smile but only managed to grimace. "I'm gonna head back," he said. "I don't like being far from the group."

"Okay," Cody said. She had every intention of letting him go, but when he turned around, surprise got the better of her.

"Hey!" She exclaimed. "You're bleeding!"

Willie glanced over his shoulder at the back of his arm, where a thin line of blood was seeping through his shirt. "Oh," he said listlessly. "Guess I should go change my bandages."

"What happened?"

"I got scratched by one of the morphs that attacked us last week," he explained. "Enwezor killed it right after."

Cody assessed his pallid complexion again, feeling a stirring of anxiety. "Are you sure it's not infected?"

Willie frowned. "It's fine," he said. "Mom said it isn't even that deep."

"But—"

"I'm gonna go put new bandages on," he interrupted. "I'll see you around, Cody."

Cody bit her lip. Willie wasn't the only person that had gotten hurt in the attack the previous week—even Captain Marcus had gotten pretty torn up. But no one that had been wounded looked pale and sick.

No one except Willie.

It might be nothing, but Cody didn't feel like it was nothing, and her mother had always told her to trust her instincts.

She jogged back to the tree she'd been using as target practice, retrieved her knives, and went to find Clio.

.  .  .  .  .

Pain. Anxiety. Exhaustion. Frustration. Suffering.

It was all pulsing around in her bloodstream at a throbbing, relentless rate, as though the overload of emotional turmoil had spilled into her veins and arteries and was seeking to escape through her skin but couldn't find a way out.

And it wasn't even *her* emotional turmoil; it was Marcus's.

By the time they stopped to set up camp for the night, Aya was at her breaking point, and, not knowing what else to do, she went in search of Solomon. It had been a long, trying day, and she was desperate for someone to talk to. She needed advice and answers, and Solomon was the only person she really trusted in the group.

She found him towards the back of the camp, conversing with a group of other, older vampires. They were talking and laughing, and Aya paused outside of their circle, not wanting to interrupt, but Solomon saw her and turned, smiling in greeting.

"Good evening, Aya," he said, his smile waning as he took in the expression on her face. He lowered his voice. "Are you all right, child?"

"I'm…in need of answers," she said, unwilling to go into detail with others so close by. "But it's not dire," she added, not wanting to be a bother. "I can come back later."

Solomon waved his hand dismissively. "Nonsense." He turned to the gathered vampires. "You'll have to excuse me, friends. I'm needed elsewhere."

"You are Aya of Clan Ayume, are you not?" Asked one of the vampires gathered there, ignoring Solomon and assessing her with curiosity.

"I am," Aya answered.

"Is it true that you've lived on your own since your clan's destruction?" Another vampire inquired.

"Yes," she replied reluctantly, not wanting to be drawn into a conversation about her past.

"And that you've slain morphs?" The same vampire pressed.

Aya glanced around at the congregated vampires, seeing the same hungry eagerness in all of their gazes. Gossip was what they sought, and Aya was too drained to take kindly to it. Still, she didn't let her exhaustion show. "Yes," she answered again.

One of the females crossed her bony arms and clucked. "Some would call that foolhardy, child."

Aya ignored her disapproval and stood tall in spite of the pain she was currently feeling. "I did what was necessary to survive," she replied levelly. "It was kill or be killed." She paused. "It still is. We may have safety in numbers today, but I have traveled and seen what horrors this world contains. The morphs seek our genocide; there will come a time when we all must fight."

"You speak with an abundance of certainty for someone so young," the female vampire replied, her lips pursing with indignation at Aya's response.

"I may be young," Aya responded, her tone neutral, "but I am not naïve. I endured my clan's destruction, and I know that many other clans have been similarly butchered since Year Zero. We are at war for our very survival—that is a fact that cannot be denied or ignored." She paused. "So yes, I speak with certainty. And I will continue to do so in the hope that what I have to share may help our people endure and prepare them for the trying times ahead."

"You are Hachirou's daughter beyond a shadow of doubt," the tallest vampire of the group stated, surprising Aya. "I met your father decades ago. He was a fine Guardian, and a wise one." He gave her a small bow of approval. "I look forward to hearing what you have to say at the conclave," he said.

"As do I," Solomon added, placing a gentle hand on Aya's arm. "Now, my friends, please do excuse us. You have detained our guest long enough."

"Hurry back," one of the women said. The rest of them nodded and murmured goodbyes, a few of them smiling at Aya as they did.

"Well handled, Aya of Clan Ayume," Solomon murmured to her as they turned away, too softly for any of the other vampires to hear. Aya nodded in response but said nothing; the interaction had left her feeling even more depleted than before.

Solomon steered them out of camp, leading them in silence for nearly half a mile before they came to the very edge of the forest. Beyond lay a flat, open, treeless valley, warmed by the light of the pale, waning sun and flanked in the distance by jagged, snow-capped mountains.

Aya stopped and stared in wonder, marveling at the utterly foreign vista.

It was as though they'd walked to the edge of one world and were standing at the fringe of another—one that Aya had never seen the likes of before. She had lived in the woods her whole life, and the sheer openness of the country before her was alien to her. The woods were beautiful in their dense greenery; this was beautiful in its barren vastness.

"What is this land?" She finally asked.

"It is the northern tundra," Solomon replied, "and *that*," he added, pointing to the mountains in the distance, "is where we are going. There is a well-protected stronghold deep in the mountain pass. The clans agreed to gather there because of its remote location and its proud history. It is one of the few places that has always been held by vampires; no human has ever set foot in those mountains."

Aya was still drinking in the sight of it all. "It's breathtaking," she said.

Solomon nodded. "It is." He turned towards her. "Now, tell me what is bothering you. We will not be overheard here."

Aya hesitated. There would be no reason to share what was troubling her if she didn't first ascertain a basis of truth. "Actually," she said, "before I do, there is something I need to ask you."

Curiosity sparked in Solomon's eyes, but he nodded. "Ask away."

Aya swallowed, feeling suddenly nervous. "What do you know about blood bonds?" She asked quietly.

Solomon's eyes widened and a look of unexpected surprise stole across his face. "Blood bonds?" He repeated. He exhaled through his teeth. "Now *that* is something I haven't heard anyone speak of in quite a long time."

Aya forced herself to ask the follow-up question, the one that had the power to change everything. "Are they real?"

Solomon nodded slowly. "Oh yes. They are an ancient phenomena, and very, very rare, but they are real."

Aya could feel her throat tightening. "Can you tell me about them? Any details you know would be helpful." She was aware that her tone was almost desperate, but she couldn't help it; she *had* to know.

"Well, blood bonds are not an exact science. There is great variability among the ones that have been documented, so it will be difficult to answer your questions." He must have seen the way her expression dropped, because he added, "But I will do my best. Do you see that fallen tree over there?" He pointed, and Aya nodded. "Let's have a seat. This may take some time."

Aya walked to the indicated spot and waited for Solomon to sit next to her on the fallen log. Once he was settled, he began.

"Blood bonds, as I said, are an extremely rare phenomena. In our entire history, less than one hundred have been recorded, and only a handful more have been passed down via word of mouth. The reasons for their formation, as well as the nature of their formations, differ from instance to instance, but there are three abiding similarities." He held up a hand, then punctuated each statement by raising a finger. "One: blood bonds are always initiated by drinking the blood of another. Two: they always occur between two individuals. And three: once formed, they last forever."

*Forever.*

That one word alone was enough to make Aya's head spin, but she held her tongue and retained her composure, not wanting to interrupt Solomon.

"Blood bonds are an extraordinary occurrence, and they only ever manifest between two individuals who have an extraordinary connection. In almost every case, the connection that leads to a blood bond is love—and I don't mean love in just the romantic sense of the word. That is usually part of it, but it is also strength of character, shared values, sameness of spirit. Some people use the term soul mates to describe it, and I am inclined to agree. The connection between two blood-bonded vampires transcends the physical. There is simply no other way to put it."

Solomon paused. "Questions so far?"

Aya had plenty of questions, but she shook her head. Better to hear it all first.

"Very well. Now, having never experienced a blood bond firsthand, I can only pass along what I've heard and read of the connection itself, so keep that in mind as I relate this to you. From what I know, it seems that two individuals, once blood-bonded, develop a kind of…almost psychic connection. They are able to communicate without words and across vast distances, and they share their emotional experiences. If one of them is in pain, so is the other. If one is joyous, the other is too. Blood bonds strengthen over time, and so do the individuals' shared emotions. It's even been recorded that in some extreme cases, when one member of the blood-bonded pair has died, the other has died too. That is the intensity of the connection."

Solomon lapsed into silence, and Aya struggled to put her racing thoughts into coherent questions. Eventually, though, she came to one that eclipsed all of the others.

"Do blood bonds always occur between two vampires?" She asked, her voice sounding infinitely small to her own ears.

Solomon gazed at her intently, as if searching for the question behind the question. "Almost always," he answered at length.

Aya pushed the issue. "*Almost* always?" She echoed.

"Well, blood bonds usually require blood to be exchanged between *both* individuals, but there is one famous exception that I know of." Solomon cocked his head. "Do you know the story of the Wanderer?" He asked.

Aya's brow furrowed. "I thought the Wanderer was a human legend, not a vampire one."

"The Wanderer is a person, not a legend, and the story is not only a human one. It is a shared history between our two races, though one that not many people alive today know."

"But you do know it?"

Solomon nodded. "I do, because my clan – Clan Kovač – was directly involved in the story." He took a deep breath. "Many years ago, shortly after the First War, there was a human girl named Anna Ross who left her people and went out into the wilderness. Some say she was running away from an abusive husband; others think she was a scientist tasked with collecting foreign data, and still others believe she was simply an explorer setting out into the unknown. Whatever the real reason, Anna left her home and eventually trekked high into the mountains, where she came across a vampire that had been badly injured. His name was Alexei, and he was of Clan Kovač." Solomon shifted slightly on the tree. "You see, even though the war was over, there was a great amount of resentment still festering between many of the clans, and attacks and raids were not uncommon. Alexei had been attacked and left for dead by vampires of a different clan, and he was bleeding out when Anna happened upon him. Instead of leaving him there, she took a risk and helped him, tending to his wounds and nursing him back to health. While Alexei was recovering, he and Anna shared their stories and grew close, and despite their obvious differences, they fell in love. Though not known for certain, their time together in the mountains was most likely when their blood bond was formed. Alexei would have needed blood in order to recover, and Anna was easily the most accessible source." He shrugged. "In my opinion, the timeline fits."

"In any case, when he was fully healed, Alexei took Anna back to his clan and presented her as his mate. As you can guess, this news was not well received among his people. The Guardian in charge at the time ordered Alexei to dispose of Anna, but Alexei refused and was banished for his disobedience. For years, he and Anna lived a nomadic life, traveling the wilderness and avoiding other clans, during which time Anna kept a running journal—a journal that I believe the humans still have a copy of to this day.

"After seven years of exile, the Guardian of Clan Kovač relented – probably because Alexei's mother never stopped begging for her son's sentence to be rescinded – and he allowed Alexei and Anna to return.

"This is when their blood bond became known, and I believe it was the reason that Anna, at least to a certain extent, was accepted by the clan. Those who spoke in her favor claimed that any human who could forge such a bond with one of their own was an exceptional individual and should be treated differently from ordinary humans. Others disagreed, but Alexei and Anna stayed and made a home for themselves there.

"Trouble came after their daughter Keira was born. Before her birth, it wasn't even known that a vampire and a human could produce offspring, and the child – living proof that a mix of their two species was indeed possible – scared and appalled most of the clan, even those who had previously supported Alexei and Anna.

"Fearing for the life of their child, the couple decided that Anna should take Keira back to human civilization. They agreed that their daughter would be safer there, and so, despite their desire to remain together, Alexei and Anna parted ways. Anna went back to her home, taking her child and her journals with her, and found asylum with her sister. I don't know the sister's name, but she helped raise Keira in secret and worked to hide the child's obvious uniqueness from the rest of the humans.

"In this, the sisters were successful, because Keira grew up and led a relatively normal life—she even married a human – Caspar Jones, I believe – and raised a family of her own, though whether her husband or any of his family ever knew the truth of Keira's parentage remains a mystery."

Aya nearly doubled over in shock. "Jones?" She repeated.

Solomon had been staring out at the tundra as he recounted the tale, but the sharpness of her tone drew his attention and he looked over at her, raising a brow. "The name means something to you?"

Aya nodded. "One of the humans I was traveling with is a Jones. His full name is Clio Jones."

Solomon's expression turned thoughtful. "And you suspect that he might be a descendant of Keira and Caspar?"

"He has to be," Aya reasoned. "Clio was one of the hunters injected with the *Metamorphosis* vaccine," she explained, "but it didn't affect him like it did the rest of the hunters. I know this because of the way the other humans treated him: they were scared because he was different, because he didn't become a morph. He became a true hybrid between human and vampire. His own people call him the Mutt."

"Hmm…" Solomon mused, lips pursed pensively, "I suppose it is possible. Blood is strong and roots run deep. If your Clio shares even distant relations to one of our kind, it stands to reason that the vaccine would affect him differently than any ordinary human." He turned his questioning gaze on her. "Do you think he is aware of his ancestry?"

"No, I don't think he is," Aya said sadly. She wished she could tell him, but Clio was far away, with Marcus and the others, out of sight and out of reach. Strangely, she missed him almost as much as she missed Marcus; Clio had become a sort of reliable, reassuring presence in her life—similar, in a way, to how she now viewed Solomon.

Realizing that she was getting lost in her own thoughts, Aya forced herself back to the present. "Whatever happened with Anna and Alexei?" She asked.

Solomon smiled sadly. "I'm afraid their story doesn't have a very happy ending," he said. "Once Keira was grown, Anna left to find Alexei, no doubt relying on their blood bond to guide her way. Around the same time, Alexei left Clan Kovač in search of Anna. But alas, the two were never to meet again. Alexei was killed by members of his own clan once they discovered his purpose, and Anna's body was discovered nearly a month later, half-buried in a snowdrift on the northern ridge of one of the high mountains, not far from where Alexei was murdered. It's likely that an avalanche killed her, but no one will ever know for sure."

Aya felt a wave of emotion roll over her at the tragedy of it all. "That's so sad," she murmured.

"It is, though one good thing did come of it. After the rest of Clan Kovač found out about what had happened, they mourned the loss of Alexei, and some even mourned Anna. While in life, the pair had been viewed as a taboo couple, in death, they were viewed as tragic lovers, and many came to regard their deaths as senseless and avoidable. The people responsible for Alexei's murder were banished, and ever since then, Clan Kovač has had a much more lenient view of humans than any of the other clans."

"Too little too late."

"For Anna and Alexei, yes. But perhaps not too late for the next couple like them." Solomon straightened up and gave her a penetrating look. "Now that you've heard it all, tell me, Aya: why are you so curious about blood bonds and the possibility of their existence between vampires and humans?"

Aya gazed at Solomon without guardedness. She could no longer delay speaking the truth, and she no longer wanted to. The nature of the bond she shared with Marcus was no longer just a suspicion in her mind; now she was certain of it.

She raised her chin slightly, in a small, subconscious gesture of defiance. "Because I formed a blood bond with a human," she answered.

To her surprise, Solomon smiled. "Yes," he said, a touch of ruefulness in his voice, "I suspect you are correct."

"You already knew?"

"I had my suspicions," he admitted. "When you spoke of the human who gave you his blood multiple times and I saw the look in your eyes when you talked about him...yes, I suspected it then." His expression took on an air of concern. "But what happened today for you to seek me out about this?"

Aya bit her lip. "What you said about blood bonds...about being able to...to sense the other person, to feel their emotions? Well, I have been. I've been feeling Marcus's pain all day, and it's different than any time I've felt his pain before. This time it's lasted, and I'm—I'm worried about him."

"Do you love him?"

"I think...I think I might," she admitted. "Even though I shouldn't."

"You cannot help who you love, Aya," Solomon said gently.

"I know, but you don't understand. Marcus isn't just a human," she continued, feeling a familiar pinch of inner turmoil. "He's a Reaper."

For the first time since she'd met him, genuine shock registered on Solomon's face. His eyes widened and his mouth dropped open. "Oh my."

Aya couldn't discern the inflection of the older vampire's response, but her own guilt bubbled to the surface. "I know," she rushed on, ashamed. "It's terrible. He's killed so many of us, led so many raids…" She bowed her head. "My feelings are a disgrace to my clan's memory."

"Aya," Solomon interjected, placing a gentle hand on her arm. "You've misinterpreted my reaction—that's not at all what I was getting at. I *am* stunned, but not for the reasons you've assumed." The corners of his eyes crinkled with kindness as he gave her a small smile. "It's not your feelings that shock me at all, child. It's your human's feelings."

Aya was at a loss. "I don't know what you mean."

"Think about it, Aya: this Marcus of yours is a Reaper, one of the most elite vampire killers in existence. His sole purpose, prior to the rise of morphs, was to hunt down and butcher our kind."

Aya hung her head in shame. "I know."

"No, child, you don't," Solomon rebuffed. "What I'm getting at is that, in spite of everything – his upbringing, his training, his mission – in spite of it all, this Reaper gave you a place in his group, offered his blood to you when you needed it, and, I suspect, he is at least partly the reason you are here now."

Aya swallowed. "He is," she admitted. "Although it is hard to believe. When we first met, Marcus bested me in a fight and took my heart—and then he used it to blackmail me into helping his group. Our deal was that he would return my heart once the group reached Fortress Ashland. I hated him so much," she recalled, thinking back to those first, bitter weeks she'd spent with the humans. The memory of the hatred was still fresh in her mind, and yet, strangely, she couldn't remember what it felt like to hate Marcus or any of the humans. Too much had happened since then. Too much had changed.

"But the hatred didn't last," Aya went on. "Things changed. We traveled together and fought together and I—I started to see him differently." Her lips twitched up sadly. "I think we started to see each other differently. And then when Esfir and the others showed up, Marcus…Marcus gave me my heart back. Just like that." In what had now become a reflex, Aya's fingers went to the leather straps around her neck. She began to fidget with them idly in an effort to distract herself from the pain of remembering that final goodbye. "It's still hard to believe," she murmured, "but that's what happened. Marcus returned my heart and told me that I should be with my people. He let me go."

Solomon had let her speak uninterrupted until then, but now he broke his silence. "And why do you think he did that?" He pressed gently, his voice soft.

"I don't know."

"You do. Why would he want you to be with your people? Why would he care whether or not you were with your own kind?"

"Because he…" Aya froze. *Because he loves me?*

Solomon had guided her to those words, and they popped into her head immediately, but Aya kicked them away.

No. It wasn't true. Marcus didn't love her. All he'd said was that he didn't hate her, and that wasn't the same thing. It wasn't even close.

She stared at the ground. "You're wrong," she murmured, refusing to meet the older vampire's eyes.

Solomon sighed, the exhale sounding almost sympathetic. "You're so young, Aya, and I know that you've endured more than your fair share of pain. Your fear of being rejected and experiencing any more pain must be great. But believe me when I tell you that I have lived long enough to recognize love when I see it. Even if you didn't share a blood bond with this human, the very nature of your relationship with each other is extraordinary anyway. If I had to guess, I'd say that your Reaper is struggling with the truth of his feelings as much as you are with yours. But that doesn't change the fact that both of you have those feelings. He may never have said the words to you, may never even have admitted them to himself, but the sheer fact that you are here speaks louder than any words ever could."

Aya felt the press of tears in her eyes, but unlike the first time she'd conversed with Solomon, this time she didn't stop them from falling below her lashes. She looked up at the white-haired vampire as they slipped down her cheeks. "Even if you're right," she said through her tears, "it doesn't matter. There is no future for us. There never was and there never will be."

Solomon regarded her calmly. "That's not necessarily true," he said. "Even Anna and Alexei, as tragic as their story was, had a few happy years together before the end. The future is what you choose it to be, and you, my dear, have a decision to make. You can stay here and try to move on, or you can go back." He gathered her smooth hands in his wizened ones. "I'm not going to lie to you, Aya. You would be much safer if you stayed. As General Crow has no doubt told you, as a Guardian apparent, you will have a special status among the vampires gathered together for the conclave. You will have influence, protection, and, I am sure, friends and admirers." He paused, squeezing her hands gently. "And I must confess that part of me hopes you choose to stay. I know we haven't known each other for very long, but I care about you. Seeing you safe and happy would bring me much joy. But it is not my decision to make." His expression twisted into one of concern. "You mentioned that the humans you were traveling with are headed to Fortress Ashland—that is west of where we were when you joined us, correct?" He asked.

Aya nodded.

"Then I suspect I know the reason why your blood bond is acting up," he said gravely. "It's trying to warn you of danger. You see, there is a morph army standing between your humans and their fortress, and your group is headed straight for it."

Aya lurched to her feet. "What?" She exclaimed, panicking. "How many days away was the army from where we were?"

Solomon stood with her. "It's impossible to say, Aya. I don't know the pace your group is traveling at, or what their exact route is. All I can tell you is that it is very unlikely that such a small company will survive if they cross paths with the morph army camped in that area."

The horror of that realization nearly made Aya double over, her whole body seizing up at the thought that Marcus and Clio and all the rest of them could end up like her people.

Slaughtered. Butchered. Massacred.

*Dead.*

She looked up at Solomon. "I have to go," she said, her voice shaking with urgency. "I have to get to them before they reach that army."

"We are a long way from your humans, Aya—miles and days. You may not make it in time."

"I have to try."

"And what about the conclave? What about your place here?"

Aya was aware of the opportunities slipping through her fingers, but she couldn't bring herself to care. Not right now. "I still have to go," she answered firmly. "I have to try and save them."

To her surprise, Solomon nodded. "Just as any Guardian would," he murmured so softly that Aya wasn't sure whether or not the words were meant for her. "Then go you must," he said at a more audible level.

Aya wavered as something occurred to her. "Should I speak to General Crow first? I don't want to cause any bad blood between us."

"I would urge you not to. You are an honored guest and a Guardian apparent, and while you are technically free to come and go just like anyone else in our party, I have a feeling that the General would find a way to...to dissuade you from leaving," he reasoned, the euphemism all too clear. "I will speak to Crow on your behalf...once you are a safe distance away."

A wave of gratitude rolled through her. "Thank you," she said.

"You're more than welcome, child," Solomon assured her. He stretched out his forearm and Aya placed hers atop his. *Wrist to wrist, vein to vein.*

"Be safe," he said.

"I'll do my best."

Solomon smiled gently. "I have no doubt of that," he replied with fervor in his voice. "I hope we meet again someday."

"As do I," Aya said, meaning it. "Thank you for everything."

Solomon nodded and released her forearm. "I wish you speed and luck, Aya of Clan Ayume," he said in farewell.

Aya said her own goodbyes and watched as the old vampire turned and headed back to camp. Then, when she was alone with nothing but the gentle wind for company, she closed her eyes and opened her mind, letting all of the feelings she'd been resisting wash over her, welcoming them with open arms.

The pain hit her first, making her gasp out loud at the force of it, but then she absorbed it and pressed on, searching beyond it, for something – anything – that she could latch on to.

And then she found it. It wasn't as strong as the emotional connection, but the thread of Marcus's presence was a faint pull in her awareness, a tug that was just strong enough to guide her in the right direction.

Aya took a deep breath and opened her eyes.

*I'm coming,* she vowed silently, the thought grounding her, and then, on silent feet, she began to run.

·　·　·　·　·

Of all of the situations they could have possibly encountered on their hellish exodus from the ruins of Easthaven, this was one that Marcus was not at all prepared to deal with.

In his time as a soldier and Reaper, he had been called many things: hero, warrior, monster, savior, murderer—the list went on and on, but never, not once, had he been forced to play the role of executioner.

Until now.

"Please..." Vivian Brandt begged for what had to be the hundredth time, tears streaming down her face as her chin wobbled with emotion. "Don't do this." She was on her knees, her arms wrapped around her sickly seven-year-old son as she stared up at Marcus with bleary, panicked eyes. "Please," she begged again. "Give us more time."

Marcus said nothing, just continued clutching the handle of his machete so tightly that his fingers started to go numb. Sloane and Enwezor were flanking him, waiting for orders that he couldn't bring himself to give, while Vivian Brandt and her husband Christopher were staring at him in horror, protectively shielding their son. Not that it mattered. If Marcus decided to go through with killing the boy, the elder Brandts wouldn't be able to stop him.

The problem was, he couldn't bring himself to do it. Will Brandt looked like a walking corpse and his eyes were already changing, but he hadn't turned yet. He was still, for the moment, a defenseless seven-year-old human boy.

Marcus thought of the little girl in the caves, the badly injured cannibal that he'd killed in Aya's stead. Breaking her neck had been nearly impossible, had nearly torn him apart, but he'd been able to do it because he'd truly believed – at least on some level – that it was the merciful thing to do.

Killing Will Brandt would not be kind or merciful. It would be murder. And yet what choice did he have? What fucking choice had the Brandts left him?

*You chose not to give your son the preventative vaccine,* he wanted to scream at them. *You knew what this fuckhole of a world was like, knew what the dangers were, and you still chose this. This is on you, you worthless pieces of shit. Your son is going to die or become a monster, and it's all thanks to you.*

And yet the blood would still be on his hands.

"Captain."

Marcus turned at the sound of Jillian's voice, flinching when he saw the look of fear in her eyes—a look directed squarely at him.

"There is another way," she said, stepping between Marcus and the infected boy. She lowered her voice. "The boy hasn't turned yet, even though he was scratched over a week ago. That means that for some reason, the change is occurring much more slowly than it usually does. So perhaps—perhaps instead of acting now, we can…wait. Maybe we'll make it to Ashland before he turns completely."

Vivian Brandt latched on to Jillian's words, her voice shaking with tremulous hope. "Yes!" She interjected. "Will is still Will—if we just wait, the doctors can help him when we get to Ashland. No one needs to die. Please, don't hurt my son."

Jillian nodded, her wrinkled face still fixed on Marcus. "She's right, Captain. I know you're worried about the group's safety, but Will is still human. Killing him is not the right thing to do, especially when there is a chance we can save him."

She was dead wrong, and Marcus knew it. Even at the slower rate of transformation, Will Brandt had a week left at most. There was no way in hell he would survive as a human all the way to Ashland; they were still a good month or two from reaching the fortress. Waiting and hoping for the best was nothing more than wishful thinking.

And yet Marcus still couldn't do it. He was tired of killing, tired of making impossible decisions and coping with the fallout, tired of people looking at him the way Jillian and the Brandts were looking at him right now.

He sheathed his machete. "Fine," he yielded. "The boy stays alive for now. But if he turns before Ashland, he dies."

Vivian Brandt broke down into shuddering sobs at his words, and her husband nodded grimly. Jillian stepped back. "Thank you, Captain. You're doing the right thing."

*No, I'm not,* he thought, but he ignored it. Maybe, by some miracle and against all odds, Will Brandt would manage to stay human until they reached Ashland.

*Yeah, and I'll shit enough gold to live like a king,* Stan's voice piped up from his subconscious. Marcus clenched his jaw and turned to Enwezor and Sloane. "Keep an eye on the boy at all times. If you notice any visible changes, come find me. Understood?"

Enwezor nodded. "Understood, Cap."

Sloane's brow furrowed. "If something happens and you're not nearby, should we…?"

Marcus thought of the look of horror on Aya's face when she had resigned herself to killing the girl under the mountain.

"No," he said. "Not if you can avoid it." The idea of Enwezor or Sloane having to wrangle with the guilt of killing a child for the rest of their lives made his stomach turn. At least *he* was already damaged goods. "Just come find me," he said. "I'll do what needs to be done."

· · · · ·

Daria awoke in a cold sweat, her slender limbs shaking badly. There was blood dripping from her nose, and she wiped it away with the back of her hand as she cast off her pallet's thin blanket and stood.

Visions always brought blood, but this time she didn't care; she was too troubled by what she'd seen to spare any concern over the state of her stained clothing. Still shaking, she ran her clean hand through her hair and stepped out of her tent, breathing in the cold night air.

She wasn't alone. Esfir must have completed her rounds or heard Daria cry out and come running, because the blonde vampire was standing just outside of the tent, eyeing Daria with curiosity. She raised a pale brow. "What did you see?" She asked.

Daria shook her head. "Bad omens."

"Anything clear?"

It had been all too clear this time—much more so than her usual visions. Behind her eyes, Daria could still see Aya on the ground, writhing in pain as she bled from her eyes and nose, could still see the light leave her face as the bleeds took her.

Still, she didn't feel like sharing that with her blonde clan mate. Esfir had been less than pleased by Aya's unannounced departure the day before, and she would no doubt relish the news that Aya was doomed to suffer the bleeds.

"No," she lied. "Nothing clear. Just blood and death."

Esfir nodded, apparently satisfied. "Do you want me to get you something to wash up with?" She asked.

It was only then that Daria realized her nose was still bleeding. She could feel the stickiness of the blood on her lips and chin, could feel the tickle where some of the drops were running down her throat. "Yes, thank you."

Esfir momentarily left her there and Daria bowed her head, watching as the blood began to fall from her chin to the ground below, her mind drawn back to the horror of her vision.

She felt a wave of sympathy for the doomed vampire. Most visions could be interpreted in various ways, but not this one. When a vampire's heart was pierced and they endured the bleeds, there was only ever one painful, agonizing outcome.

Daria closed her eyes, once more seeing the dark-haired vampire's blood and pain. The timeline was uncertain, but the eventuality was not: Aya was going to die.

She opened her eyes and sighed, staring up at the stars, uncaring of the trail of blood that once more started to run down her chin and neck. "You chose unwisely, sister," she whispered to the night. "Most unwisely."

·     ·     ·     ·     ·

Clio had told her to run for the bunker, and she was doing exactly that— running back to the bunker like her life depended on it, ignoring the screams of terror and pain all around her and blocking out the flashes of movement (morph? human?) she could see from the corners of her eyes.

None of it mattered. All that mattered was getting back to the bunker. She needed to get back and lock the door and —

Another scream pierced the air, and this one made Cody Reade come to a dead stop. *Did they just say…?* The scream that followed the first confirmed it and propelled Cody back into motion, this time away from the bunker and towards the voices. All because of the name.

She found them almost immediately.

The teenage twins – Lyle and Lucy – were cowering against a tree, and Lyle was waving a stick at a small morph that had its back to Cody.

But it didn't matter. Cody knew who it was even before Lyle once more screamed his name.

"Will, get back! Leave us alone!"

"Please, Will," Lucy sobbed. "You know us!"

Cody felt like someone had poured ice water down her spine. All of her fear at the morph attack disappeared, leaving only coldness in its wake.

"No," she said softly. "He doesn't know you. Not anymore."

The thing that had once been Willie turned at the sound of her voice, baring a mouthful of pointed fangs, his black eyes riveted to her throat, and even though they hadn't really been friends anymore, Cody felt tears welling up in her eyes.

*Why did you have to get scratched, Willie? Why couldn't you just be okay?*

She swallowed. "Willie?" She called out in spite of what she'd told the siblings, clinging to the stupid hope that somehow, he would recognize his nickname and remember who he was.

But the morph only growled at her. Willie, like so many of the people she knew and cared about, was gone.

Wiping the wetness from her eyes, Cody took out two of her throwing knives and quickly scanned the area around her. Zor and Sloane had been watching Willie for the past four days, but right now they were nowhere to be seen. It wasn't surprising, though. They'd probably gotten distracted during this latest morph attack. How could they have guessed that Willie would turn right when everything got so crazy?

The timing was terrible, and it meant that Cody was the only one around to deal with the monster that had once been her friend.

Steeling herself, she flipped the knives around in her hands, holding them gingerly by the blades, and waited, shifting into position.

She didn't have to wait long.

Morph Willie charged her after only a second, extending his claws toward her as he closed the distance between them.

*Three... two... one...*

Cody threw her knives with deadly precision. The first twirled through the air and landed in the center of Willie's chest, and the second hit him squarely between the eyes, dropping him instantly. He fell to the ground at her feet as Cody stood there shaking.

*I'm sorry, Willie,* she thought numbly.

And then she was struck from behind, the blow so forceful it sent her sprawling to the ground mere inches from Willie's body.

Startled and in pain, Cody pushed herself up to her forearms, trying to ignore the way Willie's flat black eyes were staring lifelessly at her.

"You little bitch!" Someone hollered above her. "You killed my son!"

Cody rolled over, coming face to face with Vivian Brandt. The woman's face was livid, crazed, and she had an axe in her hands.

Cody's eyes widened. "Please, Mrs. Brandt, it wasn't Willie anymore—!"

"Shut up!" Vivian shrieked, brandishing the axe. Her eyes flashed. "I'm going to kill you, you little orphan bitch!"

Cody scooted backwards, her earlier terror returning with a vengeance. She was vaguely aware that Lyle and Lucy were screaming at Vivian to stop, but neither sibling was taking action. They were either too scared or too paralyzed to intervene.

Which meant that there was nothing to stop Vivian Brandt from killing her. Cody opened her mouth and screamed.

And suddenly, in a billow of black fabric, a figure appeared between her and Willie's vengeful mother and emitted a growl so fearsome that Cody fell silent. Shock stole what was left of her voice as soon as she realized who her savior was.

*Clio.*

Cody knew that Clio was a hybrid, but this was the first time she'd ever seen him look like—like *this*. His eyes were black, grey veins bleeding down the right side of his face, and his lips were pulled back in a snarl, exposing fangs longer than those of any morph Cody had ever seen. He was anger and power and feral strength – a veritable nightmare come to life – and he had never looked less human.

"Get away from her," he hissed at Vivian. In one swift movement, he grabbed the axe out of her hands, cast it aside, and unsheathed his katana, holding the slender blade up to the woman's neck.

"But she—she *killed*—" Vivian gurgled.

Clio's black eyes flashed with murderous promise. "One more step or word and I will kill you where you stand."

That quieted the hysterical woman. Indecision warred in her eyes for a moment, but then she held her hands up in a gesture of surrender and stepped back, shooting Cody one final hateful glare as she retreated.

Clio waited until she was a few paces away and then he turned around, holding out his free hand to Cody.

Cody grasped it and began to pull herself to her feet, but then she saw a flash of silver in her periphery. "Clio!" She screamed.

What happened next transpired so quickly that Cody didn't even really see it—her mind just filled in the blanks.

Vivian Brandt must have had another weapon on her person because she lunged at Clio with a spare dagger in her hand, adrenaline and rage fueling her movements. She was fast, but Clio was much quicker. He let go of Cody, turned, and sliced, taking off Vivian's arm just below the elbow. Then he twirled once, using the momentum to bring the katana around in a sweeping arc. It was fluid and lightning fast, and in the next moment the katana was dripping blood and Vivian Brandt's head was rolling on the ground a few inches from her dead son, her mouth opened wide in a scream she hadn't even had time to voice.

Cody blinked in shock, trying to process what had just happened.

Clio dropped his bloody blade and stood there for a moment, shaking with rage, his fingers twitching at his sides.

Without being told, Cody instinctively knew that he was trying to keep his inner monster from taking over. She swallowed and, her own hand still shaking, she reached out and tugged on the hybrid's hand. "Come back, Clio," she tried to say. "It's over now." But her voice didn't seem to be working properly and all that came out was a jumble of incoherent syllables.

But Clio turned anyway and looked down at her. His chest was still heaving, but, as Cody watched, the blackness began to recede from his eyes and his fangs began to retract. Soon, he looked like his mismatched self again.

He frowned, the rage in his hazel eye giving way to concern. "Are you all right?" He asked her.

Cody's eyes darted over to Willie and his mother. Morph or not, *she* was responsible for that. Those were her knives sticking out of Willie. She'd thrown them. She'd killed him.

She shook her head, her chin beginning to tremble.

Clio crouched down in front of her. "I'm so sorry, Cody. None of this should have happened and you—you shouldn't have had to do this or see me like that. I know you must be scared."

As soon as he said it, Cody couldn't hold it in anymore. She began to cry.

Clio seemed to break as soon as she did. "Please don't cry," he said. "You don't have to be scared. I won't hurt you. I'd never hurt you."

Cody didn't understand why he was saying that, but she didn't care. She just stumbled forward and collapsed into him, throwing her arms around his neck, her tears pouring out like a flood.

Clio stiffened for a moment, but then he relaxed and began to gently stroke her hair. Carefully, he scooped her up in his arms and stood. "Come here, you two," he beckoned to Lyle and Lucy, and Cody could feel the rumble of his voice when he spoke from where she was pressed against his chest. "I'm going to take Cody back to the bunker and then I want you both to stay with her until this is all over. Understood?"

Cody didn't hear them answer, but they must have, because a second later Clio was moving, his strides long and sure.

There were still intermittent screams piercing the air in the distance and the clash of skin and steel, signs that the battle was far from over, but Cody had nothing left in her. Still shaking with sobs, she burrowed deeper into the safety of Clio's chest and closed her eyes.

· · · · ·

Long after everyone else was asleep, Marcus kept watch by the fire, waiting for any sign of Clio just as he had the previous two nights. He was exhausted and battered in more ways than one, but he couldn't sleep. After the week they'd had, vigilance was non-negotiable.

They'd endured three morph attacks in only twice as many days, and Marcus feared that the group wouldn't be able to endure a fourth.

All three Brandts were dead: Will had turned, Clio had been forced to kill Vivian, and Christopher had been torn to pieces by a morph in the last of the attacks. The ugliness of their deaths had nearly flatlined morale in the group, and then when Colleen – who had just barely recovered from her illness – had been slain, the scant remnants of everyone's hope had drained away.

Wounded, weary, and despairing, they'd holed up in the nearest bunker and Marcus had sent Clio to scout ahead because he sensed – he damn well *knew* – that the worst was yet to come.

Sending Clio off once again in such a dire time had done little to put Marcus's mind at ease, but it had been unavoidable. He was almost certain that there was a morph base camp somewhere nearby—there was simply no other logical explanation for the quick succession of attacks they'd endured at the hands of three different raiding parties. And if his suspicions were correct, finding out exactly where the base camp was located was imperative. Happening upon it by accident when they were unprepared would be a disaster.

Reconnaissance had been the wisest move, but Clio had been gone longer than he should have been, and now Marcus was beginning to fear that something had happened to the seemingly invincible hybrid.

So instead of trying in vain to sleep, Marcus kept watch for the third night in a row, hoping that, by some miracle, Clio would return and bring good news.

He waited and waited until finally, close to dawn, the first of those two things happened.

Clio returned.

He appeared, as always, like a wraith: swiftly and silently, emerging from the trees like a grim specter, and it was very clear from the expression on his face that the news he'd brought with him was far from good.

Marcus skipped the pleasantries and braced himself. "What did you find?"

Clio's lips were pressed into a thin line. "Exactly what you expected me to find," he answered. "A morph base camp. It's a hundred strong, and that's not even the worst part."

Of course it wasn't. "Tell me."

"The real problem is the location of the camp," Clio continued, stress evident in his voice. His proud shoulders slumped forward. "It's directly in our path, and because of the mountains, I couldn't find a way around it, meaning that—"

"We're trapped," Marcus finished bleakly. "We can't go back, and we can't go forward."

Clio grimaced. "Precisely." For the first time since Marcus had met him, a look of utter despair passed across the hybrid's face. "Marcus, I…I don't know what we are going to do," he confessed, his voice heavy. "These people are relying on us to get them to Ashland, but after what I saw today…" He shook his head. "I'm not sure it's possible anymore."

Marcus swallowed hard, thinking of everything that had happened since the fall of Easthaven: the storms, the morphs, the vampires, the sickness, the deaths…so much blood, pain, and suffering. Ever since they'd started out, it had felt like the universe itself was fucking rooting against them.

*And now we're stuck, trapped in this fucking wasteland of a country with nowhere safe to go.*

Marcus barked out a mirthless laugh, his breath fogging in the cold predawn air. "You know what?" He bit out caustically, all his doubts finally consuming him, "I'm not sure it was ever possible to begin with."

. . . . .

The mess hall was crowded but quieter than usual, people conversing in hushed tones and glancing furtively at the guards posted in each doorway as they ate their lunches. Once, the hall would have been a din of noise come noon, but ever since the Guard had begun increasing security and personnel around the fortress, the general mood of Ashland's populace had declined drastically. People were uneasy, concerned, and paranoid, and every mealtime was now a reflection of that.

Emmanuel was sitting by himself towards the back of the hall, idly stirring his soup, his mind occupied with other things. Because of the tightened security that his father had insisted upon at the Council meeting five days hence — for ostensibly no actual reason – Emmanuel had all but lost his freedom of movement. In the first two weeks following the day he'd administered the vaccine to the captured morph, Emmanuel had gone and monitored the morph's progress on a daily basis. Since his father's crackdown, however, he'd only been able to slip away to the dungeon once. It had been three full days since he had seen the morph, and he was more than a little worried.

*What if its rehabilitation took a turn for the worse? What if it escaped? What if it died?*

The list of negative possibilities was endless.

Suddenly, a sharp double-rap on the edge of the table pulled Emmanuel's attention and he looked up, blinking in surprise at the sight of Joben Hale standing in front of him.

The commander was angled away from him and his eyes were trained on the guard posted nearest to them. "Go at four o'clock," he whispered quickly. "I've bought you twenty minutes. You won't run into anyone."

He was gone before Emmanuel could ask for more information, and Emmanuel stared after him as he strode from the mess hall, perplexed.

He had no reason to doubt Joben's word, but he wondered what exactly the other man had done to 'buy' him twenty minutes. Emmanuel hadn't spoken with Joben since before the Council meeting, but he knew that Dex had been in contact with him, and Dex was aware of Emmanuel's trouble. It wasn't so farfetched to imagine that Dex might have requested Joben's help in the matter and in so doing put the commander at risk, and that frustrated Emmanuel. Still, though, he wasn't foolish enough to waste the opportunity Joben had somehow given him.

He finished his soup and cleared his place, then walked back to his room, making sure to walk at a pace that wouldn't attract any attention.

The afternoon passed slowly, and Emmanuel reviewed his notes to pass the time until four o'clock finally arrived.

Leaving the copy of his notes on his desk (the originals were in his makeshift lab), Emmanuel turned off the lights and opened his door, peering out to look for guards.

Just as Joben had promised, there were none.

Quickly, Emmanuel locked his door and hurried down the hallway. At each corner he searched for guards, half convinced that his luck wouldn't hold, but it did. The halls and stairwells were empty and silent, and before he knew it, he was standing before the locked door that led down to the old subbasement he was using as a temporary lab.

Retrieving the ring of keys from his pocket, Emmanuel unbolted the door and stepped inside, shivering as a wave of cold, dank air hit him.

And then he heard a voice drifting up from the stairs leading to the subbasement. Emmanuel froze in shock, his entire body stiffening.

He couldn't make out what the voice was saying, but it didn't really matter. All that mattered was that someone had gotten into the lab. Someone was down there, now.

Which meant that they knew about the morph and the unsanctioned experimentation Emmanuel was conducting.

*I could be turned out for this,* he thought in a panic, and it wasn't an irrational fear. Even if they'd only been down there for a minute, whoever was in the lab would certainly have enough damning evidence to get him convicted at a trial.

Emmanuel knew what Dex would do. *Silenced people are the best secret keepers,* he'd said in one of their early meetings, and Emmanuel had heard enough stories about Dex's exploits to know that the albino man had put those words into action on more than one occasion.

But he wasn't Dex. No matter what the situation, he'd never been a killer and he had no plans of becoming one now. Somehow, he would think of another way to solve whatever problem was waiting for him.

Swallowing against his rising fear, Emmanuel made his way down the steps as silently as he could, trying to formulate a plan. Maybe he could talk the intruder down, show them the benefits of the work he was doing, try to make them understand…

Emmanuel blinked, coming to a shocked standstill at the bottom of the stairs.

There was no one in the lab.

He was utterly and completely alone.

Except that the voice was still speaking, rattling off words and numbers, as clear as could be. And the voice was coming from…

Emmanuel nearly lost his balance as the realization hit him.

The voice was coming from the morph. The morph, which was sitting with its back pressed against the bars of its cell, was *speaking*.

Emmanuel swallowed, his throat suddenly as dry as a desert. The question *it worked? it worked?* pulsed in his brain as he slowly, cautiously, walked towards the cell. "He—hello?" He stammered, his heart pounding.

The voice stopped, silence reigning.

And then the morph turned and looked at him. It blinked once, twice, its mostly human eyes full of fear and uncertainty, its face haggard and drawn. "Hello?" It repeated in a quiet voice—and it was indeed the same voice that Emmanuel had heard before.

Emmanuel was so bowled over by the morph's transformation that he could barely get his mouth to form simple syllables. "I…" He stopped. "You can hear me—you can understand me?" He finally managed.

The morph nodded slowly and then wrapped its hands around the bars and pulled itself up to its feet, its mottled black and blue eyes never leaving Emmanuel's face.

"That—that's good," Emmanuel said, still reeling at the difference a few days had made. The morph's claws and fangs had started receding over a week ago, as had the blackness of its eyes, but it had still been animalistic the last time Emmanuel had been in the lab, had still seemed unresponsive and had still exhibited behaviors much more beast-like than human. But now, it—*he*, rather, was not a morph at all. Not anymore.

Emmanuel swallowed again. "I'm Emmanuel," he stated. "I'm a doctor here. I've been treating you for the past few weeks. Do you remember anything about that? Or anything from before?"

The man's face contorted at the question and he started to shake, his limbs trembling.

Emmanuel held up his hands in a calming gesture. "It's okay," he soothed. "It's okay. We don't have to talk about that right now. Let's start with something easier."

That seemed to relax the former morph slightly, and Emmanuel offered him an encouraging smile. "Do you remember your name?" He asked.

The man remained still for a moment, and then he nodded and opened his mouth. "Ian," he said quietly. "My name is Ian Hayes."

# A Million to One

*Sometimes, sacrifice is the only way forward.*
- Old Reaper maxim

. . . . .

Before the fall of Easthaven, Enwezor would often wake up in a good mood, ready to tackle whatever the day threw at him. Since they'd set out, however, he'd had fewer and fewer mornings like that. But even now, he would still sometimes wake up feeling like it was going to be a good day, that despite the dangers and attacks and the constant scarcity of supplies, despite the pain and exhaustion, the group would rally enough to last a few more hours until they made camp and started the cycle all over again.

Today was not one of those days. Enwezor knew, from the moment Sloane shook him awake, that something was wrong—well, *more* wrong than the shitfest of wrong they usually experienced. The shift in morale had been bad enough after the Brandts and Colleen had been killed, but today it was downright funereal. Cap and Clio had been silent and somber all day, and while that wasn't entirely unusual for Cap, it was for Clio. And in addition to that, the group hadn't pressed forward at all. Cap had given some vague reason as to why they were lingering at their current outpost for another day, but Enwezor could tell it was just an excuse—and not even a good one. The civilians had started to whisper and grumble, their paranoia increasing as the daylight dwindled, and then, just when Enwezor didn't think his own anxiety levels could creep any higher, Cap had called for the meeting during first watch.

Something was *definitely* wrong.

"Hey, Zor," Sloane said, gently bumping his shoulder with hers as she fell into step beside him.

"Hey." He glanced over at her. "What do you think Cap called the meeting for?"

Sloane shrugged, her lips pulling down in a frown. "Nothing good, judging by how weird he and Jones have been acting all day long."

Enwezor was glad that he wasn't the only one who had noticed. "Right?" He agreed. "They're acting like...like..."

"Like they're trying to find the best way to tell us that we're going to die," Sloane finished.

Normally, Enwezor would have chalked that answer up to Sloane's insufferable habit of responding sarcastically, but something in her tone made him think that she wasn't joking. His stomach turned. "You really think it's that bad?"

Sloane met his gaze, and there was an utter lack of hope in her green eyes. "Yeah, I do," she replied softly.

They walked in silence after that until they got to the campfire. It wasn't far from the bunker, but all of the civilians were inside for the night, safely out of earshot.

Cap and Clio were already there, conversing in low tones, but they stopped as soon as Enwezor and Sloane drew up beside them.

Sloane crossed her arms. "What's going on?" She asked, wasting no time.

Cap looked from her to Enwezor, his expression unreadable. "We have a problem."

Enwezor shrugged. "We've had problems before—"

"Not like this one," Cap said, cutting him off. "Clio found a morph base camp while he was out scouting. It's a hundred strong and it's directly in our path."

Enwezor's jaw fell open. *A hundred morphs?* They'd never faced even half that many at once before. "Shit," he cursed, not knowing what else to say.

"Can't we just avoid the camp—you know, go around it or something?" Sloane asked, her brow furrowing.

Marcus shook his head. "No. The morphs picked their location strategically; the camp is positioned on the only accessible road that passes through this mountain range. Their camp is our only way through."

Enwezor jumped on Sloane's earlier train of thought. "We could find another path," he suggested. "Or make a new one. Maybe over one of the peaks?"

Again, Marcus shook his head. "No, we can't. The mountains in this area would be perilous to traverse even with proper gear, and without gear they'd be impossible to climb. The peaks are too steep, the inclines too severe."

"So what are our options?"

"We don't have any," Marcus admitted. "At least, we don't have any viable ones. Either we try and fight our way through the morph camp, or we go weeks out of our way and circumvent the mountain range. The probability of failure is high no matter which we choose."

"Well, option one seems like a suicide mission to me," Sloane said. "There are only sixteen of us left, and that's including civilians like Jillian who won't be much use in a fight. So if we're putting it to a vote, I vote option two."

"So do I," Enwezor agreed. An extra few weeks of travel time wasn't great, but it would certainly beat getting massacred.

"I admit it sounds better on the surface," Cap said, "but as soon as Clio and I talked it through the problems became obvious. For example: the outposts and bunkers we've been relying on for shelter and fuel do not run north or south along this mountain range. If we circumvent the mountains, we'll be traveling hundreds of miles without food or shelter from the elements. We haven't found fresh game in weeks, and temperatures are still dropping. Unless our luck or the weather changes significantly, there's a good chance we'll either starve or die of hypothermia before we make it back around."

"Maybe," Sloane argued, "but that doesn't change the fact that if we stay and fight, we'll be massacred. There's no way our group can take on a hundred morphs. We've barely been able to fend off the latest attacks—and the most morphs we've faced at once is twenty."

No one disagreed. Sloane was right, and all four of them knew it.

And suddenly, the horrible reality of their situation hit Enwezor with such force that it nearly stole the breath from his lungs.

"We're going to die either way," he uttered as he reached the same conclusion that Cap and Clio must have reached earlier. He looked between the two soldiers, daring them to deny it. "I'm right, aren't I?" He asked when they offered no reply, hoping that one of them would contradict him.

But they didn't. A pained look flitted across Cap's stoic face. "It's very likely," he said quietly.

Enwezor felt like his world was collapsing, and apparently, he wasn't the only one.

"You've got to be kidding me," Sloane spat out next to him. She was practically shaking, her usual sarcasm and composure completely gone. "We travel nearly seven hundred miles, through all kinds of fucking hell, and for what? To die now? When we're this close?" She snorted out an incredulous huff. "This is fucking ridiculous."

Enwezor stared at his friend in shock. He had never seen Sloane act like this before. No matter the situation, she'd always been able to stay detached. Sure, she was pessimistic, but she was also cool and collected. Now it was like she'd snapped. Not knowing what else to do, he tried to place a hand on her shoulder, but Sloane shrugged him off.

"No," she barked at him, her green eyes flashing with anger. "I don't want anyone's pity or comfort." Her voice cracked. "I want to live," she choked out. "I want to make it to Ashland. I want to have a roof over my head and a meal in front of me and I want to put on some clean damn clothes, but apparently that's too much to ask for. Instead, I got to survive up to now just so I could die bloody or starve. It's a fucking joke!" She kicked at the fire, sending a flare of embers crackling into the sky. "You know, I wish we'd just gotten blown to shit with the rest of Easthaven. At least that would have been a quick way to go."

Enwezor sucked in a breath. "Wait!" He exclaimed. "Sloane, that's it!"

She looked at him sharply, frowning. "What's it?"

"An explosion," he answered, his gaze shifting between her, Cap, and Clio. "We don't have to fight the morphs," he said, his voice rising with excitement. "We can blow them up. Cap—do you remember when we were at Eden and you asked us to do a weapons inventory and stock up?"

Marcus nodded.

"Well, we did, and in addition to all of the steel we found, there was also quite a bit of—"

"Dynamite," Sloane breathed, her eyes going wide. "Shit, you're right. And we took it with us." She laughed, and this time the sound was like a bubble of hope. "Zor, you're a genius!"

But Cap didn't seem to share their enthusiasm. If anything, he seemed put off by their newfound hope.

And Enwezor understood why a second later.

"It's a good idea," Marcus said. "But we can't use the dynamite to blow up their camp."

"Why the hell not?" Sloane asked, incredulous.

"Because of its location," Cap answered. He sighed. "The pathway through the mountains is extremely narrow—the trail bottlenecks pretty drastically before it widens again, meaning that if we set off an explosion, it will likely bring down thousands of pounds of rock and debris from the mountains above it and block our route. It'll also likely cause an avalanche, and because of the snowstorms we've been having, you can bet it will be a big one."

Enwezor stared at the shorter man, the hope he'd had moments before dwindling down to bleak hopelessness. There wasn't a word strong enough to convey the demoralization he felt in that moment. "So what you're saying is that we'd effectively be destroying our only way through," he said.

Marcus nodded solemnly. "That's exactly what I'm saying. Remember how the morphs bombed us when we were in the mines under the mountain? They essentially buried us. The only reason we were able to continue on was because they blocked off our retreat but not our egress. But this isn't the same scenario. If we explode their camp, we'll be trapped on the wrong side of the debris—if we don't get killed by it to begin with."

So that was it, then. They were back at square one again, every option they had still ending with their deaths.

The heaviness of it all nearly buckled Enwezor where he stood.

But suddenly Clio, who had been a silent observer up until that point, held up a finger. "Hold on," he said, and Enwezor could see the gears turning in the hybrid's mismatched eyes. "We may not be able to use the dynamite to blow up the camp, but maybe we can still use it to our advantage."

In a fluid motion that Enwezor had witnessed many times before but still rattled him because of its impossible speed, Clio unsheathed his katana and angled the blade towards the ground. Using his foot, the hybrid cleared a small patch of snow to reveal the muddy earth beneath. "I'll show you what I mean—if you're interested?" He asked, glancing over at Marcus.

The Reaper crossed his arms over his broad chest and nodded. "All options are worth exploring at this point. Go ahead."

They all stepped in close as Clio used the point of his katana to draw an X in the mud. "If we're here," he said, "and the morph camp is here—" he drew another X a few inches behind the first and then flanked it with two mountainous shapes "—then we do have a little room to work with." He made a circle off to the right between the two spots he'd marked. "This area is where we can stage a diversion." He jabbed the tip of his blade into the middle of the circle. "Here's what I'm thinking. If we use part of our dynamite cache to set off an explosion, the morphs will likely come investigate. Think about it: the first two raiding parties that attacked us last week were only ten strong, but the final party was a double—twenty morphs, meaning that whoever's in charge realizes that we are a greater threat than they initially anticipated. When the first two raiding parties didn't return, they sent twice as many, but we killed them, too, so I'd wager that if we make our presence known with something as dramatic as an explosion, even more morphs will come. And that," he concluded with another jab of his katana, "is when we set off the rest of the dynamite."

Enwezor gawked at the brilliance of the hybrid's idea. "It's just like a mousetrap," he said, stunned. "We draw them in and then we hit 'em hard."

Clio nodded. "That's the general idea, yeah."

"But you didn't say trap," Sloane pointed out. "You said diversion."

"That's because it *will* be a diversion," Clio confirmed. "If this plan works – and I think it will – the morph forces will be split." He began to draw lines connecting his marks in the mud. "A good chunk of them will go *here*, to see what caused the explosion, while the rest remain at base. So, if we time it right, one person can set off the dynamite while the rest of the group makes for the pass. Instead of sixteen of us against one hundred, the odds will be more like fifteen against fifty or less." He paused. "Failure is obviously still possible, but at least we'd be giving ourselves a fighting chance."

Enwezor was so happy that he could have cheered—right up until he realized the one fatal flaw in the plan. "Wait," he said, his brow furrowing. "What about the person who stays to set off the dynamite? To kill that many morphs, the second explosion is going to have to be big. How will they clear the blast area in time?"

The hybrid's lips pulled up in a sad little tilt. "There's always a catch," he said.

A heavy silence descended on the group.

"So one of us has to sacrifice ourselves," Sloane eventually voiced.

Clio glanced over at Cap, meeting the Reaper's eyes so briefly that Enwezor couldn't interpret the look that passed between them.

Clio flicked the mud off of his katana and sheathed it. "Not necessarily," he said. "There is obviously a good chance that the explosion will kill the person who sets it, but if they survey the area prior to detonating the cache, they can try to find something nearby that can act as a natural shield against the explosion and then set the dynamite to their advantage. It's not foolproof by any means, but at least it will give them a few extra seconds to get away and a small margin of safety. Then, if the main group is successful in killing the morphs that remain at the base camp, the soloist can join back up with them."

Enwezor appreciated that Clio was trying to be optimistic, but he knew that the hybrid was reaching. Whoever stayed behind to set off the explosions would most likely die, and Enwezor knew without being told that it was going to be one of the four of them.

He looked around at their tiny group. Cap couldn't do it—he was the leader, and Enwezor couldn't imagine the group making it to Ashland without him. And Clio was invaluable; he was the strongest fighter next to Cap and he had also become a sort of leader to the group. As for Sloane, well, she was his friend; he didn't want her to die.

Which left only one option.

Enwezor took a breath. "I'll do it."

Sloane gawked at him. "Like hell, Zor."

"Sloane, it's gotta be one of us. There just aren't any other options."

"What about Ed?" She suggested, putting her hands on her hips. "That guy is always looking for ways to help."

"We can't ask a civilian to do this," Clio interjected. "They don't have the training and it wouldn't be right to put such a crucial responsibility on their shoulders."

"I agree," Cap added, silencing the argument. "It needs to be one of us."

Sloane's shoulders slumped. "Well shit," she uttered, glancing at Enwezor. "If you're volunteering, I guess I should too. I'm not going to let you show me up."

Her tone was flippant, but Enwezor could see the fear in her eyes. He swallowed against the lump in his throat. "You're always showing *me* up," he said with much more levity than he felt. "Let's take turns for a change."

Cap stepped forward, holding out his hands. "This isn't a democracy," he said firmly. "I'll decide who it will be. In the meantime, I need you two to go see exactly how much dynamite we have. Report back to me with a precise amount."

They both nodded and saluted and were about to turn away when Cap spoke again.

"Hold up," he said, regaining their attention. Enwezor looked back, waiting. "It was…very brave of you both to volunteer," the Reaper said. There was a strange look in his eyes, one that Enwezor couldn't define. "I know it's a moot point now, but the two of you would've made fine Rangers."

Enwezor's pride swelled at Marcus's words, despite the gravity of their present situation. "Thanks, Cap," he said huskily. "That means a lot."

Sloane snorted. "C'mon, Mule, don't go getting all sappy. We've got shit to do."

It wasn't her usual show of bravado, but Enwezor appreciated that she was trying to put on a brave face. "Right," he said, nodding. "Let's go count some dynamite sticks."

.  .  .  .  .

Marcus watched Sloane and Enwezor walk away, noting the proud way they held themselves despite the fear and anxiety they had to be feeling. It was a testament to how far they'd come from the trainees they'd once been.

"It's funny," he murmured, reflecting on how much the pair had changed in the time since he'd met them. "Those two harassed me for half a year before I finally agreed to train them, and when they started out, they were the biggest disasters I'd ever seen. But now…" He sighed. "If the Rangers were still active, I'd choose them both for my squad in a heartbeat. They're incredible kids."

Clio stirred next to him, shifting slightly. "Yes, they are." He paused. "And they have a captain worthy of them," he added.

Marcus glanced up in surprise at that, but then he shrugged. "Cap is just a nickname," he said. "I'm not even officially a ranking officer."

"You are in every way that counts," Clio countered gently. He straightened. "May I ask a favor of you?"

Marcus raised a curious brow at him, waiting.

"Will you look after Cody for me?"

Marcus frowned, confused. Why the hell would he need to look after Cody? The question didn't make any sense. "What are you talking about?" He asked.

"I'm asking you to keep an eye on Cody when I'm gone," Clio explained. "Because the odds are stacked pretty drastically against me surviving this."

Marcus was still at a loss. "Surviving what?"

"The explosions," the hybrid clarified, his human eye full of sad acceptance. "I've thought it through, and the solution is simple: *I* am going to be the one who stays behind. I'll set the dynamite. I'll be the diversion."

It shouldn't have come as such a surprise that Clio would volunteer, given that they'd agreed only moments earlier that it would be one of the four of them, but it still did.

Before Marcus could say anything, though, Clio barreled on. "Hear me out, Captain," he said. "It *needs* to be me. We've already established that it can't be a civilian—they don't have the training necessary to conduct a solo operation, but it also shouldn't be Sloane or Enwezor; they're just too young. They have their whole lives ahead of them. If they make it to Ashland, they'll have a place, a future. But I won't, because *this*—" he added, gesturing to the morph side of his face "—this won't fit in. I'd be an outcast at Ashland, just like I was an outcast at Easthaven." He dropped his hand and sighed, staring into the fire. "And all that aside, the truth is that there is no one better for this job than me. I'm adept at using explosives, I have the most field experience in the group, and I'm faster than any ordinary human." He looked back, meeting Marcus's gaze. "The truth is, Captain – whether you want to admit it or not – I am the only choice."

Marcus stared at the other man in silence. There was no doubt in his mind that Clio meant what he was saying. If Marcus gave the order, Clio would lay down his life for the group. Not that that came as a surprise. After all, the hybrid had proven his protectiveness and loyalty time and again, and he'd never once complained about the distrust he'd endured. He'd persevered in spite of it, and now he was held in high esteem by nearly everyone.

And he deserved it. Clio Jones was a better man than most, and far wiser than anyone Marcus had ever known.

But that didn't change the fact that he was wrong.

There *was* another choice, and it was a choice that Marcus had realized was the right one pretty soon after Clio had started talking.

"You're not going to stay behind," he told the hybrid. "I am."

It was clear that Clio had not been expecting that. His lips parted in surprise. "Captain, you can't —"

Marcus held up a hand. "Yes, I can," he said.

Ever the voice of reason, Clio immediately tried to talk him out of it. "Marcus, you're the leader. The group needs you."

That was the first problem Marcus had thought of, too, but the answer was literally right in front of him. "The group needs *a* leader, not me, and you're as cut out for the position as I am." He paused, thinking of the hybrid's unceasingly diplomatic nature. "Actually, you're probably a better fit."

"Captain—"

"Give it a rest, Jones. I've made up my mind, so just shut up and listen."

Clio crossed his arms, perturbed, but he didn't interrupt.

"You know the route to Ashland, you're the best damn fighter we have, and the group has come to trust you. It makes sense for you to take over; it's almost like we were preparing for this transition anyway." Marcus touched his healing ribs. "Because of this shit, you've been taking point more than I have the last few weeks." He grimaced as the press of his fingers caused a flare of pain. "Besides," he added, dropping his hand, "I don't think I have another fight in me. I'll be of more use to the group by blowing myself up and taking a few dozen of those rabid fucks with me."

"That's not true," Clio argued, his eyebrows knitted together. "You are the rock that's held this group together—and you're the only reason we had a chance of surviving this western passage to begin with. The group rallies behind you—they always have."

"They've also rallied behind you, and right now, you're in much better shape than I am." Marcus cocked a brow. "Don't believe me? Then answer this: which of us is more capable of fighting a horde of morphs right now?"

Clio dropped his gaze, withholding an answer.

Which was all the answer Marcus needed. He snorted. "Exactly. You don't want to admit it, but you know I'm right." He paused. "And besides, you have Cody to think about. You're her family now, and I expect you to be there for her. You promised Maggie as much."

In a way, it was Cody that had made Marcus realize that *he* was the one who needed to stay behind. That little girl had become Clio's family, and she would need him if they made it to Ashland.

But no one would need an injured pseudo-captain like him. He was alone, unwanted, little more than a lingering trace of an all but defunct branch of the military.

Everyone in the group had people they were trying to get home to, or people traveling with them that they cared about, but Marcus didn't. Everyone he cared about, everyone he loved, was gone.

"There's nothing for me at Ashland," he admitted quietly. "Just ghosts and memories."

Clio placed a gentle hand on his shoulder. "You have friends, Marcus. People who care about you. That won't disappear when you get to Ashland."

Marcus glanced up at the hybrid. There was conviction in his hazel eye, but it was the conviction of someone who still had something left to live for. "I know," he answered numbly. "But it's not the same." He clenched his jaw. "Besides, I'm tired of losing people. To borrow Enwezor's expression, it's my turn. This time, I'll stay behind and do what needs to be done."

Clio dropped his hand away from Marcus's shoulder. "Is there anything I can do to change your mind?"

"Nothing."

Clio pursed his lips, still troubled, still looking like he wanted to argue, but he nodded reluctantly. "Very well." He straightened up. "I disagree with you, but you are the leader and I will respect your decision, just as I respect you." He clasped his hands behind his back, his stance gaining a business-like quality. "So," he said. "What are your orders, Captain?"

Marcus straightened up as well. "Go tell Sloane and Enwezor what we've decided and then gather the group. We'll tell everyone the plan and set out first thing tomorrow."

"All right."

"But we'll keep the part about me blowing myself into the next life between us and Enwezor and Sloane."

A pained look crossed Clio's face. "Are you sure? I know it would demoralize the group, but at least you'd be able to say goodbye—and you deserve that much, at the very least."

Marcus ignored the way his heart seized up, keeping his expression neutral. "I'm sure," he said. "It's not worth it; the group needs to be as resilient as possible when they attack the morph camp, and this kind of news would only shake everyone up. Besides, goodbyes don't change anything anyway."

Clio was silent for a long time, watching him, but eventually he conceded to Marcus's wishes with a nod. "Okay," he said. "No goodbyes, then. But there is one thing that needs saying." He paused. "I wouldn't feel right parting ways without telling you, Marcus, that you are the best commanding officer I've ever served under." He saluted, holding the posture as he met Marcus's eyes. "It's been an honor, Captain."

Touched and somewhat surprised by the emotion in the hybrid's voice, Marcus returned his salute. "The feeling's mutual, Jones," he responded, meaning it. "It's why I feel confident leaving the group under your command; I know you won't let our people down." His lips tugged up slightly. "After all, you have a pretty good track record."

"Not as good as yours."

"Give it time." Marcus dropped his hand. "Now let's go tell everyone what we're up against."

·  ·  ·  ·  ·

The morning was cold and clear, and they reached the agreed upon diversion point well before noon.

Clio held up a hand, halting the group.

"All right," he said, uttering the first words anyone had spoken since they'd set out. "Drop the packs."

Sloane and Enwezor shrugged the laden packs off of their shoulders and carefully placed them on the forest floor.

Clio glanced over at Marcus, watching as the other man picked up the discarded cargo. He shouldered one pack on top of the pack he was already carrying and strapped the other onto his chest. His face remained impassive, but Clio caught the way his legs buckled slightly beneath the burden of extra weight.

He stepped in close and lowered his voice. "You okay?" He asked.

Marcus grimaced. "Okay enough to get to the job done," he replied.

"Captain," Ed called, walking over to where they were. "You sure you don't want help? Me an' Bird could each take a pack and go with you."

Aside from Ed, Bertrand – more commonly referred to as Bird – was the largest man in the group, and while somewhat skittish in social situations, he'd proven himself capable during a fight.

Of course, neither Bird nor Ed knew that their esteemed leader would be going on a one-way trip.

Marcus shook his head in response to Ed's offer. "No. Stay with Clio—we need all the manpower we have in order to wipe out the morph camp. I'll be fine." He adjusted the packs and straightened up, turning to Clio. "I hope this plan of yours works," he said.

*So do I.* "It will."

Marcus nodded, his grey eyes full of focus and determination. "Good luck."

"You too, Captain." He was about to say something else when he caught sight of Enwezor and Sloane in his periphery. They'd both reacted badly the previous night when they'd learned of the Reaper's decision, and while there had been a few volatile, emotional words exchanged between them and their captain as they attempted to change Marcus's mind, in the end they'd both bit their tongues and listened, because regardless of their personal feelings, they weren't about to disobey direct orders. But right now, neither of them looked like they were going to be able to keep their composure for much longer. If Marcus stayed, the ruse would be up, and everyone would know the truth.

Again, Clio lowered his voice so that only Marcus could hear him. "You'd better get out of here," he warned, purposely shifting his gaze to the younger soldiers as he spoke.

Marcus seemed to get the hint. He stepped away and raised his voice, addressing the group at large. "We have one chance at this," he said, "so let's make it count. When you attack, attack hard, and don't stop until every single morph is dead. Understood?"

Murmurs and cheers of assent filled the void left by his question, and Marcus nodded, satisfied. "Okay. I'll catch up with you later."

He looked over at Enwezor and Sloane, and then his eyes met Clio's one last time. A few unspoken words passed between them, and then Clio did the only thing that felt right in the situation: he saluted the man who had given him a chance when no one else wanted to, the man who had entrusted the group's safety to him, the man whom he would miss—if, of course, he and the others survived the day.

And then he watched as Marcus turned and walked away into the woods.

He swallowed against the small lump in his throat and refocused his attention to the group. *His* group, now.

"Okay," he said, rallying. "Let's get into position."

. . . . .

Every step with the weight of the extra packs was a struggle, but for once Marcus welcomed the pain. After all, soon enough he wouldn't be able to feel much of anything, so he might as well enjoy every last sensation—even the shitty ones.

Clio had paced out the decided upon location the night before and told Marcus what to look for, and well within the hour, Marcus arrived at the place in question.

It was a small clearing—probably no more than twenty yards wide in any direction. Marcus walked to the center and took off the pack on his chest, unzipping the top pocket. They'd tied the eight sticks of dynamite together with twine, making sure to keep the wicks accessible, so Marcus simply removed the bundle and placed it on top of the pack, using the simple canvas as a makeshift sheet. Then he took a single match from one of his pants pockets and held it aloft. He struck it quickly using his thumbnail—a trick that Stan had taught him years ago, and then he crouched down and gingerly lit the end of the center stick's wick. It began to fizzle and spark, and Marcus jogged to the edge of the clearing that seemed furthest from the center, hustling despite the pain in his ribs. Bracing himself against a tree, he turned and watched as the fuse shortened and the air began to grow smoky, and then he plugged his ears.

*Three…two…one…*

The boom of the explosion was deafening, and Marcus winced at the sound as the ground shook beneath him. Flames soared skyward, filling the clearing with a bright light, and a few stray birds that had been hidden in nearby trees shot out of the barren canopies, cawing in terror as they flew away.

*They had to have heard that,* Marcus thought, staring up at the chimney of black smoke curling in the air. *Maybe they even felt it.*

He wondered how long it would take for the morphs to come, and how much longer after that Clio and the others would attack the camp. Seconds? Minutes? Hours? It was impossible to know, and even more impossible to guess what would happen when they did. Marcus hoped that they would win, that they would live, but even if Clio's plan was a success, their odds were still not great.

*By sundown, I'll be ashes and bones and they'll probably be morph meat,* he thought grimly, but as quickly as it had come, he pushed the thought away. Now wasn't the time to brood on morbid outcomes; he had to focus, to make sure that everything went as planned on his end.

Marcus waited until the air and ground settled, and then he strode back to the center of the clearing, depositing the remaining two packs on top of the charred remnants of the first. Methodically, he removed the dynamite bundles and placed them side by side on the ground. Unlike the other pack, these sticks were bundled in groups of twelve, which meant that the explosion would be much bigger than the first. And judging by the blast area left by the first one, the second would likely fill the whole clearing.

It would be bad news for the morphs, but it was also bad news for him.

*Well, twerp, sometimes you gotta make sacrifices to make progress—isn't that somethin' you super soldiers say?*

Marcus snorted at the memory of his uncle. It just fucking figured that in his last few minutes on earth, it would be Stan that popped into his mind.

Then again, it was fittingly ironic. After all, he was about to follow in Stan's final footsteps.

With a sigh, Marcus stooped down and removed a single stick of dynamite from the cache, and then he walked back to the far edge of the clearing, placing the dynamite in one hand and palming a match in the other.

Now, all he had to do was wait—for the morphs and for the end.

· · · · ·

They'd split into three factions just as he'd instructed, and from his elevated vantage point atop the small bluff overlooking the valley, Clio could just see Enwezor's group to his far right and Sloane's group to his far left. Both of them were hanging well back from the morph camp, waiting for his signal.

Clio had to admit that of all the places to stage the attack, this particular valley was ideal. While not as heavily wooded as the surrounding forest above and around it, the wide valley was still filled with enough trees to give them a good measure of security. In fact, the only open, clear stretch of land was the path that led up to the morph camp itself, where it lay nestled between the bases of two jagged peaks. At one point, before nature had reclaimed much of its surface and before morphs had walked the earth, the path had been a road used by military and civilian transports alike.

*How drastically things have changed in just a few short years,* Clio thought as he monitored the activity in the morph camp below him.

Even though the bluff he'd chosen for their stakeout jutted upwards, Clio remained prone, not wanting to draw any attention to his location in case the morphs had implemented some kind of watch or patrol. His limbs were starting to stiffen from the prolonged inactivity, but Clio pushed the discomfort to the back of his awareness, focusing instead on Sloane and Enwezor and keeping one eye on the stretch of forest leading away from the right side of the valley, where Marcus was supposed to set off the dynamite.

Minutes passed, and then more minutes passed, and just when Clio was beginning to think something had gone wrong, the first explosion happened. It wasn't as big as he'd hoped it would be, but it was still a spectacle—the *boom* of it reverberating into the valley as a plume of smoke rose skyward amidst a barren canopy about a half-mile away.

Clio heard the collective gasps of his other group members standing further below him on the bluff, and suddenly Savannah crawled up next to him, stretching out and peeking over the edge. "Do you think it worked?" She breathed, her eyes bright with hopeful curiosity.

Clio nodded and dipped his head toward the far end of the valley, where the morph camp lay nestled between a break in the mountains. "Look for yourself," he said.

"I can't tell what's going on, Jones," she said with a pout. "Human eyes, remember?"

"Right." It was easy to forget, sometimes, that the rest of the world didn't share his enhanced eyesight. "They've formed a pretty big circle in the middle of the camp," he relayed. "They're talking, and some of them are gesturing towards the explosion. And now..." He trailed off, watching as a massive morph parted the crowd and held up a muscled arm, calling for silence. The thing had to be well over six feet tall, and it was built like a brick wall.

It was, without a doubt, the largest morph Clio had ever seen. And it was, also without a doubt, the commander.

"And now what?" Savannah whispered. "What's going on?"

"I think I found the leader," he replied quietly.

The large morph conversed with the others for a few minutes, and then the entire group dispersed.

Clio held his breath, praying that his assumption would be proven right.

It was.

Less than two minutes later, three units came streaming out of the camp and started off across the valley, heading for the forest.

"Thirty down..." He said absently.

Savannah jerked her head sharply in his direction. "Thirty?" She hissed, the hope in her eyes transforming into panic. "That means there's a good seventy-some morphs still at camp. We can't take all of them out!"

"More will go after the second explosion," Clio said, crawling backwards until he was far enough away from the edge to stand without being seen by anyone below. He gestured for Savannah to do the same and waited until she stood up to turn to the others.

Ed, Bird, Ralph, and Panko were already huddled up, looking at him with strained expressions. Cody was the only one who didn't look afraid—her six-year-old features were scrunched up in determination and she had her daggers gripped tightly in hand. Clio smiled briefly at her before assessing the rest of his group. With the exceptions of Savannah and Cody, each member of his group was large and beefy and had proven their worth in previous attacks. He'd intentionally selected the strongest fighters for his own team because they would be the ones leading the attack.

*The first wave always has to be strong. Knock the enemy back from the outset and then send in reinforcements to finish the job.*

It was a strategy he'd learned early on in his military training, and it was more or less today's game plan.

"All right," he said, looking from person to person and trying to instill confidence in them. "Captain Marcus has set off the first explosion, and three parties of morphs have already left the camp. We will move into position in the valley and wait for the second explosion. Based on what just happened, it's safe to assume that even more units will be deployed after the next explosion. As soon as they clear the valley, we will attack." He began walking down the path that led towards the valley. "Stay close," he said over his shoulder.

If he'd been alone, Clio would have gotten as close as possible to the morph camp to wait for the second explosion, but he couldn't trust the rest of his group to be as quiet as he was, so he halted them about fifty yards away, making sure they were shielded from sight by the trees.

Luckily, from what Clio could see, none of the morphs were paying much attention to...

Suddenly, a clamor of grunts and shouts rose up somewhere east of the camp, and Clio watched in horror as a small cluster of morphs disappeared into the trees. Seconds later, a shrill, human scream erupted into the air.

*Sloane's group!*

"Shit," he cursed, drawing his katana. He'd been specific in his instructions—telling Sloane and Enwezor not to attack until they saw his group reach the center of the morph camp, but clearly something had gone wrong.

"Change of plans," he called out to his team. "Sloane's group is in trouble, which means we need to attack now. Cody, Savannah—hang back as we discussed. Take out as many with that bow as you can," he directed to Savannah, "and Cody, you cover her if any stray morphs head this way." The little girl nodded, and Clio felt his throat tighten. He wished he could have kept her out of the fight entirely, but it simply wasn't an option. Forcing himself to push his anxiety about her aside, he turned to the others. "The rest of you, with me. Now!"

He didn't wait long enough to hear any arguments or protests. Brandishing his katana, Clio charged forward, vocal cords straining as he bellowed out the loudest battle cry he could muster in an attempt to draw attention to himself. The other men with him took it up a moment later, filling the air with a chorus of shouts that could have woken the dead.

Thirty yards, twenty yards, ten yards, five...

A group of morphs had assembled at the forefront of the camp, waiting with snapping fangs and bared claws as Clio and his group advanced towards them.

And front and center, towering above his underlings, was their imposing commander, his black eyes watching Clio with voracious wrath, his lips pulled back in a snarl to expose his impressive mouthful of fangs.

Clio narrowed his eyes and let his own fangs descend.

*You're mine,* he vowed, and then the two groups collided in a clash of steel, claw, tooth, and blood.

. . . . .

In the wake of the explosion, quietness descended on the forest, imbuing the scorched clearing with a strange sense of calm.

As Marcus waited for the morphs to come, his mind drifted, inevitably, to the past. Ever since Easthaven, he'd tried not to think of the people he'd lost, to put the grief behind him and focus on the people that were still alive, but now...well, what was the point? He was no longer in charge, and no one was relying on him to fight the good fight and persevere. Now he was a ticking time bomb (almost literally), and his exhausting battle with life was finally coming to a close.

He expected that thought to bring him peace, but it just left him with an unsettling numbness in his bones. His life had been an endless tapestry of mistakes and misadventures, each strand of it stained with blood and death and sorrow. He'd survived his family, his friends, his lover, had lived just long enough to see the world get overrun by monsters and everything turn to shit. *That* was his story, his legacy: loss, regret, shit, and misery. Sure, happiness was a concept he'd understood once, briefly, with Jocelyn, but by now he'd long forgotten what it was to feel anything but tired and depressed.

Maybe death wouldn't be so bad in comparison, even if there was nothing after it. At least nothingness wouldn't be painful.

Before he could dwell on those thoughts in any more detail, the relative silence of the moment was shattered by the sounds of heavy feet approaching. Moments later, the first morph came into view.

It drew to a halt as the trees parted, signaling to the morphs behind it to follow suit. Its black eyes roved the terrain, homing in on the scorched earth and the small bundle resting in its midst.

*Go on*, Marcus urged silently. *Take the bait.*

But the morph stayed where it was. More and more morphs came pouring into the clearing, but all of them stopped near the first, standing well back from the cache of dynamite.

Marcus had hoped – in vain, he now realized – that the morphs would go and inspect the dynamite, which would subsequently allow him to explode the lode without the need to get too close. Marcus had thought that maybe, just *maybe*, he might be able to stand clear enough of the blast to survive it.

*It was a futile hope, anyway*, he thought with grim acceptance. *I was always going to die here.* Steeling himself, Marcus took a breath and stepped from his hiding place, coming into full view of the morphs.

"Hey! Uglies!" He called out, looking on in satisfaction as, en masse, their heads all snapped in his direction. Certain that he had their collective attention, he spoke again. "Watch."

And then he struck the match and lit the fuse of the lone stick of dynamite he was holding. The wick caught and sputtered to life, causing a few of the morphs to stamp at the ground. Marcus dropped the used match and held the stick out, waving it back and forth in the air as he walked a few paces to the right. He stopped once he had positioned himself so that the morphs would have to cross directly over the bundles of dynamite to reach him, and then he waved the lit stick once more.

The nearest morph growled at him, and Marcus sneered in return. "Come and get me, fuck face," he taunted. "I'm not going anywhere."

There was a moment of stasis, and then the growling morph charged, closing the distance between them with blinding speed.

The others followed seconds later, rushing at him with murder shining in their dead, black eyes.

Marcus held his ground, keeping one eye on the morphs and one eye on the small flame moving inexorably down the length of the wick. If it was going to work, he had to time it right.

He wasn't as studied in pyrotechnics as Clio, but he'd thrown enough grenades to correctly gauge the precise moment to send them flying, and he applied the same logic now. When the hissing flame was only about three inches from the blasting cap, Marcus retracted his arm and then lunged forward, releasing the stick of dynamite. It twirled through the air, heading straight for the bundles of dynamite in the center of the clearing.

A few of the morphs stopped and turned as the lone stick arced above their heads, but most of them kept rushing forward.

It would only be a matter of seconds before the first morph reached him, but it didn't matter; the dynamite would explode before then.

Ignoring the morphs, Marcus watched as the airborne stick of dynamite began its descending spiral, and then he exhaled and looked skyward, resting his fingers on the boomerang Jocelyn had given him just as the stick landed on top of the cache.

A pause, and then...*eruption.*

There was a small blast and then a much, much larger one, and the last thing Marcus saw was a blaze of white light coming towards him. He felt the impact of a heavy body crashing into his own, blistering heat, and a blinding pain in his right shoulder.

And then the light was gone, the air was ripped from his lungs, and Marcus felt nothing at all.

· · · · ·

The humans were *everywhere*.

At least, that was how it felt to Balbo.

Their camp had devolved into total chaos in the span of a few minutes, and no matter which way he turned, his eyes were met with pandemonium. There was fighting and death and blood all around.

The audacity of the humans had taken all of them by surprise, but that surprise had been quickly displaced by panic as they realized that these humans were not like the humans they normally encountered. These humans were guerrilla warriors—fierce, fast, and seemingly unafraid, and they were everywhere, attacking from all angles. There was even a second cohort of them somewhere farther off in the forest, as indicated by the explosion they'd seen.

But despite the surprise of the multiple attacks and the boldness of the explosion, Balbo had thought that he and the others would quickly regain the upper hand. He'd felt confident, right until the *creature* had appeared on the path.

Balbo had never seen anything quite like the man-vampire that came charging towards them, and he'd never seen anyone fight like him. Without ever breaking his stride, the strange half-breed ran full force into Commander Demetrius, slender sword and fangs extended.

Commander Demetrius had a reputation for being one of the best fighters in their ranks: he was incredibly strong and brutal, and he was known for literally ripping his victims apart. Balbo had never seen anyone even come close to scratching the fearsome leader.

Until now.

The half-breed moved so fast he was almost a blur, dodging every swipe of Demetrius's claws with seeming ease while simultaneously slashing with his long sword, leaving stripes of blood on Demetrius's thick skin. It enraged the commander, but Demetrius was adaptable; he began to anticipate his enemy's moves, twisting away from the slice of the strange creature's blade until finally, he landed a blow of his own, slashing his claws straight across the half-breed's throat.

But the half-breed didn't collapse, as Balbo was expecting. He'd jumped back just far enough that the claws merely grazed his skin, and he recovered with astonishing speed. He twirled, black clothes billowing around him, and came up behind Commander Demetrius, extending his sword for a killing strike.

The commander moved out of the way just in time, growling in fury, and he rounded on the other man, lunging forward with his fangs extended while also reaching for the sword. The half-breed was able to avoid the snap of Demetrius's jaws, but the morph commander succeeded in disarming him. Balbo watched as the sword skittered away from the fighting figures, and then he watched as his commander's lipless mouth opened in the simulation of a smile.

"Got you," he hissed as he wrapped his talons around the leaner man's arms and yanked him in close. The commander gripped his victim hard and began to pull, and Balbo knew what was coming next: the ripping. Demetrius was going to literally wrench the humanoid creature apart with his massive claws.

Except that he didn't. The half-breed's grimace of pain morphed into an almost smug grin, his strange eyes beginning to weep black as the veins darkened in his face. And then, before the commander even had time to process what was happening, the humanoid creature's head snapped forward, long fangs extended, and he latched on to Demetrius's neck. The commander shrieked, eyes widening, and Balbo watched on in paralyzed horror as, in one savage motion, the half-breed tore his commander's throat out. He held it between his teeth like a trophy, watching on with unblinking eyes as blood sprayed everywhere. Commander Demetrius's grip loosened, and a second later, he crumpled to the ground, dead.

Only then did the victorious attacker spit out the dead morph's throat. "No," he muttered as blood dripped down his fangs and chin, the words just loud enough for Balbo to hear. "Got *you.*"

And then, while Balbo was still reeling from the incredible defeat he'd just witnessed, the second explosion occurred.

It was much larger than the first, the roaring *boom* of it echoing from the forest out to the valley and the camp, and Balbo watched as a large column of bright, angry flames burst skyward. He could hear a few humans beginning to cheer in the aftermath of the explosion, and then he heard Demetrius's second barking orders to Balbo's unit.

"Into the forest!" The lieutenant shouted at Balbo and the others, but his eyes were focused on the half-breed that had just killed their commander. "We'll finish up here," he vowed, guttural voice full of promise.

Balbo didn't wait to see what would happen. Still somewhat in shock, he stumbled into line with the rest of his unit and ran for the forest.

He took one last look back at the camp before it disappeared from sight, wondering if it or anyone in it would still be left when he got back.

He also began to wonder, as he listened to the crackle of burning wood and saw the smoke cloud looming before him, if he would even survive long enough to find out.

· · · · ·

The pain was excruciating, which was how Marcus knew that, despite all odds, he was still alive.

There was a loud, high-pitched ringing in his ears, and every inch of his body was aching. Wincing, he tried to draw in a breath, only to be rewarded with a mouthful of dirt. He coughed and sputtered, choking, and then, realizing what the problem was, he raised his head a few inches off of the ground, his neck protesting vehemently as he did so.

Marcus blinked slowly, trying to focus on his immediate surroundings. The explosion had pulverized the morphs, and the clearing – which was now much wider than it had been before – was strewn with body parts and soaked in ash and blood. The leafless trees nearest the impact sight had been blown back, as if the bare branches were trying to flee the scene, and a few of the slenderer trunks had even snapped entirely from the pressure of the blast wave. Many of them were scorched or burning.

As Marcus struggled to all fours, he realized that there were scorch marks on much of his clothing and a few raw patches of skin where he must have been burned, though there was no blistering. His shoulder was throbbing, and there was blood running down from the circle of teeth marks the morph had left there, but the damage was nothing compared to what it could have been.

His head was spinning, his ears were ringing, he could taste blood in his mouth, his limbs were shaking, and he couldn't breathe properly, but for some unknown reason, he was still alive.

And as a fresh wave of morph reinforcements poured into the decimated area, Marcus realized, with cruel irony, that he wanted to *stay* alive.

Using what little reserve strength he had left, Marcus pushed himself to his feet, unsheathed his machete, and unclipped his boomerang.

*You can't fight your way outta this, pipsqueak,* Stan's voice taunted him. *There's one of you, ten of them, and you're pretty much dead already.*

*Try, Marcus, try,* came the fainter echo of Jocelyn's voice.

Marcus set his jaw and squared his shoulders. He could barely grip his weapons, and he couldn't hear the morphs as they charged towards him because his ears were still ringing painfully, but he didn't care.

He might not be at his best, might not even be anywhere close to okay, but he was a Reaper. If he was going to die, he was going to go down fighting.

* * * * *

Clio had regained his katana after killing the commander's second-in-command, and ever since then he had fallen into an almost trance-like calm, slashing and striking with deadly precision as morph after morph rushed at him and the bodies piled up around him.

Which was why, when one of them grabbed his arm, Clio turned and sliced without thinking.

But this one – much smaller than the others – ducked beneath his blade.

"Clio!" It shrieked, raising its hands above its head.

Clio blinked in shock, immediately snapped out of his blood haze. *"Aya?"* He breathed, incredulous.

The vampire stood up. Her delicate features were twisted into a grimace of worry. "Where's Marcus?" She asked.

Clio glanced off in the direction of the explosion. "Over there," he said, crestfallen. "He's the one who set off the dynamite."

A determined look stole across Aya's face and she nodded grimly before turning away. Clio grabbed her arm. "Aya, don't," he pleaded. "He's—he's gone."

The vampire shrugged out of his grasp. "No, he's not," she said. "He's…" She trailed off, taking in the carnage around them, her brows furrowing as she seemed to realize the exigency of the group's situation.

The indecision she was battling was obvious to Clio, and he used it to try and sway her. "Aya, I know you're upset about Marcus, but please. Stay and fight. We need you here."

It was clear by the expression on her face that he'd said the right thing. Aya's lips pressed into a flat line. "All right. What do you need me to do?"

"Go check on Sloane's group. Something went wrong early on and they might need backup."

Aya nodded. "I'll go. But Clio, if they're okay—"

"Then yes," he yielded. "You can go and see if Marcus is still—"

"He is," she insisted, and she took off running before Clio could argue with her. Almost as sudden as her departure, the momentary lull in the battle ceased and Clio had no more time to dwell on the vampire's return or the fate of the doomed Reaper. He adjusted his grip on his katana and once more began to fight.

· · · · ·

Marcus let the boomerang fly just as the first two morphs reached him, and the double-bladed weapon sliced gracefully across one of the morph's throats before sailing back to Marcus's outstretched hand. He threw it again and then hacked down the morph in front of him, gripping the hilt of his machete with both hands and striking again and again at the junction of the morph's shoulder and neck until he finally pierced its hardened skin and arterial blood sprayed out from the wound.

Blinking against the blood in his eyes, Marcus yanked the weapon out of the morph and stumbled back, breathing hard. The next morph bowled him over, knocking the wind from his lungs and sending his machete flying away. The creature was heavy, and it nearly crushed Marcus's windpipe as it slashed and bit at him.

Trying to ignore the fresh flares of pain where the morph tore at his skin, Marcus squirmed beneath its bulk and managed to reach down and retrieve the dagger strapped to his boot. He brought the blade up and stabbed at the morph's face once, twice, and then, on the third time, he successfully plunged the short blade into one of its eyes. The creature jerked as blood and pulp ran from its ruined eye, and then it slumped over.

Leaving the dagger where it was, Marcus grimaced and heaved the morph off of him, rolling out from beneath it and sputtering as he finally managed to gulp down air and feed his starving lungs.

He looked up just in time to see the next morph come lunging for him, and Marcus crawled forward, reaching for his machete.

Not in time. The morph fell on him before he could retrieve his weapon, crushing him facedown into the ground, and a second later Marcus felt its sharp fangs on the nape of his neck.

*Fuck!* He screamed silently, realizing with horror that it had him.

But the fatal bite never came.

The morph loosened its grip and relaxed, dead weight, on top of him.

Mustering up a last bout of strength, Marcus rolled the morph off of him and then immediately realized why it hadn't finished him off.

Jocelyn's boomerang was lodged into the back of its skull.

Marcus's eyes widened in bewilderment. *What the hell...?* The last he'd seen of his boomerang, it had been arcing away for him, headed into the fray of oncoming morphs.

Maybe one of the morphs had thrown it, with the intent of hitting him, and hit one of their own instead. It seemed highly unlikely, but Marcus didn't question his lucky break. He reached out, grabbed his machete, and once more pushed himself to his feet, determined to make the most of his second chance.

And then he froze in shock, staring at the blur of movement that was currently dispatching the remaining morphs.

The familiar, dark-haired blur of movement.

The machete fell from his hand as Marcus took in the impossible sight before him. Never, not in a million years, had he ever expected to see her again, and yet here she was.

*Aya.*

It couldn't be, but it was. There was no mistaking her.

Aya had returned.

He was still standing there, staring, as one by one the morphs fell, and then, when all five were dead and the sounds of battle were over, Aya turned towards him.

She retracted her fangs as the dark veins beneath her eyes began to lighten. "Marcus?" She called out, tentatively.

*It can't be real. It can't be. No one ever comes back.*

He watched as Aya wiped the blood from her eyes and took a few steps in his direction. Her moves were cautious and slow, unsure, so different from the confidence she'd displayed moments earlier.

She stopped when she was a few yards away from him, the uncertainty in her expression giving way to concern. "Marcus?" She said again.

His eyes roved over her from head to foot. She *looked* real, solid, and yet it was so hard to believe that she was actually standing there, that she'd come back, that she wasn't just a figment his imagination had conjured up as he lay bleeding out on the ground. In fact, given the circumstances, *that* seemed more plausible than the idea that Aya – who had left weeks ago and traveled to who-knows-where with a bunch of vampires – had miraculously reappeared just in time to save him like some shining vampiric knight. Not only did that scenario seem impossible, but it also made no sense. Why the hell would Aya come back when she'd finally been reunited with her own kind?

Maybe that morph *had* gotten him, and now he was just enduring some final, cruel hallucination before the end. His life had been a cosmic joke, so why should his death be any different?

And yet, it didn't *feel* like he was hallucinating, and Aya wasn't fading away. She was still standing there, silent and somber, watching him as the seconds ticked by and blood from her morph kills dripped from her face and hands.

"You...you're real?" Marcus finally managed, heavy skepticism lacing his voice.

Aya's lips twisted and her eyebrows knitted together, as if she were wounded by the question. "I'm real." He saw her throat work as she swallowed. "I...I came back."

A million thoughts came to mind, a million questions that were all clamoring to be voiced. *When did you get here? How did you find us? Why did you leave the vampires? Weren't you happy to finally be with your own kind? Did you know we were in danger? Did you come back just to help us?*

The questions raced through Marcus's mind, but in the end, they all merged into the same, simple question, and it was one that surpassed all the others, one that made every other question seem utterly insignificant by comparison.

"Why?" He asked, looking into her dark eyes. "Why did you come back?"

She met his gaze, and the answer was there even before she spoke it, the truth radiating from her very being, so loud and so pure that Marcus's knees almost buckled.

"Because you said I should be with my people," Aya answered, her voice as soft and sure as the dawn. "And you were right."

It took a minute for the significance of her words to sink in, but when it did, Marcus's breath caught in his throat.

"I know you might not feel the same," she continued on in his silence, "but that doesn't change the truth." She smiled, and it was tremulous and small, but it was genuine, and it made Marcus's heart ache in a way his heart hadn't ached in a long time. "It took me a while to figure it out," she added in an even quieter voice than before, "but you and Clio and the others…you *are* my people."

*You are my people.*

Marcus stared at her, but it wasn't shock that he felt; it was the acceptance of something he had known for a long time but never fully acknowledged, a fundamental truth that he no longer had a reason or impetus to deny.

*You're my people, too, Aya,* he thought, and then he was moving before he'd consciously made the decision to, half-walking, half-limping towards her until he was no more than a breath away.

He looked into her eyes, hoping that she could see past the blood and grime on his face. "I'm glad you're back," he said softly, honestly, and then, propelled by some unknown instinct, he drew her in close and wrapped his arms around her.

Aya stiffened for a heartbeat, and then she relaxed into his embrace, her own arms winding around his neck. She placed her head against his, gently, and Marcus felt the slight tremor that coursed through her body as she choked back a sob.

There was so much he could have said, but Marcus was exhausted and beaten down and overcome with a wealth of emotions he usually didn't experience, so instead he just closed his eyes and took comfort in Aya's nearness.

He was wounded and in pain, but, for just a brief, transient moment, Marcus remembered what it was like to be almost happy.

· · · · ·

Balbo was watching the scene in the clearing from where he was hidden in the trees, and he looked on in shock as the vampire and human embraced.

Earlier, when the vampire had appeared like some grim specter and started wiping out his unit, Balbo had fallen back. He'd assumed that, once the vampire had killed his brethren, she would dispatch the human as well, but instead...*this* had happened.

He couldn't believe it. First the strange half-breed appeared and dispatched his commander, and now a hunter and a vampire were embracing? Balbo didn't know what to make of any of it, but he did know what he had to do.

Moving as silently as he could, Balbo retreated from the clearing and headed deeper into the forest.

# Road to Recovery

*Sometimes, it is in the quiet moments, those seemingly unimportant moments, that we discover the most profound truths about ourselves.*
- Quote taken from Queen Elisiana's personal memoirs, circa the First Vampiric War

·　·　·　·　·

Aya frowned up at the dark, hazy sky, praying that the snow wouldn't start to fall until they managed to get to the bunker, but the scattered flurries already descending from above proved that her prayer might be in vain.

Setting her lips into a firm line, she gently adjusted Marcus's arm where he had it draped around her shoulders and kept walking.

The Reaper was not in good shape. He was limping badly, favoring his uninjured leg and leaning against her to keep himself balanced. She didn't mind, but the fact that he was relying so heavily on her was not a good sign. Marcus usually eschewed all help no matter how badly he needed it, but now Aya was almost dragging him along. On top of that, he was shivering terribly beneath the ripped and burned remains of his clothing, and, excluding the angry reds of his many wounds, his skin was ashen. Worst of all, though, was his breathing. It had been raspy and unsteady before they'd even left the clearing, and it had become increasingly more labored and irregular as they trudged slowly towards the bunker.

And, of course, Aya could *feel* his pain, like a dull, ever-present ache in her own body.

The snow started to come down more heavily a few minutes later, and Aya was suddenly jerked to the side as Marcus stumbled over his feet. She managed to steady them both, but when she glanced over, she could see the exhaustion on Marcus's face. It was a small miracle he hadn't passed out already, but there was no way he would last much longer.

"How much further?" She asked quietly, her voice strained with worry.

Marcus raised his head just enough to peer out from beneath the mess of overgrown, damp hair hanging in his eyes. "Not much," he wheezed after he took a look around. He drew in a shaky breath. "A couple hundred yards or so. We should be able to see it soon."

"Okay. Can you manage?"

"Yes," came the terse reply, but Marcus didn't look at her and Aya had a feeling that he was bluffing. Still, she started forward again, bearing as much of his weight as he would allow, focusing all her energy on one step, and another, and another.

Marcus's estimation proved right, and Aya let out a breath of relief as soon as the sloped walls of the small bunker came into view. By the time they reached the door and Aya ushered Marcus inside, the snowfall had thickened, and the first inch was already sticking to the ground.

"Fucking snow can go fuck itself," Marcus muttered weakly as Aya turned and shut and bolted the door behind them.

A weak smile tugged at her lips in spite of their situation. She'd missed Marcus's colorful brand of pessimism more than she'd realized. "It *is* winter, Marcus."

He made an irritable *tch* sound. "Winter can go fuck itself, too," he rejoined dryly before collapsing against the nearest wall. He leaned his head back, and Aya could see that his eyes were scrunched tight in pain. She could also see that he was still shivering.

Concern flaring up anew, Aya gently guided him to the floor and told him to wait, and then she began searching the bunker for any useful items.

It was relatively small—only three rooms in total. One had a number of cots spread out on the floor that the group had most likely used, so Aya grabbed one that looked the least flattened and dirty and carried it back to the first room. She also managed to find a blanket, but only one. It was old and worn but better than nothing, and she carried that back to the other room as well, glancing over at Marcus as she did.

The Reaper's eyes were shut, and his head had lolled to the side.

"Marcus?"

He groaned in response but didn't open his eyes.

It wasn't a good sign; Aya didn't know a lot about medical care— she wasn't a healer and she certainly didn't have much experience aiding humans, but she knew that, between the blood loss and how cold Marcus was, falling asleep could be disastrous.

She knelt down in front of him and shook his shoulders.

"Fuck," Marcus cursed, opening his eyes to glare at her.

"You need to stay awake," she instructed. "Keep your eyes open. I'll be back in a minute."

Aya hurried through the other rooms, scavenging the storage trunks and crates for clothing and medical supplies. Eventually, she managed to find a heavy sweater, a few tins of ointment, and a scant array of gauze and bandages, but there wasn't much else. Apparently, the group had stocked up well before setting out for the morph camp.

When she got back to the room, Marcus's eyes were closed again. She rushed over to him, but Marcus held up a hand before she could shake him. "Don't," he said wearily. "I'm awake."

Aya knelt down again, sitting back on her heels. "We need to treat your wounds," she said softly.

Marcus blinked his eyes open and nodded. Then he attempted to shrug out of his ruined jacket, but between his fatigue and the tremors shaking his limbs, he didn't get very far. He cursed in frustration and gave up, stilling.

Without a word, Aya leaned forward and helped him, removing his arms from the jacket as gingerly as she could. And then, before he could protest, her fingers nimbly undid the buttons of his shirt and then she helped him out of that, too. Next, she unlaced his boots and helped him stand up. She reached for the buckle of his belt, but Marcus made a sound of protest and she stopped. Clearing his throat, Marcus undid the buckle himself and pulled the belt through the loops of his pants before he pushed the tattered fabric down his legs.

*Oh,* Aya realized, feeling a faint blush stain her cheeks. She'd been so intent on helping him that it hadn't occurred to her that she was *undressing* him.

"I'm sorry," she stammered. "I-I didn't mean to—"

"It's fine," he huffed, and then he stumbled over to the cot she'd carried in and sat down, wincing and shivering as he did.

The hazy light streaming in through the window hit his skin as he sat there, and Aya's embarrassment disappeared in an instant as she stared in shock at the Reaper.

His muscular body was a canvas of agony, tattooed with cuts and slashes and bite marks and dotted with purple contusions of various sizes. There were patches of raw skin on his arms where he'd been burned from the explosions, a circle of deep teeth marks punctured in his right shoulder, and his other shoulder was sagging at an awkward angle. There were also faded white lines trailing down one side of his chin and neck, evidence of an older attack, but no doubt the work of morph claws.

"Marcus..." Aya breathed in dismay. "You're..." But she didn't know what to say. She didn't even know how the man was still alive.

"I've been better," he tossed off, but the wheeze in his voice prevented him from sounding as nonchalant as he'd no doubt intended.

Aya went to him. "I found a few supplies. There weren't any painkillers left and there aren't enough bandages for all of your injuries, but I can at least treat the worst ones."

Marcus grunted. "We need to set my shoulder first." His steel eyes were only half-visible beneath his bangs as he spoke.

The terminology was foreign to her. "Set your shoulder?" She repeated dubiously.

"My left shoulder is dislocated," he explained. "The joint is out of place."

That must be why it was hanging the way it was, but Aya had no experience with such a thing before. She'd never seen or heard of a vampire with a dislocated shoulder, but then again, her people were notoriously hardier than humans. Perhaps dislocations were only a human injury.

"I've never done this before," she admitted. "What do I need to do?"

With a grimace, Marcus lay back on the pallet and bent his left arm at a ninety-degree angle, keeping his elbow tucked close to his side. "Put one hand on my wrist and the other on my bicep," he instructed.

Aya did as he asked, trying to be as gentle as possible and making a conscious effort to avoid placing her hands directly on any patches of burned skin.

"Good," Marcus said. "Now, slowly pull my arm out and away from me—*fuck*, slower than that." He winced as Aya stopped moving his arm.

"I'm sorry," she said, chagrined.

"It's fine." He took a breath and set his jaw. "Keep going."

She did, watching as Marcus's face contorted in pain, and just when she was about to stop and ask if she was doing something wrong, she saw the head of his shoulder pop back into place beneath his skin. She dropped his arm in surprise.

Marcus let out a choked breath, his features relaxing. "That's better," he murmured. He opened his eyes halfway, staring up at her from beneath his heavy lids. He started to say something, but then his eyes closed again, and within seconds, he was asleep.

Aya moved to wake him, but as she watched the steady rise and fall of his chest, she decided against it. Instead, she arranged the solitary blanket around his frame as best she could while still keeping the majority of his injuries exposed, and she reached for the ointments she'd found.

Gingerly, she began to dab up the blood covering his body. Most of it had dried and hardened, but some wounds were still fresh, still bleeding, and Aya's fangs stirred at the scent. She grimaced at the involuntary reaction, ashamed at her body's response. She would never, ever consider feeding on Marcus in his weakened, vulnerable state, no matter how hungry she was. He was—

He flinched in his sleep as she began to clean one of his more ragged wounds, and Aya froze. The pain hadn't woken him, but she could see it register in the furrow of his brows.

*He is so human.*

It was obvious, really, but it was something she'd almost forgotten when it came to the Reaper. His strength and determination, his seemingly implacable armor, his fearlessness in the face of anything that stood in his way…it was easy to forget that he was just a human. Flesh and blood and a beating heart. So alive. So fragile. By the very humanness of his nature, Marcus danced much more intimately with death than she did, and yet somehow, he endured anyway.

Aya had never seen such strength in so fragile a creature before.

If the rest of the Reapers were anything like Marcus, well, Aya could understand why the other humans treated them with something akin to hero-worship.

*But he's not indestructible,* she thought as she looked back down at his wounded body. *Neither of us is.*

She set back to her task with even more care than before, applying just enough gentle pressure to clean the blood away, trying not to let her hands linger any longer than necessary on the planes of his muscular body. The desire to touch him just to feel him was great, but it would be wrong to take advantage of the situation.

Besides, for all she knew, Marcus wouldn't want her hands anywhere near him. She remembered the way he'd looked at her in the beginning, the way he'd spoken the word *vampire*…like it was a vile taste he wanted to spit out. He'd been disgusted by her, disgusted by what she was.

But she also remembered the way he'd held her that night at Eden and the look in his eyes when his finger had grazed her lip. She remembered when he'd returned her heart and let her go.

Solomon was right; things *had* changed.

With a quiet sigh, Aya pushed away the tumult of complicated thoughts and refocused her effort on attending to the wounded Reaper.

•　•　•　•　•

Emmanuel was doing his best not to stare, but every few seconds he would glance up from the dishes he was scrubbing and look over at his strange house guest, his scientific curiosity to observe everything overriding his manners.

He – Ian, that was – had been sitting at the kitchen table with the bowl of porridge for over five minutes, but he hadn't eaten a single bite. A few times he had looked down at the bowl in what Emmanuel could only describe as consternation, but other than that, he'd remained completely immobile.

When there were no more dishes to wash, Emmanuel dried his hands and slowly approached the kitchen table, then slid back a chair and cautiously sat down across from the former morph.

"Aren't you hungry?" He asked as it became abundantly clear that Ian was not going to touch his food.

Blue eyes blinked up at him and then darted away. "Yes."

Emmanuel let the other man's answer hang in the air for a moment. "Do you want something other than porridge?" He ventured, even though, when he'd asked earlier, Ian had specifically asked for porridge.

A flush of color began to spread across his guest's cheeks. "No. It— it's not that." He cleared his throat. "I, uh…I don't remember how," he admitted, fidgeting in his seat.

"How to eat?"

Ian shook his head as he met Emmanuel's eyes. "How to use a spoon. Big motions are okay, but the fine motor skill stuff…not so much."

A wave of pity rolled through Emmanuel, followed quickly by shame. Of course Ian would have trouble. He'd been a morph for nearly six years; ordinary, everyday human things Emmanuel took for granted were all basically new to the other man. He should have expected difficulties and planned for them instead of letting Ian flounder.

"Not to worry," Emmanuel said gently, trying for a smile. He reached across the table, ignoring the way Ian flinched away from him, and picked up the spoon. "Like this," he instructed, turning his hand so Ian could see how each of his fingers was positioned on the utensil. Then he scooped up a spoonful of the porridge. "See?"

Ian nodded and Emmanuel placed the spoon back down. "Now you try," he encouraged.

It took a few attempts before Ian's fingers managed to close over the spoon and hold it steady without dropping it, and a few more tries before he was able to successfully dip the spoon into the porridge and get the food to his mouth, but after his first bite, his nearly forgotten muscle memory seemed to kick in and he all but devoured the remainder of the porridge.

Emmanuel watched him eat in silence, taking mental notes about things he wanted to write down later while also feeling a twinge of guilt over how hungry Ian was. It had been two days since Emmanuel had discovered him in the lab, and nearly twenty-four hours since he had brought him back to his quarters, and in that time, Ian had eaten nothing. He hadn't asked for food—hadn't really spoken much at all, truth be told, aside from asking if a Reaper he'd been friends with was currently stationed at Ashland, and Emmanuel had been so shocked by the success of the vaccine that he hadn't even thought to ask sooner about food.

*The first successful turning of a morph back to a human and I am doing nothing to aid his recovery. I'm acting like a passive observer instead of a doctor taking responsibility for his patient. Helena would be so disappointed.*

"Thank you."

The quietly spoken words pulled Emmanuel out of his guilty thoughts. "For what?"

Ian blinked at him. "For the food."

"Oh." Emmanuel gave him a small smile. "You're welcome, Ian."

The former morph flinched at the sound of his name, like a pained reflex.

It was an unexpected reaction, and it roused Emmanuel's worry. "Do you want me to call you something else?" He asked, concerned.

"No." Ian took a breath and then released it slowly. "It's just that I...I don't feel like Ian anymore. Ian was someone I used to be...before..." He looked up at Emmanuel, his blue eyes haunted in a way that Emmanuel was becoming familiar with. "Ian was confident, easygoing—likeable. Decent. He wasn't a monster," he added in a low voice.

*Oh.* "Neither are you," Emmanuel said, his voice soft but firm. "You aren't a morph anymore. You *are* Ian."

The other man's brows furrowed. "Then why do I have more morph memories than human ones? I remember everything that happened since I turned. *Everything.*" He shuddered. "But my human memories are all foggy. I couldn't even remember how to use a damn spoon."

Emmanuel pursed his lips. "Only at first," he countered. "Your human memories may be foggy, but that's only because they're less recent than your...other memories." He paused, gauging the other man's expression before continuing. "You said that you remembered everything that happened since you were turned," he chanced, and when Ian's face remained impassive, Emmanuel ventured on. "Would you be open to discussing those memories? You are the first human to transition back and your experience could shed a lot of light on morph physiology and thought processes. It could ultimately help us understand the nature of morphs much more so than we do now."

Ian slumped back in his chair, his shoulders drooping as his lips twisted unhappily. "They're not pleasant memories," he mumbled. His brow creased with pain. "I did horrible things. I killed people." He swallowed hard and then, after taking a few deep breaths, he sat up a little taller, seeming to collect himself a bit. "Look. To say I want to talk about all of it would be a lie, but if you think...I mean...do you think my memories can help other—others like me?" He asked finally.

Emmanuel nodded with conviction. "I know it."

Ian let out a breath. "Okay," he said, a flicker of determination beginning to overshadow the trauma in his blue eyes. "I guess I can try, then. If you really think it'll make a difference."

"It will make a huge difference. And I also think it will help you," Emmanuel added. "I'm not saying it won't be difficult, but I think that sharing your story and talking about what happened may have a cleansing effect. Keeping all of those negative memories bottled up inside won't help you move forward. Talking about them might."

Ian looked like he desperately wanted to believe that, but he didn't agree outright, and Emmanuel could tell that the former morph's recovery would be long and difficult. Even without knowing the details, he could see how torn up Ian was by the things he'd done, and he knew that reliving those things wouldn't be easy.

But healing was a process, and pain was often the first step.

"We could start now, if you feel up to it," Emmanuel suggested in the wake of Ian's silence.

"Now?" There was an edge of panic in the other man's voice.

"Or we could wait." The last thing Emmanuel wanted was for Ian to feel pressured into talking.

But the other man surprised him. "No...now is okay," Ian said. He leaned forward and placed his elbows on the table. "So, uh, where do you want me to start?"

Emmanuel felt a warm sort of admiration for Ian's courage. Whatever else he was or may have been, it was obvious that he was a fighter, and that was a trait that Emmanuel respected.

He quickly walked over to his desk at the far end of the room and retrieved a notebook and pen. Once he sat back down across from Ian, he opened to a blank page and looked up.

"Well," he said. "Why don't you start at the beginning?"

．　．　．　．　．

Marcus blinked his eyes open slowly, his vision sharpening right alongside the pain. Every inch of his body ached and hurt beneath the scratchy blanket resting atop him, and he winced as he pushed himself up into a seated position on the cot, his arms shaking.

Aya was sitting across from him on the floor, and though he could plainly see the disapproval on her face, she didn't say anything.

He licked his lips, swallowing at the uncomfortable dryness of his mouth. "Is there any water?" His voice was no more than a rasp of sandpaper.

Aya nodded and disappeared into another room, coming back a moment later with a half-full bottle.

He tried to take it from her, but the second his fingers tried to close around its surface the bottle slipped out of his hand.

Aya caught it before it reached the floor and unscrewed the cap herself. She was still for a moment and then she brought the bottle to his lips.

Marcus felt his gut twist in humiliation, but he didn't refuse her help. At least she hadn't asked first—words would have made it worse.

Aya was careful and attentive, letting him take a few weak sips and never pouring too much water into his mouth at once. He was so enervated that it took a few long, slow minutes to get through the bottle, but he drank it all.

It took all the energy he had left not to collapse back down on the pallet when he was finished.

Aya placed the empty bottle aside and sat back on her heels. "There isn't much food left, but —"

Marcus shook his head. "Can't eat," he mumbled. "Not yet."

It was Aya's silence that finally made him glance over at her.

Her hands were balled into fists on her lap and she was frowning down at them, her anxiety nearly palpable.

"Hey," he rattled. "What's wrong?"

She raised her eyes to his. "You," she answered. "*You're* wrong, and I don't know how to help you." She curled in on herself. "If you were a vampire, I would just give you blood, but you're... you're *human* and I have no idea how to heal you. I've never felt so helpless or so...so useless."

*Useless?*

The ridiculousness of that statement nearly made Marcus laugh. The vampire had saved his life, for fuck's safe, and she needed to realize that. "Useless my ass," he said, his crassness blundered somewhat when he started to cough. When the short fit subsided, he added, "If it weren't for you, I'd be dead."

Aya ignored his words, turning to a different argument. "I *am* useless," she insisted. "If Jillian or someone with more knowledge of human injuries were here, you would be much better off. A human would know what to do."

Marcus nearly blurted out that he didn't *want* anyone else around playing nursemaid to him, but he held back. "It wouldn't make any difference, Aya." He sighed, deciding to be honest with her. "I'm in bad shape. By rights, I should probably be morph meat. But I'm not, thanks to you, and now it's just going to take some time. Humans don't heal as quickly as vampires do."

He wrapped the scratchy blanket tighter around himself, his gaze shifting to the view beyond the solitary window. It had stopped snowing, but the carpet of white on the ground looked deep, and the sunlight was weak and dwindling, casting long shadows of grey down from the bare tree branches.

*Shit.* "How long was I out?" He asked.

"Almost all day."

An entire day, gone and wasted. Angry, Marcus tried to stand, only to be rewarded by pain so intense that he saw spots behind his eyes. He fell with a gasp, Aya's arms the only thing that prevented him from landing on his ass.

"Marcus..." She cautioned, gently easing him back down to the pallet.

"I know," he mumbled. "Clearly I'm not going anywhere." He choked out a frustrated exhale. "Fuck. I can't do this. Not knowing is worse than knowing the worst."

Aya stared at him, blinking in confusion.

Marcus sagged on the pallet. "I have no idea what happened to the others," he clarified. "For all I know, everyone is dead."

"Dead? Why would you...?" Aya's hand flew to her mouth, though it didn't quite stifle her gasp. "*Oh.* Marcus, I—I'm so sorry," she said, the words muffled. She dropped her hand to her lap, and Marcus watched as it clenched into a fist. "I was so distracted by your condition that I forgot to tell you."

His limbs might have been lethargic, but his attention was as sharp as a razor blade. "Tell me what?"

"I found the others before I found you. They were fighting, and they were winning. Clio's group had almost taken out all of the morphs at the main camp, and when I found Sloane's group, their situation was more or less the same...except for Sloane."

Marcus felt something worse than his physical pain begin to tear at his chest. He swallowed. "Is she dead?" He managed.

The hesitation before she answered told Marcus everything he needed to know.

"She wasn't when I saw her, but she..." Aya's expression fell. "I don't think she could have survived. The others were tending to her, but she'd lost so much blood and her arm...it was..." Aya shook her head, her dark eyes full of compassion. "I'm sorry, Marcus."

He knew she meant it, but that didn't lessen the impact of her words. He swallowed the lump in his throat. "And Enwezor?"

"I didn't get as far as Enwezor's group," she answered. "Once I was sure all the morphs attacking Sloane's group were dead, I came after you."

Marcus said nothing. Sloane and Enwezor, his trainees, his protégés. His responsibilities. Both possibly – probably – dead.

He'd never had a family, never had children of his own, but he imagined that the loss he felt at the moment was pretty damn comparable to how a parent felt at the loss of their child.

Sloane and Zor might not have been his blood, but hell, they were still his kids. And now at least one of them was gone, just like everyone else he'd ever cared about.

It was a good thing he'd never had kids of his own; only a worthless father would outlive all his children.

A gentle touch stirred him, and Marcus looked down to see Aya's hand resting on top of his.

"A lot of your people are still alive," she said softly, her dark eyes brimming with compassion. "And Enwezor could easily be one of them. Don't give up hope. Not now. Not when we've been through so much."

Part of him wanted to argue, to tell her that hope was just denial of reality, but he didn't. He could feel her fervor in the press of her skin on his, almost like she was kinetically passing her hope to him.

It was strange, and probably all in his head, but it made him feel…better.

It made him want to pull her closer, to gain more of that feeling, and as he looked into her eyes, he sensed that Aya would let him.

Still, he pulled his hand away. "Don't worry," he said. "You didn't save my ass for nothing. I'm not giving up." *Not yet.*

Aya seemed satisfied with his answer. "You should get some more rest," she suggested, changing the subject.

The idea had a drug-like effect, her words cuing his exhaustion. "I've never slept this much in my life," he muttered, but he lay down all the same, stretching out on the pallet and grimacing as even that amount of minimal motion set his nerves ablaze in pain.

As the throbbing and aching tapered off, something new occurred to him.

"Aya," he called, turning just his head.

She didn't say anything, just waited expectantly.

"Where did you sleep last night?" He asked.

The question seemed to catch her off guard. "I...I stayed up most of the night," she said. "To keep an eye on you. I did sleep a little, though."

His lips quirked up at her transparent evasion. "Where?" He pressed. He knew full well that this particular bunker wasn't exactly stocked—and that was before the group had stripped it of supplies.

Aya looked down at her lap, her black hair slipping over her shoulders and covering most of her face. "Against the wall," she admitted.

Marcus would have laughed if his ribs hadn't hurt so fucking much. "For a vampire, you play the martyr act very well," he quipped.

Aya glanced up at him, tucking her hair behind her ear. "What?" She asked blankly.

He sighed. "Just share the pallet with me," he said. "There's plenty of room for both of us."

She went back to staring at her lap. "It's fine," she said. "I don't need to—"

"Aya."

She fell silent.

"C'mon. Just get on the damn mattress and shut up."

"But—"

"But nothing. If you argue, I'll get up and physically move you, which will probably reopen half of my wounds. It won't exactly be good for my recovery."

Aya's expression darkened and she muttered something that sounded a lot like *you couldn't move me even on your best day*, but she stalked around to the far side of the pallet and sat down, keeping as much space between them as possible.

"Was that so hard?" He teased, his voice already thick with sleep.

Her response was a muted growl. "One more word and you can add fresh fang marks to your list of wounds," she threatened.

Marcus felt his lips tug up wryly.

*I wouldn't mind those, Aya,* he thought, and then he heard her sharp intake of breath, making him wonder if, in his delirium, he'd accidentally spoken aloud.

But then sleep overtook him and he let the thought slip away.

·   ·   ·   ·   ·

It was late, long past when most civilians turned in for the night, but the lateness of the hour mattered little to Joben Hale. Even if Emmanuel Mason had not requested to meet with him, chances were good that he would have been awake anyhow, seeing to some other business.

At precisely the time they'd agreed upon, three knocks came at the outer door of Joben's quarters. He was almost certain it was Emmanuel, but because of the precarious climate as of late, he had to make sure.

"I am not entertaining visitors at this hour," he said through the door. "Come back tomorrow."

There was a pause, and then, tentatively, "No one entertains at this hour, but business never waits."

Satisfied, Joben unbolted the door and stepped aside, letting a nervous-looking Emmanuel Mason in.

Joben steered the younger man into his office and ushered him into one of the sitting chairs. Ever since the dismantling of the Rangers, he'd lost the expansive headquarters he'd once had, but his private quarters were still larger than most, and Joben was fortunate enough to have an adjoining office. It was a luxury not shared by many other officials—especially not retired officials.

"Tea?" He asked the doctor with a lifted brow.

Emmanuel shook his head. Joben shrugged and poured himself a cup of tea and took a sip, silently appraising the man across from him. Ostensibly, he seemed okay, but on closer inspection, Joben noticed clear signs of stress. There were bags under his intelligent brown eyes that hadn't been there before and a tightness around his mouth, sure signs that the crackdowns as of late were wearing him down more than he wanted to let on.

Joben took another lingering sip and then set his cup aside. "Are you holding up all right?" He asked.

"No. We need to procure another morph as soon as possible."

The bluntness of the statement surprised Joben just as much as its content did. Even under stress, Emmanuel was always polite to a fault. *Something must be very wrong,* he thought.

He took the seat opposite the doctor, careful not to react in any way. "What happened to the morph we already have?"

"Nothing," Emmanuel answered quickly. "Ian is doing well— incredibly well. Because of him, I now know much more about morph nature. He's provided invaluable information. But he's also told me many troubling things." The doctor paused, gathering himself. "I'll share all my notes with you later," he said, "but right now, we need to capture another morph. And not just any morph."

Joben leaned back against his desk and folded his arms across his chest. "Not just *any* morph?" He prompted.

"No. Ian told me that there is a morph hierarchy," Emmanuel explained. "Ian was a lower level, lesser functioning morph, but not all morphs are that way. Apparently, there is more variation that we ever dreamed possible. Ian told me that some morphs are rabid, driven just by pure instinct and bloodlust—the other morphs refer to them as mongrels. Ian was part of the next branch up, so to speak; he was part of the horde. He retained some of his human reasoning and coordination, but only very limited speech capabilities, and his emotions were instinct driven rather than based on higher cognitive reasoning. He said that most morphs fall into this category and the mongrel category.

"But then there are other morphs—the more dangerous ones. They are capable of speech, as well as human thought and reasoning. Ian said that they are called superiors because of their elevated intelligence and strength, and that they are the captains and commanders that serve the morph force." Emmanuel paused. "And then there are the elite."

Joben felt a tremor of unease go through him. "What did Ian say about them?"

"That they are the equivalent of our Reapers, but faster and stronger. Ian said that he'd only ever seen an elite on one occasion, but that it was enough to convince him that elites are the most dangerous creatures in the world."

Joben's hand tightened on his teacup. "How many elites are there?" He asked.

The young doctor shook his head. "I asked that same question. Ian doesn't know."

Joben nodded, pondering that. "Is that why you want to capture another morph? To find out of if they know more?"

"Yes, but not to find out more about the elites." Emmanuel frowned gravely. "There are even more troubling questions that need answers." His brown eyes met Joben's blue ones. "Ian overheard a name during his time with the morph army."

"Which name?" Joben asked.

"Whitman."

A stunned silence fell over the room.

*Whitman?*

The possible implications of that began to flicker through Joben's mind at lightning speed. None were good.

He did not, however, want to project his own musings onto the doctor, so he hid his own suspicions and deferred to the younger man. "What do you think it means, Emmanuel?"

"I think it confirms what Dex has been trying to prove for years," the doctor answered. "That there are ties between the morphs and our esteemed governors."

"Perhaps," Joben mused, choosing to ignore the way Emmanuel's face twisted as he mentioned the governors, "but in what context did Ian hear Whitman's name mentioned? The morphs may have been discussing their enemies, in which case it would make sense for the names of high-ranking human officials to come up."

It was a sound point, but Emmanuel shot it down with a shake of his head. "That isn't the way Ian described it. He said that one of the superiors was discussing Whitman like we would an old friend—not with rancor or hate, but with familiarity."

"But Ian's account alone isn't enough to flesh out the truth," he surmised. "To be certain of anything, we need more than one perspective, and hopefully one that sheds a closer view on the upper ranks of the morphs."

Emmanuel nodded. "Yes, which brings me to my initial point: we need to procure another morph subject. If we can turn another morph back into a human, we may be able to fill in the missing pieces."

"But not just any morph," Joben mused, repeating Emmanuel's earlier statement as he sensed where the young doctor's train of thought was heading.

Emmanuel sighed. "Exactly," he replied. "Not just any morph. We need a higher up—one that would have had more responsibility and be more informed about larger scale morph affairs. Based on what Ian said, I don't think we have any chance of catching an elite, but a superior..." He trailed off.

"It's a good idea, albeit a vastly problematic one."

Emmanuel frowned. "That's putting it mildly."

"Yes, I suppose it is." Joben stood and placed his teacup on his desk. "We don't know where to find a superior or how to subdue one, let alone how exactly we would go about capturing one—unless you are aware of how Dr. Mortimer managed to acquire Ian while he was still in morph form?" He paused, then continued on when Emmanuel shook his head. "Right. And even if we came up with solutions to those issues, we don't have the manpower to conduct a mission beyond the walls." He drummed his fingers on the edge of his desk. "Or permission," he added quietly. "I don't have the clearance anymore to sanction this type of operation."

"No," Emmanuel agreed. "Not on your own, at least."

Joben looked up at that, catching on immediately to the unspoken implication. "You are entertaining the idea of asking Kai to allow and support a mission outside of Ashland's walls?" He asked.

"We have to entertain that idea," Emmanuel murmured unhappily. "I can't see how we can move forward without her help."

Joben pursed his lips, thinking of how his fellow commander would react at hearing their proposal. Based on past experience, Joben didn't think it was likely to go well. Then again...

"Commander Ramirez will never agree to something like this – or even entertain the idea – unless there is some viable proof that this mission is necessary and worth the risks. If you really think we need her help – and I believe you're right in that assumption – then we will have to show her something tangible."

Emmanuel's eyes widened. "You want me to show her what we've been up to?" He guessed. "As in show Ian to her?"

Joben nodded. "Yes," he said simply, and then he held up a hand before the younger man could say a word. "It is true that Commander Ramirez follows the letter of the law, and it is true that she is hotheaded and stubborn, but she is not a fool; if she sees physical proof that your vaccine works and if Ian tells her what he told you, I believe she will come around."

"And if she doesn't?"

It was a possibility Joben didn't want to consider. "She will," he replied firmly. *She has to.* For all their differences and disagreements, Joben would not want to start a war with Kai or ask Dex to intervene. She was a good commander who cared about her men, and Joben respected her.

"I'll set up the meeting," he said to Emmanuel.

The doctor didn't argue. "All right," he acquiesced. "What do we tell Dex?"

Joben pursed his lips. Dex cared nothing for Kai and would not want to involve her in any way. And even if it were somehow possible to convince Dex that involving Kai would bring about the best outcome, Joben wasn't certain that Dex wouldn't *see* to her once the mission was completed. Kai was a 'strait-laced sycophant', in Dex's opinion, and he would no doubt view her as a loose end he needed to tie up.

Which Joben would never allow. He'd crossed many lines both during and before his tenure as commander for the benefit of the greater good, but he still had limits, still had lines he refused to cross. But Dex…Dex didn't believe in the sanctity of anything aside from his own end goals. It was one of the many things that made him effective, but it also made him dangerous, ruthless.

"We tell him nothing for now," Joben decided. "We'll do this as cleanly and covertly as possible. Understood?"

It wasn't often that Joben pulled rank anymore, and in reality, he didn't really have any sway over Emmanuel. However, the skin of a feared and respected commander wasn't a skin shed so easily, and his tone and stance had the desired effect: the doctor nodded in mute agreement.

"Good," Joben said, his tone softening. "Thank you for speaking with me and for sharing all that you've learned so far from Ian. I'll let you know when I have a time and place for the meeting with Commander Ramirez. For now, I think it would be best for you to return to your quarters—before your father realizes where you've been."

"He pays little attention to me these days," Emmanuel replied as he rose from his chair.

*That's probably for the best,* Joben thought as he ushered the doctor to the door. The less Reginald Mason knew about his son's activities, the better.

Joben bid the doctor good night and then closed his door and sagged against it, releasing a weary sigh.

So much new information, and all of it bad.

*"Storm's coming,"* Francis had told him once, so long ago, on that idyllic day before the morph outbreak had changed the world forever. *Storm's coming,* he'd foreseen, and the storm *had* come. What Joben wondered now, as he pressed his forehead against the solid, cool bulk of his door, was whether the storm would ever end.

. . . . .

Marcus dreamed of Jocelyn…her smile, her laughter, the feel of her body pressed close to his…

When he roused himself enough to open his eyes, there *was* someone pressed close to him, but it wasn't Jocelyn.

Somehow, in their sleep, he and Aya had become a tangle of limbs. They were facing each other, and her head was resting against his bandaged chest, her hair tickling his skin the same way her cool breath did every time she exhaled. They were pressed together lower down, too, Marcus realized after a moment, one of her legs sandwiched between his, one of her arms around his torso, one of his arms slung across her back. It was casual, comfortable, familiar, and Marcus was reluctant to move—and not only because he didn't want to wake her.

How long had it been since he'd held someone in his arms like this, since he'd had someone in bed with him?

He'd forgotten how good it could feel.

Aya shifted slightly in her sleep, moving closer, burrowing against him a little more in *just* the right way.

*Fuck.*

Marcus groaned.

The flare of pain he felt with her body pressing against his wounds paled in comparison to the flare of arousal that flooded his limbs at having her so near.

Almost unconsciously, he reached up, his fingertips inching towards the tendrils of hair half-covering her face, seeking to brush them away.

But then Aya opened her eyes, and Marcus froze. Her gaze was unfocused, hazy, her eyelids still droopy with sleep, but as her vision came into focus her eyes widened and she gasped in surprise, instantly scooting away from of him.

"I'm sorry," she began hastily, her cheeks burning. "I don't know when I—"

Marcus caught her wrist as she began to sit up, his grip loose but firm enough to make her pause. "Don't go," he murmured. The piteousness of that request should have made him cringe in embarrassment, but for some reason it didn't.

Aya's lips parted, but she otherwise stayed completely still.

Marcus watched her, enjoying the sense of quiet he felt, in the room and in his head, and the peace of that moment gave him the clarity he needed to ask the question she'd only partially answered two days before. "Aya," he began, holding her dark gaze. "Why did you come back?"

He felt her arm tremor beneath his hand. "I already told you why I—"

He cut her off. "No." He could sense the walls going up around her and he didn't want that. He wanted the truth. The *whole* truth. "You told me part of the reason, but you're holding back. I can tell." He searched her eyes. "Tell me the real reason. Please."

She pulled out of his grip, but this time Marcus let her go since he sensed that she wasn't going to run away.

His instincts were right; Aya sat up and crossed her legs, resting her hands in her lap and physically regrouping. Then she took a breath, her shoulders moving as she inhaled and exhaled. "Do you remember when I asked you if something had changed after the second time I fed on you?"

Marcus remembered. He remembered it with perfect clarity, right down to the feel of her hips twitching beneath his fingers. He swallowed, nodded.

"Well, I lied when I said nothing was different. We...we formed a blood bond."

Even though Marcus had no idea what the hell a blood bond was, he could tell, simply by her grave tone, that it was important. Big.

"Blood bonds are extremely rare," she went on, "and usually formed between two vampires. Our situation is almost unheard of." She paused. "Our blood bond was the reason I was able to track you so quickly. It was also the reason I knew you were in trouble. I could sense it, just like I can feel your emotions. Sometimes, I can even hear your thoughts when they're strong enough," she added, her voice dwindling to a mumble.

Marcus said nothing. He wasn't one to believe in superstitious mumbo jumbo – Stan had knocked any sense of spirituality out of him at an early age – so he was somewhat surprised to find that he believed Aya completely. He'd never been able to hear her thoughts, but he certainly felt...*connected* to her on a deeper level, could feel and understand and sense her in a way that he hadn't been able to before.

But there was one detail that eluded him. "You said that blood bonds are extremely rare," he echoed. "Define 'extremely'."

"There is only one other known instance of a blood bond being formed between a vampire and a human."

Marcus could have sworn his heart temporarily stopped beating. "So how the hell did we manage to become the second pair?" He asked, not even attempting to keep the incredulity out of his voice.

Aya fidgeted, her fingers running nervously over the hem of her shirt. "The source varies," she said, "but usually it...it's love."

Marcus blanched. *Love? No way in hell,* came the instant mental rebuttal. *We hated each other.*

But that was bullshit. They may have hated each other in the beginning, but that hatred had long ago dissipated, evolved. By that cold night when she'd fed on him the second time…

An image of Aya, nervously leaning in, eyes and lips shining with want, appeared in his head, as did the sensory memory of the way her fangs had gently pierced his skin…

*Fuck.*

No, he definitely hadn't hated her anymore. He hadn't loved her, either. Had he?

*Did* he?

Grimacing with effort, Marcus pushed himself up to a seated position, mimicking Aya's position.

Sitting felt good—solid and real, a nice contrast to how surreal everything else felt. Never, not in a million fucking years, would he ever have imagined having this conversation with a vampire. Never. And yet here he was, and here she was.

And he had to know.

"Aya," he asked slowly, softly, "do you…?" He couldn't bring himself to say it, but he thought it, he felt it, and he knew, beyond a shadow of a doubt, that Aya had heard the question in its entirety.

Her gaze dropped, the black fringe of her lashes concealing whatever truth he could have gleaned from her eyes. "It wouldn't make any difference either way," she murmured at length. "We are what we are—vampire and human. There would be no future for us even if those feelings were there." She paused, her lips tightening just a fraction, just enough that Marcus caught it. "Besides," she added, "your heart belongs to another."

Marcus regarded her quietly. He wished she would look at him, but he understood her reservation. On the battlefield, she was confident, decisive. Here, with no threatening distractions, her vulnerability was palpable.

They were very, very much alike.

"I do love Jocelyn," he affirmed softly. "I always will. But Jocelyn is gone." His voice caught on the last word, that final syllable sticking in his throat. Seven years—seven fucking *years* and it still wasn't easy to admit that Jocelyn was lost to him. Dead and buried and only alive in his memories.

*Some wounds never heal.*

He'd said that to Maggie one night by the campfire, a night that seemed like a lifetime ago, when he and Aya had been linked only by blackmail and Maggie had been…

He shoved the thought away abruptly, but its implication lingered in his mind like a bitter aftertaste.

Everything had changed. Maggie was gone now, Jocelyn was gone, but Aya—Aya was flesh and blood. She was alive. She was a vampire he trusted, an enemy turned confidante and comrade. She'd been his savior on more than one occasion, and, somewhere along the way, she'd become one of them. He'd missed her when she'd left—missed her long before he'd admitted it to himself, and he was glad she had returned. He needed her, relied on her – and, he admitted as his eyes quickly flickered over the slope of her shoulders and the graceful curve of her waist and down to the slight flare of her hips – he wanted her in a way he hadn't wanted anyone since Jocelyn.

Articulating any of those small epiphanies eddying through his brain was next to impossible, but he owed it to Aya to try. She looked so downcast, so forlorn sitting there across from him, and it was his fault.

"I care about you, Aya," he said finally. He didn't know if he loved her, and he sure as shit wasn't in the right mental state to go figuring that out at the moment, but he knew one thing for certain, and he said as much. "And I feel this…this bond between us, too. And I'm glad it's there."

*That* made her look up. "You are?" She asked, her porcelain brow crinkling in disbelief.

"I am," he answered, nodding, feeling the truth of it settle in his very marrow. "You've given me strength, Aya," he went on, feeling uncharacteristically emboldened. "Alone, I always doubted our odds of making it to Ashland, but with you, I…it seems possible."

Aya's lips tilted up sweetly. "You don't give yourself enough credit," she argued. "Under your leadership, the group always had a good chance of making it to Ashland, despite the odds."

"Half of them are dead."

"And half are still alive."

"Not quite half," he mumbled bitterly.

Aya reached out and squeezed one of his hands. "Marcus," she chided. "Don't. Don't do that to yourself."

He obliged her, falling silent for a while. At some point, he realized that he was idly brushing his thumb across her knuckles, gently caressing the smooth skin of her hand, and a new thought occurred to him.

"Are you staying?" He asked as casually as he could manage.

He felt her hand flinch beneath his touch as the rest of her body stiffened. "I was planning to," she replied, her tone full of wariness, "but if you don't want—"

Marcus tightened his grip on her hand. "I want you to," he answered firmly.

He felt more than heard her exhale. "Oh," she said softly. "Good." He could almost hear a hint of a smile in her tone, but it was gone when she spoke again.

"What happens when we get to Ashland?"

That was a question he didn't have an answer to. "I don't know," he admitted. Soldiers in all three fortresses had a standing kill-on-sight order in regard to vampires and morphs, but maybe, since Aya was traveling with him, the rules would be slightly different.

"It won't be easy, but if we make it as far as Ashland, I'll vouch for you. I have an old friend there who will listen, and if he hears how you basically saved all of our asses time and again, I think he'll speak on your behalf, too."

Aya's eyebrows rose. "He must be quite an important friend."

"He's an idealistic bastard, but he's also a military commander. And a good man. I trust him."

"Then I will, too," Aya said.

Marcus didn't say anything else. Even with Joben's support, he knew that seeking amnesty and asylum for a vampire would be a monumental struggle, but he didn't want to dwell on it. He couldn't. That was a problem for a day three hundred miles west of where they were, after they were back with the others and after they'd faced and survived whatever trials still lay ahead of them.

*No use worrying about tomorrow's shit since tomorrow ain't a certainty. Survive today and then deal with the next today.*

That was one piece of Stan's unsolicited advice that Marcus happened to agree with. With the constant dangers, it made sense to live one day at a time.

He would find a way to solve the Ashland problem when, or rather *if*, they made it there. But for now…

His stomach rumbled painfully. "You said there wasn't much food left?" He asked, dealing with the most present problem.

Aya pulled her hand from his grasp and stood up. "No, but there's a few dried fruit stuffs left in the other room. I'll get them for you."

She was gone and back in the blink of an eye, and Marcus was pleasantly surprised to discover that his appetite had returned. He finished off the three small servings she'd brought him in record time.

Aya looked simultaneously pleased and worried as she watched him, but the latter emotion was all he could see swimming in her eyes by the time he was done.

"You need more," she observed grimly, her lips pulling down in a frown. She sighed. "I'm going to go out and see what else I can find," she said. "Will you be okay here by yourself?"

Marcus scoffed with more bravado than he felt. "I'm a Reaper, Aya. I'm sure I'll manage, even if I have to freshen some of these bandages without my doting nursemaid."

His sarcasm didn't mollify her, but it did seem to draw out a spark of anger in her dark eyes, which was a nice departure from the worry she'd been radiating. "Reaper or not," she responded tightly, "you shouldn't be so cavalier. You almost died two days ago and you're still barely able to move. If something happens while I'm gone—"

"I'll manage," he insisted again, this time without the sarcasm. "But at this point, food is more important. So go," he added more gently. "I'll be all right."

Aya's lips pressed together. "I won't be long," she promised.

Marcus watched her leave, feeling a strange tug of loss at her departure. He wasn't, however, worried about her. If anyone could handle herself – even alone in a morph-infested wilderness – it was Aya. She'd proven herself to be pretty incredible in every situation they'd been caught in so far.

The thought made him cringe a bit. Hell—his emotions might have been the equivalent of scrambled eggs, but maybe he *was* a little in love with her.

He wondered what Stan would've said about that.

More accurately, he wondered how long it would've taken for Stan to bash his brains in for even entertaining that possibility.

It didn't matter now, of course. It didn't matter at all, truth be told. Sorting out the jumble of his feelings was a problem also for some vague day in the future. For now, he needed to work on getting his strength back.

Taking a breath, Marcus forced himself to his feet.

To no avail.

He fell immediately, landing hard on his hands and knees, the pain ricocheting out from his palms and kneecaps with such force that he gasped.

*Come on,* he urged himself. *Get up.*

Gritting his teeth, he once more pushed himself up. His legs began to wobble again, and his head reeled with vertigo, but he reached out and used the wall to steady himself, taking one breath and then another and then another until he felt his equilibrium slowly start to return.

He let go of the wall and this time, he didn't fall. *Guess that's progress,* he mused, and then he took a step forward.

His whole body shook, but he remained standing, and inch by inch, step by step, he crossed the room. Then he turned around and did it again. By the time he collapsed back down on the pallet, he was drenched in sweat and breathing hard.

And he was thirsty.

Fuck.

Well, external motivation was a good thing, he supposed. He waited until his heart rate settled and his breathing was back under control, and then, the goal of water in mind, he stood up once more.

This time, his legs stayed steady.

. . . . .

Emmanuel hadn't seen Kai since the time he'd confronted her about changing her Council vote all those weeks ago, but even so, he wasn't sure that enough time had passed for her to cool off. She'd been livid when he'd brought up her family, and Kai had a reputation for holding grudges.

Which was why, when he heard three sharp raps against his front door a little before midnight, Emmanuel stiffened.

*We need her,* he told himself as he forced his feet to move. *We need her on our side.*

It was sound logic, but he still had to take a deep breath before he unbolted the door and turned the knob.

"Commander Ramirez," he greeted quietly with a nod of his head.

Kai was dressed in her usual austere ensemble of all black, and her expression matched. "Dr. Mason," she greeted coldly.

Emmanuel stepped aside and gestured for her to come in. "Please," he said, holding out his arm. "Make yourself at home."

Kai strode past him and Emmanuel shut the door, steeling himself for the coming encounter before he turned to face her.

Still, he managed a meek smile when he caught her eye. "Would you like some coffee?" He asked, trying to ignore how out of place Kai looked standing in the middle of his kitchen. "Or tea, perhaps?"

She didn't even give him the courtesy of a refusal. "What I would like, Dr. Mason," she answered instead, "is to know why Joben Hale insisted that I meet with you here and at this hour."

Emmanuel groaned inwardly. *This is going to be an uphill battle.*

Kai's posture may have been nonchalant – shoulders back, arms at her sides – but it was clear from the tone of her voice and the curtness of her words that her figurative fists were up. She wasn't in a mood to hear anything he had to say, and it made Emmanuel nervous.

Not nervous enough to give up, however.

"He arranged this meeting because we've had a breakthrough," he said.

Kai raised one of her full, curved brows. "What kind of breakthrough?" She asked, placing her hands akimbo.

Emmanuel decided to sidle into a response instead of answering bluntly. "Please hear me out before you condemn my actions," he said. "I know genetic experimentation is illegal, and I know that you yourself have upheld the ban against aiding research regarding morphs in the past," he added, then took a breath, "but what would you say if I told you that we were no longer working on suppositions? That if you give us the help we need, we will be able to save many of the citizens we lost? That we have concrete proof that it is possible to reverse the effects of the *Metamorphosis* vaccine?"

Kai was unmoved. "Other than saying you should be imprisoned for breaking the law? I would say show me the proof."

This time, instead of forcing a smile, Emmanuel had to hide one. "Fair enough," he said, feeling a modicum of victory. Then, in a louder voice, he called, "Ian, please come here."

It wasn't often that Kai's resting mien of displeasure could be affected, but the surprise on her face when Ian walked into the room a handful of seconds later was sincere. She looked him up and down, and Emmanuel could see the gears turning in her head.

"Who is this?" She asked at length.

Ian shifted from foot to foot, looking incredibly uncomfortable beneath Kai's scrutiny.

Emmanuel gave him a reassuring smile. "This is Ian Hayes. He was a Rangers soldier who received the *Metamorphosis* vaccine six years ago."

Kai's full lips parted in disbelief. "That isn't possible," she said, her brown eyes widening.

"Despite the current law, Dr. Mortimer has never given up on our citizens—on *any* of them. She has been working on a cure for years," Emmanuel went on. "Using her notes, I was able to finish it. The results speak for themselves."

Kai's gaze drifted back to Ian. "Is this true?" She asked him. "Were you a morph? Did Dr. Mason turn you back?"

"Y-yes, ma'am," Ian stammered, his gaze flitting from Kai to the floor. "Both of those things are true."

"Can you prove that?"

Wordlessly, Ian pulled up the sleeve covering his left arm, showing off the unmistakable mark of the original vaccine.

"I see," Kai said finally. There was no longer any trace of skepticism in her voice. "And now that you're human again, do you still remember what it was like to *be* a morph?"

Ian flinched. "All too well." His tone was haunted, hushed.

Something shifted in Kai's eyes, then, a softening that Emmanuel had never seen before. "I can't imagine what it must have been like to go through that," she said softly. "I'm sorry."

Ian shrugged his shoulders and scratched the back of his head. "It's okay," he responded. "I mean, it's not, but…" He exhaled. "If I can make up for it, for what I—" He faltered, pain flashing across his face. "For what I did while I was…like *that*," he carried on, "then I want to. I want to help."

Kai nodded, her hands slipping back to her sides. "All right." She turned to Emmanuel. "You have my attention, Dr. Mason. Tell me what you want."

Emmanuel hoped the disbelief wasn't showing on his face. "We need to capture another morph," he confided. "In order to make sure the cure is viable, we have to test it on more than one subject. We also need more information on the morphs. Ian has provided some insight into morph affairs and the makeup of their forces – which I will share with you – but we need more. We cannot rely on his testimony alone if we wish to regain the upper hand. And in order to do all this," he added, "we need soldiers. *Your* soldiers. And your support." He paused. "There is no way we can move forward without you, Commander Ramirez."

Kai was quiet for so long that Emmanuel could feel nervous sweat breaking out on his forehead. Finally, just when he was about to break the interminable silence, Kai spoke.

"I take it that you have no intention of going to the Council with this or trying to find a legal loophole."

It was a statement, not a question, and a perceptive one at that. "That is correct," Emmanuel answered honestly. "Given my father's actions as of late, we decided it would be in our best interest to involve as few people as possible."

Kai didn't miss a beat. *"We?"* She echoed.

"Commander Hale and I," he answered. He said nothing of Dex.

Again, Kai nodded. "Very well. I do not condone clandestine activities, but I do recognize that this is a...unique circumstance and needs to be dealt with as such, especially since any and all genetic experimentation is outlawed." She rolled her shoulders back. "In spite of my sense of duty, I will help you. I do not abide breaking the law, but you have proof—material proof, and I want to save our citizens. I will give you the manpower you need to capture another morph. On one condition."

The sense of victory that had bubbled up in the pit of Emmanuel's stomach fizzled out. "What is your condition?" He asked warily.

"When my assembled team leaves Ashland, Ian goes with them."

Emmanuel blanched. The thought of sending Ian back out into morph territory when he'd already endured so much trauma was unthinkable. He couldn't agree to that. He wouldn't. "I don't think that's—"

"I'll go."

Kai and Emmanuel both stopped, looking over at the blue-eyed former morph. "Ian," Emmanuel began. "You don't have to—"

"Yes, I do," the other man interjected. "It makes sense. I know the landscape. I know the routes the morphs travel on. I know where the army bases are and where the units are camped. I know the places that are overrun with mongrels. I know where to go and where not to go. And I know how to find the kind of morph you need."

Kai seemed pleased. "Then it's settled," she said. "I'll organize and debrief my team and let you know when the mission will commence." She headed for the door, but turned back, the unbraided half of her hair falling in waves behind her shoulder. "I want complete files on everything you've discovered and discussed concerning the morphs."

"Of course," Emmanuel assured her. "I will bring them by your headquarters tomorrow. I can't risk making you your own copies, but you can peruse them at your leisure while I'm there."

"Fine. Was there anything else, Dr. Mason?"

It was the closest thing to an amenable question that she'd ever asked him. "No, Commander," he replied. "Thank you—for believing us and for helping us."

Kai's stiff demeanor seemed to lose a bit of its rigidness. "I know we have our differences, Dr. Mason, but what you've done here is incredible. I know you may feel I've stood against you in the past, but that is because I refuse to risk my soldiers' lives on foolish errands. This is not a foolish errand. If there is even the slightest chance that these results can be duplicated and that we can save some of the citizens we lost, it is worth the risk."

Emmanuel bit his tongue, not wanting to say that sending men to Easthaven to track down potential survivors would have hardly been a fool's errand. It wasn't the time or place, and Kai had just agreed to help them; the last thing he needed to do was stir her anger. So instead he politely inclined his head. "I'm glad you feel that way."

Kai nodded at him. "Good night," she said. "I'll see you and your files tomorrow." Then she briefly nodded to Ian. "I'll be in touch soon." She paused. "Welcome back," she added, and then she opened the door and disappeared into the hallway.

Emmanuel let out the tense breath he'd been holding.

"Wow. She's uh, a bit…" Ian trailed off, apparently unable to find a word to describe the Guard commander. "Is she always like that?" He asked instead.

"At least in public," Emmanuel replied quietly. He eyed the other man carefully. "Are you sure you are well enough to go back out there? It was brave of you to volunteer, but you can still change your mind."

Ian gave him an attempt at a nonchalant shrug. "Thanks for saying so, but I need to do this. I need to face what happened. I need to face what I was."

There was something so genuine, so earnest, about Ian that Emmanuel found himself believing what the former hunter was saying. "All right," he yielded. "As long as you feel that way, then I'll stand by your decision."

Ian smiled, the warmth of it reaching his eyes in a way that made him seem younger—boyish, almost. "Thanks." He colored slightly.

"Uh...I know it's late, but would you mind if I ate something? I'm kind of hungry again."

Emmanuel chuckled. Out of all Ian's dormant human traits, it was definitely his appetite that had woken up first. And it had woken up with a vengeance. "Sure," he said, heading over to his pantry. It had been stocked a few days ago, but now its shelves were mostly bare. "I think there's enough left here for me to make us some soup. Does that sound okay?"

"Yeah," came the embarrassed reply. "Sorry about, you know, eating all your food."

"Don't be," Emmanuel said as he placed his gathered ingredients on the counter. "You're a walking miracle, Ian. I think the least I can do is spare you some food."

In reply, Ian granted him another warm smile. "Can I help?" He asked.

Emmanuel blinked. First Kai had agreed to help them, and now Ian was ready to try his hand at something new. It was shaping up to be quite the night. "Of course you can," Emmanuel answered, realizing that, for the first time in recent memory, he felt happy.

He also felt hopeful that maybe – just maybe – things were beginning to turn around for the better.

·   ·   ·   ·   ·

It was strange to think that a week had passed since she'd half-carried Marcus into the bunker. In some ways it felt like they'd just gotten there, and in other ways it felt like they'd been there for a lifetime.

They'd fallen into an easy kind of routine: she would go out and scavenge for food in the mornings while Marcus exercised and worked to get his strength back, they would spend their afternoons patrolling (she did it alone the first three days until Marcus insisted he was well enough to go outside with her), and then they would curl up on their shared mattress in the evenings and fall asleep beside each other. Although they never fell asleep that way, more often than not they would wake up in each other's arms, and the last two mornings Aya had been content to stay there. Somewhere along the way, she'd gotten used to the feeling of having him near.

It was a glimpse at another life—a quiet, domestic kind of life, and Aya half wished that it didn't have to end, that they could just go on existing in the small bubble they'd created for themselves, far from danger and pain and judgment.

But it was time to leave.

She heard Marcus return from the river, the sound of the bunker door opening rousing her from her daydream, and she finished securing the packs she'd been stocking. There hadn't been much left in the bunker, but she'd found an assortment of basic provisions that could prove useful in their travels.

One of the floorboards squeaked as Marcus entered the room she was in, and Aya zipped up the smaller pack and stood up, turning to hand it to him.

Except that he was closer than she was anticipating, and she ended up smacking him in the chest with it.

Marcus expelled a surprised gasp and Aya instinctively reached out, steadying him as her face began to burn. "Sorry," she murmured, silently cursing her stupidity.

But Marcus seemed amused, his lips curving wryly. "I didn't realize you were so impatient to leave that you were ready to fling things at me." He chuckled. "Warn me next time."

Aya shouldered her own pack, willing the color to leave her cheeks. "I didn't realize you were standing so close," she said lamely. "And I'm not impatient to leave." The veracity of that statement cooled her embarrassment. She looked up at him, noting the humor glinting in his eyes and the way the curling ends of his overgrown hair were clumped together, still damp from his impromptu bath in the river. "If anything, I wish we could stay a little longer," she added quietly.

An emotional change seeped into the atmosphere of the room. "Me too," Marcus said softly, his gaze sobering. "Being here…with you…it's been a nice break." His eyes flickered down to her lips, making Aya's stomach twist into nervous knots.

She didn't even realize she was leaning towards him until she heard his sharp intake of breath. "Aya…"

She looked into his eyes. There was something burning there, something she recognized as hunger, but it wasn't the same kind of hunger she was familiar with. It was something darker, headier, more…

She parted her lips, her fangs twitching.

And suddenly Marcus's hands were on either side of her neck, cupping her face, the rough pads of his fingers raising goosebumps on her delicate skin.

She sucked in a breath, her own hands coming to rest on his chest, her fingers curling into the fabric of his sweater.

Marcus groaned, the sound sending a shivering thrill down Aya's spine. His grip tightened. So did hers.

She wanted…

*Touch me.*

She thought it, felt it, radiated it, and she could feel Marcus responding, could see a fissure begin to crack in his control…

But then, as suddenly as it had started, it stopped, and Marcus's hands were gone and he was stepping away from her.

"We should go," he said eventually.

Aya reeled, feeling unsteady on her feet.

What had happened? What had *almost* happened?

"Marcus?" She said tentatively, searching his eyes for some kind of explanation.

But she found none. His gaze was still dark, hungry, but his voice was under tight control. "We should go," he repeated.

"But…"

"Aya." His tone was huskier this time, more labored. "We can't stay here," he ground out, his jaw clenching. "We can't waste any more time—no matter how tempting it is," he added as he tore his gaze away from her, his voice dropping pitch.

Aya swallowed. She felt empty, similar to how she felt when she hadn't fed in a long time, but not quite the same. It was a different kind of emptiness, one that made her whole body ache.

Then again, she *hadn't* fed in a while; maybe it was nothing more than hunger.

And besides—Marcus was right. They needed to leave. They had to find the rest of their group, had to return to the world and all of its responsibilities.

But the desire to ignore all that, to reach out to Marcus and find out what would have happened if he hadn't pulled away was immense.

And apparently she wasn't alone in her struggle.

Marcus was staring at her, the same conflict she was experiencing warring in his eyes. But the soldier in him was winning—she could see it in the way his posture straightened and in the hard set of his mouth. "We can't," he said. "Not now. When we make it to Ashland…maybe then. But not now."

Aya couldn't argue with him. Marcus was a leader, a soldier, a fighter. Of course the mission would come first. He wouldn't be him if it didn't.

And Aya loved him all the more for it.

"Later," she agreed, not even knowing quite what she meant.

*Later.*

As they stepped out into the snow beyond the bunker and left their quiet, simple shelter behind, the word lingered in her mind.

*Later.*

She wondered if later would ever come, or if the promise of that word was, like their short time at the bunker, just a glimpse at a life she'd never have.

# Building Tensions

*Never make the mistake of thinking that peace will last forever; no matter how strong or unshakeable it seems, peace is nothing more than a spinning top, and like all spinning tops, it is not sustainable. One day it will falter.*
- Quote taken from a speech made by Commander Dante Pole, later published in his posthumous biography

. . . . .

Louisa Mason was feeling every bit her age this particular morning as she stared into the vanity mirror above her dresser. The item was an antique, and one of the few things that she'd kept after her separation from Reginald. Usually its presence reminded her of better days and happier times, but now, all she could see was her tired reflection staring back at her. Fine lines now creased her once-smooth dark skin, and her deep brown eyes had lost some of their vivacity. Even her thick black hair seemed to have lost its shine.

*I used to be beautiful,* she thought wistfully. *I used to be someone.*

Once, she'd been the darling of the people, Ashland's first lady who stood beside her husband but still had a voice of her own. Now she was the governor's ex-wife, and her fall into obscurity had been swift. Fame was a fickle thing, after all.

Still, she wouldn't go back. Even though she missed the sense of importance, dealing with Reginald in the later years of their marriage had worn her down in an irrevocable way. Watching him flaunt his dalliances in front of her had been the tipping point, but even before that, seeing Reginald treat their son like he was so much muck on his boots year after year had eroded whatever affection and esteem Louisa had once felt for him. She only wished that her younger self had seen past his charm and confidence and realized that in every way that mattered, Reginald was blind.

"Mom."

Louisa started. She'd been so lost in her thoughts that she hadn't even realized she was no longer alone. She turned to greet her son and then frowned when she saw the expression on his face. "Manny? Is everything okay?"

In lieu of answering, he strode forward and slapped his hand down on her dresser, releasing the paper that had been balled up in his fist. "Read it," he barked.

Completely baffled, Louisa slowly reached out and grabbed the paper. She opened it, smoothing out the copious wrinkles as she did, and then she held it up to the light.

*~Phase one is complete. Phase two is scheduled for 30-6. Everest will be in contact. Isolation in place until then. – L*

She read it twice and then looked up at her son. "Is this supposed to mean something to me?" She asked, still at a total loss.

The hostility in Emmanuel's eyes frightened her, and it reminded her, uncomfortably, of Reginald. "Did you write this?" He asked.

She blinked. "I don't—"

"Did you write this?" Her son demanded again, in a louder voice.

Louisa took a step back. "I refuse to be spoken to like this," she said sharply. "You are my son. You will not barge in here and interrogate me."

Something broke in Emmanuel's expression, but he didn't back down. "Mom, please, just—just answer the question. After everything I've discovered these last few weeks..." He shook his head. "It's been hell. So please, *please*, just answer the question."

Louisa shook her head. "No, I did not write this. I've never seen this before in my life."

"So you're not 'L'?"

"No." She felt a pang of worry shoot through her. "Where did you get this, Manny? And what do you mean by 'after everything I've discovered these last few weeks'? What are you talking about?"

Her son only chose to answer her initial question. "I found it," he said quietly.

Louisa pressed her lips together. "Where?" She followed up, resisting the urge to tap her foot in irritation like she'd done when Manny was little. "On the floor of the dining hall? Dropped by one of your patients?"

"Dad's office."

"When did your father give you permission to go in there?"

"He didn't."

Louisa paled. "You broke into your father's office and stole this?" Her brows furrowed together. "Manny, your father is not the kind of man you steal from. Why would you do something like this?"

"Because he's lied to me my whole life!" Emmanuel snapped. His shoulders started to shake. "He pretends to be this noble man, this inspiring leader, when in reality he's a killer. I've spent my whole life trying to please a killer, trying to make a murderer proud of me."

Louisa felt as though she'd been seized by paralysis. "A killer?" She repeated dubiously. "What are you saying, Emmanuel? What are you talking about?"

Her son's shoulders sagged. "I think he knew, Mom," he answered, voice cracking. "I think Dad knew what was going to happen in Year Zero. I think he knew that the vaccine wasn't going to work, and I think he stood by and let thousands die anyway. All because he wanted power. And you..." Emmanuel met her gaze, his own swimming with warring emotions. "The other governors knew too, and some of their wives did as well. I didn't want to believe you were involved, but when I found this and saw the signature, I thought..."

Louisa reached out and took her son by the arms. "Emmanuel."

He met her gaze again, with obvious reluctance.

"Where did you get all this information?" She questioned. "How do you know any of it is true?"

Her son's expression turned wary. "I...I can't tell you. But I know it's true, Mom. I just know it."

She didn't doubt the veracity of his words, but the fact that he couldn't share what proof he had or where he'd obtained said proof made Louisa's stomach tighten. "Manny," she said, lowering her voice. "I find it hard to believe that talk of sabotage and conspiracy are running rampant through the medical wing. What exactly are you involved in? And who told you these things?"

Her son pulled back from her touch. "I can't—" He stopped himself. "I'm just trying to fix things. I'm trying to make things right."

"By breaking into your father's private office? By accusing him of murder?"

"I can't explain right now, Mom. I'm sorry." He reached out and took the paper back from her, once more crumpling it into a small ball. "But just—just tell me, once and for all: were you ever aware of something my father did that he shouldn't have done? Did he ever talk to you about anything, tell you to keep any secrets?"

*Our marriage was built on secrets*, Louisa thought immediately, but she held her tongue. The secrets had all belonged to Reginald, after all, not her. "No," she replied firmly. "Whatever you've learned or think you've learned of your father's past deeds, it's more than what I know. Communication was never one of our strengths as a couple."

A small wave of relief seemed to wash over her son. He exhaled. "Okay." His expression turned sheepish. "I'm sorry for coming here like this," he apologized. "I just needed to know. I will not come here like this again. I promise."

He turned to go, but Louisa called after him. "Emmanuel."

Her son stopped.

"You're a doctor, Manny. A healer. You're not a spy. Whatever you're doing, whomever you're working with, stop. Your father is a powerful man. Don't give him a reason to take action against you." *I already lost him. I can't lose you too.* "And you should put that note back where you found it. Before your father realizes it's missing."

Emmanuel nodded once. "I'll put it back," he agreed, but he was careful not to promise anything further.

"Manny," she pressed. The turmoil she could see on her son's face made her heart ache. "Are you sure you don't want to tell me what's going on? You can confide in me—about anything. You never know; I might even be able to help you."

But her son kept his silence. "I'm sorry, Mom," he replied. "I can't." And then he turned and left.

Louisa sank down on the edge of her bed once her son departed, feeling even older and wearier than she had when she'd been looking at her reflection in her vanity mirror.

Had Reginald really known what would happen in Year Zero? Had he been involved in it somehow? Her ex-husband had always been ambitious, but it was hard to believe that his desire for power would motivate him to do something so evil.

Still, Louisa racked her brain, trying to think back, to recall any conversations that had passed between them that would coincide with Emmanuel's claims.

And then something came to her, and Louisa's hand flew to her mouth to stifle the gasp of realization.

Reginald had taken them to Ashland *before* the morph outbreak. He'd claimed that he'd been assigned to do a sweep of the fortress (*standard procedure, dear*) and he'd taken her and Manny along with him for no real reason. It hadn't struck her as strange at the time, just fortuitous, but now…

*Did you really choose to let humanity fall, Reginald? Is our son right about you?*

She thought about the wrinkled note with its cryptic message, trying to recall exactly what it had said. Something about phase one and phase two…the name of a contact, isolation…all unclear and vague. And signed by a person with the same initial as her own name.

Not damning in of itself, but certainly strange enough to raise questions.

*And now Emmanuel is somehow involved in whatever this is.*

Louisa was suddenly filled with ominous foreboding. Reginald was already disappointed in his son. What would happen if he found out what his son was doing behind his back?

The answer made her shudder.

.     .     .     .     .

"And you're not to tell anyone what you are doing and where you are going. If asked, say that you are under orders not to speak a word. *I* will handle the fallout, if there is any."

Brianne's lips turned down as a deep furrow appeared on her dark, smooth forehead. "You are putting yourself at risk, Commander. Are you sure you would not rather have us claim we are working independently, without your knowledge?"

Samar perked up at that, the idle rhythm he'd been tapping on the table with his fingers momentarily ceasing. "Brianne has a point," he added, leaning back in his chair. He was the only one seated at present, so he had to tilt his head up to catch Kai's eyes. "Many believe us to be common mercenaries anyway, so it wouldn't be out of character for us to take on a job from an independent contractor behind your back."

Kai sighed, resting her hands on the top rail of the chair in front of her. "Except that it would," she said, looking between her two subordinates. "Your past reputations are just that: *past*. The two of you are the most faithful, trustworthy people I know; I will not have the integrity of your characters sullied to shield my own reputation. Even if you are willing."

Samar shrugged. "So be it," he said.

Brianne, however, was not as easily deterred. She stepped forward from where she'd been leaning against the wall, walking over until she could rest her fists on the conference table. "Kai," she said gently, "do you really believe this endeavor is worth the risk? If the governor finds out, we could all be turned out for our involvement."

Kai said nothing at first. She knew that being turned out was a possibility—she'd known it from the second that Emmanuel Mason had spoken of his plan. The good doctor might not have realized the gravity of what he had asked, but Kai was not naïve. Involving military personnel for scientific gain would be viewed as a power play, and Mason would not take kindly to it.

But Ian Hayes was living proof that things could be different, that the doomsday path humanity was on might be diverted, and Kai did not value her life more than that chance.

What hurt most was knowing that if something went wrong and Dr. Mason's plans did not succeed, Brianne and Samar would go down with her. The two ex-cons were more than just her most trusted subordinates—they were her confidantes, her friends, and, since she'd lost her biological one, the closest thing to family that she had. To say that she cared for them deeply was an understatement. She loved them like the brother and sister she'd lost.

And knowing that they were willing to die on her orders, without so much as questioning her, only made this decision all the harder to make.

But the decision still had to be made.

"Yes," she said eventually, heavily. "We could all be turned out for this." She looked between Brianne and Samar, gauging their expressions carefully. "But think of what we could gain by taking that risk. We're talking about thousands of saved lives and a chance to live outside again, a chance to be free of walls and isolation." She released the top rail from where her hands had been gripping it. "If Ian Hayes is courageous enough to face the reality he lived with for six years because he believes there is hope for humans like him, I do too. And if we don't succeed, well...maybe we will open the doors for someone else to try and do better." She paused, her voice dropping slightly. "Sometimes, sacrifice *is* the only way forward."

Everyone was quiet after that, until Samar broke the silence. "You sound like your sister," he said.

Kai stiffened, but not in anger. The only people she felt comfortable discussing her family with were here in this room, but that didn't change the fact that even after so many years, she'd never properly dealt with her grief.

"Maybe my sister's beliefs were not so wrong after all," she said softly.

Three tentative knocks broke the mood.

Kai nodded at Brianne, and the dark-skinned woman walked over and opened the door, stepping aside to let Emmanuel Mason and former morph Ian Hayes into the conference room.

Ian's reaction at seeing the six-foot-tall, muscular Brianne was close to comical. He looked the woman up and down from her bald head to the combat boots on her feet, his gaze lingering on the wicked scar bisecting her cheek, and then he swallowed visibly.

Kai repressed a smile. It wasn't the first time she'd seen someone stare upon meeting Brianne for the first time. "Ian, meet Brianne. Brianne, Ian."

The black woman extended a hand, which Ian took. "Welcome back," she said.

"Uh...thanks," Ian replied, trying to muster a polite smile.

Kai gestured to Samar, who had at last risen from his chair to face their visitors. "And this is Samar."

The lean man inclined his head. "So you're the morph, huh?"

A wince passed across Ian's face. "Former morph," he corrected quietly.

Samar crossed his arms. "Right," he acknowledged unapologetically. "And do you really think you gleaned enough useful information while in your...*other* nature to lead this little operation?"

"Well, I remember everything pretty clearly and I was out there for almost six years, so yeah, I think I can help."

"That's not what I asked."

"Samar," Kai interjected sharply. Her subordinate fell silent and she turned to Ian. "Please forgive my subordinate's attitude. I imagine this can't be easy for you, Ian, but I hope you understand that Brianne and Samar are putting their lives at risk to undertake this mission with you. They will naturally have questions, which is why the three of you will be spending the next forty-eight hours together. I expect you to give them all the information you can on what to expect beyond the fortress, and they will refresh your memory of combat techniques." She paused. "Questions?"

Finally, Ian looked up. "Will Dr. Mason be staying with us?" He asked hopefully.

"No. I believe that you need to develop a rapport with my subordinates prior to leaving Ashland, and that can best be done if the three of you operate as a unit. Dr. Mason and I will check in with you, but other than that the three of you will be on your own."

Ian tried to hide his crestfallen expression, though he didn't quite succeed. "Oh. Okay, I guess."

Brianne stepped forward, making Ian nearly jump out of his skin. "I'll show you where you'll be bunking," she said, and then her eyes met Kai's. "Is there anything else, Commander?"

Kai shook her head. "No. You're dismissed."

Brianne and Samar left without any further prompting, ushering Ian along with them, but Kai called out before the doctor followed suit.

"Dr. Mason—a moment, please."

The governor's son turned back, waiting.

"I have a question for you, and I would like a straight answer."

"Very well," the doctor replied, a touch of wariness creeping into his voice. "What is your question?"

"I remember when you were inquiring about Dr. Mortimer around my soldiers, so I am well aware that you were looking for her journals and notes. My question is: who returned those notes to you?"

Kai had been seeking a candid reaction, and a candid reaction was exactly what she got.

Emmanuel Mason's face paled and his lips parted in surprise. "I...are you doubting my ability to discover a cure on my own merits?" He said after a pause, evading her question by going on the offensive.

Kai felt her mood darkening. "I don't appreciate the deflection, Dr. Mason," she said, letting coldness seep into her voice. "And my memory is apparently a bit sharper than yours. You told me in no uncertain terms that Dr. Mortimer's notes aided you in discovering this cure. So, answer my original question." She cocked a brow at him. "Or do you have something to hide?"

She was pushing him, willing him to break, to confess whatever it was that she was sure he was concealing. She already knew that he was hiding something. What she wanted was confirmation—and a name.

"Very well," Emmanuel said at last. "If you insist on knowing, it was Joben who recovered the notes and returned them to me. I wanted to know where he'd found them, but he told me not to ask so I respected his wishes and didn't push the issue."

He was lying; Kai could see that as clear as day, but it was also obvious that he was going to cling to his lie, even if she continued to dig for the truth. Her lips tightened. "Be careful who you trust, Dr. Mason. Not everyone who aids you is a friend."

"Do you doubt Joben's integrity?"

That struck a nerve. "I'm beginning to doubt yours," Kai answered, bristling. "You and I both know that I was not referring to Joben Hale. Just because you offered his name does not mean that I believe you. Do not insult my intelligence by thinking that I will accept everything you say at face value." She clenched her fists, keeping her anger in check. "So, unless you are going to divulge the real answer to my question, I have nothing more to say to you."

For a brief second, the doctor almost looked ashamed, but then he collected himself and nodded. "You have the real answer," he insisted, his gaze steady. "I will be back tomorrow to check on Ian's progress with Brianne and Samar. Good day, Commander Ramirez."

Kai watched him go in silence, fuming inwardly.

It was clear enough why he wouldn't tell her the truth—either Emmanuel Mason was involved with someone that she wouldn't approve of, or the person he was involved with wouldn't approve of her. After all, if the mystery person were a friend or comrade, there would be no need for secrecy.

Which meant that the person in question was not a friend *or* a comrade.

*Friend or foe, friend or foe, if you have to ask…*

Kai sat down at the empty conference table, drumming her fingers on the table as Samar had been doing earlier.

*Who are you protecting, Dr. Mason?* She wondered, feeling uncharacteristically uneasy. *Who?*

. . . . .

Even with Marcus still healing, traveling as a team of two was much easier than traveling with a large group of people. They covered a lot of ground every day, making more progress than the group they were following—as evidenced by the increasing freshness of the tracks. Aya was confident that they would reach the others in a few more days.

It would be good to see them; she'd genuinely missed the humans, and she was restless over not knowing whether or not they were all right. Tracks could tell you a lot, but they couldn't reveal an exact number of people or tell you which people they were unless you were trained in the art of tracking, which Aya was not. The only small consolation prize was that one set of tracks was noticeably smaller than all the rest, which meant that Cody must still be alive.

A twinge of guilt rolled through Aya's stomach as she thought of Maggie's little girl. During their time in the bunker, Aya had had a lot of time to ponder her actions the day she'd returned, to rethink her decisions. She'd been so single-minded in getting to Marcus that she'd left Clio and the others in haste and probably prematurely. Someone could have needed her help, and she hadn't made sure everyone was safe before heading into the woods. What if someone had died because of her rashness?

*But Marcus would have died if I hadn't left exactly when I did.*

She'd spent a lot of time musing over that thought as well, and she couldn't deny that it was true. She'd arrived in the bombed-out clearing not a second too soon—one more moment and Marcus would have been morph food.

Still, the fact that she'd left the others in possible danger didn't sit well with her, and she couldn't get away from the sinking feeling in her gut that if someone had died because she hadn't been there, Marcus would never forgive her for it. He never put himself first, and he wouldn't have wanted her to put him first, either.

Aya was brooding over it all so deeply that it took her longer than usual to realize that Marcus was watching her.

"What is it?" She asked.

He stopped walking, wincing slightly as he stilled. "Let's make camp here for the night," he suggested.

It was nearly an hour earlier than they usually stopped, but Aya could see Marcus's fatigue and – now that her mind was not whirring a million miles an hour – she could feel her own fatigue as well.

"Okay," she agreed. "Why don't you rest? I'll get started."

Marcus shook his head, his lips setting in a stubborn line. "I can help, Aya."

She didn't have enough energy to argue with him, and in the end, she knew that he was right. She had to trust that Marcus knew his own body well enough to make judgment calls like this; if he thought he had enough strength to help set up their camp, then he did.

They set about their tasks in companionable silence, and in short time, their pallets were spread out beneath the makeshift shelter of overhanging branches and they had a small fire going.

Aya watched Marcus portion out a third of his remaining food, ignoring the way her own stomach rumbled. She couldn't remember the last time she'd fed, and her fangs were aching.

"I can tell, you know," Marcus said eventually. He had almost finished his meal, and he was pushing the remaining smattering of berries, jerky, and other small morsels around with the tip of his index finger.

"Tell what?"

His eyes flickered to hers, then away. "I can tell how hungry you are," he said quietly. "I can feel it."

Aya swallowed. Of course he could. She forgot, sometimes, that their blood bond went both ways. "It's been…a while since I fed," she admitted, deciding not to deny it.

"Yeah, and it shows." Marcus tucked the remainder of his food into the small knapsack and stashed the knapsack back in the larger pack. "I didn't request an early stop today for my sake. You're dragging, Aya."

She felt her shoulders sag at his words. "Only a little," she hedged. "But I'll be all right."

Marcus sighed. "I'm stronger than I was a week ago," he said. "Strong enough for you to take blood if you need to."

The suggestion made her recoil as much as it tempted her. "No." The word was firm on her lips. "Maybe in another few days, but not now. You're still recovering."

"Aya—"

"I'll be okay. Really. I've gone this long before without feeding."

He was quiet for a moment. "What happens," he finally asked, "when you go *too* long without feeding?"

The question surprised her—not because it wasn't a logical question to ask, but simply because Marcus so rarely asked questions about her nature.

"Vampires can starve to death just like humans can," Aya answered. "But it's more likely that bloodlust will set in before then. I've seen starving vampires snap before." She paused, giving Marcus a sidelong glance. "Why? Are you afraid that I might go rabid?"

She asked it with a trace of sarcasm, but it didn't seem to amuse Marcus at all. He frowned. "No. I'm just..." He shifted. "Worried about you," he finished, not looking at her.

Aya felt a flush of warmth squeeze her chest. It meant a lot, having someone care enough to worry about her. She had been alone for so long that she'd almost forgotten what that felt like.

She studied Marcus's profile, her eyes drawn first to the steady pulse at his throat and then to the faint white lines running from his chin to his shoulder, frowning at the way they glowed in the firelight.

"How did you get those?" She asked softly, her voice a curious murmur.

It only took Marcus a second to realize what she was talking about. He shrugged. "The usual. Morph attack. The thing caught me by surprise. It happened while you were gone."

On an impulse, Aya scooted towards him, closing the distance between them until she was kneeling just to his left, and then she reached up and ran her fingers over the lines running down his throat, tracing the path the morph's claws had made in his skin. They were jagged in places and raised slightly, still in the process of healing.

"They're deep," she commented, her brow furrowing.

Marcus stopped her fingers from completing their journey, holding her hand captive against his neck, stilling her. "I've had worse," he said slowly, and the look in his eyes – that trademark blend of somberness and weariness that only appeared in those who had endured long-time suffering – made her believe him.

It also made her ache for him. "I'm sorry," she whispered.

"Don't be." The words were gruff. "You've been through shit, too," he added. "Everyone who's survived in this world has been through shit. That's the nature of life."

Aya swallowed against the rising lump in her throat. She didn't want to be so affected, but Marcus's words made her indescribably sad. Feeling defeated, she rocked back on her ankles, dropping her hand away from Marcus's neck. "Is that really all there is?" She said eventually, the words small and fragile even to her own ears.

*Pain? Suffering? Death?*

Those were certainly the elements of life she'd known best over the last six years, so maybe it was true. Maybe there was really nothing else to look forward to.

It was a depressing thought.

Marcus shifted slightly, moving his legs to either side of Aya's knees. "No," he said firmly, as if he could sense the bleakness of her thoughts. "It's not."

Aya was about to ask him what he meant when she realized that Marcus was still moving, shifting forward.

Her eyes widened as one of his hands came up and cupped the nape of her neck. "What are you—?"

"It's not all there is," he said, and then he gently pressed his lips to hers.

It wasn't a long kiss—his lips lingered on hers just enough for Aya to feel their softness and warmth, but it was a match struck, a fire kindled, and when Marcus pulled back, Aya's only thought was to chase the sensation.

Without even being fully conscious of her actions, she brought her hands up to Marcus's chest and leaned towards him.

*I want...*

She kissed him, harder than he'd kissed her, her lips driving against his with all the fervor she'd kept at bay for weeks.

The answering groan she received from Marcus only spurred her on, and she melted into him, momentarily forgetting his injuries until he groaned again – this time in pain – and the hand he'd had on the back of her neck slid up into her hair and tugged.

Aya gasped, breaking off their kiss. "Sorry," she said breathily.

Marcus's eyes were dark. "Fuck sorry," he said, leaning his forehead against hers. "Some things are worth a little pain," he added in a murmur, catching her bottom lip between his teeth.

Aya shuddered. *"Marcus..."* She said weakly as he tugged on her lip before releasing it.

Marcus chuckled, his steel eyes full of dangerous humor. "You're not the only one who can bite, vampire," he teased, letting his lips skate down to her throat.

Aya arched into his touch, bringing her chest flush to his while one of her arms slid around his back, clutching at him like an anchor. She was trembling from the mere whisper of his lips on her fragile skin, and when he parted his lips and she felt the wet press of his tongue against her neck, she was all but shaking, her fingers curling into his worn sweater restlessly, her budding arousal heightening as one of his hands slid down the curve of her waist and gripped her hip, urging her closer to him.

Aya wondered, vaguely, the thought skittering across her consciousness, if this was how Marcus had felt before she'd fed from him: wanted, needed, aching to be possessed in a way that couldn't really be described. She'd felt the stir, the intimacy of it herself, but those feelings had been overshadowed by the need to feed, by her need for blood. But now, even though she was hungry, all her awareness was focused on the physical: the flick of his tongue and gentle suction of his mouth, the way her body felt pressed into his, the way his grip on her hip was solid, sure, *tightening.*

As if reading her mind, Marcus scraped his teeth against her jugular, running them from her collarbone up to her jawline and back before he pressed an open-mouthed kiss into the hollow of her throat. "Yes," he said softly. "That's how it felt."

He leaned back enough that Aya could search his eyes, and she found nothing but honesty there.

Honesty and that tantalizing hunger that was becoming all too familiar to her.

She licked her lips, feeling her fangs stir and a touch of wetness much further down, instantly reminded of their last day at the bunker.

She'd never had a lover, never had someone she'd even come close to being with aside from a few stolen kisses and fumbling gropes shared with her by other vampires in her village, but this thing she felt for Marcus – this desire that went far beyond any simple craving for blood – made her wonder if *this* was what it was like to desire someone. The actualization of it all was foreign to her, but the raw need for something…something *more* made her instinctively want to press closer to Marcus, to kiss him again, to touch every inch of him as she sank her fangs into his neck and…

Marcus's sudden tenseness roused her faster than the sound of a snapping branch did, but in a matter of seconds the heady mood was forgotten and they were both on their feet, standing back to back and scanning the forest around them.

It didn't take long to locate the source of the intrusion—a lone morph was coming towards them from the west, probably drawn by the light of their fire. When it saw them, it attacked, but it lacked any kind of finesse and Aya took it down with one blow before it managed to get within ten yards of their camp. When it was done, she retracted her fangs and claws, staring down at the corpse for a moment before walking back to where Marcus was putting out their fire.

"Just in case," he said by way of explanation.

It didn't matter to Aya one way or the other—it wasn't like she needed the warmth to survive. But Marcus did.

"Are you sure you'll be warm enough without it?"

Marcus grunted out an affirmation as he stamped down the last of the embers, sending a few orange sparks flying into the air. "It hasn't snowed in a few days and it doesn't feel as cold tonight. I'll be fine." He gave her a look. "You, on the other hand, won't be fine if you don't feed soon."

So, they'd circled back around to *that* conversation. Aya sighed, relenting in the face of Marcus's stubbornness. "Okay," she yielded. "You're right. I need to feed. And I will," she went on before he could interject, "as soon as we catch up to the others. It would be too much of a risk for me to take blood from you now. We're alone, you're still healing, and if we had to defend ourselves against more than just a single morph like tonight, we would both need our strength. I am uninjured; I can easily manage my hunger for a few more days."

After a heavy pause, Marcus nodded slowly. "All right. But if things change…"

"I'll tell you," Aya promised. She paused, feeling suddenly self-conscious. "Marcus," she began. "About what happened before the morph showed up. We…"

"I shouldn't have kissed you," he cut in, the words landing like knives in Aya's heart. "We're exposed out here, and that was reckless, stupid. I'm sorry."

"*I'm* not," Aya countered bravely, even though she felt incredibly small in the wake of his regret. "I've wanted to know what that would feel like since we left the bunker. And even since before that," she admitted quietly.

Marcus approached her. His expression was controlled save for the slight heat in his gaze. "Make no mistake," he said softly, huskily. "I'm not sorry it happened, only about the circumstances. I'm smarter than that—we both are. But sometimes…" His eyes traveled down her neck and roamed lower before he seemed to catch himself. He closed his eyes for a second, a muscle clenching in his jaw. "It's hard to stay in control." He brought a hand up to her cheek, his thumb brushing gently against her skin. "I want you, Aya," he whispered. "More than I've wanted anything in a long time."

Aya leaned into his touch, bringing a hand up to cover his. "I'm right here," she murmured.

Marcus's hand tightened beneath hers. "I know," he said, and then he let his hand slip away from her. "And when we get to Ashland and we've bathed the grime of this fucking ordeal off of us and we don't have to be on guard all the time, *trust* me—I plan on taking full advantage of that fact."

His voice had dropped in pitch towards the end, full of some dark promise that made Aya's stomach flip, but it was something else, something much more innocent, that made her smile.

"You said when," she observed.

Marcus blinked at her in bemusement. "When?"

"You said *when* we get to Ashland, not 'if'."

For the first time since she'd met him, Aya saw a small but genuine smile brighten Marcus's face. It softened his features, made him appear younger and more boyish than she'd ever seen him look before.

And it was utterly, completely endearing—a glimpse at a happier, more hopeful version of the hunter she knew.

Marcus chuckled. "So I did," he agreed dryly. He shrugged. "Huh." He shot her a look from beneath half-lifted eyelids. "Guess you've given me something to look forward to, vampire." His smile faded, although the levity remained in his voice. "C'mon," he said. "Let's go get some rest."

Aya followed him back to their pallets without arguing, but she knew that, judging from the way she was tingling from her head to her toes, she was much too awake to get any rest that night.

And she didn't care at all.

.     .     .     .     .

It had been a week of unexpected events, starting with finding the coded message in his father's study and followed up by witnessing Ian training with Brianne and Samar and clearly gaining the respect of Kai's two most trusted subordinates.

But the most unexpected part of Emmanuel's day occurred when he unlocked his apartment door and found Dex lounging in his armchair.

The albino man was sitting with his legs crossed and his hands folded across his lap, and he looked entirely at ease, as though breaking and entering were a perfectly acceptable thing to do.

Then again, Dex probably thought that it *was* an acceptable thing to do.

Emmanuel mastered his surprise and closed the front door behind him, resisting the urge to ask the other man how exactly he'd gotten into the locked apartment, mostly because he had a feeling that Dex would just offer a sly smile and refrain from answering anyway.

So instead, Emmanuel cleared his throat and asked, "What's happened?"

Dex cocked a pale eyebrow. "Happened?" He echoed. "What would make you think that something has happened?"

"Well, we do have a scheduled meeting in three days, so I'm assuming that if you have something to discuss that couldn't wait until then, it must be important, or something must have happened."

"Hm." Dex raised one of his hands and began to inspect his fingernails, his whole demeanor one of complete disinterest. "No," he said after a pregnant pause. "Nothing has happened." His grey eyes flickered up to Emmanuel. "I merely wanted to stop by and say hello to your houseguest. You can imagine my surprise when I discovered that he was no longer here."

"Ian is—"

"With Commander Ramirez's lackeys," Dex finished. "Yes, Dr. Mason, of that I am already aware. My question is: why?"

It was unsettling enough that Dex knew that Ian had been staying with him instead of at the lab, but it was even more unsettling that Dex knew where Ian was now—especially considering that the only other person who knew was Joben, and Joben had agreed not to mention it to the albino.

Emmanuel kept his tone casual. "Ian expressed interest in regaining his military fitness," he said, injecting his lie with grains of truth. "Now that he is human again, he is trying to figure out where he fits in. Since he was in the military before, it seemed like a natural enough place to start."

"Ah." The word was so nondescript that Emmanuel couldn't glean anything from it. "Why go to Commander Ramirez, then, and not to our dear friend Joben Hale?" Dex asked.

It was a logical question, and Emmanuel struggled to come up with a believable answer. "Ian is..." His mind raced. "Ian is, well...he is affected by what happened to him. He associates the Rangers with the vaccine. I was worried that renewing any kind of bond between the two could trigger post traumatic stress or cause him to regress, so I suggested he get a true fresh start—with new people and a newer, still active branch of the military."

"So, Commander Ramirez knows what Ian is."

The displeasure Emmanuel detected in Dex's voice made him uneasy. "Yes," he admitted slowly. "She knows."

With the fluidity of a cat, Dex rose from the armchair and stepped forward, nonchalantly straightening the bottom of his starched button-down as he did so. But when he stopped well within Emmanuel's personal space and his grey eyes bored into Emmanuel's brown ones, there was nothing nonchalant about his gaze. It radiated coldness, anger, and predatory threat, and Emmanuel had an instinctive urge to step back, to retreat away from the danger he sensed there.

"Perhaps I was not clear before, Dr. Mason," Dex said, his voice soft but as stinging as the feel of ice on skin. "Everything I do is a game of chess, and you agreed to play this round. But just because you are involved does not mean that you are the king. In the future, if you wish to make a move, you will clear it with me first. Otherwise, I may have to sacrifice your piece. Knavishness and secrecy are things I do not tolerate."

Emmanuel swallowed. "I never meant to go behind your back," he said. He could feel dampness on his palms. "I would have told you about all of this at our next meeting—you just beat me to it." It was a blatant lie, but Emmanuel sensed that right then, he needed to placate Dex. The albino man may not have been as physically intimidating as the soldiers and bodyguards within Ashland's walls, and he may not have shared Kai's alpha-like aura, but he radiated a coldness that was unparalleled. There was no doubt in Emmanuel's mind that, when he looked at Dex, he was staring into the eyes of a killer.

"Telling Commander Ramirez that you broke the law and have been actively conducting genetic experiments was risky enough, but exposing Ian to her..." Dex made a *tsking* sound, as if he were a teacher expressing his disappointment to a student. "Dr. Mason, your gamble truly surprises me. Commander Ramirez could have arrested both you and Ian, and we would have lost everything. It was not worth the risk. And yet what distresses me even more is that you also put me at risk. If Commander Ramirez ever discovers that *I* am involved in any of this, she will work to shut you down completely. She is not a fan of mine. She would interfere with your work if she knew I had any part in it, and that we cannot have." He lowered his voice. "So, if I find out that she *does* learn of my involvement in your project, what happens next will be on you."

Emmanuel flinched at the implication. "I will not say a word," he vowed.

"Good. And I expect to hear of any other interactions you have with her going forward."

"Of course."

Dex stepped back, giving Emmanuel some much needed breathing room. "Do not try my patience again, Dr. Mason," he said, and then, without another word, he brushed by Emmanuel and strode to the door.

Emmanuel listened to Dex open the door and leave, frozen in place until he heard the sound of the door latching closed, and then he sank to his knees.

*I should never have gotten involved with him,* Emmanuel thought miserably. Every time he had an encounter with the albino man, one thing became more and more certain to him: not everyone involved in Dex's schemes was going to survive the coming tribulations.

Maybe none of them would.

·  ·  ·  ·  ·

Quintus regarded the cowering, pitiful creature kneeling before him in silence, weighing the implications of the story the underling had shared.

The large tent they were in was full but silent, all of the gathered soldiers waiting on Quintus to speak. It was one of the many perks of being one of The Seven—no one ever dared to cross him, even in the minutest of ways.

Usually, that knowledge and the certainty of his power over all other morphs gave Quintus great pleasure, but right now, his disquiet was dampening all other sensations.

He looked down at the underling again. "You're sure?" He asked, his voice rumbling.

The thing nodded up at him subserviently. "Yes, sir. A vampire and a hunter."

Quintus snarled. It was a bad omen, and it also meant that he and the others were not as on top of current events as they should be. If allegiances between vampires and hunters were forming, there was no telling what else might be brewing in the cesspool of humanity. And the humanoid creature the underling had mentioned…? The fact that it had been strong enough to slay Demetrius, a superior, was cause enough for alarm, but the fact that no one had ever seen a creature that matched its description before was even more troubling. The attack on Easthaven had been successful because they'd had the upper hand; in order to take down the remaining human strongholds, they needed to retain the upper hand, or, judging by these unforeseen complications, regain it.

"Very well." Quintus motioned at two of his commanders, and they came forward immediately, each bending a knee.

"Prepare my horse and choose ten soldiers," he instructed. "I am going to speak with Primus."

His commanders bowed their heads. "Yes, General," they rasped, each hurrying away to do his bidding.

Quintus then gestured towards the underling at his feet. Two more soldiers came forward, each grabbing one of the creature's arms.

"Rend him."

The morph paled and started to jerk in the soldiers' grasp, struggling. "Please no," he begged.

Quintus looked down at him, feeling nothing but apathy. "You have brought useful information, and for that I am grateful. But you abandoned Commander Demetrius and your unit during battle. You are a deserter, and you know the penalty."

"Please!" The creature screamed, struggling harder. "Mercy!"

Quintus turned away without deigning to reply, ignoring the screams and shouts for leniency that followed after him. It had been months since a rending had been carried out; a brutal reminder of just how gruesome it was would do wonders for cultivating more obedience in the ranks. He would have liked to stay and watch it for himself, but there were more pressing matters to deal with.

He strode out of his tent and hoisted himself up on his waiting horse, giving it a swift kick in the flanks to spur it forward, listening to the sound of hooves as the ten soldiers he'd requested galloped after him.

It was a full day's ride to Primus's base. Usually, when Quintus needed to speak with the head of the elites, he would send one of the superiors in his stead to act as envoy.

But not this time.

This information called for a personal visit and immediate action. With a furious growl, Quintus urged his horse on faster.

# Almost

*Sometimes, it may feel like the storm is over, that you've made it through, when really the calm is not the end of the storm but its eye. It is a deceptive calm, and a cruel one, for you are not through the storm but at its heart, and the worst trials are yet to come.*
- Reflection taken from a recovered diary found in Tifist District, author unknown

. . . . .

It was a cold night, though that wasn't anything Enwezor wasn't used to at this point. Shivering beneath the thin layers he'd piled on, feeling goosebumps rising and chafing against the stiff fabric of his perpetually damp underclothes, wincing as his toes and fingers stung like cold fire before the numbness settled in, breathing in the air that seemed to frost his lungs from the inside out…these were all sensations that had become routine, expected. What he wasn't as used to yet was the other kind of coldness, the one that had settled in his chest ever since the day they'd attacked the morphs, since the day Cap had sacrificed himself to save the rest of them. Since the day that Enwezor had *let* Cap sacrifice himself to save them.

The dark hours dragged on as Enwezor turned the events of that day over in his mind, and just like the previous night and the night before that, Enwezor couldn't console himself with memories of what had gone right. Yes, they'd beaten the morphs, and yes, Clio's plan had gotten them through what should have been a massacre. But now the group was without its captain. A good man was gone. Dead.

The closer they got to Ashland, the more Enwezor felt the injustice of it. They were within a hundred miles – a hundred *fucking* miles – of the fortress, and everyone in their group had survived so much hardship, had come so far. There wasn't a single person there who didn't deserve to set foot within the walls, who hadn't earned the right to survive long enough to feel safe again. But apparently that didn't matter in this world. Getting *so close* wasn't the same thing as getting there.

"Hey."

Enwezor looked up. Clio was standing in front of him, frowning, his arms crossed across his lean chest. Enwezor hadn't heard him approach, but then, he never did; utter silence was one of the hybrid's many talents.

Enwezor straightened up, marginally. "There's...nothing to report," he shared glumly. "Area's clear."

The taller man didn't move. "Okay." He paused. "Would you like to get some sleep? I know you relieved Ed earlier than we agreed, so I could take the rest of your watch."

Enwezor shook his head. "Thanks, but no." It wasn't like he would be able to get anything resembling a peaceful rest anyway. He looked up at his stand-in captain. "I'd rather have something to do," he admitted honestly. "Makes me feel like I have a purpose."

Clio was quiet for a moment. "Are we at Ashland yet?" He asked finally.

Enwezor frowned at the question. "No?" He answered, not really knowing what the other man was getting at.

"Then you do have a purpose." There was compassion in the hybrid's human eye, but also resolve. "This group of ours has suffered unimaginable losses, Enwezor, I know, but we don't get to give up or regret what's happened. The sacrifices that our friends made – the sacrifice that your brave captain made – those were not in vain. We owe it to everyone we've lost to press forward and see the rest of these people safely to Ashland." His voice was fervent. "That is your purpose,

Enwezor Balogun: to survive. To help others survive. Whatever grief and darkness you're grappling with…you need to let it go."

It might have been the truth, but it didn't make Enwezor feel any better. Still, he gave Clio a wry upward tilt of his lips. It wasn't convincing as even a ghost of a smile, but it was the closest thing to a *'thanks for the advice'* he could muster.

"Yeah." He cleared his throat. "I guess I'll, uh, get back to patrolling." He was worried for a second that Clio would offer to keep him company, but as usual, the hybrid was much more perceptive than that.

"I'll relieve you in a couple hours," Clio said with a nod. And then, softly, he added, "Hang in there. It does get easier."

The hybrid disappeared as silently and suddenly as he'd arrived, and once again, Enwezor was left alone with the biting cold and the heaviness of his own thoughts.

He began walking in the opposite direction he'd been patrolling before, his eyes scanning the surrounding area but his mind miles and days away.

Until he saw something that shouldn't have been possible, and he was ricocheted back into the present moment with enough force to steal his breath.

Not twenty feet away, there was a vampire.

She'd seen him too, clearly—her fangs were bared and she was staring back at him, her black eyes as wide as Enwezor's brown ones must have been.

And she wasn't alone. There was another vampire with her, a broad-shouldered male, his form slightly shadowed by the darkness of the nighttime forest. Both of them began moving towards him.

Enwezor screamed for help.

The figures stopped, which seemed rather bizarre, but then Enwezor saw them more clearly, their features coming into sharper focus, and he realized that the second vampire wasn't a vampire at all and all his thoughts about their strange behavior faded to white noise.

He froze, blinking a few times. And then he blinked a few more times, convinced his eyes were deceiving him.

*No,* he thought. *No, this isn't possible. I'm seeing things. I must be.*

"Enwezor?" The apparition questioned.

Enwezor stumbled back a pace, his hand moving reflexively towards his knife. "You're dead," he wheezed, unable to process the impossibility that stood before him.

"I should be," the man said, stepping forward. "But I'm not."

Enwezor trembled. He wanted the ghost to be real. He wanted to believe. "Cap?" He whispered, just as Clio materialized at his side. A few seconds later, Ed made a much louder, more noticeable entrance.

The hybrid and the burly man both drew in sharp breaths. "Marcus? Aya?" Clio said, his voice rife with incredulity.

"Holy shit," was Ed's contribution between panting breaths.

Enwezor's fingers slipped away from the hilt of his knife, his knees buckling. "Cap?" He said again, louder this time.

The familiar sigh of irritation made Enwezor's chest swell with hope. "Yes, Balogun," Marcus grumbled. "I heard you the first time. It's good to see you, too."

Enwezor half-laughed, half-sobbed in reply. "But you...you were dead."

Marcus was close enough now that Enwezor could see the sobriety in the man's steel gaze. "I would have been, if Aya hadn't shown up when she did," his captain said. "She saved my life."

In response to that admonition, Aya lowered her gaze, her hair slipping forward to cover her face, as if she were somehow embarrassed by Marcus's frankness.

But Enwezor didn't care. Aya might have been the strangest, most self-conscious vampire he'd ever seen, but she was also the impossibly strong creature that had saved his captain's life, and, in doing so, she'd unknowingly saved a piece of him, too. So, without even thinking about it, Enwezor stepped towards her and did something he never thought he'd do: he reached out and hugged a vampire.

Aya stiffened in surprise, but Enwezor didn't let go. He squeezed her gently in his arms. "Thank you, Aya," he said huskily. "You are one crazy, amazing vampire."

He pulled away to find the pretty vampire staring at him in surprise. "You're welcome," she said.

Clio showed much more restraint than he had, but Enwezor still caught the warm smile that flashed across the hybrid's face. "Welcome back," he said, looking first at Aya and then at Marcus. "We missed you. Both of you."

"Ain't that the truth," Ed supplied, now that he'd finally gotten his breathing under control. He whistled through his teeth. "We've got a lot of muscle in our group, but the two of you...hell. You're living legends. I can't believe you're alive and here, but damn am I glad."

Aya's lips pulled up into an embarrassed smile. "I'm not sure about us being legends of any kind, but thank you. It's good to be back."

Enwezor found himself smiling too, the happiness at being reunited infectious.

Only Marcus seemed to be immune, and it was then that Enwezor realized how battered the man was, his visible skin covered with wounds in various states of healing, his posture not the impeccable military stance it usually was. Before he had time to comment on it, however, Marcus cut in.

"Have you been taking Sloane's shifts?" The Reaper asked quietly, effectively changing the direction of conversation.

He'd been addressing Ed, and the burly man nodded. "Yeah," he said. "Can't say I'm too fond of the lack of sleep, but I'm happy to contribute." He scratched idly at his head. "Hey, how'd you guess the shift change? You just got back."

Marcus's voice remained impassive, but Enwezor could see a hint of pain in the man's lidded eyes. "Aya was there the day of the attack. She told me about Sloane."

"Oh." Ed shot a look of surprise in the vampire's direction before he shrugged. "Yeah, well, Sloane's had some trouble, uh...*adjusting* since then. Clio thought it'd be best for me to stand in for a while. 'Til she gets her bearings and what not."

Marcus's entire demeanor changed. "She's had some trouble adjusting *since* then?" He asked, the emphasis on the penultimate word as sharp as a knife.

And finally, Enwezor put the pieces together. *He thinks Sloane is dead,* he realized with a shock. "Cap," he said tentatively, "Sloane...she's not dead—she survived."

It was like a dam had burst, Marcus's stoicism suddenly overcome with a flood of disbelief and shock. "Sloane is alive?"

"Yeah," Enwezor affirmed. "She's alive. She lost her arm during the fight, but it's Sloane; an arm's not gonna stop her. She had a pretty rough couple days after it happened, and she still bitches and complains a lot, but she'll be okay."

Marcus looked so affected by that news that Enwezor thought, for a ridiculous second, that the legendary Reaper might actually hug him.

He didn't, of course, but Enwezor smiled anyway, glad that for once, he'd gotten to deliver some *good* news.

Cap - as always - mastered his emotions quickly. "And the others?" He asked, his tone once again all business. "Did we lose anyone else?"

This time, Clio was the one to deliver the good news. "Not a one, Captain," he replied. He gestured to Enwezor and Ed. "We didn't run into too many problems after we attacked the morph camp, but when we did, we kept our people safe."

The Reaper was quiet for a moment, looking between all three of them with an unreadable expression, and then he did something that Enwezor never would have expected him to do: he saluted them.

It wasn't quite as shocking as a hug would have been, but Enwezor thought it was pretty damn awesome anyway.

.　.　.　.　.

"Yeah, and then this asshole walks up like some mutant version of the Grim fucking Reaper and tells Jillian 'step out of the way' in this scary voice and draws that sword. I swear my life flashed before my eyes."

Clio smiled wryly at Sloane's description of him. Every time the redheaded hunter told this story – and she was very fond of telling it – the tale got more dramatic and her name-calling became more colorful.

"I saw the blade come down," Sloane continued, pausing to gaze around the campfire at her rapt audience, "and the next thing I knew, I was short one arm. One slice and it was gone—just like that." She punctuated her finale with a snap of her fingers and then tossed a teasing glance in Clio's direction. "It's not fair, you know. Now I can only flip you off with one hand." She did. "See? It doesn't have the same effect."

Clio chuckled. "And here I thought you didn't appreciate me," he said sardonically. "I should save your life more often. Your gratitude is overwhelming."

Sloane snorted. "Save it, Jones. You could have at least warned me first."

An image of Sloane on the ground, her right arm a crushed, bleeding mess, flashed before Clio's eyes. A pool of blood had been spreading around the pulpy mess of her ruined limb, and he could still vividly recall the way the light was fading from her terrified eyes. There had been no other way. If he hadn't amputated her arm and gotten the stump wrapped in a tourniquet posthaste, she would have bled out in a matter of minutes. Probably sooner. "If I remember correctly, we were a little short on time," he said with more sobriety. Then he eased up. "But don't worry: next time I'll give you a three second warning."

Sloane's green eyes widened. "If that sword of yours even comes close to my remaining arm, I will make you pay. Starting with that bun."

Clio reflexively touched the knot of hair on top of his head. "Why does everyone always threaten the bun?" He grumbled.

Sloane laughed. "Savannah has a big mouth."

Savannah was sitting at the second campfire with the other civilians, but that didn't stop Clio from shouting "damn you, Wix!" from where he was sitting. His exclamation was met with a very confused "what did I do?!" which elicited a chorus of laughter from everyone except the confused pregnant woman.

Clio took that moment to look around at the people gathered around their own campfire. Sloane and Enwezor were sitting side by side and looking happier than he'd seen them look in weeks; Ed was beside them, still tucking into his dinner with a passion; Aya and Marcus were sitting opposite the others, their fingers almost touching where they rested on the ground; and then there was Cody, of course, her little body tucked into Clio's side. She was half asleep, her head lolling forward every few seconds and her eyes never fully open, but she'd wanted to stay up to hear everyone's campfire stories and Clio had relented. It was hard to say no to Maggie's daughter, especially after all of the heartache she'd endured. If she fell asleep and Clio had to carry her over to her pallet next to Jillian, well, he could think of worse duties.

For now, having Cody there with him and the others, part of their impromptu reunion dinner, was about as close to a perfect night as any he could imagine.

Even after seeing Aya on the day of the attack, Clio had not expected that a reunion would ever occur, and he'd certainly never expected that the vampire would somehow save Marcus. The fact that the two of them were alive and here, and that, against all odds, their group was together again, was incredible.

"Have you been practicing with your left hand?" Marcus was asking Sloane when Clio tuned back in.

The waifish girl sighed. "Yeah, but it's been difficult. My aim is all off and I'm used to generating everything with a right lead. Now everything feels backwards."

Marcus nodded in understanding. "Keep practicing. It'll get easier."

"Please do," Ed cut in. "I'm not cut out for nightly watch duties. I need my beauty sleep."

Sloane smirked. "Ed, you could hibernate and it still wouldn't be enough sleep to make you beautiful."

Enwezor choked on the water he was drinking and Ed stood up, kicking a stray stick into the fire. "Could say the same thing about you, One Arm," he said, and even Clio had to smile at the look of surprise on Sloane's face. She wasn't used to being outdone.

"Touché," she admitted. She stood up too. "Tell you what: how about we take watch together tonight? I won't be much help, but I promise I'll insult you enough to keep you awake."

Ed chortled, his wide maw splitting into a toothy grin. "Why not," he said.

Clio watched as the unlikely pair shuffled off into the night.

"Clio?"

Cody's voice was more yawn than word. She blinked up at him, her eyes not quite opening at the same time. "I'm..." another yawn "...tired."

Clio smiled down at the little girl. "All right," he said, standing up and stretching. "C'mon, Miss Reade. Time for bed."

To his surprise, though, Enwezor interrupted before he could pick Cody up.

"I'll take her over to Jillian," the younger man said. "I'm pretty tired myself."

Clio relented, giving Cody a pat on her head.

The little girl swatted his hand away. "Don't," she said sleepily. "You'll mess up my bun."

Clio smiled in spite of himself. "Sorry," he said, eyeing the frizzy, tangled mess crowning the girl's head. The thing was already beyond help, but Cody had been attached to it ever since she'd coerced Jillian into doing it for her the previous morning. She'd even shoved one of the twins when they told her she was being a copycat, which was quite a reaction considering that they'd just been teasing her about her hair.

Clio bit back a smirk. He certainly didn't need three guesses to figure out where she'd acquired *that* little defensive quirk.

*Maybe I'm not having the best influence on her*, he mused as Enwezor took Cody's hand and led her away.

"Clio."

The hybrid turned back and took his seat again, peering at the Reaper across the fire. "Hm?"

"Thank you," the other man said. "For everything."

Further explanation wasn't necessary. Clio smiled. "Just doing my job, Captain," he said. "And thank you for coming back. This group wasn't the same without you." He caught Aya's gaze. "Without either of you," he added.

The three of them sat in silence after that – an easy, companionable silence – simply keeping each other company and listening to the dwindling crackle of their fire and the neighboring one until Marcus excused himself in order to go check in on the now-sleeping civilians and Sloane and Ed.

Clio would have gone with him, but he sensed that Aya had more to say, so he remained where he was.

The vampire was fidgeting a little, but she didn't say anything, so Clio took the reins. "Are you planning to stay with us?" He asked.

"Yes." Her dark eyes were troubled. "I'm not sure it's the right choice, but I...I can't leave. Not now."

Clio could sense her trepidation, her doubt. It was rolling off of her tense shoulders in waves, cascading down to where her hands were clenched like two fists of marble in her lap. "Staying might be the harder choice, but that doesn't make it the wrong choice," he countered gently. He watched the dying embers of the fire smolder out to smoke, the charcoal tendrils drifting into the night sky. "Were you unhappy with the other vampires?" He finally asked.

Aya tucked a strand of hair behind her ear. It had gotten longer since Clio had last seen it, the glossy ends now hanging well past her elbows. "I wasn't unhappy," she answered. "But I missed all of you. More than I thought I would."

It wasn't too difficult for Clio to read between the lines. "And one Reaper in particular?" He chanced.

Aya looked up at him, clearly surprised by his forwardness. But she didn't deny it. "Yes," she admitted. "I missed Marcus." She bit her bottom lip, worrying at it for a moment before she spoke again. "I'm...bound to him," she went on. "We're bound to each other. One of the older vampires explained it to me." Her eyes found Clio's again. "It's called a blood bond. They're very rare and very strong. Marcus and I—we're tethered to each other for life."

*That* was quite a revelation, although it made a lot of sense. It certainly explained the way the two had always seemed to gravitate towards each other. But Clio sensed that wasn't the whole story. "And?" He prompted.

"And I love him," Aya said quietly. "And I think he feels...something for me, but lately I'm not sure if that's because of the bond or because his feelings are genuine."

Clio leaned forward onto his elbows. "Does it have to be an either or, Aya?"

"No," she ceded. "I suppose it doesn't. But I...I want him to love me for me." A pained look crossed her face. "I want him to love me the way he loves Jocelyn."

Clio felt for her, truly. This was a much different conversation than the last one he'd shared with Aya around a campfire. She'd hated the Reaper, then, when he'd literally had her heart. Now he figuratively had it and her feelings were just as strong in the opposite direction.

The irony of it was not lost on him, nor was her sadness. "Give him time," Clio advised. "I haven't known Marcus for very long, but from what I've observed it's obvious that when he cares, he cares deeply. He might always love the woman he lost, but that doesn't mean he won't feel the same way about you one day."

"Perhaps you're right."

"I'd wager I am," he tried to assure her. "We'll be at Ashland in a few days," he added, suddenly realizing that, after all this time, their journey was finally coming to an end. It was an uplifting thought. "Things will be different when we're not constantly on guard and under attack; you'll have time to figure things out."

The troubled look on Aya's face didn't dissipate, but it seemed to lessen slightly. "I hope so," she said.

Clio stood up. "I'm going to go relieve Marcus," he said. "You can stay here, if you'd like."

"Clio, wait."

He did.

Aya stood up too, walking around the fire until she was standing in front of him. "There's something else I found out while I was with the vampires," she said. "Something about you."

Clio's eyebrows flew towards his hairline. "Something about me?" He repeated dubiously. Those three words were the very last that he would have expected to hear from her.

Aya nodded. "Do you know the story of the Wanderer?" She asked.

Clio thought for a second, unsure where exactly this conversation was going. "Vaguely," he said after a moment. "I remember being told the story when I was a child...the human girl that left her people and went out into the wilderness. There were all kinds of myths regarding what happened to her."

"What happened to her wasn't a myth, and neither was she," Aya said. "Anna Ross was a real person, and during her travels she fell in love with a vampire named Alexei. They had a child together, a daughter, and she was raised by Anna's human family." Aya paused. "A daughter who grew up and married a man named Caspar Jones," she added.

Caspar Jones.

Casper *Jones.*

Clio stood there, rooted to the spot, a lifetime's worth of insecurities and uncertainties suddenly snuffed out within the span of a few sentences. It was the truth he'd been waiting to hear his entire life, the answer to a question he'd never quite been able to voice aloud but one that had consumed his very blood from time immemorial.

*Who am I?*

He didn't question what Aya had revealed to him because he didn't need to. He knew it was true. He'd seen his family tree before, knew that it traced itself all the way back to a simple blacksmith named Caspar Jones. And even if he hadn't, the veracity of his lineage was in the very nature of what he was, as clear as could be.

"So I really am a hybrid," he said once he'd regained the use of his voice. "I always have been."

"Yes."

More pieces were falling into place. "That's why the vaccine affected me differently," he surmised. "Because my DNA wasn't strictly human. I'm an anomaly because I've always been an anomaly."

He looked down at Aya, feeling a budding smile twist at his lips. "Wow," he commented dryly. "A mutated half-breed and a vampire who is bound to a Reaper. We're quite a strange pair, aren't we?"

Aya returned his half smile. "I prefer the term unique," she replied. "And lucky, too. Not everyone gets to find a place where they fit in, a place where they're accepted, but here, with these humans, I...I feel like we belong." She looked up at him. "Is that crazy?"

"No." It should have been, but it wasn't. "I feel that way too. I feel like we're family."

"Family..." Aya repeated, the word filled with nostalgia. "I never thought I'd have that again."

Clio thought of everything he'd lost, of the grief he hid deep down in the recesses of his memory where no one else could see it. "Neither did I," he added quietly. "But here we are."

"Yes," Aya murmured in reply. "Here we are."

They stood there for a suspended moment, silhouetted by the dappled moonlight shining down through the canopy of bare branches above them, not saying anything until Clio felt the urge to tell her one more thing. "I know I've already said it," he began, "and so has everyone else, but I'm really glad you're back."

"Thank you," Aya responded quietly. "I...I needed to come back." Her voice grew even softer. "A Guardian's place is with her people," she added.

Clio was no expert in vampire lore, but he remembered hearing the term *Guardian* before. From what he could recall, they were leaders, defenders, warriors. And judging from the solemnness in Aya's voice, Clio guessed that she must have been a Guardian herself—or at least had been related to one.

It wasn't at all surprising; Clio recognized exceptional people when he saw them, and Aya was definitely exceptional, in more ways than she probably even realized.

"We're lucky to have you," he said, and then, wanting to lighten the mood, he clapped his hands together. "All right," he said. "Enough chit chat. I know that you are immune to the cold, but I am not. I need to move or I'm going to freeze in place." He rubbed his hands together to create some warmth. Speaking about being cold made him realize how cold he actually was. Go figure. He exhaled and dropped his hands to his sides. "Let's go find your Reaper and do something productive."

He pretended not to notice the way Aya blushed at his choice of words, but for the second time that day, Clio couldn't suppress a small smile of amusement.

He really was glad to have her back.

· · · · ·

"You're sure you're ready to do this?"

Ian looked up at the bald woman and gave her a nod that he hoped conveyed more self-assurance than he felt. He needed to project at least a bit of moxie. After all, it was *his* plan they were following. "Yeah," he said. "I'm ready."

Brianne nodded and then motioned to Samar. "Okay. We'll be at your six and twelve. If something goes wrong and you need us to intervene sooner than we agreed, shout loudly."

"Okay."

Brianne's lips pressed into a tense line. "Good luck, Ian," she said, and then she jogged away, Samar doing the same in the opposite direction.

And then Ian was alone in the clearing.

His fears resurfaced instantly, the terror of his morph years awakening like a sense memory: the sounds and smells of the forest, the pounding of his heart in his ears, the knowledge that there were others out there, the insatiable urge to tear and bite and kill...

He took a deep breath. *No. I am not that thing anymore. I am Ian Hayes, I am human, and I am on a mission to help humanity. I've got this. I am not afraid. I'm not.*

He was.

But he was also not one to back down from something just because he was scared. Besides—he'd always thought that the best way to get over his fears was to face them head on.

Feeling a rush of determination, Ian began to set up his camp. He made sure to be as noisy as possible, dragging branches across the ground, snapping twigs, even coughing from time to time. After he was done assembling everything he needed, he constructed a small fire and lit it, throwing the darkening forest into crackling illumination.

*Okay. Step one done.*

Now all he had to do was wait.

He sat down and bent his knees, wrapping his arms around them as he stared off into the darkness around him. If he were still in morph form, he would've been able to discern shadow from form even as dusk turned to night, but his human eyesight was limited. There was a very good chance that, even if the plan worked, he wouldn't see the morph coming. He also no longer had enhanced hearing, and morphs – especially superiors – could be stealthy when they wanted to be.

There was so much that could go wrong.

Now, as he sat in front of his fire, Ian realized that acting as bait had seemed a lot safer when they'd only been discussing it.

But there was no turning back now.

He went over the plan again in his head to distract himself from nerves. *First, set a trap. Next, lure the morph in and capture said morph with assistance from Samar and Brianne. Finally, transport it back to Ashland without being spotted by soldiers on patrol.*

During planning, figuring out that last part had proven exceptionally tricky for two reasons: one, Guard soldiers were trained to shoot first and ask questions later when it came to any and all nonhuman beings; and two, their three-man mission had not been formally approved. But Commander Ramirez had given them a key that would open a back gate into Ashland—one that wasn't monitored on the regular patrol route. So, if they managed to succeed in capturing a morph (way easier said than done, no matter how badass Samar and Brianne were), their reentry should be taken care of.

As for the problem of transporting the captured morph, Dr. Mason had given Brianne and Samar special darts to use. Each one was filled with a potent drug mixture meant to render even a strong morph unconscious, and even though the drug had only ever been tested on large mammalian predators, Ian was confident that the darts would work. He hadn't known Dr. Mason for very long, but the lanky man had saved his life, and Ian thought that counted for a lot. He trusted the doctor.

The minutes ticked by, with no sign that the ruse was working. Feeling antsy, Ian stood up and kicked idly at the fire, sending a shower of sparks skyward. He watched them flicker out and then sighed, stuffing his hands into his pockets.

The clearing around him was still silent and empty, and there was— Wait.

Ian squinted into the darkness, his body tensing.

*Did that shadow just move?*

Tentatively, he took a step forward, and then, when nothing happened, he took one more. "Hello?" He called out. Speaking went against every instinct he had, but he was supposed to be bait. If there was a morph out there, he needed to lure it to him. "Hello?" He called again, a little more loudly.

There was a rustle in the trees, and then the shadow that had moved earlier stepped forward, detaching itself from the surrounding darkness.

The morph opened its maw and bared its teeth.

And then a second morph stepped forward. And a third.

All three were horde morphs. The superior they'd been tracking was nowhere to be seen.

Ian felt his throat go dry. Something was wrong. "Help!" He shouted as he reached for the dagger he'd brought along. "Multiple targets!"

The only response was a bloodcurdling scream that cut off much, much too soon.

It came from behind him, so Ian backed up a few paces, put the fire between himself and the three morphs, and turned around.

What he saw nearly made him stumble into the fire.

The superior they'd been tracking, the one Ian had been hoping would fall for his trap, was standing at the opposite end of the clearing, grinning at him. Samar's head was in its left claws, two of its talons speared through the back of the man's skull and poking out of his eye sockets. There was blood dripping from the severed neck, and the soldier's mouth was opened wide, as though he were still screaming from beyond the grave.

Breaking into a cold sweat, Ian flipped the dagger around in his hand and shifted into a defensive position. "Brianne!" He shouted in a panic, but there was no reply. Maybe she was dead, too.

The morph shook Samar's head off of its claws and looked past Ian. "*Get him,*" it spoke, its voice a guttural rasp.

The three morphs behind Ian came charging, needing no further prompting.

Aware that a lone dagger wouldn't be enough against three morphs, Ian grabbed a long stick that was only half in the fire, holding out the flaming side. He pointed it at the three morphs on his left and then aimed his dagger at the superior calmly walking towards him from the right.

*Maybe I can get out of this,* he thought desperately. *I just have to stay calm. I can fight them. I can win.*

But then Ian heard movement from directly behind him and he realized that there was, in fact, no way he could win.

.  .  .  .  .

When they set out that morning, it was still dark and cold, the sky a hazy grey and the air still retaining its nighttime bite. Aya could see rain clouds in the distance, heavy charcoal monsters that loomed maybe a dozen or so miles away from where they were. All in all, it was promising to be another bleak day of traveling, filled with little sun and lots of rain.

The mood of the group didn't reflect this, however; everyone was expectant, hopeful, energized, like there was an electric current fueling each of them. Nobody had complained about the early set out time, and everyone was walking with a spring in their step. There was no talk of cold or lack of provisions or sore muscles. The predawn morning was filled with anticipatory silence and the feeling of everyone holding their collective breath, and the reason was obvious.

Today was the day they would finally reach Ashland.

It was surreal, in a way. After endless months of traveling, the journey itself had become a way of life, and day by arduous day, the reality of ever reaching their intended destination had become more like a distant horizon—present, but never attainable, simply something to strive for. Walking, fighting, surviving…that was everything. The time before was a disappearing dream, and there was no after. There was only the pain and struggle of the now.

Only that was no longer their reality.

Ashland was less than twenty miles away, and the terrain had leveled out considerably, meaning that the remainder of their journey - provided there weren't any unforeseen complications - would be a relatively easy one.

*We're nearly there. We're going to make it.*

Those thoughts played like a mantra in Aya's mind as the day wore on, as ever present as the warring emotions she couldn't shake.

On one hand, she was as excited as the humans. Being able to truly rest in a dry, safe place without having to be on guard all of the time…oh, it would be indescribable.

On the other hand, her trepidation was growing with every closing mile. The concerns she and Marcus had discussed before rejoining the others, the things she'd promised herself she wouldn't worry about until it was necessary—those concerns were now valid. Ashland was a *human* fortress, after all, and she wasn't human.

"Aya."

Marcus had dropped back, slowing his stride to match hers. His steel eyes were regarding her closely.

"I'm fine," she said in reply to his unspoken question.

She had a feeling that he wasn't relying on the blood bond to see through her lie. He reached out and squeezed her hand. "Try not to worry," he said. "We'll figure it out when we get to Ashland."

His words didn't make her nerves settle, but they did help, as did the simple comfort of having him near.

Which was why, when he made to move back to the front of the group, Aya stopped him, her anxiety getting the better of her. "Marcus." She bit her lip. "Could you...?" *Could you stay here with me, just for a little while?* She stopped herself from fully asking the question, partly out of embarrassment and partly because she realized that she was being silly—there was no excuse for her neediness.

But Marcus knew what she wanted anyway. He nodded and looked over his shoulder. "Clio," he called back to the hybrid. "Take point for a while."

"Sure thing, Captain," the hybrid called back. A few seconds later, Clio's tall, black-clad figure came into view. He gave Aya a knowing smile as he passed by, which made color creep onto her cheeks, but Cody's appearance saved her from any further chagrin.

"Are we really gonna get to lead the group?" The little girl asked. She was holding hands with Clio, staring up at the hybrid with wide eyes.

Clio pursed his lips. "Tell you what: how about *you* lead the group? I'll be your second."

Cody beamed and then darted ahead of Clio a few feet, setting her face into a solemn grimace of determination. Clio followed her like a shadow, standing far enough back so that Cody could really feel like the leader but close enough to act as a shield.

*He is going to be a wonderful surrogate father,* Aya thought, and then she pushed that thought and every other thought away, focusing on the trek and Marcus's comforting presence at her side.

They caught up to the rain clouds by midafternoon, and despite everyone's earlier excitement, the weather did put a damper on their progress in more ways than one.

As she watched the humans around her shiver as the cold rain soaked their clothing, Aya felt grateful that temperature was one element she didn't have to contend with. Everyone in the group seemed uncomfortable and miserable.

Until Cody shouted a single, attention-grabbing word.

"Look!"

She was pointing to something through the trees in front of her, and Aya saw it through the rain at the exact same moment that everyone else did.

The imposing, unmistakable façade of a very large, very high wall.

"Ashland!" Someone else shouted, and then they were moving as one unit, running with renewed energy, the finish line they'd been waiting so long to cross finally in sight.

Aya stood in shocked stillness for a moment as the rest of the group raced past her, listening to the rising chorus of whoops and hollers and cheers, and then she broke into a smile and jogged after them, Marcus at her side.

More of Ashland came into view as they drew closer, the high outer wall spanning some fifty meters across. It was also probably some thirty meters tall and fortified, capped by turrets and lookouts, all completely encaged with barbed wire.

Aya didn't know much about the fortress itself, but from first glance alone, she could tell that it was definitely a step up from Easthaven in terms of security.

At this point, the group was a mere thirty yards away from the wall, Aya and Marcus trailing just a few yards behind them, and almost all of the humans were waving their arms above their heads and screaming for joy, their rain-drenched, muddy clothes completely forgotten. A few of them were literally jumping up and down.

"Hey!" The first few shouted as they reached the wall, banging fists and arms against its unyielding surface. "Let us in! Let us in!"

Aya was watching them – grinning at the sight of Ed trying to literally muscle his way through solid wall – when she heard Marcus bark a curse at her side.

She stopped in surprise, just in time to see Marcus's face go white. "NO!" He roared, and then he shoved her, roughly, to the right.

Startled by the suddenness of Marcus's action, Aya never even thought to break her fall. She landed hard in the mud, wincing at the impact. A second later, she felt another, fainter jolt in her left shoulder.

She blinked in confusion, just as she heard Marcus cry out in pain. He was on the ground next to her, clutching at his own left shoulder. There was an arrow a few feet behind him, bloody water dripping from its shaft.

*He's hit!*

The thought surfaced with a sense of dread but was immediately overshadowed as Marcus crawled to her side and began pushing at her. "Run!" He yelled as he struggled to shove her away. There was raw desperation in his voice. "Run, Aya!"

Too late, Aya processed what he was saying.

Too late, she looked towards the wall and saw the guard in the watchtower, reloading his bow.

Too late, Aya reacted.

The arrow came sailing towards her, arcing through the sky just as she rose to her feet, a tiny projectile that seemed so small compared to the vastness of the sky it was flying through.

It hit her squarely in the chest.

Aya stumbled back, her dark eyes widening as her awareness narrowed to the tiny tip of lead protruding from her chest.

No—not her chest.

Her heart.

The realization drew a stunned gasp from her lips.

It was impossible, almost defying belief, and yet it had happened. The arrow had found its one tiny, devastating mark.

It was a true shot in a million.

Reeling, Aya fell to the earth, landing face-up in the mud, clutching at the pierced leather pouch through her shirt. She could already feel the blood on her face, could feel it starting to stream from her eyes and her nose, could see the red of it where it was seeping out from beneath her fingernails.

*The bleeds…*

The pain took hold then, and Aya screamed. She had endured pain before, had suffered greatly, but *nothing* compared to this. Every millisecond was excruciatingly intense. It felt like her body was being shredded from the inside out, felt like someone was holding a live wire up to all of her nerve endings at once. Every limb, every muscle was screaming in agony, and her body was spasming in reaction, unable to contain the pain.

Aya had no idea how her grandmother had endured the bleeds with such dignity; it was unbridled, unmitigated torture.

Belatedly, Aya realized that she was being cradled, and she blinked through the haze of blood and tears until she could see Marcus's stricken face hovering above hers. He was brushing the blood away from her eyes and he was speaking to her, but Aya couldn't hear past her own blistering screams.

With an anguished sob, she bit her tongue, willing herself to regain control.

She saw Marcus break off the shaft of the arrow and then slip the leather strings from around her neck, saw the look of horror on his face as he drew the tiny pouch out from beneath her shirt and saw the arrowhead embedded in it.

"What can I do?" He said in a rush. "Blood? Bandages?" His hands were shaking. "Fuck, Aya, what should I do?"

She opened her mouth and then coughed violently before shaking her head. She could feel blood pooling in her throat, choking her.

Unable to explain, she reached up – the simple motion taking most of what little energy she still had – and placed her hand on Marcus's cheek. *Nothing,* she told him, speaking through their bond. *You can't do anything, Marcus.*

"Fuck that!" He barked, his face contorting in anger and pain. "This is not happening! It's not!" He reached up with his free hand and pressed it against his bloody shoulder, then brought the dripping hand to her lips. "Just take my blood—fucking take all of it," he growled. "Please, Aya."

A few drops fell onto her lips, but Aya made no move to drink.

*It won't make a difference,* she said silently. *There is no cure for the bleeds, Marcus. You know that.*

Before he could respond, a cacophony rose up in their periphery, and Aya was dimly aware of people shouting and the sound of heavy boots pounding on the ground.

*Guards,* she thought, from a place that seemed very far outside of her own body. *The guards are coming to finish the job.*

She raised her head an inch, moving just enough so that she would be able to see her attackers before they descended upon her.

What she saw instead was Clio drawing his katana, standing defensively in front of the place where she and Marcus were huddled on the ground, the rest of the Easthaven group flanking him.

"Back away," she heard him say, his voice low and threatening.

There was the sound of a brief struggle, followed by the sound of a body hitting the mud.

"I said *back away,*" Clio hissed, accentuating his command with a warning slash of his katana.

The others had formed a protective circle around her and Marcus, and some of them had even followed Clio's lead and drawn weapons. Even tiny Cody Reade had her knife in hand.

"It's a vampire!" An unfamiliar voice shouted. "We have orders!"

"I don't care about your orders," Clio responded. "No one touches her."

"Why are you protecting it?" Another unfamiliar voice called.

This time, Sloane spoke before Clio could. "Because she's one of us, you dolt," the hunter said. "Now listen to the hybrid and back the fuck up."

"You can't—"

"Yes, we can," Enwezor said. "You heard the lady. Aya is one of us. If you want to hurt her, you're gonna have to go through us."

Clio bared his fangs. "*All* of us," he warned.

The tenseness of the situation was escalating - that much was obvious - and the hope of reaching a peaceful resolution seemed to be slipping away. More and more people were speaking and arguing, but the rest of the words were lost on Aya. There was a ringing in her ears now, something high-pitched and fuzzy, and it was drowning out everything else.

*It's almost over now,* she thought. *It has to be.*

The tears streaming from her eyes were now more water than blood, and she blinked them away as best she could. When her vision cleared slightly, she took one long, final look at the circle of people around her.

It was an incredible sight.

The humans were protecting her.

Her *family* was protecting her.

Aya was hurting, worse than she could ever remember hurting, every breath literal agony, but for a fleeting second, all of her pain was blotted out by a sense of fullness. If her heart could have stuttered, it would have, because in that singular moment, Aya felt happier than she had in a long, long time.

She was dying, yes, but her family was surrounding her. All of the people she still cared about in the world were with her, and she was in the arms of the man she loved.

*I'm not alone anymore,* she thought through her tears. *I found a home.*

There were certainly worse ways to die.

The thought was enough to grant her a modicum of peace, but then she looked up at Marcus and what was left of her bleeding heart shattered completely.

The Reaper, *her* Reaper, was crying.

He was rocking back and forth where he knelt on the ground, his overgrown hair dripping rain onto her face as he cradled her head in his hands. "*Aya...*" He gasped, his whole face contorted with a sorrow so deep that Aya could feel the coldness of it seep into her dying bones. "You *can't,*" he choked out through his tears. "Just—just hold on..." He crumpled above her, resting his forehead against hers as he wept. "Fight it," he begged. "*Please...*"

Aya didn't have enough strength left to move. She didn't even have enough strength left to speak.

*Our story was always destined to end in blood.*

She'd found solace in that, once, and now cruelty didn't seem like a strong enough word to describe the irony of it. She wanted to stay with Marcus, to stay with her people, to live, to experience the future that had almost been hers.

But she'd never get the chance.

Her time was up.

She'd been holding on, but she couldn't any longer. Feeling consciousness slip away, Aya finally succumbed to the pain and fatigue and closed her eyes. *I love you, Marcus,* she thought in her final moment. *I wish we could have had more time...*

. . . . .

The arrival of the commander brought a decisive end to their standoff, and it didn't happen a moment too soon.

Coming up from behind the Ashland soldiers, the Latina woman barked a short order and her men immediately stepped aside, making way for her. She marched up to Clio, her brown eyes taking in the ragged group before her with tactical swiftness.

"Tell me who you are and what you are doing at our gates," she commanded, directing her demand at Clio.

Clio retracted his fangs and skipped the introductions. "We are survivors from Easthaven seeking refuge. Your men shot one of our group members and then refused to back down after we explained the situation."

"That's because the *person* we shot is a vampire, Commander! And so is this guy!"

The woman held up a tattooed arm, silencing her subordinate. "Is that true?"

"I am a unique product of the *Metamorphosis* vaccine," Clio answered. "Not a vampire. Aya—" he gestured behind him "—is a vampire. She is also one of us. She aided and protected our group during our long journey."

A flash of disbelief stole across the commander's features, which quickly settled into a severe expression. "We do not harbor vampires here," she said. Her voice was quiet, but Clio could still hear the hatred in her words.

He could also hear the ragged breaths Aya was drawing on the ground behind him, getting shallower and sparser.

He didn't have time for this. "Commander, please. I promise to explain everything to you as soon as our group members – Aya included – have received medical attention." Clio paused. The woman looked unconvinced, so he decided to offer an incentive. "We have a great amount of sensitive information regarding what happened at Easthaven and what is going on in the outside world. With morphs *and* vampires. We will share everything we know with you. All I ask in return is sanctuary for our group. If you feel unsafe, we will happily agree to be quarantined until you are satisfied that we are not a threat to the citizens of Ashland, but please, Commander, we need a doctor *now*."

She stared at him for a long, unreadable moment as the rain continued to fall, and then she nodded once. "You have a deal." She motioned to her nearest subordinates. "Ry, Silas, Jamila—lead the foreigners inside and lock them in B Ward. You may bring them food and water but make sure they stay put. No one enters the inner gate until I give the all clear. Miller, Deirdre, Cole—escort the wounded to medical. I will find Dr. Mason."

The commander left without a backward glance, her men immediately hastening to complete their orders.

Clio motioned for the others to sheathe their weapons. "Go with the soldiers and do what they say," he instructed, and then he whirled around and knelt down in front of the Reaper and the vampire, still inwardly reeling at how quickly the day had turned from joyous to tragic in the course of one awful moment.

*We made it. We were safe. This should never have happened.*

Clenching his jaw against the onslaught of anger he felt, Clio placed a hand on the captain's shaking shoulders. "Marcus," he said gently, concealing his own inner turmoil. "Let me take her. Please."

The Reaper didn't move. "She's dead," he rasped.

Clio felt a chill settle in his stomach at the hollowness of Marcus's voice. "She isn't," he said, though he wasn't entirely sure if that was true. Vampire hearts didn't beat like human hearts, so there was no easy way to tell whether Aya was still hanging on to life. Judging from how bad she looked, Clio knew it was more than probable that Marcus was right, but he clung to the alternative anyway. "Please," he tried again. "Let me take her. You're wounded. I'll be able to carry her more easily."

Reluctantly, Marcus released his grip on the vampire and Clio gingerly picked her up. She was dead weight in his arms, and she was unresponsive. Those were bad omens, as was the fact that her blood began to seep into his clothing almost immediately. Clio shifted her slightly and, trying not to draw parallels between Maggie's final moments and now, he looked down at Marcus. "Can you walk?" He asked.

The Reaper met his gaze and nodded. His expression was harrowed, and his face was covered in Aya's blood and wet with rain and tears, the skin beneath white from shock.

"Good," Clio answered, ignoring the pang of sympathy he felt for the other man. "Get up. You need to come with me to medical. Now."

Marcus stood up, staring at Aya's inert form. "My shoulder will be fine," he mumbled.

"I'm sure it will," Clio said through his teeth, exasperated. "Now walk with me. Quickly, dammit!" He added when the Reaper made no move to follow him. "There isn't much time." *We might already be too late.*

Finally, Marcus fell into step beside him, still looking dazed and shocked. "Time?" He repeated listlessly.

Clio hastened his pace. "I have an idea," he said, gaze focused forward on the open gate before them. "Now rally, Captain. For Aya's sake."

The shorter man listened, and Clio sped up even more, hoping that maybe, just this once, luck would be on their side.

# Faces from the Past

*When the dust settles and the sky clears*
*There still will be you and I*
*Months may pass and years may change*
*But our love will never die.*
- Stanza taken from *'Ode to Us'*, the final recorded work of poet Inigo
Black, dated Year 12 B.M.

. . . . . .

"Not you."

Savannah paused midstep, looking up in surprise at the female soldier standing between her and the gateway the rest of the Easthaven group was passing through. "Excuse me?" She asked, confused.

The woman gestured to Savannah's stomach. "You're pregnant. You need to go to medical."

Adam had been in line ahead of her, but he turned back once he realized Savannah wasn't right behind him. "Hey," he said, throwing a curious glance at her over the soldier's shoulder. "Is everything okay?"

The soldier answered without turning to him. "She needs to go to medical. She'll join you later if the doctor clears her." She motioned to one of the civilian volunteers that had been giving water and food to the Easthaven group. "Charlotte will take you," she told Savannah.

The girl in question came up and gave Savannah a tentative wave. She was young and slender, her long brown hair secured in a braid that trailed down her back. "Come with me, please," she said.

Savannah gave Adam a parting look and followed after her guide, relieved that the girl wasn't walking too quickly. It had been a long day and Savannah was lightheaded and exhausted; Charlotte's slow gait was a blessing.

The furtive glances she kept giving her were less of a blessing, however. They made Savannah feel self-conscious. Finally, though, they reached their destination and Charlotte stepped aside, holding the door open so Savannah could pass through. "Here you are," she said.

Savannah gave her a small smile. "Thanks," she replied, her smile waning as the girl flinched away from her when she walked by.

*Geez. Do you I really smell that bad?* She wondered. *I know I haven't had a proper bath in a long time but it's not like I've sprouted extra limbs made of dirt.*

Adam probably would have found that amusing, but Savannah didn't.

She didn't have time to dwell on it, though, because a nurse came up to her almost immediately. "I'm Ginny," she said brightly as she escorted Savannah to another room within the facility. "I'm just going to check your vitals and do a few routine tests before the doctor comes to see you."

Savannah didn't protest, but as she watched the nurse set about her tasks and saw the way her bright demeanor sobered after each successive part of Savannah's physical, Savannah began to worry.

"Is there, um, something wrong?" She asked.

Ginny's bright smile reappeared, though this time it looked more forced than before. "Oh, nothing to worry too much about!" She hastened to assure her. She jotted a few more notes down on her chart and then walked to the door. "Wait here, please," she requested. "Dr. Mason will be in shortly."

When the door closed, Savannah exhaled and leaned back on the examination table. The metal was cold against her back, and the only sound (once the click clacks of Ginny's shoes faded) was the quiet hum of the overhead lights. There was no wind, no crunch of snow, no pitter-patter of rain, no rustling in the distance, no cadence of voices, no sound of nature at all, and its absence was almost unsettling. Even when they'd stayed in the bunkers, it had never been this quiet. Now, though, it was like Ashland's walls had muted everything except for the thoughts in Savannah's head and the artificial thrum of the lights.

Savannah put her hands on her swollen stomach, trying to dispel the loneliness she felt.

"It's different, huh?" She whispered aloud to her unborn child. "Being inside." She brushed her hand back and forth across her abdomen as she looked up at the lights above, thinking about how different their light was from sunlight.

She sat up hastily when the door opened a few minutes later, but to her surprise, it wasn't the doctor.

"Jones?" She said as the hybrid closed the door behind him and turned to face her. He looked tired—more tired than she'd ever seen him look, his hazel eye full of weariness.

"Hey, Wix." There was one visitor's chair in the room, and Clio sank into it. "I heard you were here. Thought I'd come check on you, see how you were doing."

Savannah ignored the implied question. "I think you should answer that yourself," she replied, her brows drawing together in concern. She'd never seen him with so much as a fleck of dirt marring his clothes, but now the dark fabric of his shirt was stained badly, discolored by large, splotchy patches of dried and drying blood. His face was also paler than usual, his human skin nearly a matching shade to his vampire side. "You look like crap," Savannah commented unhappily.

Clio leaned forward on his elbows and sighed. "I feel like crap," he murmured.

Savannah shifted. "Is Captain Marcus here?" She asked tentatively. She hadn't seen the Reaper since...

"He's here," the hybrid answered. "So is Aya."

*Aya.* Tears sprang to Savannah's eyes as the events from the previous day replayed in her head. She'd been with the others, shouting ecstatic nonsense at Ashland's wall when she'd seen the arrow go flying above their heads. And then when she had turned around...

Savannah would never forget the look of shock on Aya's face as the vampire had crumpled into the mud.

"She deserved better," Savannah said aloud, blinking her tears away. "So much better." She looked over at Clio. "I saw you carry her inside. Is she…?" She stopped, unable to finish the question.

Clio shook his head. "It's hard to say, but it doesn't look good. I had an idea, something I thought might make a difference, but she's—she's unresponsive." He put his head in his hands. "Today should have been a joyful day, but instead…" He sighed. "God, what a mess."

"Yeah." It wasn't really an appropriate answer, and Savannah wished that she could have thought of something better to say, but she couldn't. 'Mess' pretty much summed it up.

Suddenly, Clio looked towards the door.

It opened a few moments later, revealing the nurse who had been there before. She stepped into the room and then openly gaped when she caught sight of Savannah's visitor. She retreated a pace, and Savannah saw the hurt register on Clio's face a split second before he bowed his head.

It made her want to slap the smile off the nurse's pretty face.

"I apologize," the nurse said, "but Dr. Mason will not be able to see you today after all." She walked over – widely avoiding Clio – and handed Savannah a small piece of paper. "This pass needs to go to Commander Ramirez. You can give it to one of the soldiers. And this one—" she handed Savannah a second slip "—is for tomorrow, so you won't have any trouble being readmitted to medical. There's been some rule-tightening lately, so we have to keep everything very official."

Savannah climbed down from the metal examination table. "Okay."

"Did Dr. Mason say why he wouldn't be able to see Savannah today?" Clio interjected.

The nurse blinked a few times, as if she were surprised that Clio was speaking. "Um, well, yes," she managed. "He is tending to other patients and is in the middle of a delicate procedure that couldn't be interrupted."

A spark of something dangerously close to hope appeared in Clio's human eye. "By 'other patients' I take it you are referring to my two companions?"

The nurse frowned but offered a nod of affirmation, and then she walked over and opened the door, holding it open and looking very eager to disengage from the conversation. "They're preparing a welcome dinner for the other Easthaven guests in the dining hall," she said, addressing Savannah. "You are welcome to join them. Charlotte— the girl you met earlier? She will show you the way."

Savannah wasn't about to abandon Clio. "I'm sure my friend is hungry, too," she said.

The nurse's kind mien seemed to falter. "Oh, well, I'm sure that would—"

"Actually, Wix, I'm gonna hang here," Clio cut in. "See if Dr. Mason needs any assistance." He gave her a small smile. "But save me a slice of cake if they have it, okay?"

It was a joke completely lost on the nurse, but it made Savannah smile. She remembered the early days of their friendship, the 'cake day' visits she used to make to him when he'd been holed up in Easthaven's basement. The formidable hybrid had had quite the sweet tooth.

The fact that Clio was making a joke about it now meant that he was feeling better, which could only really mean one thing: not all hope was lost after all.

Her own worries falling by the wayside, Savannah gave Clio a quick side-hug. "I'll be back later with your cake," she said. She gave him a pointed look when she pulled away. "In exchange for answers and updates."

Clio gave her a mock salute and then Savannah followed the nurse out of the room.

When they were almost back by the entrance to the medical facility, the nurse leaned towards her. "I can't believe you traveled with that man and the vampire for so long," she whispered. "Weren't you scared?"

Savannah stopped. "Actually, Aya and Clio are two of the reasons I *wasn't* scared," she answered, anger coloring her voice. "They're also the reasons that me and the other Easthaven survivors made it here."

The nurse seemed taken aback by her tone. "I'm sorry, I didn't mean—"

"Yeah, you did." Savannah exhaled, trying to curb her emotions. "Listen, I know they may not look like you and me, but that doesn't matter. They're heroes, and Clio and Aya deserve acceptance just as much as every other Easthaven survivor."

The nurse looked far from convinced, but Savannah was too tired to try and talk some sense into her, and her stomach had been rumbling ever since the first mention of food. "Just...be nice to him, okay?" She said, and then she walked over to where Charlotte was waiting for her. The girl was still regarding her with the same wariness she'd displayed earlier, and Savannah wondered, as she fell into silent step behind the young volunteer, if this was what it felt like to walk a day in Clio's shoes.

. . . . .

The head hadn't started to rot yet, but that could be attributed to the cold. Bodies – and parts of bodies – kept better in the lower temperatures.

Sextus put a foot on the severed head and rolled it facedown. He didn't want to look at the mangled features or the bloody eye sockets if he didn't have to; unlike many of his brethren, he found the sight of death repugnant.

Feeling uneasy, Sextus moved toward the remnants of the small fire in the center of the clearing. It had burned down to nothing but charred logs and ash, cutting out a circle of mud on the otherwise snowy ground. A few yards away were the only tracks he could find—multiple prints scuffed in haphazard lines and circles, most likely the signs of a struggle. There were drag marks in the snow leading out from the chaotic scene, but they disappeared abruptly a few steps later. Sextus could almost make out two sets of footprints leading away from that point, but new snowfall made it impossible to say for sure. Aside from the severed head and the fact that Bruzo was missing, what had happened here remained a mystery.

"Sir."

Sextus turned to see one of his underlings approaching, a hunchbacked creature missing one eye. Everyone in the regiment had started calling him Cyclops, and Sextus had long since forgotten the morph's real name.

"We found the body," Cyclops rasped, gesturing over to the right. "In the woods."

Well, heads had to have bodies somewhere, Sextus supposed. Why the human had been out here - days from shelter - wasn't clear, but at least the head was no longer a mystery. Bruzo had a taste for decapitation.

"And Bruzo?" Sextus inquired. "Or his cohort?"

The underling shook its head. "No sign."

Sextus pondered that, once more looking at the remains of the camp. It was a strange location to make camp, and it seemed almost deliberately exposed.

*The humans are up to something.*

Quintus had alluded to as much in the note he had sent. Apparently, an eyewitness had seen a hunter and vampire fighting together shortly after Commander Demetrius's camp had been wiped out. Quintus had gone to speak with Primus about it, which meant that it was serious. No one bothered Primus unless it was absolutely necessary.

With a jerk of his clawed hand, Sextus motioned for his underlings to head back to camp. They obeyed immediately. Sextus followed, intentionally lagging behind them a bit as he contemplated all of the recent happenings.

First, survivors from the Easthaven fortress had caused problems for multiple raiding parties sent to deal with them, including the group led by Duro, who had been quite the formidable leader until his broken body had been discovered on the sheerer side of a cliff face. Then there had been the explosions and the decimation of Demetrius's entire camp, including Demetrius himself at the hands of a creature some were calling the Two-Faced Demon. Then the rumors of a vampire and a hunter working as allies, and now this: a potential trap laid by humans, with no clues as to what had happened except a decapitated man and one missing superior.

Something was brewing—that much Sextus was sure of. Morphs of the caliber of Duro, Demetrius, and Bruzo didn't just get killed and they didn't just go missing. If the humans had been able to get the better of them, it meant that humankind was getting organized and strengthening their offense. Maybe they knew more than he, Quintus, and the rest of The Seven had given them credit for.

*We adapt faster than the humans do,* Primus had said once, but maybe he was wrong. If the humans had been shaken badly enough after the attack on their fortress, maybe they had begun to do some adapting of their own. Why else would a vampire and hunter ever find themselves fighting on the same side?

Regardless of whether any of Sextus's speculations were correct, the amount of evidence spoke for itself: the humans were up to something, and it couldn't be explained away by simple coincidence.

When Sextus returned to camp, he called for Cyclops.

The hunchback shuffled over to him, waiting attentively for his orders.

"Get me parchment and a raven," Sextus commanded.

Primus was too far away for Sextus to go to him directly as Quintus had, but he would still send word about Bruzo and the strange scene in the woods. As their leader, Primus had a right to know about any and all suspicious activity.

And in addition to making Primus aware of what had happened near his camp, Sextus would also suggest that they move up their timetable for the second large-scale attack.

The sooner another fortress had fallen, the better.

· · · · ·

As far as welcomes went, the dinner they were having in Ashland's main dining hall was among the more subdued ones. It was their second night in the fortress (but first official night there, since they'd been penned up in B Ward waiting to get clearance into the main fortress the night before), and no one aside from the fourteen of them was there to celebrate with them—not that much celebrating was going on. It should have been an evening filled with laughter and conversation and reunions, but instead it felt like everyone was holding their collective breath and waiting for the other shoe to drop.

*Or like everyone's waiting to hear that the doctors couldn't help Aya,* Enwezor thought more accurately.

He hadn't seen her go down. He'd been with the others, pressed up against Ashland's walls and cheering like an imbecile, oblivious to the drama playing out behind him. It wasn't until Clio had turned back and shouted for help that he'd realized something was amiss.

That was when the celebration had ended for Enwezor and all the rest of them. The perks of being once again inside of a fortress—showers, soap, fresh clothes that didn't have holes in them and actually fit, beds with real pillows…it was all great, it really was, but Enwezor couldn't help but feel hollow inside. All seventeen of them should have been enjoying Ashland's comforts, and all seventeen of them should have been here now, sitting around a table and sharing food. But they weren't.

The cook and her assistants were pleasant enough when they brought out the food for Enwezor and the rest of the Easthaven group, but Enwezor wasn't the only one who had a hard time smiling and thanking the Ashland crew for their hospitality.

Their appetites got the better of them, though, and pretty soon most of them were tucking into their plates with gusto. Aside from the sounds of forks and knives and chewing, though, everyone stayed quiet.

Until Ed took a second helping of stew and Sloane said, "Seriously?"

Ed, as always, was unfazed by the judgment in her tone. He shrugged. "I'm hungry," he stated simply.

Sloane had been poking at her food with the fork she was clutching somewhat awkwardly in her left hand, but at that she put the utensil down and closed her hand into a fist on the table. "Well, think with something other than your stomach," she snapped. "This whole thing is bullshit."

Enwezor swallowed the bite in his mouth and frowned. "I know this isn't how we expected it to be when we got to Ashland, but they're trying—"

"To what?" Sloane cut in. "First they shoot Fangs, then they pen us up like cattle for hours on end and grill us with questions like we're fucking terrorists—"

"Sloane," Jillian scolded softly, her eyes darting over to the kitchen.

"No. Don't 'Sloane' me. I don't care if they hear. They shot one of us, locked the rest of us in what was basically a holding cell, and then, when they finally let us out, we're not allowed to see our friends and family who live here because of some fucking *curfew*?" She snorted. "Yeah. They're trying. Trying to make us wish we'd gone to Stowe or Ballater or Deepwynne instead."

"The rules aren't everyone's fault, though," Lyle said.

"Yeah," his sister chimed in. "I'm sure our cousins want to see us just as much as we want to see them—just as much as I'm sure all of your families want to see all of you, but people like us don't make the rules."

"We had to put up with annoying rules at Easthaven, too," Lyle finished as he slurped up a spoonful of stew. "Maybe you've just forgotten, Sloane."

The redhead's eyes narrowed. "I haven't forgotten." Finally, she lowered her voice. "But you guys have to admit this is above and beyond the usual bullshit," she said. "We didn't have a curfew at Easthaven, and there definitely weren't as many restrictions about where we could go and when we could go there."

Enwezor found himself agreeing. They'd been in Ashland less than forty-eight hours, but it was obvious that Governor Mason kept everyone on a much tighter leash than Governor Carter had at Easthaven. That alone certainly begged the question of *why*, but it wasn't fair for Sloane to lash out in as general a manner as she was doing.

"Lucy has a point, though," he voiced. "People don't make the rules, Sloane."

Sloane didn't respond, just flashed him a look of irritation that he'd seen many times before.

*New place, same old Sloane.*

He was about to make a snide comment about it when one of the little kitchen girls came tiptoeing up to the table. She was gripping a small piece of paper and she looked spooked, which wasn't surprising given that Sloane was still fuming, the anger radiating off of her in waves.

Enwezor cleared his throat. "Sloane," he said, inclining her head. "I, uh, think she needs to talk to you."

The 'who?' died on Sloane's lips as she swiveled around on the bench and saw the young girl. "Oh," she said instead.

The girl held out the paper. "Mrs. Jeremiah asked me to give this to you," she said in a rushed squeak.

Sloane snatched the paper. "Mrs. Jeremiah?" She repeated dubiously. She unfolded the note. "I don't know any Mrs...." It was like someone had flipped a switch on the redhead's emotions. Sloane froze, and a look of utter shock came over her face.

Enwezor stared at his friend, perplexed. He had no idea who Sloane knew at Ashland, let alone whom she would get a note from that would elicit this kind of bizarre reaction, but then again, Sloane never said anything intentionally substantive about herself. Maybe she had a whole slew of friends and family here that she'd never mentioned before.

Sloane stared at the paper in her hand for a few more pregnant moments, and then she pushed her chair back and stood up. "Excuse me," she said distractedly, not really looking at any of them, and then, without another word, she walked out of the dining hall.

Everyone stared after her, but only Ed lacked the discretion to keep his mouth shut. "What was that about?" He asked. "Who is Mrs. Jeremiah?"

"Not a clue. Maybe a relative of some kind?" Enwezor answered.

Ed shook his head. "She said she doesn't know anyone named Mrs. Jeremiah. You tend to keep track of people's names when they're kin."

Enwezor shrugged. "I don't know, then." He picked up his spoon again. "Do you have any family here, Ed?" He asked, in an effort to change the subject.

"Nah, my family's all at Ballater. Got some friends here, though, people I'll try and look up tomorrow."

Enwezor nodded. "Me too." He thought of his parents, wondering if they knew about Easthaven, wondering if they thought he was dead. He'd have to try and get a message to them tomorrow when Ashland's morning curfew ended. Hopefully, the post guys would be open to bribes.

"We all have people scattered at the different fortresses," Jillian added, shaking Enwezor from his thoughts.

"I don't."

It was the first time Cody Reade had spoken at the table — the first time she'd really spoken at all since they'd gotten to Ashland, and the somberness in her eyes made Enwezor sad.

"You've got us, though," he offered with a smile, trying to cheer her up. "And Clio."

The little girl's expression didn't soften. "Maybe," she said. "But they shot Aya and I haven't seen Clio since we got here." She set her utensils down on her empty plate and stood up, fixing Enwezor with a knowing stare that was much too wise for a six-year-old. "They don't really want us here," she said. "Not all of us. They're going to break up our family."

She walked away before Enwezor or anyone else could say anything, and after a moment, Jillian gave a tired sigh and put her spoon down in her nearly finished bowl of stew. "I'll go after her," she said. She stood up, and Enwezor could hear her joints popping in protest from across the table. "The rest of you: *behave*. We are guests here, and we don't need to stir up more trouble than there already is."

*Here, here,* Enwezor thought sarcastically. *Everybody raise a glass. That's some toast-worthy advice right there.*

Silence reigned again after Jillian's departure, and aside from Adam and Savannah inquiring about dessert, everyone's appetites seemed to wane after that point, too. Even Ed's.

As everyone shuffled off to bed, Enwezor walked by the kitchen and thanked the cook, and then he headed back to the temporary room he'd been assigned, pondering Cody Reade's parting comment.

*They're going to break up our family.*

He could have dismissed her words away as a six-year-old's illogical fear, but Enwezor knew there was truth in what she'd said.

It made him think that maybe they weren't out of danger yet, and *that* made his stomach twist uncomfortably.

*Our fight's not over yet,* he realized with a sinking feeling. *Maybe it never will be.*

．　．　．　．　．

Charlotte watched as the Easthaven survivors shuffled out of the dining hall, her eyes following after them even as Marge the Barge started scolding her.

"Get a move on, children!" She was hollering. "Those dirty dishes aren't going to clear themselves!"

Charlotte rolled her eyes (although she waited until she was facing away from the Barge to do it) and grabbed her friend Nancy by the hand. "C'mon," she mumbled. "We'd better do as we're told."

Marge might have weighed close to fifteen stone (hence the name everyone called her behind her back) but the woman could move like a cat when she wanted to, and Charlotte had gotten smacked in the ears enough times to realize that it was in her best interest to listen to the fat lady's directions the first time she spoke them.

Still, it was hard not to stand around dumbly and gawk at the new arrivals. In Charlotte's twelve years, she'd never seen anything quite like them.

"Did you see how skinny they all were?" Nancy asked as they began to stack the dirty dishes into piles.

Charlotte nodded. Even the biggest man at the table had been too thin to fill out his clothes, and some of the others looked like skin and bones. The oldest woman's eyes had been so sunken in her face that she'd looked like a corpse someone had dug up and dressed.

"And the way they *ate*," Nancy went on. "It was like they'd never seen food before."

"Well," Charlotte reasoned as she straightened her stack and picked it up, "they were out in the wild for months. I doubt they had any proper food."

Laden with the first set of dishes, Charlotte headed back to the kitchen and Nancy fell into step beside her.

"It makes you wonder how they survived, doesn't it?" Nancy whispered conspiratorially. "Do you think they ever…ever ate people?"

Charlotte made a face. "Ew, Nancy, that's gross."

Her friend shrugged. "Doesn't mean it isn't possible. I read in one of the history books in school about this family that ate the youngest kid during a cold winter so that the rest of them wouldn't starve."

"You did *not* read that in a history book."

"Fine," Nancy huffed. "But I heard it from Old Jim, and he's like a walking history book so it's pretty much the same thing."

They set their stacks of dishes down on the counter as Marge the Barge stared on disapprovingly, and then they scurried back out into the dining hall.

"You took one of them to medical, didn't you?" Nancy asked.

Charlotte thought of the pregnant woman. "Yeah. I was there when they got let in, too," she added.

Nancy's eyes widened. "Really?" She breathed. "Then spill! I want details."

"Well, they were kind of…um, they kind of scared me," Charlotte admitted. "They had so many weapons with them and some of their clothes were bloody and…" She shuddered. "There was a girl even younger than us, and *she* had a knife. They didn't just look like survivors, they looked like…like killers."

Nancy seemed to process that as she stacked the glasses together. "They probably *are* killers," she finally said. "Otherwise they would've died. Mamma says it's kill or be killed outside the fortresses, and that's why we need to stay inside."

Charlotte was about to reply when one of the serving platters fell from her hands and clattered to the floor.

Quick as a cat, Marge the Barge's face appeared in the kitchen doorway. "Careful!" She yelled at them. "If either of you girls breaks anything, I will tan your backsides, do ya hear?"

"Yes, ma'am," they both muttered.

Charlotte didn't drop anything else, and she and Nancy worked in silence for a while until they were sure Marge the Barge was no longer monitoring them.

"So," Nancy said under her breath as they began to wipe down the table with rags. "Did you get to see the vampire?"

Charlotte shook her head. "No," she said, and she was glad for that. She'd never seen a vampire, and she didn't want to. "I was helping out in B Ward, but they took the vampire straight to medical. I didn't see her or the Reaper, but I heard the others talking about them."

"What about the two-faced man?"

"I didn't see him, either."

Nancy pouted. "Too bad," she said. Then her face lit up. "Hey—what if we snuck out later and took a peek in medical? Everyone is dying to hear details and we'd be super popular if we had some."

"Are you kidding?" Charlotte whispered back. "If we break curfew, we'll get in trouble. The Guard would catch us and take us to Commander Ramirez or Governor Mason or something, and we'd lose even more privileges." *Or something worse would happen.*

"Only if we get caught."

"We *will* get caught. We can't even get away with stuff in front of the Barge."

Nancy let out a huff. "*Fine,*" she said, elongating the word into a sigh of exasperation. "You're no fun, Charlotte."

Maybe she wasn't, but Charlotte had heard rumors about what happened to people who broke curfew, and she didn't want to find out firsthand if they were true. "Sorry," she said to her friend. "I just don't want to get in trouble."

"Whatever."

An idea occurred to Charlotte. "You know, you could always ask Taylor to go take a look for you."

Nancy's cheeks turned bright red just as Charlotte knew they would. "I could not."

"You could. Taylor likes you. He'd go if you asked."

"Maybe," Nancy said noncommittally, and the girls finished wiping down the table in silence until Nancy changed the subject. "Hey," she began. "What was that note all about? The one Mrs. Jeremiah gave you?"

Charlotte shrugged. "Dunno. Mrs. Jeremiah didn't say. She just asked me to do her a favor and pass the note along to the redhead from Easthaven."

Nancy twisted her rag out, squeezing the dirty water into the bucket. "Hmm. What do you think it said?"

"I didn't ask."

Nancy placed the rag on her shoulder when it was no longer dripping and stood up, grabbing the bucket in her free hand. "Maybe she was asking the one-armed lady to kill the governor," she hypothesized.

Charlotte froze. "Why would you say something like that?" She asked, appalled by the idea.

Her friend shrugged. "Everyone knows that Governor Mason has enemies—that's what Mamma says. She also says that there are a lot of people who want to see someone else take his place as governor. Maybe Mrs. Jeremiah is one of those people."

Charlotte grabbed her friend's arm and pulled her close, the water sloshing in the bucket as she did. "Don't say things like that," she whispered firmly. "If anyone hears you or your mom talking like that, you'll be turned out."

Nancy smiled in a way that made Charlotte's stomach twist into knots. "Only while Governor Mason is in charge," she whispered back, and then she jerked out of Charlotte's grip and carried her bucket back to the kitchen.

Charlotte stood there, staring after her friend in stunned silence until she heard Marge the Barge hollering at her to hurry up, and then, not wanting to get her ears boxed in or earn a spanking, she pushed the conversation with Nancy to the back of her mind and did as she was told.

· · · · ·

Kai Ramirez left the Guard's private gym well past midnight. She was soaked through, her clothes clinging to her trim frame as though she'd been standing out in the rain. In reality, of course, she hadn't felt rain on her skin (aside from the other day) in nearly six years; her clothes were drenched because of the sheer brutality of her workout.

Kai had a reputation for pushing herself harder than her soldiers, for maintaining a level of fitness that was daunting to everyone else, but even by her standards, tonight she'd pushed herself to the brink of exhaustion.

She'd needed to, after listening to hours of first-hand accounts from the Easthaven survivors. Their stories were incredible, admirable in many ways, but certain parts...

Not wanting to think about it just then, Kai headed for the communal showers, hoping that a quick soak would clear her head. She stripped, leaving her wet clothes in a pile on the floor and stepping beneath the cold spray. There was hot water available in Ashland, but Kai never used it. She liked the clarity she found in the cold water.

Tonight, though, she found no peace, and finally, when the suds from her soap had disappeared down the drain and she was a rash of goosebumps from head to toe, she turned off the water and toweled herself dry.

She stopped briefly in the laundry facility to dump her clothes, and then she donned a pair of drawstring black pants and a black tank top before wandering towards the dining facility.

Governor Mason had started enforcing curfew for the citizens weeks ago, but Kai – along with a few select personnel – was exempt. Kai had no idea how long that freedom would last, but tonight she aimed to indulge in it.

There was no one in the kitchen at such a late hour, so she went about heating water for herself and brewed a cup of tea, eschewing her normal choice of green tea in favor of a stronger black tea. When it was ready, she wandered into the dining hall, intending to enjoy the unusual solitude of the large space.

To her immense surprise, however, there was someone already there.

Kai paused only for an infinitesimal moment, taking in the familiar stranger's disparate features before she kept walking and sat down at the end of a long table.

She put her mug of tea down in front of her, watching the steam curl into the darkness of the high ceiling above. She hadn't bothered to turn on any lights, so the only illumination in the large room came from the faint glow of the kitchen lights she'd left on.

"Technically," she said, eyes still on her tea, "civilians aren't supposed to be wandering around at this time of night."

The man walked towards the table Kai was sitting at and shrugged. "Well, good thing I'm not *technically* a civilian, then."

Kai looked up at him, noting the way the pale half of his face seemed almost translucent in the dim lighting. "Or technically human," she added, remembering the fangs he'd sported the day before. Gossip had already spread through Ashland about the katana wielding stranger with the alien face, fearful whispers that had put even Ashland's staunchest men on edge.

Kai, however, was unaffected by such inane chatter. She knew the man's real identity, knew the things he'd done in service to humanity, and even the jarring change in his appearance didn't rouse her fear. Actions mattered much more than appearance to her—always had, always would.

"True." Clio Jones gestured to the bench opposite her. "May I?"

Kai inclined her head and took a sip of her tea. The flavor was so distasteful to her that she almost didn't swallow. But it was still better than drinking green tea—*his* tea of choice.

"Thank you for allowing me to stay in medical today," the hybrid said when he was seated. "I assume you've talked with everyone else?"

Kai nodded. "Everyone except for you and the Reaper." Her lips twisted. "And *it*."

"So you know our story."

"Yes." She took another unsatisfying sip of tea. "I've heard your story. I know how the sixteen of you fought and struggled to survive over the past six months. I know what you've lost. And I know that all fourteen of the civilians and soldiers who arrived here today looks to you with respect and admiration." She paused. "As do I, Lieutenant Jones. The fact that you managed to keep those people safe under such horrifying conditions for so long...you are a testament to a breed of soldier not often seen."

The hybrid smiled. "No one's called me *Lieutenant* in a long time," he said. "It sounds strange, now." He arched a brow. "How did you know about my rank? None of the Easthaven group knows except for Marcus, and you just said you hadn't spoken to him. So, I know you didn't hear it from them."

Kai traced a finger across the rim of her mug. "I remember you from the Rangers." She hadn't recognized him immediately when she'd met him and the others beyond Ashland's walls, but as soon as one of the civilians had mentioned the name Clio, she'd known who he was.

The man's mismatched eyes trailed over her. "Really?" He said dubiously. "Pardon my saying so, Commander, but you seem much too young to have been in the Rangers when I was a member."

"I was a trainee at the time, but my older siblings were already fully-fledged hunters. They mentioned the Wraith on more than one occasion."

It wasn't a lie; everyone had talked about the Wraith in the years before the vaccine. He had been the source of wild gossip in the Rangers—more so than even the Elite Five. And Kai remembered the way people had whispered about him, too. Hunters had either wanted him, wanted to be him, or feared him. Personally, Kai had always admired him. After all, anyone who was strong enough to complete solo mission after solo mission was someone who deserved respect.

"Ramirez..." The name rolled off his tongue in a pensive manner. "Were your siblings—?"

"Gone, now, like so many others," Kai interjected quickly.

"I see," Jones replied. He didn't ask any of the follow-up questions that people usually asked. Maybe he remembered the other Ramirez soldiers and what had happened to them. Or maybe he was just perceptive enough to realize that it wasn't something Kai wanted to discuss.

Either way, she was grateful.

"May I ask you something, Commander?" The hybrid ventured after the silence between them had stretched on for some countless number of minutes.

Kai lifted a brow expectantly.

"Now that you've heard the truth of our journey from fourteen separate sources, why do you still refer to Aya as an 'it'?"

Kai clenched her teeth together so tightly she was sure her jaw would snap. "I will never view a vampire as anything other than an 'it'," she said. "And neither will the rest of Ashland."

"Aya was integral to our survival. Without her, very few of us – and possibly none of us – would be here."

Kai could see the truth of it in his hazel eye, but it didn't soften her opinion. Nothing ever would. "Maybe so," she replied tersely, "but that does not change the fact that your *Aya* is a vampire."

"So am I, to a certain extent."

"It's not the same."

"Isn't it?" He challenged.

"No." Kai pushed her mug away and stood up, tossing her still-damp hair over her shoulder. "And if you try and liken the two of you in order to gain clemency and asylum for the vampire, as I am guessing you are intending to do should she survive, I promise you that you will only succeed in convincing the Council and the people of Ashland that *both* of you should be turned out." She pursed her lips. "I intend to speak on your behalf should the Council question your humanity, but I will not be able to sway them if you insist on pointing out parallels and similarities between you and your vampire."

Jones frowned up at her. "I'm grateful that you would speak on my behalf, Commander, and saddened by the fact that you think it might be necessary to do so, but please, answer me this: if you intend to do nothing to help Aya, why did you allow us to bring her inside the fortress in the first place?"

"I honor my agreements, Lieutenant. You asked that she receive medical attention, and I acquiesced. What happens subsequently was not part of our spoken deal."

"Will you at least speak with her when she wakes up?" The hybrid asked. "Aya deserves your time."

"And if she lives, she will get it," Kai replied. "At the trial."

The hybrid's voice sharpened. "The trial?"

Kai could see the disbelief on the man's strange face, could see him trying to figure out why someone he esteemed as a hero would have to face a tribunal. She understood his perspective, to a certain extent; he'd been in the outside world for more than half a year, where nothing mattered except his group's collective will to survive.

But the focus in Ashland was different, and things besides survival *did* matter.

"If you alter your perspective, Lieutenant, you'll realize that life inside the walls is very different than life outside of them. Ashland has been an enclosed society for nearly six years—an enclosed *human* society. Your vampire may have served a purpose in open territory, but here, its presence will only cause upheaval. A trial, should the vampire survive, will be inevitable—as inevitable as its outcome," she added with dark gravitas.

"You can't know that for sure, Commander," the hybrid argued. "People can change, can show acceptance where there previously wasn't any. Our group is proof of that."

"What your group proved," Kai countered, "is that people fighting for their lives are willing to be open-minded if it will help their odds of survival. Nothing more." She grabbed her tea and started towards the kitchen, but even though she knew she ought to leave, the question that had been burning inside of her all day got the better of her.

She turned back. "Is it true," she asked, careful to keep her voice neutral, "what everyone is saying—that the vampire and the Reaper are...close?"

The hybrid regarded her curiously. "Yes," he answered slowly. "Why do you ask?"

Kai gripped the handle of the mug so hard she thought it would break. "Idle curiosity," she said, and then, her anger a full-blown hurricane inside of her, she left her mug in the kitchen, told the hybrid to turn off the lights when he left, and headed back to the gym.

. . . . .

It was cold in the medical facility, cold in a way that made Marcus acutely aware of each of his chilled limbs, but it was nothing compared to the cold he'd experienced on the journey west. That had been bone-numbing cold, the kind that seeped into your clothes and your skin and settled in your bloodstream until you were more frozen than liquid inside, the kind of cold that made your fingers and toes painfully stiff and so icy that they burned. Unlike that, the cold here was manageable, but neither it nor the outside cold compared to the ice Marcus felt in his heart as he stared at Aya's still, pale form.

She was alive, at least, thanks to the determination of the skinny black doctor named Emmanuel Mason and the creativity of Clio Jones. If Aya pulled through – and it was still a big if – Marcus would never be able to thank those two men enough, especially Clio. The hybrid's idea had been ingenious.

Marcus looked at the side table, where Aya's heart was connected to an IV of his blood. It was such a small thing, so fragile and strange, nothing at all like the hearts that resided in human chests. It resembled a kind of medium-sized, oval nut with a diaphanous, fine skin stretched over it, and it was glowing softly amidst its nestled spot in the dirt they had saved from Aya's ruined pouch. Marcus had never seen anything like it, but it was almost beautiful, in a strange, alien way. The only thing disrupting its beauty was the IV feeding Marcus's blood into its center, into the area the arrow had pierced. He watched the blood drip down, as he had been doing for hours, marveling at how little he really knew of Aya's nature.

If she survived, he would get to know her better. He vowed it.

*Please, Aya,* he silently pleaded for the countless time that day. *Please survive.*

But the vampire remained silent, and so did their blood bond.

It was strange, really; ever since the bond had been formed, Marcus had *felt* Aya, in a way, and yet he'd never been crowded by her presence, by the way he could sense her at the fringes of his awareness. She was simply there, a piece of him, fused to his very cells and as necessary as bone and blood.

It made her absence now all the more painful, all the more felt.

"...Marcus?"

The voice stirred him, a voice that was as familiar as it was unforgettable. Marcus turned in his chair, straightening up. "Hello, Joben," he said quietly.

The blond man looked older than Marcus remembered, his hair gone grey at the temples and his athletic figure slightly thinner than it had been during the glory days, but the intensity of his eyes hadn't dulled, and right now they were filled with a mixture of warmness and concern. "Dr. Mason wasn't exaggerating," Joben commented, his thick eyebrows drawing together as he looked Marcus up and down. "You're in bad shape."

*Not as bad as the shape Aya's in*, Marcus thought, but he didn't say it. "I've been worse," he answered instead.

Joben chuckled. "And better." He smiled, fine lines crinkling at the corner of his eyes. "It's good to see you, Marcus," he said fondly. "When I heard about Easthaven, I feared the worst, but when I found out that survivors had arrived on our doorstep, I knew you'd be one of them."

"Did you?" Marcus asked dryly. "Well, Stan always said I was like a cockroach," he added. "Unsightly and hard to kill."

Joben's gaze turned inquisitive. "Your uncle...?"

Marcus knew what he was asking. "Dead," he said. *Dead like everyone else.* "He bought us the time we needed to get out of Easthaven during the attack."

Joben sighed. "I'm sorry, Marcus. Truly. I know you and Stan weren't always on the best of terms, but I know losing him must have been difficult."

"Yeah," Marcus said because he didn't know what else to say. He changed the subject. "Where is Rita?" He asked. He was surprised she hadn't come to see him yet; they hadn't been the closest of the Elite Five, but she was still a fellow Reaper, still a friend.

"Rita isn't here."

Marcus felt something ugly begin to brew in the pit of his stomach. He knew Rita had been stationed at Ashland. If she wasn't here, then... "Is she dead?"

Joben hesitated. "She's gone."

"How?" Marcus pressed. "When? I want answers, Joben, not your tactfully worded ambiguities. Tell me what happened."

"I will, Marcus. Soon. We have a great many things to catch up on. But please...for today, at least, let's deal with the more pressing matter." He gestured to Aya's dormant figure. "So, this is the vampire," he stated.

Marcus stared at the older man for a drawn-out moment before finally giving in and moving their conversation in another direction. "Aya," he supplied. "She's one of the only reasons we made it here, and she *is* the only reason I did. But now..."

"Don't lose hope, Marcus. Dr. Mason seems optimistic, despite having never done a procedure like this before, and I trust his word. Emmanuel is a brilliant physician and very innovative. If there is a way to save her, he will find it."

"Maybe, but she was dead, Joben. All of this is just…" He waved his hands at the wires, needles, and monitors affixed to Aya and her heart. "Complicated guesswork."

Joben was quiet for a moment. "I heard you threw yourself in front of her," he said at length.

There was a question in his statement – there always was when it came to Joben – and Marcus decided not to be evasive. After all, on the wild chance that Aya did pull through, he'd have to tell Joben everything anyway to ensure that he would speak on Aya's behalf.

"Yes," he admitted. "I did. And if I could've taken the arrow that did this to her as well, I would have. She deserves to live." He swallowed against the huskiness in his voice. "She…she's one of the most amazing people I've ever met, Joben."

"One of the most amazing *vampires*, perhaps," Joben amended.

Marcus shrugged. "Semantics."

Joben regarded him with thinly veiled surprise. "That's quite something, coming from a Reaper." His gaze moved to Aya's inert form. "I hope she pulls through, too," he said. "Anyone that is special enough to earn your trust is someone I'd like to know."

Marcus frowned. "I trust people."

"You trust *select* people," Joben insisted. "It took you years to warm up to me, and I always had your best interest at heart."

Marcus gave his older friend a look. "You were a manipulative bastard then, and you still are. You're lucky I put up with your shit."

The smile reappeared on Joben's face. "I suppose I am." He placed a hand on Marcus's shoulder. "Eventually, I want to hear your story, but right now, I am here as a messenger on Dr. Mason's behalf. He said you've been here since your arrival and that you've refused to eat or leave the vampire's side. I understand your concern, but Marcus, you need to take care of yourself, too. I meant what I said—you're in bad shape."

Marcus shrugged his hand away. "I'll be fine."

"With food and sleep, I agree with that statement."

"Joben—"

"Would it help," the blond man cut in, "if I told you that I would personally stay here while you took a break? I'll make sure she's safe."

Marcus's eyes widened. "You'd...you'd do that?" He asked. "Without knowing her?"

Joben's gaze was resolute. "If you trust her, then I trust her, Marcus. Some things don't change."

Gratitude wasn't a strong enough word to describe the sensation of relief that coursed through Marcus's cold, stiff body at Joben's words. He'd been afraid to leave Aya's side, afraid to leave her alone, worried that she would either take a turn for the worse while no one was there or that someone would come and try to harm her. There were too many people who knew about her already, and too many people with reasons to seek vengeance against a vampire. Joben himself was one such person, but Marcus trusted him; if Joben said that he would watch over her, Marcus believed him.

He stood up, wincing slightly at the pain that shot through his legs. "All right," he said. "I...I'll be back soon."

Joben nodded. "Of course."

"Okay." Marcus took one last, lingering look at Aya, pushing out through their bond again, but still, there was nothing but silence.

"Go, Marcus," Joben urged gently. "She won't die on my watch."

Reluctantly, Marcus nodded. "If you say so, Joben," he mumbled, and then he headed for the door.

Unlike being outside, it was hard to tell what time of day it was inside of Ashland. There were lights on all the time, buzzing dully overhead, and there was no change in temperature from day to night. Still, as Marcus found himself wandering the halls in search of the temporary quarters he had been assigned earlier that day, Marcus had a suspicion it was either very late or very early. The corridors were deserted, and no voices echoed down the halls ahead or behind him.

The loneliness afforded Marcus too much time to think, and nearly all of his thoughts were of regrets, losses, and the vampire he hadn't realized he'd loved until the arrow had pierced her heart.

*Too little too late.*

Everything he loved turned to ashes and dust.

He pushed the painful thought away, too tired to carry the guilt of it just then.

The layout of Ashland was much different than the layout of Easthaven, and Marcus realized very quickly that he should have asked Joben for directions. He took more wrong turns than right ones, and before long, he was ready to kick a wall and give up. But then he heard footsteps.

*Fucking finally.*

Hopefully, whoever it was would be able to point him in the right direction, or at least point him back to medical. Maybe he'd been wandering around long enough that Joben would believe he'd taken a nap and gotten something to eat.

Hurrying his steps so as not to miss the other person, Marcus rounded a bend in the hallway. It opened into a much larger corridor— its width indicative of a main thoroughfare, and as Marcus stepped forward, two things happened in quick succession.

First, he felt Aya open her eyes.

Second, his own heart nearly stopped.

There was indeed someone in the corridor, headed away from him, but it was a mirage, a lie, an impossibility, because Marcus knew, beyond a shadow of doubt, that the person he was looking at was dead. He'd never seen her body, had never had that final bit of closure, but the stories and evidence and Stan's word had been proof enough of her death, which meant that the being in front of him now could be nothing more than a ghost.

And yet the ghost walking away from him looked solid and real, and Marcus could hear the thud of her boots on the ground with each step she took.

*It's impossible. It's not her. It's not.*

But she'd always been unmistakable—everything about her was striking in a formidable way, from the way she wore her hair to the way she walked, and Marcus felt his throat constricting with every passing second and with every step she took away from him.

Swallowing against seven years of grief and loss and repressed emotions, Marcus found his voice just as the woman reached the end of the hall.

"Jocelyn?"

# New Beginnings

*Sometimes, fresh starts blossom from rebirth and rejuvenation. Other times, fresh starts only bloom from the ashes of what came before. Never forget that for a new dawn to rise, an old age must pass away.*
- Reflection taken from Selene Wyatt's book *Eugenics: Humanity's Way Forward*, dated Year 5 B.M.

. . . . .

Commander Kai Ramirez finally decided that she needed to call it a night. Her body was exhausted, and after Cole had come to talk business with her when she was leaving the Guard showers for the second time that night, she was mentally drained, too. Cole was a reliable but needy soldier who usually reported to Brianne, but seeing as Brianne wasn't in Ashland at present, he'd taken it upon himself to report to Kai. He'd prattled on for a stream of endless minutes about minutiae that didn't really interest her, and then he'd asked, as he'd been doing daily, when Brianne was coming back from medical leave. Having to repeatedly lie was bad enough, but Kai's worry over her missing subordinates was worse. Brianne and Samar and Ian should have been back by now, and they weren't. Either something had gone wrong, or...

*There is no 'or'*, Kai's inner voice insisted. *Something's gone wrong and they're not coming back. I sent them to their deaths.*

The thought of it tore her heart to shreds, as did the fact that, even knowing their fate ahead of time, she'd still make the same decision. Brianne and Samar were all the family she had left, but their lives weren't worth more than the future of humanity.

She'd always criticized Joben Hale for viewing the little men as expendable, for pursuing the ends at the cost of the means, but as Kai walked the desolate halls of Ashland at four o'clock in the morning, her boots echoing softly on the floor, she realized that maybe they shared that unforgivable trait.

*Maybe all leaders do.*

She wondered if her sister or brother had ever been in a similar situation, wondered if they'd known what it was like to send soldiers out into the field fully aware that those same soldiers would never...

*"Jocelyn?"*

Kai froze, the whispered name coursing through her like a shock wave. There was no mistaking that voice—*his* voice. She'd known that this meeting would be inevitable, but she'd hoped it would happen later. Much, much later.

Bracing herself, Kai slowly turned and looked into the face of a man she hadn't seen in six years. He was the same – steel eyes, hard expression, coiled muscle – and yet he wasn't. He was thinner than she remembered, his brown hair longer, his posture wearier. But there was no mistaking him.

"Hello, Marcus," she said, her voice thick with all the emotions she'd been choking down since she'd first learned that he was among the group of survivors.

She watched in slow motion as the disbelief and the pained flicker of hope on his face settled into a look of crestfallen recognition. "Kai," he said, and the sadness in his voice made Kai's insides twist. "I thought...I thought you were..."

"I know what you thought." Kai swallowed. "It's an easy mistake to make. We haven't seen each other in years."

Marcus nodded. "The last time I saw you, you were just a kid. Now, though..." He shook his head in a dazed way, as if he couldn't quite believe that she'd grown up in the six years since they'd last laid eyes on each other. "You look like her," he added softly.

"I know," Kai said again, her voice nearly as soft as Marcus's. "Even when I was a little girl, everyone said I was the spitting image of my sister."

A flash of pain stole across Marcus's face, a mirror to the pain Kai felt every time she thought about Jocelyn or Finn. Even years after their deaths, thinking about her siblings was still incredibly difficult. The older Ramirez children had more or less raised Kai, and despite the large age gap, the three of them had been closer than most. Losing them had been devastating beyond words.

"You didn't have any tattoos the last time I saw you," Marcus observed as he took a step towards her. "But now you have more ink than Jocelyn did. It's quite the collection."

Kai idly traced one of the larger ink patterns on her forearm. "I suppose," she said. Though who knew how many Jocelyn would've gotten if the universe hadn't seen fit to steal her away. "I got one for every year of training I completed." *Just like Jocelyn used to do.*

Marcus paused. "Training?" His brows drew together. "I thought the Rangers was all but disbanded."

"It was," Kai responded. "Aside from Joben's reserve unit. The Guard is the dominant military branch now."

Something indefinable flitted across Marcus's steel eyes. "So you're a soldier?"

"I'm the commander, actually. At least of Ashland's branch."

Marcus chuckled lightly. "Guess I should've figured as much. High ranking was always a trademark Ramirez trait."

"I'm not the only one who followed in family footsteps," Kai replied. She tugged at the hem of her shirt, her mind drifting to the one face noticeably absent among her interviewees. "What happened to Stan?" She asked quietly. She already knew he wasn't among the Easthaven survivors, but details mattered.

"He blew Easthaven's dynamite cache to buy us time to escape," Marcus answered. "He...he went out on his own terms."

The ghost of a smile played at Kai's lips. "Sounds like him," she murmured, and then she stiffened as Marcus moved towards her. The closer he got, the more Kai's warring emotions threatened to overwhelm her. Part of her wanted to embrace him, to cry with relief that Marcus had somehow survived and reappeared in her life against all odds, but another part of her wanted to smash her fists into his face until his features weren't recognizable.

Marcus stopped when he was directly in front of her. "It's good to see you, Kai," he said, and she could tell that he meant it.

Which only made her hurt worse. "I wish I could say the same, Marcus," she replied. "But after the stories your group members told about you..." Suddenly, the slim vein of composure she'd clung to burst. "God, Marcus." Her voice was shaking. "What were you thinking, making a pact with a vampire and then bringing it here? Have you lost your mind?"

Marcus stiffened. "Kai—"

"No," she interjected swiftly. "Let me finish. You don't know what it was like for me to learn about the attack on Easthaven, to think that the one person from the old days I still cared about had been slaughtered. It was..." She couldn't find the words. "I grieved for you, Marcus," she confessed. "Almost as much as I grieved for my siblings." She blinked back tears. "So, imagine my shock and joy, when all these months later, I find out that not only did you survive, but that you also crossed a thousand miles and showed up at our gates. When one of your civilians shared the news that you were the one who'd led them here, I was overwhelmed. It was the happiest I can remember being in a long time." Her heart was a drum in her ears. "When we first found out that Easthaven had been attacked, I always hoped that you'd somehow make it, that you'd somehow survive, but I...I didn't let myself dwell on it. I couldn't." She took a breath to steady herself, to no avail. Having him there, seeing him standing before her in the flesh...it was too much. She couldn't have held anything back if she'd tried. "You were my brother in every way that counted, Marcus," she went on. "Aside from Jocelyn and Finn, I looked up to you more than I looked up to anyone else. I wanted to be like you when I grew up—I used to dream about it. And then you go and do something like this." Her hands balled into white-knuckled fists. "Do you have any idea what it felt like to learn that my childhood hero, the man my sister loved, had returned—with one of *them*?"

"Kai—"

"Do you deny it?"

Marcus said nothing, and Kai barked out a mirthless laugh. "That's what I thought," she spat, the tears starting to fall. "How could you, Marcus?" She cried, her voice breaking over his name. "They took everything from us! And you—you promised me you would get revenge for my brother and sister." She closed her eyes in an effort to stymie her tears. "I remember that day…that awful day…you came to my room to tell me that Jocelyn and Finn had been…had been killed, and you, you *vowed* to me that you wouldn't stop until you'd destroyed every last vampire who had the audacity to exist in our world. You promised me that." She opened her eyes to look at him, and his face was blurry through the haze of her tears. "I was fourteen years old when they died, and I didn't think I'd make it to fifteen. Your promise was the *only* thing that helped me survive the loss of my family." Now, facing the man she'd once idolized, Kai felt like that gangly, fourteen-year-old girl again as she angrily wiped the tears from her eyes. "So can you imagine," she continued, "can you possibly imagine the betrayal I feel right now? Can you?"

Marcus looked as though she'd struck him. "Kai," he said, holding up a hand. "Please listen. If I ever found the vampires who murdered Jocelyn and Finn, I would not hesitate to uphold the promise I made to you—*believe* me. But Aya isn't one of the vampires responsible. She's—"

"I know what she is," Kai said with barely concealed fury. "She's the vampire you saved, the vampire that your Easthaven friends all say you're in love with." She crossed her arms, grateful that her sorrow was morphing into anger. At least *that* was an emotion that could serve to strengthen instead of shatter her. "Is it true?" She challenged. "Do you love this vampire you've brought here?"

Marcus exhaled. "Yes," he admitted, and what was left of Kai's heart broke at the honesty in that lone syllable.

"My sister deserved better than you," she said acerbically, her voice full of hurt.

"I loved Jocelyn—"

Kai slapped him across the face, the force of her palm snapping his head to the side. He recovered quickly, but just as the shock of what she'd done registered on his face, Kai slapped him again, equally as hard. Marcus stumbled back a pace, but he didn't retaliate. He just stood there numbly, watching her with a pitying expression that made Kai want to tear him apart.

Instead, she decided to hit him with all the emotions threatening to consume her. "Don't you dare say you loved my sister," she growled. "If that were true, you would never defile her memory by taking a vampire for your lover." She took a step closer to him and lowered her voice, something occurring to her. "But maybe…maybe you just don't know."

"Don't know what?"

"The truth." Kai paused, searching for the strength to bring up the thing she was most loath to ever, ever discuss again. "Did Stan ever tell you how Jocelyn died?" She asked. "The real story?"

She could tell by the wary look in Marcus's eyes that he wasn't sure. "I know what happened, Kai," he said, but his words were as unconvincing as his gaze.

"I don't think you do," she snapped back. "You see, after you came and told me what happened, I couldn't accept it. People like Jocelyn and Finn don't just get killed out in the field—especially not people as skilled as my sister. So I went and found Stan and I demanded to hear the details. He told me to piss off at first, but eventually I wore him down and he told me everything." In point of fact, it had taken her four hours to wear him down, at which point Stan had shoved her into a chair, cracked open a bottle of scotch he'd been muttering about saving for a special occasion, and poured both of them a drink.

"It wasn't just a mishap in the field, Marcus," she went on. "It wasn't just an accident. Apparently, the vampires my sister's squad was tracking found out that Jocelyn was a Reaper. They butchered her group while she was out scouting ahead and took Finn hostage."

Marcus's lips parted. "What?"

*So he doesn't know.* All the better. "Your uncle's squad was acting as a sweeper, and Jocelyn met up with them after she realized her squad had been killed. She wanted to take Stan's men and go after Finn since he wasn't among the dead, but Stan refused, said it was too dangerous. But you know what Jocelyn was like—she would never have left anyone behind, least of all our brother. So she went alone, defying a direct order to retreat. When she didn't return by the next morning, Stan took one member of his squad and tracked her."

"I know this part," Marcus said. "Stan told me he was the one who found her."

"More like he found what was *left* of her," Kai corrected. "The vampires didn't just kill her, Marcus. They drained her dry and ripped her limb from limb. Stan said that by the time he got there, even her eyes had been gouged out."

Horrified was too light a word to describe Marcus's expression. "*What?*" He breathed.

"That's not all," Kai continued in a strained voice. She'd retched up the alcohol Stan had given her when she'd first heard the truth, and even talking about it now was enough to make her physically sick, but Marcus needed to know. He needed to understand the bloodsucking breed of evil he was trying to defend. "When Stan found her, there was a vampire violating her corpse, laughing about having its way with a Reaper. Stan took its head off while it was still inside of her."

The visible way in which Marcus crumpled should have brought her some measure of satisfaction, but it didn't. Kai just felt cold and numb and broken. "That's why Stan didn't bring her body home," she added in a quiet hush. "He couldn't...he didn't want anyone to see her like that."

Marcus ran a hand through his hair, his fingers shaking. His breathing was audible and strained, and he looked like someone was slowly gutting him. "Stan..." He finally choked out. "Stan told you this?"

His eyes were begging her to deny it, pleading with her to lie and grant him some scintilla of peace, but she couldn't. She wouldn't.

"Nearly word for word," she avowed. She swallowed against her own pain and attempted to take a calming breath. "Do you understand now?" She asked him softly. "Do you understand why we can never suffer a vampire to live, let alone offer one sanctuary?"

She glimpsed a hint of the old Marcus in the wake of her question, a fragment of the hardened Reaper that had made that promise to her so long ago in her bedroom while she'd sobbed inconsolably in his arms. But as quickly as she glimpsed it, that vestige of his old self faded, and when Marcus met her gaze, his eyes were tortured but resolute, and the rage and hatred Kai felt weren't visible in them.

"One day," he said, his voice chillingly calm, "I will track down each and every one of the monsters who did that to Jocelyn. I gave you my word seven years ago, and I'm renewing it now. But judging an entire species based on the actions of a few is not fair, Kai." He paused. "I used to feel like you did—I fucking loathed them, thought they all should be chopped up and used for firewood. But then I met Aya, and believe me, if there are other vampires like her, our way of thinking needs serious modification. It's not as simple as us being the good guys and them being the bad guys anymore. It can't be."

Kai couldn't believe her ears. "Even if your Aya is somehow a glaring exception to her species, you can't seriously think that there is such a thing as a 'good' vampire. Especially not after what I just told you."

The look on his face told her that he disagreed.

Kai was so livid she could see white spots behind her eyes. "Fine," she hissed. "Be a traitor to your own kind. Just know that you'll be on the losing side, in the end."

"Kai—"

She sucker-punched him, her fist making contact so quickly and solidly that Marcus fell to his knees, gasping. "Don't," she said coldly. "Don't say my name, don't say my sister's name, and don't talk to me. You're betraying me and everyone else over a bloodsucker, even though you know the atrocities they're capable of. I don't want to hear anything more you have to say."

She turned away as Marcus clambered to his feet. "Kai, wait," he wheezed behind her. "Don't leave things this way. We're not blood, but we're...we're as good as family. Please hear me out. Give me that much."

"I'll give you nothing." Kai didn't turn and face him. She couldn't. "You're dead to me," she said over her shoulder. "And when your vampire goes to trial, I will make sure the verdict comes down in my favor."

He might have said something else, but Kai was deaf to it. She marched to the end of the hallway and then she broke into a run, and she didn't stop until she was back in her own quarters and the door was shut and locked. Then she fell to her hands and knees and, overcome by anger and pain and betrayal, she wept until she had no more tears to cry.

· · · · ·

Savannah woke up in a cold sweat, the vestiges of her nightmare still clawing at her as she sat up and wiped away strands of damp hair that clung to her brow. She was shaking beneath the thin nightgown she was wearing, and the fabric was sticking to her clammy spine. Her head and lower back were aching painfully.

She didn't know whether it was the tremors or her heavy breathing that woke Adam, but suddenly he was sitting up in bed next to her, his brow furrowed with concern. "Savannah?" He voiced tentatively.

"I'm okay. It was just..." an image of the dream morph devouring her baby flashed behind her eyes "...just a nightmare."

Adam put a hand on her back and began moving it in soothing circles. "Yeah, but nightmares can be bad," he said gently. "I know. I get them too."

Savannah looked over at him even though it was too dark in their shared room to see his face clearly. "You do?"

"Yeah. Dreams about losing my mom and my siblings and dreams about...dreams about losing you."

Savannah searched for his hand, found it, and squeezed it. "I'm not going anywhere," she promised. "We made it. The hard part's over."

He sighed, his hand stilling momentarily on her back. "I know. I get that. But I guess I just thought it would feel...better, you know?"

She did know. Her expectations about what it would be like to finally get to Ashland and the reality of it were so different than she hadn't emotionally recovered yet. They were safer, sure, but in so many ways, the end of their journey felt like a massive letdown.

"Do you want to tell me what your nightmare was about this time?"

Savannah almost dodged the question, but she'd made a personal vow not to hide things from Adam anymore, so she answered as honestly as she dared. "It was about the baby. I—I lost it."

Adam resumed the circles on her back. "We're not gonna lose this baby," he said gently. "You and me and Olivia are gonna be just fine."

Savannah put a hand on her swollen belly. "Olivia?" She repeated.

"Well, we don't have to call her that, but I just thought you might want to name her after your mum. I remember you mentioning it once."

"You think it's a girl?" Savannah asked.

"Yeah. Just a feeling I have. And I think she's gonna be strong like her mom."

Tears sprang to Savannah's eyes, and she leaned forward and placed a kiss on the corner of Adam's mouth. She'd been aiming for his lips, but her eyes hadn't adjusted to the dark.

Still, she could feel the way his lips pulled up into smile beneath hers and it made her happy.

"Do you like the idea?" Adam asked. "Of naming her Olivia, I mean?"

"I love it. And I love you."

Adam had been right—she *had* mentioned that she'd like to name her first child after her mother, once, when they'd been doing laundry in the middle of the night at Easthaven and talking about all sorts of nonsensical things they'd like to do ten or twenty years from then. The fact that he remembered that wasn't surprising, because he always remembered things like that. It was one of the many reasons Savannah loved him.

Adam leaned forward and kissed her back, doing a much better job at locating her lips than she'd done in finding his. When he pulled back, he pressed a tender kiss to her damp brow and then crawled out of bed. "I'm gonna go get you a glass of water and a towel. Want anything else?"

"No; that sounds perfect."

Savannah listened to him shuffle out of their room and shut the door, and then she swung her legs over the side of the bed and stood up, flicking on the bedside lamp as she did so. She padded over to the mirror bolted above the dresser, frowning as she took in her appearance.

There were still clumps of damp hair matted to her face, and aside from the bruise-like circles beneath her eyes, her skin was pale.

Suddenly, a violent pain seized her abdomen, and Savannah gasped, reflexively gripping the dresser so as not to lose her balance. It didn't last long, even though it felt like eternity stuffed into the space of seconds, but then the dizziness struck, and Savannah felt her legs turn to wet rubber and…*wet?*

She looked down, gaping in confusion at the red-tinged water running down her legs. Oh God, was she bleeding? Had her bladder let go? She hadn't even needed to…

Realization came through a fog of renewed pain and dizziness. *The baby!*

Her eyes widened in horror. "Adam!" She screamed. It was too soon, much too soon for the baby to be coming. She was weeks away from her due date. At least, she was supposed to be. And there shouldn't have been blood. That was wrong, wrong, wrong. Savannah thought of her dream…

Another blinding dose of pain raked through her, and Savannah stumbled to her knees.

*Olivia!* She thought desperately, and then everything around her faded into darkness.

· · · · ·

Sloane fidgeted as the three little boys gazed up at her, feeling wildly uncomfortable. They were technically her half-brothers, though she'd never met them before. They certainly didn't look like her. All three seemed to be mesmerized by the fact that she only had one arm.

"What did I say, boys?" Mrs. Jeremiah said as she rounded the corner and came into the kitchen. She was holding two mugs of some steaming substance in her hands. "Go to bed. You can talk to your sister tomorrow."

*Sister.*

The word made Sloane squirm.

"Coffee?" Mrs. Jeremiah asked when her three young children scampered off, holding out one of the mugs to Sloane.

Sloane shook her head. "I don't drink coffee. Never have."

The smile on the older woman's face faltered. "Right. Of course. I must have forgotten." She put both mugs down on the counter and gestured for Sloane to take a seat. "Please," she added when Sloane made no move to sit.

Reluctantly, Sloane lowered herself into a chair. She moved to run a hand through her hair, but when she noticed Mrs. Jeremiah motioning to do the same thing, she stopped. An awkward silence fell.

"So…" Mrs. Jeremiah finally said. "How did you, um, well…" She paused. "What happened to your arm?"

"A morph crushed it."

There was a gasp. "One of those horrible things attacked you?"

"Lots of times. This particular one just got the better of me."

Mrs. Jeremiah flinched. "I'm sorry."

Sloane shrugged and stared down at the table. "Wasn't your fault," she muttered.

"Well, no, but I'm still sorry. It must have been terrible."

"Pretty much the whole journey here was terrible."

There was a long pause before Mrs. Jeremiah spoke again. "Did the doctors look at it for you—is it healing properly?" She asked at length.

"Yeah." Sloane began tracing an idle pattern on the table with her index finger. "Some doc checked it out when I first got here. He wasn't concerned. Clio did a good job cauterizing the wound after it happened."

"Clio?"

"The hybrid with the sword." Sloane looked up at the older redhead, feeling a sudden surge of anger. "Why did you write that note?" She asked bluntly. "Why did you ask me to come here?"

The older woman blinked, and then her eyebrows drew together in consternation. "I just…" She swallowed. "When I heard that you were one of the survivors from Easthaven, I wanted to see you. It's been so long."

Old hurts began to knot in Sloane's stomach. "And whose fault is that?" She asked, raising a brow in challenge. "Huh?"

It was Mrs. Jeremiah's turn to look uncomfortable. "Well, we weren't placed in the same fortress. You can't blame me for that."

"I don't. I blame you for all the years before that. I blame you for this—" she added, waving her arm around the room, "—and I blame you for those snot-nosed kids."

"What are you talking about?"

Sloane could feel the sting of tears in her eyes, and it made her even angrier. She pushed back from the table as she blinked the wetness away. "Here you are, clean and sober, with three new kids and a new last name. You have a family and a home, and for once it looks like you have your shit together." Sloane clenched her hand into a fist. "Do you know how much I would've killed for just one of those things growing up?" She huffed. "But no. You didn't even try. Why? What was so wrong about me that you couldn't bring yourself to care—not even a tiny bit?"

There were tears slipping down Mrs. Jeremiahs' cheeks. "Sloane, I— I'm so sorry," she stammered, her green eyes brimming with anguish. "I wanted to get clean, but I was so alone after your father left. I just didn't have the strength."

Sloane looked down at the floor. "Yeah. That was pretty fucking obvious. You just dumped me with your parents and left me behind like so much trash."

"That's not true!" Mrs. Jeremiah exclaimed, rising to her feet. "I know you may not believe me, but I did care about you, Sloane. I still do. I wasn't fit to be a mother to you, and for that I'm sorry. But I got my second chance, and I took it. And I know this is years too late, but I asked you to come here because I wanted to tell you that there's still room in this family for you."

Sloane thought of the three little boys, the half siblings that looked nothing like her. "That's a nice sentiment," she said quietly, "but the Jeremiah family seems pretty full to me."

It seemed like Mrs. Jeremiah was about to argue to the contrary, but a sharp rap on the door interrupted her. "Yo! Sloane, you in there?"

More than grateful for the distraction, Sloane moved towards the door, throwing it open before her mother could object.

She'd never been so happy to see Enwezor's face in her life. "What's up, Zor?" She asked.

"It's Savannah," he said. "She's…something's wrong and the baby's coming."

"What?" The word came out as sharp as the sting of a whip. "Where is she?"

"Medical. So is everyone else. I thought you'd—"

"Yeah, yeah, I do." Sloane turned back to Mrs. Jeremiah. "I have to go. One of our friends is in trouble."

"Oh." Mrs. Jeremiah gave her a hopeful look. "Will you come back?"

Sloane said the only thing she could say. "I honestly don't know."

The crestfallen expression on her mother's face almost made her reconsider her answer, but Enwezor nudged her. "C'mon, Sloane," he said with urgency. "We've gotta go."

Sloane nodded, and then she left the Jeremiahs' family quarters with Enwezor. Her dark-skinned friend gave her a searching look, but Sloane shook her head. "Don't ask, okay? I don't want to talk about it."

"Well, if and when you do…" Enwezor replied without breaking his brisk stride.

"I know. Thanks."

And then they continued on in silence, and Sloane let her worries over Savannah blot out any more thoughts of the Jeremiah family.

．　．　．　．　．

The hospital bed was a sea of blood. Or, at least, that was what it felt like to Adam as he watched the woman he loved scream in pain as she pushed for what seemed like the thousandth time since he'd found her on the floor of their temporary quarters and carried her to medical. She was squeezing his hand with bone-crushing strength, but all Adam could focus on was Savannah's pale face and the amount of blood soaking into the sheets between her legs. Everything else—the pain in his hand, the doctor and nurses offering instructions as Savannah worked to birth their child, the array of machines beeping in the background—it was all a blur.

Every second was a millennium, and each time Savannah's teary, pained gaze met his, Adam felt like his heart was being shredded. *Help me*, she seemed to be silently pleading, but as usual, he couldn't. All his worthless hide could do was hold her hand and watch.

"She's losing too much blood," one of the nurses muttered to Dr. Mason at some point during the ordeal.

Adam would have lost his shit if it hadn't been for the group. While they weren't admitted all at once, occasionally the doctor would allow one of them to come in and hold Savannah's other hand. Clio was first, followed by Enwezor, then Sloane, then Clio again, and finally even Captain Marcus. Then Jillian came and shooed the rest of them out, and she'd been standing opposite Adam ever since, wiping Savannah's brow and murmuring soothing words over the laboring woman. Hearing the old woman's voice and knowing that his friends and companions were near, waiting and watching over Savannah with him, was the only solace Adam found as the hours dragged by, and words would never be able to express his gratitude.

He had no idea what time it was when Savannah finally cried out in a long, agonized wail and their daughter's head appeared between her bloody legs.

Adam watched, stricken and hopeful, as Savannah continued to push and Dr. Mason skillfully extracted the child.

His child. Their child.

Adam felt a swell of pride before he realized that the baby was a sickly shade of blue and looked somehow…*off*.

"What…what's wrong with her?" He stammered.

Dr. Mason was all business as he turned to one of the nurses. "Get me oxygen. You—go prepare an incubator. Quickly." He looked at Adam as he motioned for one of the other nurses to clip the umbilical cord. "She's not breathing on her own," he relayed. Then, to the nurse, who'd frozen in place and was staring at the newborn— "I said: *cut the cord.*" He kept a careful eye on the child after the umbilical cord was severed, but after nearly a minute, whatever change he was hoping for clearly didn't happen because he began doing tiny chest compressions on the blue newborn.

"Is…my baby…alive?" Savannah gasped, tears running down her pale face. Jillian squeezed her hand and wiped her brow, soothing the new mother as best she could, but Adam could see the fear in the old woman's eyes.

One of the nurses arrived and affixed a small oxygen mask to the baby's face, pumping air into the child whenever Dr. Mason said to do so. After nearly two agonizing minutes, during which Adam was sure he would also cease breathing, his daughter coughed and took her first rattling breath.

Dr. Mason leaned back and exhaled. "Get her to the incubator— quickly," he told one of the nurses. He looked at Savannah. "I need to try and stop the mother's internal bleeding."

Adam felt light-headed. "Internal bleeding?" He repeated daftly.

*I could lose them both,* he realized in a panic. *I could lose them both.*

The room swirled and suddenly Adam was falling. He had just enough awareness left to register that Clio had reentered the room and somehow caught him before he slipped into unconsciousness.

. . . . .

She was in the old Rangers archive room when Clio finally found her, her small frame pressed against the lone window as she stared out into the darkness of the night. She'd redone her bun, combed through the tangles and tied it up with a new piece of leather, but she was still wearing the clothes she'd had on the day before.

Clio walked towards her and held out the roll he'd taken from the kitchens. "Here," he said, tapping it against her arm. "You missed dinner."

Cody took it and looked up at him, her features suffused by the pale glow of moonlight. "So did you," she said, tearing it in half.

Clio took the smaller half and smiled. "Thanks, Ms. Reade. Good to know you have my back."

Cody smiled in return, but it was a fleeting gesture, and it didn't reach her eyes. "How's the baby?" She asked as she took a bite of the bread.

"Alive. She wasn't breathing at first, but Dr. Mason knows what he's doing. I think she's going to pull through." Savannah, on the other hand...

"What about Savannah?" Cody asked, as if she could read his mind.

Clio thought of his friend's pale, clammy face and weak heartbeat, his own heart sinking. "It's hard to tell at this point," he answered honestly. "But if anyone can pull through, it's Savannah. She's strong."

"Yeah," Cody agreed. "She's definitely a fighter. Like you." Her voice deepened slightly. "Like Mom."

"And like you," Clio added with a soft nudge to her arm. "You're your mother's daughter, Cody. Never forget that. Her strength lives on in you."

Cody nodded thoughtfully between bites and then grew quiet, once more directing her gaze out the window. "I made up my mind about something today," she said eventually, her voice soft.

Clio waited, knowing there was more to come.

"If you get kicked out of Ashland, I'm coming with you."

Clio's lips parted in surprise. "Cody..." He swallowed. "*If* that happens, and I'm hoping it doesn't, I don't know if that will be possible. As much as I'd want you with me, you'd be safer here. You have inner reserves of strength and courage that amaze me, but don't forget that you're still only six."

"Seven," Cody replied. "My birthday was last month. I missed it."

Clio didn't know what to say to that.

"And you're wrong." Cody turned to face him, her amber eyes filled with a determined resolve that reminded Clio of Maggie. "I used to think that walls kept people safe," she went on. "But they don't. Easthaven's gone, and Ashland or one of the other fortresses could be next."

"You don't know that, Cody," Clio reasoned gently.

"Not for sure," she countered, her eyes losing none of their fire. "But I bet I'm right, and I'd rather be outside with you than stuck in here if something bad happens." Her little eyebrows drew together, and, in a rare moment, she looked her age. "Please don't leave me behind, Clio."

The fear in her voice twisted at Clio's heart. He knelt down in front of her, placing a hand on her cheek. "Hey," he said. "You listen to me, Cody Reade. I made a promise to your mother that I would keep you safe, and I'm not one to break my promises. No matter what happens here, even if we get separated, it won't be for forever. You have my word that I will never leave you behind." He smiled. "Besides," he added huskily, "I couldn't even if I wanted to. You've got my heart, kid."

Cody's cheek began to wobble beneath his thumb, and then she walked forward and threw her arms around his neck, hugging him tightly. "I love you, Clio," she whispered.

Clio closed his eyes, momentarily overcome by the power those four whispered words had over him. Other than Savannah, it had been years since Clio had heard those words spoken to him, and the fact that this brave little girl was the one uttering them gave him strength, made him believe that maybe - just *maybe* - he was good enough, human enough, to live up to the promise he'd made to Maggie before she'd died in his arms.

*Now and always. I haven't forgotten, Maggie. I never will.*

"I love you too," he murmured into her mouse brown hair, squeezing her back.

They stayed like that for a moment, until, with a sniffle, Cody pulled away. She wiped at her eyes and crossed her arms. "I meant what I said, though. If you have to leave, then I'm going, too. Okay?"

Clio wanted to argue with her, but a sliver of intuition kept him from doing so. After all, walls *hadn't* kept them safe when Easthaven had fallen; if he left her here and morphs attacked...

He sighed, relenting. "Okay."

Cody didn't look convinced. "Do you swear it?"

"I swear it."

"On your bun?" She pressed, completely serious.

Clio chuckled and stood up. "Yes," he said. "I swear it on my bun."

Cody's shoulders relaxed slightly. "Good."

They stood in silence then, watching the dark world beyond the window, and Clio wondered if, like him, Cody missed the feeling of being out beyond the walls. There had been dangers everywhere and the entire journey west had been beyond harrowing, but there had been freedom in it, the likes of which one would never find in any of the fortresses.

*I wonder if it will ever be safe to live outside again.*

Long before Year Zero, Clio had lived on his parents' farm. First with his family, and later, after they'd died, with…a friend.

It had been a humble place that the previous generation of Jones's had cultivated themselves, and even though the acreage hadn't been impressive, that modest plot of land had brought Clio a lot of happiness over the years. It was funny, really, how a small barn, a smattering of livestock, and a lake stocked with fish could be the source of so many good memories, but that was the truth of it.

Clio would've traded nearly anything for one more day on that farm.

*Well,* he thought as he looked down at the somber little girl standing next to him, *almost anything.*

Maybe he would go back to his family's farm one day. Maybe he'd even get to show it to Cody. For now, though, there were other things to worry about.

"I'm going to go check on Savannah," he said into the stillness of the room. "You want to come?"

Cody shook her head, still gazing out into the dark. "I want to stay here a little bit longer."

"All right. Just do me one favor, okay?"

Cody glanced at him over her shoulder, raising an eyebrow.

"Check in with Jillian at a reasonable time. If I find out she had to wander all over this fortress looking for you again, I am not going to be happy. I might even let Sloane give you a spanking—I hear she's itching to break in her left hand."

Cody smirked. "She'd have to catch me first."

"Cody…"

The little girl sighed, but her smirk remained in place. "I'll go find Jillian soon and I'll stay with her tonight. I won't wander off. I promise."

"Fair enough." Clio smiled. "Goodnight, Ms. Reade," he said, and then he headed back down the way he'd come.

·  ·  ·  ·  ·

The pain was what brought Savannah back to agonized consciousness, and she gasped, her eyes fluttering open to a room that was too bright.

Instinct made her try and sit up, but the motion brought a tidal wave of knifelike sensations to her lower body that made her head reel and her jaw clench.

"Savannah?"

A hand was suddenly gripping hers, clammy and shaking.

She took a steadying breath and focused her gaze.

"Adam?"

Tears of relief sprang to her boyfriend's eyes and poured down his cheeks. "Oh my God, Savannah," he sobbed. "I thought...I thought..."

She smiled tremulously, touched by his raw emotion. "I'm okay," she managed. "Sore, but okay."

More of the room came into focus, as did the events that had led her there, and suddenly her calm was replaced by an overwhelming fear. She pressed Adam's hand where it gripped her own and licked her chapped lips. "Adam...where is our baby?" She asked. "Where is Olivia?"

Adam met her gaze, and his silence seemed to last an eternity.

Savannah felt like her world was crashing down as she waited, the worst of the worst running through her mind, the sudden fear eclipsing her physical pain completely as she waited. And waited.

Finally, Adam took a breath and spoke three words: "Olivia is alive."

Savannah sobbed. *My baby,* she thought, jubilant, *my baby is alive.* A laugh bubbled from her lips. "We did it, Adam," she said, her eyes filling with tears. "She made it. Our little girl made it."

Adam was quiet.

Savannah's jubilation started to dim. *Why isn't he overjoyed like me? What is going on?*

She swallowed. "Adam...tell me."

His brown eyes were troubled, but he held her gaze. "Olivia is alive," he repeated, "but there are...complications."

Savannah felt a stirring of irritation. Here she was – emotional, in pain, recovering from a pregnancy and birth that had almost killed her – and Adam was making her pry the truth from him one syllable at a time. "What complications, Adam?" She pushed. "Where is she? I want to see her. Tell me what's going on with our baby right now. Bring her to me. You know what—never mind. I'll just go see her myself." She started to push herself up and pain lanced through her again. "Shit," she cursed, wincing.

Adam stood up. "Just hold on, okay? I'll go get Dr. Mason. He…he'll be better at explaining everything." He looked down at her, his expression twisting. "Please just rest here, okay? You've been through so much. I'll get the doctor."

He was gone before she could argue, and Savannah sank back into her hospital cot, feeling more anxious and on edge than she ever remembered feeling before. All she wanted to do was see her baby. Hold her baby. Have Adam tell her it was okay, that everything was okay.

But clearly everything *wasn't* okay.

Adam was only gone a minute, but it felt like years had passed when he reappeared with Dr. Mason in tow.

The skinny doctor put a hand on Adam's shoulder, squeezed it briefly, and then moved past him and took the chair Adam had recently vacated.

"Firstly," he said, "I want you to know that Olivia is alive, and her vitals are healthy. There was instability at first, but I do think your daughter is going to pull through."

Savannah relaxed at his words, but only slightly.

"I feel like there is a huge 'but' coming," she murmured.

Dr. Mason nodded. "You're right," he said candidly. "There is." He took a breath. "Savannah, your daughter…she…well, she doesn't appear to be entirely human."

Savannah shrank at his words. "What is *that* supposed to mean?" The words came out in a rush of heated breath.

"Olivia wasn't responding as newborns usually do, so I ran some tests. The results were inconclusive, but she seems to have some strange abnormalities in her DNA."

"I don't understand."

"To be perfectly frank, neither do I," came the doctor's honest reply. "All I can tell you is that Olivia seems to share some cellular commonalities with the morph subjects I've studied."

The words were like stones. Savannah swallowed, but her throat was suddenly as dry and tight as a reed. "Are you saying my daughter is a...a...?" She couldn't finish the thought. She wouldn't.

Dr. Mason shook his head. "No—Olivia is not a morph. But she also isn't like any other human baby I've seen." He paused. "Savannah, I can't imagine how difficult it must be to process this, but I do need to ask you a question: did you sustain any injuries during your journey, anything that could have affected the pregnancy somehow?"

Fresh tears burned her eyes. "You're the doctor," she said, her voice trembling. "Shouldn't you have answers instead of questions?"

"I should," he conceded with a nod. He leaned forward in the chair. "This is uncharted territory for me," he admitted, "and I know it's not fair. But I do need you to answer my question. The more I know, the better chance I have at making sure Olivia survives these first few uncertain days."

Savannah glanced at Adam for support. He nodded his encouragement and offered her a small, pained smile. "Go on," he urged. "I'm here with you."

Savannah looked back at the doctor. "I was scratched," she said, guilt thickening the words. "During one of the attacks, a morph scratched me pretty badly." A tear rolled down her cheek. "I thought I was fine, though. I thought the baby was fine."

Dr. Mason reached out and gave her arm a gentle squeeze. "Where were you scratched?"

"Across my stomach." The sense memory made her wince. "I...it happened so fast."

"Do you remember feeling any differently after that? Did you notice any symptoms?"

Savannah nodded. "My pregnancy...I got sick a lot more. I couldn't keep food down."

A spark of something caught in the doctor's brown eyes. "Okay. Thank you, Savannah. Anything else?"

She racked her brain. "Not that I can think of at the moment..."

Dr. Mason squeezed her arm again. "That's fine. This information is very helpful." He stood and gestured to Adam. "Why don't you sit here with Savannah for a while?"

"Can I see my baby?" Savannah blurted out, interrupting him.

"Soon, yes. Right now, Olivia is still in the incubator and I have her hooked up to a machine that is helping to regulate her breathing. When it is safe to move her, I promise you will be the first to see her. If you're feeling up to it in a couple hours, you and Adam can go visit her."

"Can I visit her now?"

"Right now, you need to rest. It was a difficult birth, Savannah; as anxious as I can imagine you are to see your daughter, as a physician, I have to insist that you stay in bed for now. All right?"

She nodded.

Dr. Mason turned to Adam and said something else, but Savannah's mind was too busy churning to catch the words. A moment later, the doctor left, and Adam once more took the seat by her bed.

Feeling lost and small, Savannah reached out her hand. Adam gripped it tightly.

"Did I mess up our baby?" She asked.

Adam's free hand came up and stroked her cheek, brushing away her tears. "No. You saved our baby. No matter what happens, you remember that, okay?"

"Okay," she replied, not really believing it.

But then her guilt and anxiety were overshadowed by something else. "Adam?" She said, her voice the strongest it had been since she'd woken up. "Promise me something."

"Anything you need."

"If…if Olivia isn't fully…if she isn't like…like us, I need you to promise me that you'll protect her anyway. No matter what. Because I don't care what she is. She's our daughter and we need to keep her safe. Even if no one else understands. Even if everyone else is afraid. Can you promise me that? Will you help me keep our daughter safe?"

There was no pause in Adam's reply this time, no hesitation at all. He leaned forward, pressed a gentle kiss to her temple, and said: "I promise. No matter what."

•　•　•　•　•

The world was still there, but she shouldn't have been. She shouldn't have been able to feel the oxygen in her lungs, shouldn't have been able to smell the blood in the tubes around her, shouldn't have been able to open her eyes and see lights, colors, shapes...*life.*

The bleeds had taken her. She had died.

And yet as Aya took a second breath and blinked beneath the haze of the artificial lights above her, she was forced to accept reality as it was instead of reality as it should have been.

Somehow, some way, she was alive.

She could have spent days wrapped around that simple, impossible truth, but a slight ping in her awareness drew her attention and she glanced to her right, her claws instinctively shifting beneath the skin of her fingers.

There was a skinny man in medical scrubs standing by her bed, staring at her, his brown eyes wide and his mouth agape.

Obviously, she wasn't the only one surprised by the fact that she was alive.

The man recovered his composure after a moment. "You're awake," he stated, as if trying to convince himself that his eyes weren't deceiving him.

"Yes," Aya answered, testing her voice. "Alive and awake." It felt strange to speak, like the words were in her head but getting them to move from her brain to her lips required lassoing them and pulling them forth with great resistance.

The human moved towards her and Aya shrank back, readying herself for a fight.

The man paused when he noticed her defensiveness. "Forgive me," he said. "You must be so confused. I'm Dr. Mason, a physician at Fortress Ashland, which is where you are. Your friends brought you to me to treat your..." He pursed his lips. "Condition," he finally settled on. "I'm not going to hurt you, but now that you're awake, I would like to test a few basic responses and assess any damage you might have sustained as a result of your wounds. Will you allow me to do so?"

The simple courtesy he showed by asking assuaged Aya's immediate concern. She nodded.

He was gentle and kind, always asking before he touched her, always thanking her when she did what he asked—looking this way, turning her head just so, blinking into a light. Soon enough, the doctor finished the examination and stepped back, hastily jotting a few notes down onto the clipboard by her bed.

Aya swallowed, cringing slightly at the sawdust texture of her throat. "Does everything seem okay?" She asked.

Dr. Mason put the clipboard down and assessed her candidly. "Miraculously, yes. You seem to be healing quickly and completely."

Aya's gaze trailed down to the small bowl of earth where her heart was nestled, eyeing the tube protruding from it. "But my heart…"

"Yes." A small divot appeared between the man's brows. "It's Aya, right?"

Again, she nodded.

"Aya, I am a man of science. If I'm being honest, there is no way you should be awake and speaking with me right now. And I must confess that initially, the only reason I agreed to treat you was out of curiosity; I didn't harbor any hope that I could save you. But your friend Clio was so insistent…" The doctor shook his head. "When the treatment started to work, I was shocked. I've never seen anything like it."

Aya wanted the details, wanted to know exactly what had happened between her loss of consciousness and now, but before she could muster the words, a nurse appeared in the doorway.

"Dr. Mason," she said in a panic. "You need to come quick. It's that woman with the pregnancy complications. She…"

The doctor held up a hand. "Show me." He turned back briefly to Aya, just long enough for her to see that his kindly countenance had given way to a look of determination. "Rest. I'll be back later to check your vitals and answer any questions you might have."

*What's wrong with Savannah?* Aya wanted to ask, but the doctor disappeared through the door before she had a chance to.

After his footsteps faded, it grew quiet and stayed that way for a long time. Minutes and hours slipped by, and Aya's worries gathered and darkened like storm clouds in her head the longer she was left alone. Was Savannah okay? Had something happened to her unborn child? Was everyone else okay? Was Marcus…?

*Marcus.*

His name sparked an idea, one that Aya couldn't believe hadn't occurred to her sooner.

Closing her eyes, she pushed out through their connection, and…

*"Let me take her," Clio was saying. "Please."*

*"She's dead."*

*She was cradled in Marcus's arms, still and quiet, bathed in blood and rain, and Marcus was having trouble breathing past his shock.*

*"She isn't," Clio insisted. "Please. Let me take her."*

It was so real that Aya wanted to reach out and comfort him, but before she could hold onto it, the scene faded, and then they were inside Ashland, in the room Aya was now resting in.

*"I'm sorry." The same doctor she'd spoken to earlier was shaking his head. "She's…she's dead, there's nothing I can do."*

*Marcus drew his dagger and lunged forward, steel eyes wild and murderous, but Clio held him back. "Marcus, stop! Violence isn't the answer here." To the doctor, he said, "There's still time. We can use the blood bond to save her. I have an idea, please just hear me out…"*

Again, it changed:

*"You should get something to eat," Dr. Mason said. "Sitting here hour after hour will not change her recovery. I promise to come find you if anything changes."*

*Marcus didn't move. "I'm not leaving her." He was exhausted, physically and emotionally, but he wouldn't budge. He couldn't.*

*"Is there anything I can do to change your mind?" The doctor pressed.*

*The Reaper's answer was resolute. "No. I'm not leaving her," he said again.*

Once more, the scene shifted:

*Marcus was speaking to a Latina woman Aya had never seen before. She was young and pretty, and so angry that her rage was a palpable current. "Is it true?" She asked in a cold voice that belied her youth. "Do you love this vampire you've brought here?"*

*Marcus's hesitation was nearly nonexistent. "Yes."*

Aya gasped and opened her eyes, breathing hard. She was shaking slightly, and even her lower lip was trembling, her physical self as affected as if she'd been bodily traveling through Marcus's memories instead of witnessing them secondhand.

As soon as her mind stopped spinning, Aya assessed what had happened. Never – not once – had it been so easy to establish a connection between herself and Marcus. She had reached out and instantly been flooded with him: his feelings, his memories, his thoughts...they'd all been right there, slipping onto her like a second skin. And they'd been powerful, clear in a way they'd never been before, as though she were reliving her own memories. But even that didn't quite describe it, because the scenes hadn't felt like memories at all; they'd been almost tangible in their realness, as if she had been transported back to watch them as they occurred.

And he *loved* her.

Her cheeks warmed at the thought, her spirit soared, and her heart...

Understanding hit her as solidly as the arrow had.

Of course. It was Marcus's blood that had saved her, Marcus's blood that the doctor had pumped into her dying heart, Marcus's blood that must have undone the work of the arrow and reversed the bleeds. Her very essence had been mixed with his blood, and the strength of their blood bond had dramatically increased.

Again, Aya took a breath and reached out, but this time she did so gently, her will no more forceful than a whisper in the wind.

Images popped up, as before, but they weren't overwhelming, and instead of letting herself be pulled randomly, Aya searched for something that felt like now, until...

*"Go get some rest," Marcus was saying. "That's an order. I'll stay here with Adam until Dr. Mason is sure Savannah's stable again."*

*Enwezor and Sloane looked tired but unconvinced.*

*"Are you sure?"* Enwezor said. *"I could probably—"* he yawned *"— probably stay up a while longer."*

*"I'm sure. Go get some rest, Balogun. You too, Sloane."*


"How are you feeling?"

The question wasn't part of Marcus's conversation, but it took Aya a moment to return to herself.

When she opened her eyes, Dr. Mason was standing in front of her once more, holding a clear medical bag filled with blood in his hands.

"How is Savannah?" She countered, ignoring the doctor's initial question.

The black man smiled. "She's weak, and there was a recent scare, but she is stable now. I believe that she and her newborn will pull through."

"She had the baby?" Aya asked in surprise. "So early?"

The doctor's smile dimmed slightly. "Yes," he answered. "It wasn't an easy birth, and your friend Savannah lost a lot of blood, but mother and child are both alive." He sighed. "All I can say is that it's a good thing Savannah didn't go into labor on your journey. I'm not sure the outcome would have been the same." He shook his head as if to clear his thoughts, and then his small smile reappeared. "Now," he said, "how are *you?*"

"Fine," Aya answered. "Actually, I'd like to test my strength, if that's okay."

The doctor placed the blood bag next to her on the hospital bed. "I don't see any harm in that," he said. "But please, if you wouldn't mind, eat first. You haven't had anything since you arrived here."

"That's not really true," Aya replied, looking pointedly at her heart. "You used quite a bit of Marcus's blood to mend my heart."

The doctor's eyebrows rose. "You can tell it's his blood?"

"Yes. All blood is unique, to a certain extent, but Marcus's is...unmistakable."

Curiosity blossomed in the doctor's brown eyes. "Is that because of the blood bond you share? Would other vampires share your opinion of his blood?"

Aya remembered hunters talking about the taste of a Reaper's blood as though it were some kind of divine elixir, but how much of that had been speculation and male posturing versus legitimate truth remained a mystery. After all, no one in her clan had ever actually tasted a Reaper's blood...until her. "I don't know," she answered truthfully. "Although I suspect that no one else would feel exactly as I do. Blood bonds are rare things."

To dissuade him from asking any more questions at present, Aya propped herself up to a seated position, pushed the covers off, and eased her legs over the side of her hospital bed. To her surprise, aside from a few residual aches and pains, she didn't feel particularly weak. And when she put weight on her feet and stood, she didn't experience even a hit of dizziness. She felt almost refreshed.

A bolt of concern shot through her. "How much blood did you take from Marcus?"

"A little less than one liter, which is more than I normally would have taken from any one person, but not enough to put him at any risk. And I made sure he replenished his fluids throughout the course of the extractions. Why do you ask?"

Aya took a few steps across the room. "Because I feel...strong. Stronger than I've felt in a long time."

"Well," the doctor went on as she began to lap the room, "how much on average were you feeding prior to now?"

Aya paused. "I suppose..." She trailed off, thinking. Aside from Marcus, she'd only accepted blood twice when she'd been with the group of vampires, and before she'd joined up with the humans, her diet had subsisted mostly of animals and scavenging. "I suppose I've been blood rationing on and off for the last few years," she realized with some surprise.

Dr. Mason frowned. "Is that normal?"

"No. But finding fresh blood sources is very difficult these days. Morph blood makes vampires sick, and humans are locked in their fortresses, so aside from vampires drinking from one another, animals are really the only viable food source. And that's only if they're uninfected."

"Interesting. I'd love to speak with you in more detail about all of this at some point, if you'd be willing to talk to me. I've never treated a vampire before, and I feel that there is so much I could learn just by talking with you."

Aya sensed that he was being genuine, and she gave him a smile. "I'd be happy to," she said. "You saved my life; answering a few questions seems like the least I can do."

"Thank you, Aya." He pointed to the all-but-forgotten blood bag. "I'll leave you now, but please consider eating. Even if you feel strong, you've been through quite an ordeal and I'm sure your body is craving nutrients."

Aya eyed the red contents warily as the doctor left. She didn't particularly want the blood and she didn't like the idea of drinking something when she didn't know its source, but perhaps he was right: her body still needed blood.

She got through three mouthfuls before she put it down, grimacing. It tasted like thick, cold sludge sliding down her throat, and she wasn't sure she could stomach any more.

"Aya?"

She hadn't realized just how desperately she'd missed Marcus's voice until she heard it. She turned, her eyes filling with tears at the sight of him.

"Hi," she said lamely, a tremulous smile touching her lips, and then they were moving towards each other, drawn like magnets.

Aya wrapped her arms around him, squeezing him tightly, though she noticed his grip on her was much looser. "I won't break," she whispered, and she smiled as she felt him pull her closer.

They stayed like that for a long time, just holding each other, and Aya could feel Marcus's relief and happiness as strongly as she felt her own, their bond heightening the sense of comfort and joy both of them were feeling in their moment of reunion.

Aya blinked her tears away as they finally pulled apart. She looked up, surprised to find Marcus's steel eyes full of emotion as well. "I thought I lost you," he said, tenderly stroking the side of her face.

Aya covered his hand with hers. "I'm only here because of you," she murmured. "You saved my life, Marcus."

As always, the Reaper shrugged off her gratitude. "Clio and Dr. Mason had more to do with it than I did," he replied. "I just supplied the blood." He let his hand fall from her face and glanced over at her heart and the partially full blood bag. "And not enough of it, apparently."

"Dr. Mason brought that for me in case I needed it, but honestly, your blood healed me. I feel strong, and that stuff…" She made a face. "Well, it doesn't taste the best. And it isn't fresh."

Marcus chuckled. "I had no idea you were such a picky eater, vampire," he teased.

Aya felt a smirk tugging at her lips. "I guess you've spoiled me, Reaper." Her levity settled somewhat. "How is Savannah?" She asked.

"She lost a lot of blood, but she was awake when I left and is doing okay. So is the baby, it seems, although I know Dr. Mason is still running tests. And thanks to Clio, Adam won't have a lump on his head."

"What happened to Adam?"

Marcus rolled his eyes. "Never mind. The important thing is, as long as Savannah stays stable, she, Adam, and Olivia are going to be fine. Which, given everything, is kind of a miracle," he added.

*Olivia must be the baby*, Aya realized.

"Would you like to see them?" Marcus asked.

Aya nodded. "I would. I would also like to leave the hospital for a while, if you think Dr. Mason won't mind. I'm tired of feeling like a patient."

Marcus shrugged. "What the doc doesn't know won't hurt him. C'mon."

They looked in on Savannah first, who was sleeping again, and while she looked thin and pale, her chest was rising and falling in a consistent pattern and her heartbeat sounded steady, which put Aya at ease somewhat.

The newborn was in a different room, in a machine Marcus called an incubator, which apparently helped babies who couldn't yet breathe on their own or had other complications. Like her mother, Olivia was sleeping, her small pale form occasionally moving as she clutched at the air with her tiny fingers.

It was one of the most beautiful things Aya had ever seen, a miracle of nature.

*How was there ever a time I wished death on all of humanity?*

"Are you okay?" Marcus asked when he noticed how quiet she'd gotten.

Aya shook her troubled thoughts away. "Yes," she answered. "She's just so...so..."

"Amazing?"

Aya smiled. "Yes. Seeing her there, I feel like it gives meaning to everything we endured over the past months. It gives me hope for the future."

Marcus nodded. "Me too," he said. He glanced around the room. "Still want to get out of here?" He asked under his breath.

Aya nodded, and she followed Marcus as he led her from the room and down a series of hallways. He always checked to make sure no one was around first before motioning her forward, which made Aya think that Dr. Mason wouldn't, in fact, have been okay with her leaving medical, but she didn't complain about Marcus's rule breaking. If anything, she was grateful for it.

Before they got to the entrance, however, Marcus glanced over his shoulder at her. "Is it okay to leave your heart here?" He asked.

Aya smiled inwardly at his naiveté. "As long as my heart is touching earth and out of the sunlight, it will be fine. I don't need it with me all the time, as you already know."

Guilt flashed across Marcus's face and Aya instantly regretted her choice of phrasing. "I didn't mean it like that," she assured him.

Still, the guilt didn't completely ease from his features until they'd arrived at their apparent destination.

They were standing in front of a door that simply read TEMP Q22.

"What is this place?" Aya asked.

"My room, for the time being," Marcus answered. He retrieved a key from his pants pocket and turned it in the lock. "I'd take you for a tour of Ashland, but given the climate right now, I think it's best if we keep you more or less out of sight." He gave her an apologetic look as he held the door open for her, but Aya understood; she wasn't a welcome guest here. Dr. Mason may have treated her kindly, but the arrow that had pierced her heart was proof that others weren't as ready to let her in.

The accommodations were simple but clean, the room furnished with a bed, chair, desk, standing lamp, and small dresser. Jocelyn's boomerang was resting on the desk, but other than that, Marcus hadn't adorned the room with any personal effects. And just as in the medical facility, there were no windows. It gave the room a somewhat cell-like feel, but it was still more comfortable and private than her hospital bed.

Aya hadn't really moved into the room, so Marcus walked past her and opened the top drawer of the three-drawer dresser, pulling out a bath towel and a pair of drawstring pants identical to the ones he was currently wearing. He handed both to her. "There's a shower room down the hall," he said by way of explanation. "I know Dr. Mason did his best to clean you up, but I don't think he managed to get all of the blood and dirt off of you. I know there aren't any showers in the medical facility, so I thought you might want to make use of one of the showers here."

At his words, Aya realized just how dirty she was. She could feel dried blood on her skin, along with other souvenirs of the mud and bleeds she'd encountered at Ashland's gates. She grimaced and took the proffered towel and pants. "A shower would be lovely," she said, feeling slightly embarrassed.

To her surprise, Marcus chuckled. "Save your embarrassment. Everyone in our group was more mud than man when we got here, and considering the fact that you literally came back from the brink of death, I think you get even more of a pass than the rest of us." He rummaged in the second drawer and pulled out a slightly wrinkled crew neck t-shirt. "Here." He tossed it to her without looking, and Aya caught it instinctively. "It's the only other shirt I have, or I'd offer you something nicer."

Aya added it to her bundle and clutched it to her chest. "It's fine," she assured him.

Marcus showed her where the showers were, handed her a bar of soap, and then stood there, staring at her with a bemused expression on his face.

"Marcus?" Aya said questioningly.

"Sorry," he murmured. "I just…" He gave her a look reminiscent of one she'd seen only once before, one that softened his features and made him appear almost boyish. "It's still hard to believe that you're here, that you're okay. I never thought…" He cleared his throat. "Sorry," he mumbled again. "I'll, uh, leave you to it."

Aya watched him shuffle down the hall and round the corner before she stepped into the shower room and closed the doors. There were three stalls, and she chose the one closest to the back wall since it had a shelf big enough for her towel and both her clean and soiled clothes.

She'd never worked a shower before (her clan hadn't had such modern amenities), and once she finally figured out the mechanism, the force of the spray startled her, making her jump as water suddenly gushed out and pelted against her exposed skin. Once she got used to it, however, the rhythmic flow of water felt good on her tensed, knotted muscles, and she ended up standing there for a few long minutes before it even occurred to her to wash herself.

The soap smelled faintly of lemon, which wasn't Aya's favorite scent, but she scrubbed every inch of herself with it anyway, from the roots of her hair down to the mud-caked space between her toes, washing away weeks of grime and blood until the water running down the drain finally ran clear again, and then she soaped herself up one more time just to be sure.

She took her time drying herself off, too, seeing as it had been years since she'd been able to pamper herself this way. For once, she had time and quiet and solitary space, and she took the opportunity to enjoy the sound of the towel rustling against her scalp and the sight of water droplets slowly rolling down her body. By the time she dressed herself in the clothes Marcus had provided, Aya was feeling more relaxed than she had since the nights in her formative years when her grandmother would sing her to sleep.

Marcus was still awake when she returned to his room, sitting on the lone chair and staring down at his hands. He glanced up as she entered, his distracted focus clearing slightly as he took in the sight of her.

Aya placed the folded bundle she'd made of the towel and her dirty clothes on his dresser and then walked over to the side of the bed closest to his chair and sat down facing him, feeling a strange, nostalgic kind of déjà vu that reminded her of their time at the cabin.

"You're troubled about something," she stated.

Marcus sighed. "Yeah."

Aya thought back to the images she'd seen when she'd tapped into their blood bond earlier, and the memory of the young woman sprang instantly to mind. "Does it have something to do with the angry woman you were speaking with?" She guessed.

Marcus's head snapped up. "You know about that?"

"Only fragments. Our bond…" She thought of how to put. "I think our bond is stronger now that your blood has been infused directly into my heart—at least on my end. It isn't just feelings and sensations that I can pick up on; it seems to be memories and experiences too."

"I see." Marcus's expression soured. "So how much of that conversation did you wind up hearing?"

*Do you love this vampire?*

Aya clasped her hands and stared down at them, letting her damp hair fall forward into her face. "Not much."

Marcus snorted in reply. "Blood bond aside, you really are a terrible liar, Aya."

Aya forced herself to meet his gaze. "I'm not lying. I didn't hear much, just enough to know that she was angry with you."

"Angry is an understatement. Kai is livid, and part of me can't blame her for it."

"Kai?"

Marcus's gaze was almost wary, as if he didn't really want to tell her. But he still did. "Kai Ramirez. She's the commander of the Guard." He paused. "She's also Jocelyn's younger sister."

*Oh.* Aya shifted slightly. "Is it…is it because of me?" She asked, thinking of how hostile the woman had been when asking Marcus about his feelings.

A pained look flitted across Marcus's already unhappy face. "Yes." He exhaled harshly, running a hand through his hair. "Kai hates vampires because of what they did to her sister and brother, and after she told me the details regarding Jocelyn's death, I…" His voice broke, and Aya felt his emotional turmoil acutely as he continued. "I didn't know how it happened until today. My uncle, he—he never told me, but he told Kai, and...now I know." He swallowed. "I wish I could unhear it," he admitted wretchedly.

Aya knew better than to ask for details.

"But Kai," he went on, "she's lived with this for seven years, and I get it. Grief, anger, guilt, sorrow, blame...it's easy to funnel all of that shit into hatred, and that's what Kai's done. Hating vampires is what's kept her going all these years, and I can't blame her for feeling that way."

The fragment she'd heard out of context was beginning to make sense now. "But she's blaming you for *not* feeling that way," Aya surmised.

"Yes." Marcus looked up at her. "She blames me. She looked up to me, and now I've shown up on her turf with one of the creatures responsible for murdering her family. You may not have had anything to do with Jocelyn's death, but all Kai cares about, all she can see, is that you're a vampire. She called me a traitor to my own kind for bringing you here, for defending you to her."

Aya could tell how much that pained him, and not just because of their blood bond; the anguish was etched all over his face.

"I'm sorry," she murmured, meaning it. "I never meant to be a source of contention between you and anyone you care about."

"You don't need to be sorry," Marcus said immediately. "None of this is your fault." His expression softened. "Before I met you, I *was* Kai. Hatred was what kept me going, and my single-mindedness about butchering your kind was the only thing that kept me from drinking myself into an early grave. But now...now I know how empty it all was."

His words were a balm to Aya's anxiety. "You're not the only one. I hated your people just as much." She could still remember that awful night with vivid clarity, when she'd stood watch over the burning pyre of her clan's remains and vowed to make the humans pay for what they'd done.

She shook off the remembered loneliness and emptiness with a small shudder. "You changed the way I see the world, too," she admitted.

"But Kai wasn't with us," Marcus said. "And neither were the people of Ashland. We've changed, but let's face it: nothing else has."

*Not yet.* "Just because we were the first doesn't mean that we'll be the last," Aya reasoned. "Sometimes change happens one person at a time."

Marcus glanced over at her, looking doubtful. "You really believe that?"

Aya thought of Solomon. "Yes," she answered. "I really do." She stood up. "Dr. Mason must be wondering where I am by now," she began with some reluctance. "I should probably—"

"Stay." Marcus stood up and walked over to her. "So the good doctor might be looking for you. So what?" His eyes were fierce. "After everything Ashland has put you through, I think you're allowed to fuck with their protocols a little."

Unconsciously, Aya's gaze shifted to the bed, and Marcus noticed, jumping to his own conclusions. He took a step back, giving her space. "I'm not..." The fierceness in his eyes faded to chagrin. "I'm not expecting anything, Aya. I swear I'm not. I just..." He gave her a telling look.

*I just want you close.*

She heard it even though he hadn't spoken it, and it was a sentiment that mirrored her own feelings. "I'll stay," she said.

Marcus's relief was almost palpable, despite the fact that he shrugged it off with a simple "okay".

Aya eyed him for a moment as he stood there, and then she made a decision. She closed the distance between them and brought her hands up to his chest.

Marcus breathed into her touch, and Aya could feel the steady, rich beat of his heart beneath her palms. She curled her fingers into his shirt.

"Aya?" Marcus's voice was questioning, and when she met his gaze, it was filled with uncertainty and a spark of something else, something she'd seen at the cabin and again after they'd shared a kiss. It might have been indefinable, but that look made her throat go dry just as it had before.

Urged on by a strange stirring in the pit of her stomach, Aya slid her hands up and wound them around his neck, and then, slowly, she closed the rest of the distance between them and, stretching up on her tiptoes, gently pressed her lips to his.

Marcus pulled back, even as his hands came to rest on her hips, the contradictory motions mirrored in the warring tide of his eyes.

Aya knew what he was asking. "You said there was more, Marcus," she murmured into the stillness of the room. She leaned in again and brushed her lips over his in a whisper of a touch. "Show me more," she said, surprised at the huskiness of her own voice.

She felt Marcus's heart stutter as if it were her own. "Are you sure?" He whispered back.

"Yes. Please."

Marcus's grip on her hips, at first uncertain, now tightened as his fingers anchored onto her, and without another word, he captured her lips with his.

Aya slanted her mouth against his and opened to him, her lips parting as she felt his tongue pressing against their seam, and while he was gentle at first, the second Aya made a small sound in the back of her throat, the mood shifted.

Marcus yanked her body against his so hard that Aya could feel every ridge of his muscular frame, and the gentle prods of his tongue became insistent, needy, as though he were trying to drink her in. It was exciting in a way Aya had never felt before, and she arched into it, seeking more, needing more. She moaned into Marcus's mouth as she felt his hands move from her hips and continue south, uttering a little gasp as he cupped the curve of her backside and dragged her flush against him.

Their mouths broke apart as Marcus nibbled down her chin and neck and latched onto her jugular, his teeth scraping along the places his tongue traveled, his lips sucking at her as though he were trying to feed.

Aya's fangs stirred at the sensation and her hips rocked involuntarily against Marcus's, and she gasped again as she felt the growing bulge in his pants, her cheeks flushing as she realized what it was.

Marcus made a sound against her throat that was more growl than groan, and he hoisted her up, guiding her legs to wrap around his waist as he moved them to the bed.

He laid her down gently and made to move away, but Aya wasn't ready for the loss of contact, and she grabbed at him, pulling him down above her. She registered his surprise even as he chuckled against her, but his chuckles turned to curses as she rocked her hips against his and let the very tip of her fangs skate along the skin of his neck.

She could feel him fighting for control, and she rebelled against it, using their blood bond to convey her hunger.

*Lose control,* she urged as she found his lips again. *Let go,* she begged as she lifted one of her legs around his hip and instinctively opened herself further to him.

She felt his desire growing, physically and through their bond, and the voracity of it was so intense that Aya felt herself growing damp. She moaned, and Marcus's hand came up behind her raised leg and grabbed the back of her knee, angling her *just* so…

Aya's whole body seemed to flush as the change in angle made her feel something entirely new, as the rigidness and weight of him rubbed against the dampening part of her she'd only ever touched on her loneliest nights. Spots danced in front of her eyes, and she rocked against him without prompting, wanting, *needing* the friction he'd teased her with.

Marcus let her, pushing back against her as he took her mouth with a vengeance, his tongue probing deeper and deeper, thrusting against hers in a way that could only be described as carnal.

But just as Aya began to feel something building within her, Marcus ripped himself away, propping himself up on his arms and putting a few inches between them.

He was breathing hard and his eyes were blown black, shining down at her with a mixture of desire and hunger that made Aya squirm, but he held her at bay when she reached for him.

"Do you trust me?" He asked.

Aya reached up and put her hand on his cheek. "You know I do, Marcus," she answered honestly.

Marcus closed his eyes at her touch and took a breath, and then he rocked back on his heels. "Sit up for me," he said.

She did, but her nerves got the better of her when his hands moved to the hem of her t-shirt. "I've...I've never..." She licked her lips. "There's never been anyone," she admitted quietly.

The look of surprise that flitted across Marcus's face was fleeting, and then he leaned forward and kissed her gently, soothing her fears. "Let me show you," he said, his hands once more catching the hem of her shirt.

This time, Aya let him pull it over her head.

Marcus was so quiet and still that, if it hadn't been for the blood bond, it would have been hard to discern what he was thinking as he gazed upon her bare form, but Aya could feel something akin to awe flowing between them, and all her embarrassment faded away.

Gently, Marcus pressed her down again into the coverlet, his hands beginning to trail down her form with such light touches that Aya had to arch into them to increase the skin-to-skin contact. His mouth followed, tracing the lines he made with his hands, kissing over her skin from her collarbone to her navel. He didn't touch her breasts the first time, so when his mouth suddenly latched onto a nipple, Aya cried out, feeling an answering gush of wetness below as his finger tweaked the other.

"Marcus..." She whispered.

She felt him smile against her skin as he switched breasts and then continued downwards, and she shivered when she felt his breath at the waistband of the drawstring pants. Like two hooks sure of their prize, Marcus curled his fingers into her pants and began to push them down, moving slightly to slip them off of her feet when they tangled around her ankles.

She was bare beneath the pants, and even though she wanted Marcus to see her, she felt nervous butterflies take wing in her stomach as his eyes roved over her nakedness. And when his hand trailed towards the place that was already wet with want for him, Aya squeaked and sat up, trapping his hand between her thighs.

Understanding blossomed in Marcus's lust-filled eyes. "Relax, Aya," he breathed, his lips rubbing along her jawline and finding her ear. He nibbled it gently, making her shiver. "Open for me," he whispered.

She obeyed, slowly, staring at him with sinful innocence. He held her gaze as his long fingers found her, as he touched her. She gasped, and then she leaned her head back, her eyes fluttering shut as he began rubbing her in small circles.

Her body began to tighten, and her fangs began to ache, and when Marcus smeared some of her wetness lower and dipped a finger inside of her, Aya's mouth opened in an involuntary cry.

Marcus caught her cry in a kiss, gently stroking her tongue with his as he continued to move his fingers over her and inside of her. By the time he added a second finger, Aya was squirming, moaning into his mouth as she tried to rock against his hand.

Abruptly, Marcus slipped his fingers away from her, but before Aya could feel disappointment, Marcus slid down her body and replaced his fingers with his mouth.

Aya bucked against him, her hips jerking so violently that Marcus had to use his hands to still them. Once he had her thighs securely pinned, he began to drink from her, his tongue sweeping against her in flat strokes and circles, alternating pressure and speed. Aya watched him at first, marveling at how erotic it was to watch him kiss her there, wondering if she looked as erotic when she drank from his neck.

When he began to use his fingers in conjunction with his mouth, however, Aya fell back against the bed, overcome with the overload of sensation.

And then, suddenly, the tightening in her body reached a tipping point and everything began to uncoil in a brilliant, unexpected shock wave that ripped a startled gasp of pleasure from Aya's throat and drew an answering, shocked groan from Marcus.

When she was able to blink her eyes open however much later, she saw Marcus staring at her with that same boyish wonder she'd seen earlier. His body was shaking as much as hers, and she could hear the stutter of his heart.

"Did you feel that?" She asked, her voice breathy in a way it had never been before.

Marcus nodded. "That's never..." He shook his head. "I *felt* you, Aya, almost like I was the one..." He shuddered. "I didn't realize the bond was so strong for me," he added. "But..." He looked down at her, the boyishness leaving his features as his hunger returned. "I want you." The words were both certain and supplicating, spoken with dark fervor. "So fucking much."

Aya leaned up and kissed him. She could taste herself on his tongue, but despite the strangeness, it only fueled her desire. Mimicking what he'd done to her earlier, Aya reached for his pants and began to push them down. Marcus helped her, standing up briefly to kick them off and toss his shirt over his head.

Through the haze of their combined need, Aya felt a brief swell of tenderness at the sight of Marcus's scarred skin, her eyes drawn to all of the reminders of the suffering he'd endured. The only other time she'd seen his bare form, he'd been asleep, but now, Marcus crawled towards her and once more eased her down on the bed. "It's all right," he said, knowing where her train of thought had gone. "We all have our fair share of scars."

Aya gently trailed her hand over the faint white lines on his neck. "But you've suffered more than most," she said, compassion making the words stick in her throat. "Enough for a lifetime."

Marcus caught the hand that was touching his scars and brought it to his lips. "So have you," he murmured as he kissed her knuckles. "But here we are." He released her hand and reached down between them, teasing her with a practiced hand until fresh wetness began to coat his fingers. He kept his eyes on her the whole time, his dark gaze riveted to her face, watching her reactions as he stirred her desire.

When Aya felt him change positions, parting her legs with his own and settling between them, she shuddered in naive anticipation. Marcus rubbed himself against her and Aya bit her lip to suppress a whine, caging it behind her teeth as a wave of pleasure rocked through her.

"*Please...*" She breathed, not really knowing what she was asking for but knowing she needed it. She was aching, empty, wanting, the dual nature of her hunger threatening to drive her mad if Marcus didn't find a way to satisfy her craving.

And then he moved lower, pressing into her instead of along her outer lips, and Aya's breath caught as she felt him gain entry and push deeper. He was gentle and slow, moving inch by inch as her body stretched in an unfamiliar way, soothing her with open-mouthed kisses to her neck as she tensed beneath him and murmuring words of encouragement as she gradually relaxed.

Aya felt fuller than she'd ever felt as he at last settled completely within her. Her lips trembled. "Marcus…"

He pulled out just as slowly, almost completely leaving her body before he once more pressed home. He repeated the motion, continuing at the halting, frustratingly slow pace until Aya raised her hips and let her fangs descend.

Her eyes flashed as she caught his gaze. *More,* she demanded. *Give me more.*

She channeled her desire through their blood bond, sending a surge of lust through their connection, and Marcus's already dark gaze turned animalistic. He thrust into her much harder than he had initially, drawing a satisfied gasp from Aya's lips, and then he was moving faster, more violently than before.

It still wasn't enough.

Aya's fangs were burning, itching to pierce and drink, the need so dire that it was almost painful.

Marcus drove himself deep and paused, her desire mirrored in his eyes. "Do it," he growled between his teeth. "Please…"

Aya leaned up and found his jugular, pressing her mouth over the lines the morph had left. *No one gets to mark you but me,* she thought, and then she opened her mouth wide and sank her fangs in deep.

The answering moan that tore from Marcus's throat was so broken and intimate that Aya couldn't help but suck greedily from the pinpricks she'd made, but even then, she nearly lost her hold on him as Marcus began to move inside of her with abandon. His thrusts grew shorter and faster until he was pounding into her at a blinding pace, and Aya drank from him until the world began to spin around her.

She could hear the sounds of their joining in her ears, could hear their mingled breaths and groans and the frenzied drumbeat of Marcus's heart, and the feeling of drinking from him while he took her so ruthlessly was indescribable. Both of them possessing each other, both of them being possessed...Aya had never felt anything even close to it before.

When Marcus began to swell within her, Aya drew her fangs from his neck to release a pent-up cry, and then she dug her fingers into his shoulders as Marcus hoisted her legs up higher on his back and pushed himself as deeply inside of her as he could go. He thrust into her two more times and then spasmed, the force of his release triggering her own and pushing Aya over the edge a second time.

They stayed like that for a suspended moment, joined as deeply as possible, pressed flush against each other and panting, both of them coated with a sheen of sweat. Pleasurable aftershocks pulsed through Aya, and she could feel Marcus's as well, as fiercely as if they were natural extensions of her own.

When his heartbeat slowed slightly, Marcus pulled back and slipped himself out of her, making Aya whimper as he slid against her hypersensitive flesh.

She gazed up at him through a haze. "Is it...always like that?" She asked.

"No," Marcus said eventually. "It's not. This was..." He ran a hand through his mussed hair as he rolled off of her and sat up. "Something different." He touched his fingers to the tiny pinpricks on his neck. They were still dripping blood, and his fingers came away red.

Aya sat up and reflexively grabbed his hand, licking his fingers clean. Marcus watched her, shuddering as her tongue slid up and down his index finger. "Careful," he said, his voice little more than a rasp.

Aya licked her lips and gave him a wicked smile. She could feel the spark of desire her actions had caused, and she relished it more than she thought she would. "Or what?" She teased.

"Are you sure you feel healed?" He asked.

Aya wasn't sure what he was getting at. "Yes," she assured him. "I told you earlier, I feel fine. Strong."

A dark smile teased at the corners of his lips. "Good," he said, and then he tossed her onto all fours with a surprising show of strength and proceeded to show her exactly what 'or what' entailed.

. . . . .

It was impossible to tell what time it was when she woke up, but Aya guessed that a good number of hours must have passed between now and whenever she and Marcus had finally fallen into an exhausted sleep after…

She sat up in bed, a lazy smile forming on her face as she took in the sight of the rumpled bed sheets and the sprawled form of Marcus sleeping next to her. He was facedown, his limbs stretched out haphazardly, and his mop of overgrown hair was sticking out like someone had zapped it with an electric current. Knowing that her hair was most likely in a similar state of disarray only made Aya's smile widen.

Her small movements roused Marcus, and he blinked his eyes open, glancing up at her sleepily before he sighed and pushed himself up to a seated position. "Morning," he rasped.

"Good morning."

The expression on his face held a peaceful kind of familiarity as he looked at her, and it made Aya think of something she'd meant to ask him the other day.

Marcus sensed that she had a question before she voiced it. "What is it?" He asked.

Aya shifted slightly on the bed. "I told you I didn't overhear much of your conversation with Kai, and that was true. But I did hear something I wanted to ask you about." She swallowed. "Kai asked if you…if you…" She couldn't get the words past her lips. Even after everything they'd been through over the past few months, even after the intimacy they'd shared last night, and even though she'd heard it secondhand, Aya still feared that her own feelings wouldn't be reciprocated.

*And where will we go from here if he doesn't feel the same way I do?*

The possibilities scared her.

"Aya."

Reluctantly, she met his gaze.

"Just tell me what's bothering you. I promise I'll be honest with you, no matter what it is."

*That's what I'm afraid of.*

She took a breath. "Kai asked—"

Two urgent knocks sounded on Marcus's door.

Both of them jumped a little, the suddenness of the intrusion startling them. When two more knocks sounded, they clambered out of bed, hastily pulling on their discarded clothes from the previous night.

Aya barely had time to smooth her hair down before Marcus opened the door.

Dr. Mason was standing there, and Aya could tell, just from the urgent, panicked look on his face, that he wasn't there with good news.

He looked past Marcus without saying anything to him. "Aya," he called to her. "You need to come with me now. If you don't, they'll send soldiers for you and drag you out of here in chains."

Aya felt her fangs and claws stir at the implied threat. "What?" She gasped, startled. "Why?"

"You're to face a tribunal today," he said. "Depending on the outcome, the Council will then decide what to do with you."

Marcus barred the door with his arm. "Like hell that's going to happen," he snarled at the smaller man. "Let the soldiers come. I can already tell you who will win that fight."

The doctor didn't back down in the face of Marcus's hostility. "Please listen to me," he insisted. "I know this is a terrible situation, but if Aya doesn't come willingly, this will turn into a blood bath." He paused. "And even if you do win," he continued when Marcus made no move to yield, "the people will deem you – *all* of you – a threat and vote to have every single Easthaven survivor turned out. You'll doom your entire group."

Aya put a hand on Marcus's arm. "He's right, Marcus. We need to do this their way."

Marcus shot her a look like she was crazy. "And then what, Aya? Let them decide to give you the bleeds a second time?"

Aya swallowed against her rising fear. "We'll plead my case and tell our story," she said. She looked at Dr. Mason, searching for a silver lining. "Do you think there is a chance I will be pardoned?" She asked levelly.

There was no hesitation in his answer, but the flatness in his brown eyes belied the hope he tried to give her. "Yes, I do. There are a great many stubborn people here, but there are also people with vision who will listen to you with open ears. I believe you have a chance. What you don't have," he added firmly, "is a choice."

Aya nodded and pried Marcus's arm away from the door. "Then I'll come with you," she said to the doctor, which elicited a bout of vehement protestations from Marcus.

She turned back to him and silenced him with a look. "We've been through worse," she said, trying to be brave.

*Bullshit,* his eyes screamed, but he nodded tersely. "I'll go talk to the others. We'll come up with a game plan to get you out of this shit."

"We have to go *now*," Dr. Mason insisted.

Aya took a steadying breath. "Very well," she said, and she followed the doctor out into the hallway, trying to resist the urge to run, to fight, even as her sense of intuition filled her with the sickening feeling that she wasn't really heading to a trial.

She was heading to an execution.

# The Trial

*Truth is so often simply that which we choose to believe; truth is rarely a reflection of things as they are.*
- Reflection taken from the prison diary of Nadya Beaumont, former Reaper of the Original Order and condemned traitor, dated 450 B.M.

. . . . .

The courtroom was buzzing with excitement, the large circular space packed like never before. People were crammed into the three civilian sections like sardines, scrunched shoulder to shoulder, and the latecomers were standing in the aisles, wedged into every available inch of space. Some of the more aggressive onlookers were pushing their way down towards the rows closest to the center of the courtroom, causing others to stumble and curse as they bulled their way through.

Dazed by the deafening din and the air of excitement permeating the space, Charlotte simply allowed Nancy to tug her along by the arm, following blindly.

She was so distracted by the chaos around them that she only realized Nancy had come to a stop when she bumped into the other girl.

"Hey," Nancy said, casting her an angry look. "Watch it!"

"Sorry," Charlotte murmured.

They were in the very top row, far from the center of activity, and it wasn't until Nancy beckoned for Charlotte to step up onto the bench that she was able to see anything.

The adults closest to the girls gave them disapproving looks, but no one told them to leave, and Charlotte swallowed down her anxiety.

*We're not going to get in trouble,* she tried to convince herself. *It's going to be fine.*

No one under the age of sixteen had been invited to the trial, but she and Nancy weren't the only underage children to sneak in. As Charlotte gazed around the room, she spotted some of their classmates and friends sandwiched between the older adults, hiding in plain sight, and no one was scolding them or escorting them out. And Charlotte knew why: the simple fact was that no one wanted to miss out on the most exciting thing to happen since Ashland had shut its gates six years ago.

Feeling more at ease about their rule breaking, Charlotte turned her attention to the doors at the top of the courtroom to their right, watching as they opened and the Council members began to file in. The men entered first, dressed in their black robes, followed by the women, filling in the rows from the bottom to the top but leaving the lowest row empty, as was customary. Once they were all seated, Governor Mason appeared, heavy gavel in hand, followed by Commander Ramirez and Commander Hale.

They took the front row, and Governor Mason held up his hand. The cacophony dwindled to a susurrus and then ceased, and once everyone had fallen silent, the governor and commanders took their seats, and the civilians followed suit.

Charlotte and Nancy sat down too, though Charlotte sat on her knees, needing the extra few inches of height to see past the taller people sitting on the row directly below her. From a hidden door at the bottom of the courtroom, a guard entered.

Governor Mason nodded to him, and the man disappeared. A moment later, he reappeared with his prisoner, and Charlotte got her first glimpse of a real-life vampire.

So did everyone else, and cries and screams broke out across the courtroom.

Governor Mason banged his gavel onto the railing in front of him. "Silence!" He ordered, and slowly, the cries fizzled out. He beckoned the guard and prisoner forward. "Bring it in," he said.

The guard shoved the vampire ahead of him, leading it to a wooden box of sorts in the middle of the floor that Charlotte had once heard someone refer to as a defendant's cage. The guard ushered the vampire through the half door and locked it inside without a word. The box was only waist high, constructed to keep prisoners in place while allowing the audience to observe them. Usually, prisoners were left to stand there without any other restraints, but for this unique situation, Charlotte watched as the guard fastened a chain to the joint connecting the vampire's handcuffs and bolted it to a small iron ring on the top rail of the defendant's cage.

The vampire let itself be restrained. Its face remained emotionless even as the guard yanked on its chains to test their secureness.

Charlotte watched it all with wide eyes, feeling oddly mesmerized by the vampire. It looked almost human and it was sort of pretty, really, with its pale skin and dark hair and slender frame. Charlotte couldn't see any claws or fangs from where she was sitting, though she did catch a glimpse of its black eyes as its gaze traveled around the courtroom— the only discernible sign that the creature was not human.

"It's hideous, isn't it?" Nancy whispered next to her.

*Not really,* Charlotte thought with a frown. "I guess," she said.

"State your name," Govern Mason ordered down below, his eyes on the vampire before him.

"Aya," it spoke.

"Last name?"

A pause. "My clan name is Ayume, sir."

Governor Mason gestured to his secretary to make a note of it. "Then I, Governor Mason, Protector of Fortress Ashland, hereby call this tribunal to order." His words echoed throughout the courtroom. "Two days ago, survivors from Fortress Easthaven arrived at our gates," he continued. "With them was the accused—a vampire and known enemy to humankind, who was admitted inside our walls under some duress. Our duty now is to reach a decision about how to proceed. As has been our custom here at Ashland since Year Zero, we will listen to witness testimonies in support and opposition of the accused, after which time votes will be cast and a verdict will be reached." The governor glanced to his left. "Commander Ramirez, you volunteered to make an opening statement on behalf of the prosecution. The floor is yours."

Charlotte watched as the tattooed commander of the Guard stood up, shrinking slightly in her seat even though the imposing woman's attention was not on her.

"People of Ashland," she began. "Since long before Year Zero, vampires have been our mortal enemies. They require our blood to survive and they have attacked and murdered us ruthlessly throughout the ages. The creation of the morphs six years ago has not changed the nature of vampires. This creature standing before you now is a threat to our safety and to our future. Granting it asylum here would put the citizens of Ashland – yourselves and your children – in danger." She paused, glancing around the courtroom at the gathered crowd. "We have endured so much and lost so much because of vampires. Think back—remember your losses. Remember why the *Metamorphosis* vaccine was created in the first place. If we allow a vampire to live, or worse, allow it to coexist with us here at Ashland, we would be doing a grave disservice to all those who gave their lives to protect us from its kind, and we would be welcoming a predator into our midst. So, citizens of Ashland and members of the Council, I urge you to stand firm in the convictions we've held dear for generations and continue to put our safety and well being above any compassion you might feel for this creature and its plight." She paused as her gaze drifted to the row reserved for the Easthaven survivors, and even from her perch in the top row, Charlotte could see the tension in the commander's hands as she gripped the railing in front of her. "In conclusion, I ask that you find this creature guilty of that which it cannot deny: its nature as a blood drinker and killer of humans —its nature as a vampire."

She sat down to a chorus of *here, here!* and *kill the vampire!*

"Thank you, Commander Ramirez," Mason intoned, silencing the crowd. "And now for the defense." He turned to the right, gesturing towards the row of Easthaven survivors. "Marcus, you requested to give the opening statement on behalf of the vampire. The floor is yours."

As soon as the man in question stood up, a rash of hushed whispers broke out in the courtroom, and Governor Mason once more had to pound his gavel against the railing to call for silence.

"You didn't tell me that *he* was the Reaper from Easthaven!" Nancy squealed excitedly in Charlotte's ear.

Charlotte gave her friend a look. "I didn't know," she said. "He didn't come in with the rest of them." She looked around at all the people still pointing and gawking and surreptitiously whispering about the man. "Why is everyone so worked up about him?" She asked Nancy quietly.

"Seriously?" Her friend gave her a stupefied look. "That's *the* Captain Marcus, leader of the Elite Five," she revealed. "People say he's the strongest Reaper since Damon's time. They say he's singlehandedly killed more vampires than the rest of the Reapers combined."

Charlotte looked down at the man again and decided that she didn't doubt it. She'd seen Reapers before — first a man named Thom and then a woman named Rita, and as intimidating as they had been, neither of those Reapers had even come close to matching the intensity of this one. Captain Marcus, from his bearing to his unwavering, piercing gaze, looked every inch the notorious killer Nancy claimed he was.

*So why*, Charlotte wondered, *is he the one defending the vampire?*

As if in response to her unspoken question, the Reaper began to speak. "In my years of service to the Rangers, first as a soldier and later as a Reaper, I killed well over a hundred vampires," he said. "And of those kills, I never regretted a single one. I was brought up hating their kind just like the rest of you, taught that they are our enemies and should be shown no mercy. When I crossed paths with Aya shortly after the destruction of Fortress Easthaven, I only spared her life because I saw how effective she was at killing morphs and I sought to use her to my people's advantage. I blackmailed her into escorting us to Ashland, stole her heart, and inflicted physical pain on her in order to bend her to my will." There was a strange harshness creeping into his tone, one that Nancy could only describe as disgust. Whether it was directed at the vampire or himself was less certain.

"I treated her like a dog, and my intent was to kill her after she'd served her purpose. But things changed. For the first time in my life, I found myself working alongside a vampire instead of fighting one. Aya may not have been a willing ally at first, but from day one, she saved lives. She repeatedly put herself in harm's way to protect us, and many of the people you see sitting here —" he gestured to the Easthaven survivors "—are only here because of her." His gaze flickered briefly to the chained vampire. "And if you think that she acted as she did only to save herself, you are mistaken. A few months into our journey, we encountered a group of vampires. If Aya had given the word, they would have attacked and killed us, but she didn't. She protected us." He paused. "The vampires offered Aya a place in their group, but she declined their invitation. Why? Because she cared about us. She cared enough to throw away a chance to be with her own people in order to make sure we were safe. For that, I returned the heart I stole from her and told her to leave with them. She resisted at first, but I insisted, so she went." He paused, and even from her seat high in the courtroom, Nancy could see the Reaper's throat bob as he swallowed.

"But Aya came back," he went on. "She had her freedom and she'd found her own people, but in spite of that, she *came back*. People of Ashland: this vampire is only standing here before you because she chose to be loyal to me and to the survivors from Easthaven. She chose to be a guardian to us, and I speak for my entire group when I say that she is one of us. All I ask is that you give her the chance she deserves, the chance she's earned." He paused. "I'll conclude with one final thought," he added. "I've commanded many soldiers over the years, taken many men and women into combat. Among those hundreds of capable soldiers, a small number have stood out for their strength, their courage, their loyalty, and I count Aya among them." His gaze drifted towards the chained vampire, his eyes and voice softening in such a way that Charlotte got the impression that he was speaking more to her than to the court at large. "Vampire or not, there is no one I'd rather fight beside than her. I trust Aya with my life, and if I could take her place in this trial, I would. I, a Reaper, value her that much." He looked back towards the Council. "I ask that you open your ears to the testimonies you'll hear today and grant Aya asylum. She is already family in our eyes. Let her be so in yours."

There was silence in the courtroom when he finished speaking, and as Charlotte looked around at the gathered crowd, she saw a myriad of shocked, confused, and troubled faces. The chorus of support that had been audible after Commander Ramirez's opening statement was noticeably absent.

"Thank you, Marcus," Governor Mason stated. "Now we will here testimonies both in opposition of and on behalf of the accused."

The antis went first. There were four of them, all passionate speakers, all with tales of woe and horror caused by vampires. Charlotte found herself cringing at some of the gorier details, and it was easy to see that the older civilians shared her distaste.

"He knows how to pick them, I'll give him that," Nancy whispered when the third speaker, a boy of eighteen, finished telling the grizzly tale of how his baby sister had been sucked dry by a vampire when he was only eight years old.

Charlotte's brows wrinkled. "What are you talking about?" She whispered back.

"Governor Mason, of course," Nancy responded. "He may be a slime ball, but he made sure to pick speakers that everyone would sympathize with."

Charlotte processed that, frowning. "But he's supposed to be..." She struggled to remember the word. "...Impartial," she finished.

Nancy rolled her eyes. "Yeah, but it's not like he *wants* the vampire to have a fair chance at winning," she said. "And I don't blame him. I think Commander Ramirez is crazy for even letting it inside our walls."

Charlotte looked down at the vampire again, trying to view the situation from Nancy's perspective. In the end, though, she couldn't. The thing just didn't look evil.

"Order, order!" Mason was shouting, the loud smack of his gavel against the railing in front of him shaking Charlotte out of her thoughts.

Whatever the fourth speaker had said while she and Nancy were whispering had caused an uproar, but the din faded to a simmer in the wake of the governor's shouting.

"We will now hear from the defense," Mason continued, gesturing towards the Easthaven group. "You may begin."

The hair on Charlotte's neck rose as the two-faced man stood up, her mouth going dry with fear as she looked at him.

She wasn't the only one. Gasps and exclamations rippled through the courtroom, and within seconds, people were shouting for the guards to do something and hurling slander at the strange man. Cries of *morph!* and *vampire!* were the most numerous.

To Charlotte's surprise, it was Commander Ramirez who stood and called for order this time. The people quieted immediately, clearly more intimidated by the austere woman than by the governor. Charlotte shrunk back when she felt Ramirez's acidic glare travel over the row she and Nancy were occupying.

"That is enough," she said, the measured clip of her voice doing nothing to mask the coldness behind the words. "This court will not tolerate such behavior. Clio Jones is not on trial, and if any of you degrade the proceedings here by shouting obscenities and making a mockery of our judicial system, you will answer to me." She paused, her gaze scouring the crowd. "For those of you who are unaware, the man standing before you is *Lieutenant* Clio Jones, a respected soldier of the former Rangers who, like so many other brave hunters, volunteered to be a recipient of the *Metamorphosis* vaccine six years ago. Despite his altered appearance, Clio Jones remains human, as you can well see by his bearing. He is sound of mind and should be shown the respect he deserves. Reflect on what he has done in service to humanity and remember how *you* are expected to act at official proceedings such as this—lest I be forced to aid your memory." Her eyes flickered to the man in question. "Lieutenant," she said with a brief nod of her head, indicating that he could begin.

"Thank you, Commander Ramirez," Jones replied. He took a breath and surveyed the crowd. "*'Reflect on what he has done in service to humanity'*," he said, repeating the commander's words. "Insightful words. Wise words." He stepped out of the front row and onto the floor, beginning to walk around as he spoke. "Indeed, we should all reflect on our deeds." He paused before a row of observers, watching them calmly as they shrunk back from him. "Appearance can be jarring, I know," he said, stepping back and giving the squirming citizens some breathing room. "However, appearance is not what defines us." He paused. "Ever since I volunteered for the vaccine, people have looked on me with fear and mistrust, even people I once felt close to. I became the Mutt, and that was all anyone bothered to see." A flicker of pain crossed his mismatched eyes. "But this—" he said, gesturing to his face, "—never changed this." He pressed a hand to his heart. "I am still the man I was, just as Commander Ramirez said on my behalf moments ago, and I am not on trial." He continued walking. "However, if I were on trial, I would want you to judge me based on my deeds, on my actions, not on features that mutated beyond my control." He paused, turning to face the section where the Council members were seated. "Are there any among you who disagree? Are there any among you who think a person on trial ought to be judged and condemned according to their appearance instead of according to their character?"

Mason gave a dismissive wave. "We are not here to banter ethics and speak of philosophical matters, Lieutenant," he said, a slight sneer in his tone. "Make a relevant point or take a seat."

"I beg your indulgence," Jones replied smoothly. "What I am speaking of does have relevancy to this case, as you will see momentarily."

Mason leaned back. "I had better."

"People of Ashland, here is what I am getting at: take Commander Ramirez's words and apply them here, to Aya. Reflect on what she has done in service to humanity and judge her based on that instead of on her appearance." He slowed his steps. "You see, if Aya were human, this trial would not be happening. She would have been praised, lauded, considered a hero by all of you. Well, discard your prejudices! A pair of fangs doesn't change the fact that she *is* a hero. She may be different than us, but that does not make her evil. And I can prove it." He turned back to his comrades. "My fellow Easthaven citizens, I ask your help in a demonstration. I would like any of you who feels threatened or endangered by Aya to stand."

Silence descended in the courtroom as everyone waited, all eyes trained on the Easthaven citizens, but after a prolonged moment of bated breath, it became clear that no one was going to stand up.

"There you have it," Jones said slowly, punctuating each word for dramatic effect. "Not even one person." He paused before once more addressing his comrades. "All right. Let's change things up. I would now like any of you who owes your life to Aya to stand."

One by one, the Easthaven survivors rose from their seats, until every single one of them was standing. Charlotte's eyes widened at their show of solidarity.

Clio Jones turned to the gathered crowd and spread his arms open. "Ladies and gentlemen, there you have it: thirteen humans who owe their life to the vampire standing chained before you. Thirteen living examples of Aya's services to humanity." He paused, letting his words and the powerful visual display sink in.

*He's good at this*, Charlotte mused, feeling somewhat swayed herself.

"Thank you," Jones said, gesturing for the Easthaven group to retake their seats. Once they did, he continued. "Now, I realize that many of you feel that this is not enough, that by her mere nature as a vampire, Aya should be condemned. Well, that is where you are showing prejudice and greatly skewed bias, neither of which has a place in this courtroom." He turned to the Council members. "I have always believed in our judicial system and in the fairness of the courts. In fact, I found myself fascinated by trials growing up. I attended as many as I could and researched even more, and despite the various outcomes, there was one commonality between them all: each accused person was judged solely based on the evidence brought to light in court. Each was judged according to his own actions. I never saw a man judged for crimes committed by his family or friends, or by humanity at large." He arched a brow. "Am I mistaken about these conclusions?"

"Of course not," Mason answered, clearly irritated by the lieutenant. "Get to your point."

Charlotte saw the two-faced man's lips tilt up, as if he were vaguely amused by the governor's irritation.

"My point is this, people of Ashland," he said, turning back to face the gathering at large. "Judge Aya according to our laws and traditions. Just as this court would never condemn a man for the crimes of another, it stands to reason that this court also cannot condemn Aya for the crimes committed by other vampires. She is not on trial for her species; she is on trial for herself. The accounts of violence you've heard so far today from the opposition have been moving - poignant and tragic and terrible - but Aya was not responsible for any of those acts; do not let the pain and pity you feel for those who shared their stories transfer into hatred for Aya. Hear this instead: from almost the moment I met her, I knew Aya had a heart capable of great love and compassion, and she proved it time and again during our journey. I watched her save the lives of my fellow citizens and listened to her give prudent counsel to Captain Marcus. She has been a leader and a friend, and I am grateful to know her." He turned slightly to give the vampire a tender smile, and Charlotte, greatly surprised, saw a sheen of tears glistening in the vampire's dark eyes.

For a confusing moment, Charlotte felt sympathy for the vampire. She tried to harden her heart, tried to remember all the bad things about vampires, but all she could see was a girl on the verge of tears, and that was very, well...*human.*

"Before I give the floor to my comrades," Jones was saying, "I would like to once again urge this court to judge Aya based on her character and actions *alone.* Listen to the rest of the testimonies and then judge her based on only that which pertains specifically to her. Prove that this court has the integrity and impartiality I've always believed it to have. That is all."

Governor Mason was practically seething as Jones retook his seat. He took a moment to calm himself, then jerked his head towards the other Easthaven survivors. "The rest of you may offer your testimonies now," he said tersely.

The Easthaven citizens spoke amongst themselves for a moment, ostensibly to decide on an order for their testimonies, and after a brief deliberation, a short, curly-haired man stood up, his gaze skittering timidly around the courtroom. "My—my name is Adam," he said, and Charlotte wondered how someone who seemed so scared to speak in front of people had ever survived outside in the wild.

"My fiancée Savannah would be here with me, but she just gave birth to our daughter," the man went on. "She's better with words than I am, but I promised her I would speak for both of us today." He clasped his hands in front of him and took a breath. "Aya is, well...from the very first night we met her, she's been like a guardian angel to us," he said. "She protected us from a morph before she even knew who we were, and later, she defended us and was badly wounded while doing so. I offered her my blood as thanks, but she didn't take it. She didn't want any thanks at all." His voice grew stronger. "If it weren't for Aya, my daughter would never have been born. My family would have no future. We wouldn't even have our lives. It doesn't matter that she's a vampire; she *saved* us." He looked at the chained vampire. "Aya, I'll never be able to find the words to tell you how grateful I am for all you've done, but after speaking with Savannah, we both decided that no matter what happens here, Olivia will grow up to know you and all that you've done for us." He looked back towards the Council members and cleared his throat. "Er, thank you," he said. He sat down.

The next person to speak was the one-armed girl Charlotte had given the note to at the welcome dinner.

"I hated Aya when I first met her," she began, her hard voice booming throughout the courtroom. "So much so that I plotted behind my captain's back to kill her. I thought I was doing the right thing." She paused. "I spent most of my waking moments watching her while I waited for the opportune moment to get rid of her, but the more I watched her, the more I realized that killing her would be a shit idea."

"Language," Mason chastised, shooting the maimed girl a harsh look.

"Sorry." She cleared her throat. "I realized killing her would be a *disastrous* idea," she amended. "You see, I hate vampires just as much as all of you probably do, but Aya was one of the only things standing between us and death, and I begrudgingly had to admit that to myself. She fought for our lives just as hard as any human among our numbers, and she didn't hold it against us when we treated her like shit." She paused. "Like garbage, I mean," she corrected before Mason could once more call her out for inappropriate language. "Sorry. Anyway, Aya was never spiteful, never vindictive, and even in the beginning, when it was clear she wanted to bite Cap's head off for stealing her heart and basically enslaving her, Aya never raised a hand against me or anyone else. She just did her best to protect us. She's pretty much a saint, and if someone as stubborn as me can realize that, all of you should be able to, too."

"One arm or not, I would *not* want to get on her bad side," Nancy whispered in Charlotte's ear as the slim redhead retook her seat.

Charlotte didn't disagree. All of the Easthaven group were intimidating in their own way...except for maybe the small man named Adam, but even though public speaking hadn't been his forte, there had still been resilience in his gaze.

One by one, Charlotte listened as the other Easthaven survivors spoke on the vampire's behalf, and by the time the last one had taken their seat, it was clear that the atmosphere in the courtroom had changed. Many people were still whispering and pointing, but the fearful and hateful looks had dwindled down to a scant few, replaced by confusion and compassion.

"I think she's going to win," Charlotte admitted to her friend.

Nancy nodded. "I think you might be right."

Mason looked decidedly unhappy as he surveyed the crowd, but then, when a guard entered the room and came over to whisper something in his ear, his dissatisfaction turned to smugness. He held up a hand and the room quieted. "It has just come to my attention that there is one more who wishes to testify on behalf of the prosecution," he revealed. "I realize it is late in the proceedings, but I am inclined to honor this request. Please welcome Corporal Becker."

Charlotte watched as the doors at the far end of the courtroom opened and a handsome, muscular soldier walked in. She'd seen him before, and she knew who he was—everyone did. Rolfe Becker was an up-and-comer in the Guard, a man with lots of ambition who was admired by many. There were rumors that he'd been expecting to be promoted to captain, but Commander Ramirez had apparently given the open position to another candidate.

"Thank you for allowing me to testify," Becker said as he stopped next to the defendant's cage, giving a slight bow to Mason. He straightened and turned his aquiline features towards the vampire, sneering disdainfully as his eyes traveled over her. Then, without warning, he lunged forward and smacked her hard across the face, the sound of his palm striking her skin reverberating through the courtroom.

A pained gasp came from the vampire, echoed by others around the courtroom.

Captain Marcus was on his feet immediately, murder burning in his eyes just as the two-faced man shouted "objection!", but before either of them could do anything more, Becker once more struck the vampire, this time with more force and a closed fist, his knuckles drawing blood.

And then he got the reaction Charlotte was certain he'd been hoping for: the vampire hissed at him, her fangs descending and the veins beneath her eyes darkening as she shifted defensively away from the corporal.

A ripple of startled gasps spread through the courtroom.

Becker smiled coldly. "You see?" He said, stepping back from her. "Beneath her calm exterior, this is what she really is."

"Objection!" The two-faced man cried again, rising to his feet. One hand was on the railing in front of him while his free arm was restraining the Reaper. "The corporal is violating every code of conduct and is deliberately provoking the defendant. He should be held in contempt and dragged out of this courtroom."

"Overruled," Mason said evenly. "We are here today to draw out this vampire's true nature, and while Corporal Becker's methods may be unorthodox, I find them necessary."

The Reaper broke free of Jones's grasp and moved forward, his steel eyes glittering.

"One more step and I will hold *you* in contempt, Marcus," Mason threatened. He looked back at Becker. "You may continue as you deem fit."

The corporal gave another obsequious bow. "Thank you, Governor Mason." He turned his attention to the vampire, frowning slightly as he realized she'd retracted her fangs. "Holding back now, are we?" He taunted. "Well, it makes no matter. You've already showed us the anger that lurks just beneath that porcelain complexion." His handsome face roved the crowd. "Ladies and gentlemen, I ask you this: what do you think would have happened just now if this vampire had not been restrained?"

"Objection!" Jones cried again. His hazel eye was full of fury. "Becker is speculating on something that never occurred."

"Because the murderous creature is chained!" Becker shot back.

Once more, Mason said smugly, "Objection overruled."

Becker cocked a brow at the vampire. "Aya, is it?" He said. He waited for a beat but continued on when she gave no reply. "Tell me, then: while on this journey of yours, what form of nourishment sustained you?"

She pressed her lips together.

"You will answer the question," Mason commanded.

A muscle clenched in her jaw. "Blood."

Becker smiled. "*Human* blood?" He pressed.

"Yes," the vampire admitted reluctantly.

"Ah. And where did you get this human blood?" The corporal asked.

A pregnant pause followed his question. "Captain Marcus," she finally said.

Gasps and murmurs erupted throughout the courtroom, even as the Reaper sprang to his feet again. "I offered my blood to her!" He shouted. "She didn't take anything that wasn't freely given!"

Mason pounded the railing so hard Charlotte thought the gavel would shatter. "Guards, remove Marcus Warren from this courtroom immediately." He glared at Marcus with menace. "And if you resist, *Captain*, I will hold the rest of your friends in contempt as well."

For a moment it seemed that the Reaper would defy Mason, but before things could get more out of hand, Jones bent down and whispered something in the captain's ear. A second later, the Reaper gave a terse nod, and, still seething, reluctantly allowed himself to be led from the courtroom.

As soon as the door closed, Becker spoke again. "You see?" He said. "This vampire drank a Reaper's blood and bent him to her will. If we allow her to stay, how many others will she corrupt? How many of your children will bear her fang marks in their skin?"

"I would never drink from a child," the vampire said hotly, and even from her place in the back of the courtroom, Charlotte could see the way the vampire was shaking.

"You may claim that," Becker replied, "but answer me this: can you survive without blood?"

The vampire once more lapsed into stony silence.

Becker chuckled cruelly. "That's what I thought." Then, in a louder voice: "People of Ashland, this vampire has showed you her fangs. She has admitted to sinking those fangs into a human being, and she has not denied that she needs blood to survive." He addressed the vampire once more. "If you were granted asylum here, among an entirely human population, tell me: where would you get your blood from?"

"No one but Marcus," she insisted.

Becker raised a brow. "And after you've drained him?" He pressed. "Who will be your next victim?"

"I would never drain Marcus or anyone else!"

Becker shook his head. "Lies," he said contemptuously. "Didn't you all notice how pale our esteemed Reaper was? How ill and thin he looked? This vampire is slowly murdering him."

"Objection!" Clio Jones shouted, even as Governor Mason once again banged his gavel to silence him. "Captain Marcus is pale because of a medical procedure that Dr. Emmanuel Mason performed two days ago, and he is thin because of malnourishment due to harsh conditions out in the wilderness." He pointed to the row of Easthaven survivors. "Aya never drank from anyone but Marcus, and yet if you look at us, we are all recovering from a long period of malnourishment. The corporal's logic is inherently flawed."

"That may be," the governor intoned, "but he is still correct. This vampire needs blood to survive. Human blood." Before Jones could interject, Mason brought the gavel down on the railing one final time and then set it aside. "This court is now adjourned for deliberation. Once deliberation has concluded, we will reconvene and deliver our verdict."

A cacophony rose immediately in the wake of Mason' decision, but the governor ignored everyone and stood, the commanders and the Council following suit as was custom. A good number of them glanced back at the vampire as they filed out of the courtroom, some looking on her with pity, others with coldness.

Once they were gone, the same guard that had brought the vampire in came back and unlatched her chains from the defendant's cage, giving her a harsh tug as he led her out.

As people stood up in the rows below and around them, Charlotte lost view of the vampire, but she stared after her anyway, lost in thought.

"C'mon," Nancy said, nudging her. "We should leave." When Charlotte gave no move to do as she requested, Nancy frowned. "Hey— are you okay?"

Charlotte looked over at her friend. "I wish we hadn't come," she said truthfully. She'd wanted to see the spectacle, wanted to be entertained and have something to gossip about, but after witnessing the treatment of the vampire, Charlotte just felt sick to her stomach.

*She's going to lose,* she thought sadly. *And she doesn't deserve to.*

So much for the fairness of the courts.

. . . . . .

Marcus was pacing the narrow confines of his holding cell, trying to contain his anger, when the door at the far end of the cell block opened and a large female guard appeared, followed closely by Clio.

"Five minutes," she said to the hybrid, and then she left the two men alone, locking the outer door behind her.

Marcus stopped pacing and immediately strode forward and gripped the bars of his cell. "Well? What else did that dick of a corporal say?" He demanded.

Clio shook his head. "Too much," he said gravely. "It was all conjecture, but it was enough to reawaken some of the fear and suspicions we'd stamped out."

Marcus's knuckles whitened on the bars. "Did they reach a verdict?"

"Not yet." Clio's brows were drawn with concern. "I'm going to do my best to smooth things over, put words in the right ears."

Marcus released the bars with a growl of frustration and stepped back, placing his hands on his hips. "It won't fucking matter," he spat out. "Becker ruined our chances—you saw the effect his bullshit had on the crowd."

"On the crowd, yes, but not on the Council. Not completely, anyway. I think there were many there who realized that he was reaching, that he was trying to stir up trouble where there wasn't any. And don't forget one very important thing."

Marcus lifted his head. "What?" He said sharply.

"Aya didn't bite Becker. She didn't even attack him. She may have bared her fangs, but she held back, and people noticed."

Marcus exhaled. He was furious and tired and beyond worried, and he wanted to rip Becker limb from limb, but he trusted Clio. "Do you honestly think there's still a chance the votes will come down in our favor?" He asked, searching the hybrid's eyes. *Do you even think there was one to begin with?*

"I do," Clio said, his eyes clear of subterfuge. "We know that the governor will vote against Aya, and from what you and I have discussed of Commander Ramirez, it's fairly certain that she will as well, but you said that Commander Hale will support us. From what I observed, I also believe there's a chance that the men and women of the Council might be swayed to vote in Aya's favor. I aim to speak to as many of them as I can."

Marcus shook his head. "You won't be able to," he said. "Council chambers will remain closed throughout the deliberation process—it's standard procedure."

Clio didn't look bothered by this. "I know that, but there's always a way," he said confidently. Then, in a quieter voice, he added, "But we need to discuss what will happen if the votes are cast and the verdict is not what we hope."

Marcus could all but feel his heart freeze in his chest. "I am not going to let them execute her," he vowed with dark promise.

"Of course not," Clio said immediately. "But we need to have a game plan—a *smart* game plan. If we act rashly, we could all find ourselves turned out."

Marcus bit back a curse because he knew Clio was right. Ashland's slime ball of a governor would no doubt find a way to punish all of the Easthaven survivors if he could; Marcus apperceived that, despite how some of the citizens felt and despite appearances, Mason would be much happier if they'd never showed up at his gates, and he'd be looking for an opportunity to send them packing.

"What are you suggesting?" He asked the hybrid.

"If the tribunal moves for Aya's execution, we go along with it at the moment and then sneak Aya out before they have a chance to carry out her sentence."

Marcus nodded, contemplating that course of action. "And if someone sees us helping her escape?" He asked, knowing that if any of them were caught, it would be all the excuse Mason would need to have them all convicted of treason.

Clio gave him a half smile. "You're a Reaper, Marcus, and I wasn't known as the Wraith for no reason," he said. "No one will see us."

Despite his misgivings, Marcus did think Clio was right. But there was still another alternative, one that didn't have a simple answer.

"What if we lose and Mason orders Aya's immediate execution?" He asked, voicing the final, most disturbing possibility. "What then? How would we help her without damning our entire group?"

For once, Clio looked to be at a loss for words. He sighed, pinching the bridge of his nose with two long fingers. "I don't know, Marcus. I pray it doesn't come to that."

"But it might."

Clio gave him a weary glance. "I know. I've considered it. I originally thought you might be able to intervene, but…"

"But then Mason held me in fucking contempt," Marcus said miserably. He stepped forward and once more gripped the bars of his cell, realizing fully the ramifications of his earlier outburst. His stomach turned. "I won't be able to help her," he said as the truth dawned on him. "I'll be stuck here when they release the verdict, completely useless." He pressed his head against the bars. "Dammit!" He shouted. "I should've held my fucking temper earlier, but I…" He thought back to the look on Aya's face after Becker had struck her. "I couldn't."

"It's not your fault, Marcus. Becker was out of line and Mason acted disgracefully by letting him continue on as he did."

"Still."

The door at the end of the cellblock opened, cutting into their conversation, and the guard from earlier who'd let Clio in reappeared. "Time's up," she said. "Let's go."

Desperate, Marcus grabbed Clio's sleeve through the bars. "Clio, if…"

Clio stepped in close. "I will not let her die," he promised in a rushed whisper. "I'll figure something out."

"I said *let's go*," the guard repeated in irritation, crossing her arms across her expansive chest. Clio pulled Marcus's hand from his sleeve and headed towards the guard. "Coming, ma'am," he said.

Marcus listened to the sound of their retreating footsteps and then sank down wearily against the bars of his cell. He put his head in his hands, feeling a wave of hopelessness wash over him.

He trusted Clio, and he knew the hybrid would keep his word, but a sick sense of intuition told Marcus that it wouldn't matter, that Aya's fate was already sealed.

*And you're surprised by that?* The taunt came in the form of Stan's voice. *Hell, Marcus, did you really think you and some bloodsucker would get to live happily ever after or some shit? Get a grip. You're going to lose her, just like you lost Jocelyn, just like you lose everyone.*

Marcus squeezed his eyes shut. "Shut up," he said to Stan, to himself. "Just shut up." But no matter how hard he willed it, he could not silence his doubts.

. . . . .

Emmanuel stared in shock at the trio before him, not quite able to believe his eyes. "We thought…" He began, faltering.

Brianne adjusted the clawed arm of the massive morph where it hung about her shoulders, gritting her teeth as the thing's entire bulk shifted. "That we were dead?" She finished. "We nearly were. Multiple times."

"Brianne saved my life," Ian said. He was supporting the morph's other arm, and he looked fatigued beyond words. Bruises in various colors of healing distorted his face and arms, and his blue eyes were dulled by weariness. He took a breath, the exertion of holding the morph's weight audible in his strained inhale. "It all…it all went wrong. When we finally managed to find a superior and formulate a plan, the morphs saw through our trap and set one of their own. I'd been acting as bait, and they attacked me before I realized what was happening. If it hadn't been for Brianne…" He closed his eyes, trembling slightly. "I was outnumbered when she showed up," he went on. "I actually thought she was another morph at first, coming up from behind, but instead I got the best surprise of my life." There was humble admiration in his tone, and, beneath the fatigue, a trace of gratitude appeared on Ian's face. If the muscular soldier beside him noticed it, she didn't let on. "Brianne fought off the low-level morphs with me," Ian finished, "and your serum saved us after that. We had to use nearly twice what you'd hypothesized would be an adequate dosage to put this guy out."

All Emmanuel had to do to believe him was look at the unconscious monster draped between the two soldiers. His firsthand experience with morphs was limited, but he had never even imagined that they could be so large. This one was a wall of muscle, his torso nearly as thick as a tree trunk. And the size of the talons sprouting from the ends of his arms…

Emmanuel shuddered. "How long ago did you last dose him?"

"Before the sun went down yesterday," Brianne answered. "We used the last doses of your tranquilizers to do it."

A bolt of panic shot through Emmanuel. "So long ago?" They would need to act quickly, then. "Okay. Let's get him into one of the reinforced cells. Now." Judging by the morph's size and weight, even the powerful tranquilizers Emmanuel had given them wouldn't keep him out much longer. And if he woke up before he was securely chained…

Emmanuel didn't want to think of what would happen.

The strange group made their way as quickly as they could through the winding hallways and into the dungeon where Emmanuel had once kept Ian locked up. Ian and Brianne dragged their unconscious companion along with some level of difficulty, though neither of them complained. Amidst his anxiety, Emmanuel felt a twinge of guilt; he wanted to offer assistance, but even at his strongest, he knew he wouldn't be able to shoulder the morph's considerable weight.

When they made it to the dungeon, Emmanuel quickly unbolted the cell door and Brianne and Ian laid the morph inside, both soldiers releasing a pained exhale as their weary limbs were relieved of the thing's bulk.

"Wait," Emmanuel said as Brianne and Ian made to move away. "Bolt its wrists to the chains hanging from the wall," he instructed, just as an extra precaution. Neither soldier questioned him. Ian lifted its wrists one by one as Brianne secured them to the heavy metal rings. Once it was done and they'd cleared the cell, Emmanuel locked the cell door and stepped back, and only then did he take his first real exhale since Brianne and Ian's surprise return a half hour earlier.

"Where is Commander Ramirez?" Brianne asked, breaking the silence. It was the same question she'd uttered when Emmanuel had stepped into his lab and first found them, but this time, he chose to answer her.

"In the middle of a tribunal," Emmanuel said. "Disturbing her now would raise questions we can't afford to answer. We need to wait until deliberation has concluded before we speak with her."

"Who's on trial?" Ian asked from where he was slumped against the nearest wall.

"A vampire who arrived along with a group of survivors from Fortress Easthaven. They showed up at our gates a day or two after you left."

Brianne frowned. "Why hold a tribunal? In my experience, we execute vampires on sight."

"This one is…different," Emmanuel said, not really having the heart to get into it with the soldier. His guilt over Aya's fate was heavy enough; hearing yet another person condemn her wasn't something he was ready to stomach. There would be enough of that going on in the court upstairs…which was the main reason he'd decided not to attend the tribunal.

He changed the subject, bringing up a question he'd been meaning to ask much sooner. "What happened to Samar?"

Brianne and Ian's silence in the wake of his question spoke volumes, and Emmanuel knew, without hearing it, that the taciturn man must have met with a bad end.

"Samar is gone," Brianne finally said. She didn't offer anything further, and Emmanuel didn't push for answers.

"Dr. Mason…!"

The note of panic in Ian's voice drew their attention. The blued-eyed hunter was back on his feet, staring at the cell.

Inside the cell, the morph was also on its feet, staring back at them.

Emmanuel's throat went dry. There had been no warning, no indication that the thing had woken up, let alone moved. The fact that a creature so massive could be so silent made Emmanuel's blood run cold.

As did the fact that the morph had woken up so soon after they'd imprisoned it. *If we'd been a minute slower...*

"What should we do?" Ian breathed, looking at Emmanuel.

Emmanuel didn't pull his gaze from the morph. "Get two of my syringes and load them onto the extendable prod," he ordered quietly. "I'll go and fetch more of the tranquilizer from the other lab so we can put it out again." He would also bring a dose of his latest batch of the cure to inject it with after it was unconscious, because the sooner they were able to change this morph back into a human, the better. "And while I'm gone, Brianne...don't take your eyes off of it."

"I won't."

The morph's cold, black gaze shifted to Emmanuel. It pulled lightly on its chains, as if testing their secureness, though it made no move to try and break them. It simply tugged for a moment or two and then relaxed, and Emmanuel found its calmness deeply unsettling.

And then its lips pulled back and it spoke, a deep rumble full of threatening promise. *"Soon."*

The hairs began to rise on the nape of his neck, and Emmanuel stepped back as a chill spread through his body. Without another word, he turned and swiftly left the dungeon, waking purposely towards his old lab. Distance didn't grant him breathing room, however. *Soon* echoed after him, lapping at his heels like a shadow he couldn't shake.

*Soon. Soon. Soon.*

It had been a promise, Emmanuel knew, but it had also felt like a premonition, and while Emmanuel wasn't a superstitious man, he still found himself trembling at the terror that one ominous word had brought him.

．　　．　　．　　．　　．

The dawn was cold, and Quintus could see his soldiers' breath fogging in the air as they crested the hill. With a single gesture, he halted their march, then urged his horse on another step, peering down into the haze of the valley below.

While indistinct, he could see a mass of bodies moving towards them, and at their helm, another figure on horseback.

Satisfied, Quintus stilled his horse and waited. It didn't take long.

The morph on horseback reached Quintus first, and his maw widened into a grin. "Quintus," he rasped. "It's been a long time."

*Not long enough,* Quintus thought. He inclined his head. "Tertius."

The other elite gave a cackle. "Still as serious as ever, I see."

Quintus made no reply. Out of all the elites, Tertius was by far the cruelest and most vicious. Primus appreciated Tertius's bloodthirstiness and violence, as did Quintus, but the way Tertius relished the pain and misery of anyone who stood in his path was unprofessional.

Still, every leader needed a creature with a black heart by their side, someone capable and willing to do whatever needed to be done without hesitation or remorse.

Tertius was such a creature.

"How many are you?" Quintus asked, putting his dislike of the other elite aside.

"Two thousand strong," Tertius answered.

Quintus nodded. "Good." He had a similar number in his own army, and once they combined forces with Sextus, the second fortress would never stand against them. It would be over swiftly.

Quintus turned his horse. "We should ride for Sextus. It will take us days to reach our reconnaissance point."

Tertius grumbled, even as he urged his horse alongside Quintus's. "Primus should have set this task to the two of us. Sextus will be an unnecessary addition."

"Primus commanded it so."

"Yes, but Sextus is weak. He *feels.*" The derisive emphasis on the last word was impossible to miss.

Quintus was actually inclined to agree with Tertius; Sextus was certainly the most *human* of the elites, prone to embarrassing moments of emotion. However, he was clever and commanded a force double the size of any other elite. Like it or not, they needed him.

"He has the numbers," Quintus stated simply.

"True. But Septima would have made a better ally."

Quintus hid his distaste. "Septima is busy in the north."

"Unfortunate, but also true," Tertius conceded. He surveyed the landscape ahead of them. "How many days do you think it will take us to reach him?"

Quintus had only traveled the distance once before. "Forty, if we take into account the heavy snows."

Tertius gestured for one of his commanders. "Tell the army we ride for Sextus with haste. Anyone who lags behind us will be rended."

The commander nodded and moved away, no doubt to convey Tertius's orders.

Quintus frowned. "Most of our forces are on foot," he said. "It will take them longer than us to reach Sextus."

The grin reappeared on Tertius's face. "Not if they run." He dug a heel into his horse's flank. "I am impatient to begin. Blood and mayhem await us, Quintus."

Once more hiding his distaste, Quintus kicked at his own steed's flank. "Aye," he said, and he and Tertius rode forward, their combined army following behind them.

. . . . .

When the heavy doors opened and the guard led her once more into the courtroom, every seat was already filled, and there was an aura of hushed stillness in the air. Aya took a breath and dutifully followed, her eyes flitting only briefly towards her Easthaven friends. Clio gave her a small, tight-lipped smile, but between his palpable anxiety and the lack of Marcus's presence, Aya didn't have it in her to return the gesture.

She kept her eyes downcast for the remainder of her walk to the defendant's cage and waited meekly as the guard once more secured her wrists in chains, not wanting to see the expression on his face or anyone else's. She had hoped, earlier, that the testimonies on her behalf would soften the hearts of those who would soon judge her, but Corporal Becker had destroyed her chances. It was maddening, frustrating, and bitterly unfair. Were all these people really so blinded by hatred that they couldn't see how manipulative Becker had been?

Were they so deaf to truth that the words of her friends had had no impact on them?

Aya was afraid to look up and see the answers to those questions staring her in the face. But she had never been a coward, so she raised her eyes anyway, taking a breath to steel herself against the sea of disgusted faces she was sure to see.

To her immense surprise, however, many of the faces she saw were not filled with hatred or disgust, and some were even filled with compassion.

For the first time since Becker's appearance, Aya felt a tremor of hope fill her chest.

Which was precisely when Governor Mason banged his gavel. "I call this tribunal back to order," he said. His dark, unfriendly eyes met hers. "Aya of Clan Ayume, we have deliberated amongst ourselves and our now ready to reveal our votes and issue a verdict." He paused. "As is customary, the Council members will give their votes first."

Aya watched as a tall, robed older man stood up in the second row. "The men of the Council vote against the vampire and move for execution," he said, the words slipping as insipidly from his lips as if he'd been reciting a dry verse of poetry.

Aya swallowed, feeling the small glimmer of hope she'd felt begin to fade.

"Thank you, Councilman Orwell," Mason said. "A vote for execution. And now we turn to the women of the Council."

A plump, white-haired woman stood up with some measure of difficulty, her robes clinging to her expansive frame. "The women of the Council vote in favor of the vampire and move for amnesty," she said in a reedy voice before sinking heavily back down onto the bench.

The governor's full lips twisted unhappily. "Very well," he muttered. Then, in a louder voice, "Thank you, Councilwoman Tioga. A vote for amnesty." He shifted in his seat and shot a glare in Aya's direction. "As for my vote," he said without standing, "I side with the men of the Council and move for execution, which puts our count at two to one in favor of execution. Commander Hale, please share your vote."

A tall blond man stood up—Marcus's friend, if Aya remembered correctly. He was older but still very handsome, and he moved with a grave sense of dignity. Unlike the Council members who had delivered their votes, Commander Hale looked at her before he spoke, and there was kindness in his piercing blue eyes. "I side with the Councilwomen," he said, and Aya felt a wave of relief roll through her. "I vote in favor of the vampire and move for amnesty."

Governor Mason's face darkened, but only slightly, as if he'd been expecting Commander Hale to vote as he had. "It seems we now have a tie," he said. "Two votes in favor of execution and two votes in favor of amnesty." He turned slightly and looked at the final vote caster. "Commander Ramirez, I believe the deciding vote is yours."

Aya felt her throat go dry as the Latina woman she'd first seen through Marcus's memories stood up. Her brown eyes weren't filled with pain and anger as they had been when she'd been speaking with Marcus, but there was no warmth there, only an emptiness that stirred Aya's pity even as it roused her fear.

*She gave the opening statement against me,* Aya remembered with a sinking feeling. *And she blames me for what happened to her sister. My fate is sealed.*

There was silence in the courtroom, a silence that dragged on for some moments before Aya realized that it was due to the fact that the commander had not yet spoken. Confused, Aya looked briefly around the room before glancing back at the governor and lastly at the commander, meeting the other woman's unreadable gaze once more.

"Yes," Commander Ramirez finally said, breaking the silence. Her voice was haltingly quiet in the stillness of the courtroom. "The deciding vote is mine."

# Some Things Never Change

*It's true that some things never change, but it is also true that some things do change, and that is an important thing to remember as we make our way in this world.*
- Reflection taken from the teachings of the vampire historian Solomon of Clan Kovač, date unknown

. . . . .

Life had always been straightforward for Kai, even if her version of 'straightforward' didn't line up with everyone else's version of the word. She saw things in black and white and acted accordingly, and while that bothered some people, Kai didn't care. In fact, when she'd been a child, going against the grain had been more or less her default. If everyone said yes, she said no. If everyone decided a certain song was rubbish, she'd usually wind up humming the tune for days. She wasn't into conforming, and she usually didn't care what anyone else thought of her.

But there had been a few times, in her much younger years, that she *had* cared.

Once, when she was seven, she'd cut her own hair. She'd wanted to look like Bladed Jax, her comic book hero, and she'd been cutting her nails for years; surely, cutting hair should have been just as easy.

It wasn't.

She'd mangled it, and she'd been so embarrassed by the mess she'd made that she'd angrily shaved off all of the remaining tufts, only stopping when she was as bald as the day she'd been born. Then she'd sat down on the bathroom floor and cried.

Jocelyn had found her like that, hours later. She hadn't said anything at first—she'd just sat down next to Kai and draped her arms on her knees.

*"Aren't you gonna ask?" Kai had eventually mumbled.*

*Her sister had shrugged. "No. But you can tell me if you'd like to."*

*Kai had shaken her head. She didn't want to talk about it. "Everyone's gonna make fun of me," she'd muttered lamely.*

*Jocelyn had raised a brow. "Since when do you care what anyone thinks, sis?"*

*It had been Kai's turn to shrug. "I don't. But I also don't want to get laughed at."*

*At that, Jocelyn had stood up. "Well," she'd said, "I may not be able to grow your hair back, but I think I can help you with that."*

*And she'd picked up the scissors Kai had discarded and proceeded to cut off her long, beautiful hair. "See?" Jocelyn had said when she'd finished, giving Kai a smile and reaching out a hand to pull her to her feet. She pointed to their reflections in the mirror. "Now you're not the only one. We're a pair of trendsetters."*

*"But your hair was so pretty, Joc—"*

*Jocelyn had placed a hand on Kai's shoulder, her expression sobering. "It's just hair," she'd said. "It doesn't matter. And neither do bullies. Don't let them get to you, Kai, and don't let their teasing or your desire to be accepted convince you to do things you don't want to do. Just be yourself and remember that I love you the way you are."*

It was amazing, really; her sister had always known exactly what to say, what to do. She'd always been sure of herself, and as Kai stared at the vampire chained in the defendant's cage, feeling the press of everyone's eyes on her as they waited for her to give her vote, Kai wished that Jocelyn were there with her, guiding her.

But her sister was dead, just like her brother and parents. There was no one left to guide her or give her advice or stand beside her and place a reassuring hand on her shoulder. She was alone.

And she had a decision to make.

She could sense Mason's impatience, but she didn't care. He could wait, and so could the rest of them.

As she'd done countless times that day, Kai studied the vampire before her. She cut a somber figure, standing there in the dull, factory-made clothes they'd given all of the Easthaven survivors, chained to the railing in front of her. Her black eyes were watching Kai closely, waiting, and there was tension in her posture, but there was a calmness about her too, as if she'd resigned herself to accept whatever verdict was reached.

Kai's hands tightened into fists. Part of her wanted to take her revenge out on this vampire because of what she was, because of what her kind had done to the Ramirez family. But unlike Mason and the men of the Council, Kai wasn't deaf to the testimonies given on the vampire's behalf. When she'd forced herself to put aside her anger over Marcus's betrayal and listen with open ears to what the others had said, she'd reached the surprising conclusion that, in spite of what the bloodsucker was, this particular vampire had done nothing to deserve a death sentence.

But the alternative…

Kai pursed her lips. *What do I do?*

The question seemed to stretch out before her, reaching into the unseeable distance. Part of her wished she could consult Clio Jones about it—the hybrid seemed to possess an uncanny amount of intuition, and he certainly knew how to present a case to the court. But she couldn't talk to him, just like she couldn't consult her long dead sister.

Unbidden, though, Jocelyn's words to her seven-year-old self once more came to Kai.

*Don't let them convince you to do things you don't want to do. Just be yourself.*

And suddenly, Kai knew what her vote had to be.

She took a breath. "I cannot vote in favor of granting the vampire asylum," she said, her voice ringing out in the courtroom. Out of the corner of her eye, she saw the governor's face break into a smile, but it dimmed as she went on. "However," she continued, "in light of the testimonies heard today, I also cannot vote in favor of the vampire's execution. Therefore, I present a new vote." She ignored the gasps and murmurs and the way Mason's hand tightened on his gavel. "I vote for exile; I vote that the vampire be turned out." She paused, turning to face the Council members seated behind her. "I present this vote as a new alternative to asylum and execution, and I now urge you to reconsider your current votes."

"This is highly irregular, Commander Ramirez," Mason said, seething.

Kai didn't so much as blink. "Highly irregular, yes, but not unheard of. There is precedent for introducing an alternative sentence before all votes are cast. Would you like me to present you with examples?"

"No. I know which cases you're referring to." Still fuming, Mason closed his mouth and sat back in his chair, his face as dark as a bloodstain.

Kai waited, watching as the Council members turned to one another and discussed the new turn of events. She knew her move had been a gamble, but she also knew it had been the right thing to do. Now, at least, the vampire's fate was out of her hands.

Minutes went by, but finally, the deliberation ceased, and Council representatives Orwell and Tioga rose once more.

Councilman Orwell nodded to Councilwoman Tioga, giving her the floor. "The women of the Council retract our earlier vote and move for exile," she said.

Kai nodded, but her attention was focused on Orwell. After all, unless the men changed their vote, the vampire might still be executed.

The old man's eyes darted briefly to Mason before settling on Kai. "The men of the Council also retract our earlier vote and move for exile," he revealed.

Hiding her reaction, Kai once again nodded. "Thank you, Council members." She turned to Mason and Joben. "Governor? Commander?"

Joben spoke first. "I too retract my earlier vote and move for exile."

Mason, of course, merely shook his head, still livid.

Kai turned to the court at large. "Let the record now show that all votes are cast," she said. "Four to one in favor of exile. A majority vote has been reached."

For a moment, Kai thought that Mason would ignore trial procedure and mandate that the vampire be executed anyway, but instead, after shooting Kai the blackest glare he could muster, he raised his gavel one last time. "Aya of Clan Ayume, I hereby sentence you to be turned out. As is customary, you will be held overnight and released at dawn. Should you ever try to return to this fortress or seek refuge at any other human fortress, you will be executed for treason." He brought the gavel down with a final *thwack* and gestured for a guard. "Take her to a holding cell." He stood up. "This tribunal is now concluded," he finished, and he brushed by Kai without another word.

.   .   .   .   .

Enwezor made his way down the empty corridors with as much stealth as he could, looking around every corner before rounding it, walking on careful, silent feet. He even held his breath a few times when he thought he heard something or someone, but each time it proved to be no more than his imagination, which had always been more active than he would've liked and had refused to chill the fuck out after the ordeals of the trip west.

As he reached the corridor that contained the holding cells, Enwezor clutched the steel rod more tightly in his hands, preparing himself, but surprisingly, there was no one there when he rounded the final corner. The place was deserted, and the heavy door leading into the cellblock was unlocked.

Aya's cell was at the far end of the empty block, and the walk there was long and dark, the hall lit only by a few dim fluorescent lights. When Enwezor finally reached the vampire's cell, he drew in a breath.

"Clio?"

The hybrid and Aya were seated together on the floor and had been speaking in low tones, but they paused their conversation once they noticed Enwezor.

Enwezor lowered the steel rod. "Where…where's the guard?" He managed.

Clio smiled wanly at the makeshift weapon before meeting Enwezor's eyes. "I bribed him," he explained. "Though to be honest, he didn't need much persuading. He was at the trial and I don't think he agrees with how Aya was treated. He was very malleable when I asked for permission to keep her company tonight." Clio paused. "I assume that's why you're here as well?"

Enwezor nodded. "Yeah." He looked over at Aya. "I just…it seemed wrong that you'd be alone tonight."

The vampire gave him a smile. "That's very kind of you, Enwezor." She gestured to the cell door. "Please, come in. It's unlocked."

Enwezor moved forward and took a spot on the floor opposite Aya and Clio, leaning back against the wall. His mouth twisted as he looked at the vampire. "This isn't right," he muttered, his earlier anger resurfacing. "That trial was a joke."

Aya raised her shoulders in a slight shrug, but the gesture seemed somewhat forced. "Honestly," she said, "it turned out better than I was expecting it to."

Enwezor frowned at her choice of words. *Turned out.* "You know what it means, right? Your sentence?" He asked.

Aya gave a sidelong glance at Clio and nodded. "Yes," she answered softly. "I know what it means."

Enwezor looked at Clio. "And you're okay with this? You're okay with the fact that Aya can never again set foot in a human fortress—*any* human fortress?"

"Of course I'm not okay with it," the hybrid answered. "But my being unhappy doesn't change the verdict, Enwezor."

Enwezor crossed his arms and looked down at the floor. "I know that." He exhaled. "I just—"

"Well shit, who would've thought *I'd* be the one late to this little party?"

Enwezor blinked, startled to see Sloane standing just outside the cell. She opened the door and closed it behind her, then leaned back against it. "So, what's the plan?" She asked, directing the question at Clio.

Aya answered. "There's no plan, Sloane," she said. "I'm going to leave at dawn as I was ordered to, and I'll stay away."

Sloane waved an incredulous arm at Clio. "And you're just going to let her?"

Clio made a face. "Why does everyone keep insinuating that I have control over Aya's actions?"

"Because you're the boss," Sloane replied simply. "What you say goes."

A look of genuine surprise bloomed in Clio's hazel eye, and a moment later, he chuckled lightly. "That's a nice sentiment—especially coming from you, Sloane, but this is Aya's decision, and I respect it. You both should do the same."

Aya tucked a piece of hair behind her ear. "If I obey the verdict, then all of you will get to stay. You'll be safe, and you'll be with your own kind." Her gaze shifted between the three of them. "You all deserve that much and more, after everything you've been through."

"After everything *we've* been through," Enwezor corrected. "Don't exclude yourself, Aya. You're part of our group, too. We need to do what's right for everyone."

Sloane slid down to the ground and crossed her legs. "Zor's right," she said. "We're in this together, Fangs."

Aya smiled, and there was a nostalgic kind of sadness in it. "We were," she said. "But now things are different. We've all made sacrifices for each other in the past, and now it's my turn. As much as I want to stay with all of you, as much as I'll miss you, I'm doing this for us—so that we all can have a future."

Enwezor didn't know what to say. Aya's words contained an ugly amount of sense. "But where will you go?" He finally asked. "What will you do?"

"I'll go north," Aya answered with resolute immediacy, and Enwezor could tell from her tone that she'd reached that decision long before he'd gotten there. "I think I remember the way back to the place I parted course from the vampires. I'll try and reach them and then hopefully rejoin them."

"Are you sure that's what you want?" Sloane pressed.

Aya shifted. "Many of the vampires I was traveling with were kind," she said, hedging. "I will be glad to see them again. And I can't deny that my existence there will be easier than my existence would have been if I'd been granted asylum here," she added.

They all fell silent at that. No one could deny that she was right, after all.

Enwezor didn't know how long the silence had dragged on when a thought suddenly occurred to him. "Hey," he blurted out. "Where's Cap?"

"In Ashland's secondary prison block," Clio answered. "He was held in contempt, so he won't be released until the morning."

Enwezor's gaze darted involuntarily to Aya. "So that means…"

"Cap won't get to say goodbye," Sloane finished for him. She snorted. "Of all the bullshit I've witnessed in the last seventy-two hours, this might just take the cake. Mason is a fucking rat."

Clio's lips twitched. "I believe that's an insult to rats," he murmured.

Aya still hadn't said anything, and her eyes were carefully downcast. Enwezor felt a fresh stab of pity for the vampire. "Aya, do you want me to…I don't know…pass Cap a message or something?" He cringed at how juvenile his offer sounded. "Or, I mean, I could…" He trailed off.

Aya saved him from further verbal stumbling. "Thanks, Enwezor, but it's okay. Marcus and I are…bonded. I'll say goodbye to him in my own way."

Something in the way she said *bonded* made Enwezor think there was more to that particular story, but he didn't ask. It wasn't his place. "Okay," he said simply.

Their conversation drifted to other things then, with a little prompting from Clio, and soon the mood in the small cell was much lighter. Enwezor even managed to make Aya crack a smile at one point, which made him feel a little better about life.

He rested his head against the wall, thinking. It was funny, really, how easily conversation flowed between the four of them. It twisted this way and that, crossed all kinds of topics, and it never required any great amount of effort to keep it going. It reminded Enwezor of his school days, of the times he and his group of friends would loaf around and share their stolen pack of smokes. They could spend hours just sitting and talking, discussing dreams and sharing stories about everything and nothing, totally oblivious to the world outside of their little circle.

This felt like that.

Unlike his younger self, though, this time Enwezor recognized how lucky he was to have people in his life like Sloane, Clio, and Aya. Real friends weren't something you came by every other day, and they were something to be cherished—especially when you'd been to hell and back with them.

It made the pain of knowing that he'd be saying goodbye to one of them forever all the more acute.

Unfortunately, that wasn't the only pain Enwezor felt at that moment. The stiffness of his limbs had been a mild annoyance since he'd sat down in the cell, but now it was getting too difficult to ignore. He made a face and adjusted his legs. "Shit," he complained. "My legs are not fans of this floor."

Sloane shot him an incredulous look. "Really, Mule? You're complaining about the floor?" She shook her head and sighed. "Typical. We've been in Ashland for three days and the creature comforts have already made you soft."

Enwezor could feel himself getting hot around the ears. "Shut it, Sloane," he muttered. He was about to tell Clio to go stuff it, too, because he could see a tiny smirk on the hybrid's face, but then Clio reached behind him and pulled out two pillows. He tossed one to Enwezor and the other to Sloane. "Here," he said.

Enwezor tucked the pillow under his numb backside, instantly feeling a twinge of relief shoot down his legs. "I'm surprised they give you more than one pillow in these cells," he commented as he worked some feeling back into his limbs.

"They don't," Aya said. "Clio brought extras." She gave the hybrid a small smile. "I really didn't think we'd need them."

Clio returned her smile. "I told you they'd come." His voice softened. "That's what family does, Aya. They're there for each other— no matter how hard the floor is," he added, a good-humored twinkle flashing in his human eye.

Enwezor sighed. "You know, you're all impossible. I mean it." The sentiment would have been more believable if he hadn't smirked, but Enwezor couldn't help it; as much as it sometimes rankled him when Sloane needled at him, tonight he found it as annoying as he did endearing, and when he saw the way Aya had to bite back a laugh at Clio's comment, whatever sourness he might have felt dissipated entirely. Aya – sort of like Cap, Enwezor had come to realize – wasn't naturally disposed to be humorous, so it was always nice when someone made her smile or laugh. It was nice to see her happy.

*And now she's going to leave. Forever.*

Enwezor's smile faded, and for a moment he wondered how Cap must feel. Enwezor would miss Aya dearly, but Cap...well, none of them – not even Clio – had bonded with Aya the way Cap had. Enwezor didn't know exactly what had been going on between the two of them, but he knew it was something different, something deeper, than what Aya shared with the rest of them.

It was almost enough to make Enwezor ask Aya again if there wasn't something he could do, something he could give to Cap on her behalf, but as he saw how genuinely happy Aya looked at that moment, Enwezor decided against it. There was no reason to pull her out of her brief happiness and remind her of the fate that awaited her come morning.

So instead, Enwezor adjusted his pillow, sighed softly, and joined back into the conversation, forcing himself to forget about the world outside of their tiny cell and family, forcing himself to just *be* and to enjoy the dwindling time he had left with Aya.

And for a few wonderful, peaceful hours, he did.

. . . . .

When Joben wound his way to the back of the old archives room, Kai glanced over at him, and the look on her face made it clear that she wasn't happy to be disturbed—least of all by him.

She was sitting by herself at the conference table, a half empty bottle of scotch in front of her. That in of itself was surprising, given that liquor was banned and that Kai wasn't one for breaking rules, but her presence in the archives room at such an early hour of the day was even more surprising.

"I made it very clear that I wasn't to be disturbed unless there was an emergency," she said, looking back towards the pale dawn light coming in from the window. "Has something happened?"

Joben closed the door behind him and walked over to the table. "No," he said as he took a seat adjacent to Kai. "Nothing's happened. Brianne told me you were up here."

A muscle clenched in Kai's jaw, and she raised the bottle of scotch to her lips. She took a generous mouthful and then coughed as she swallowed it down. "What do you want, Joben?" She asked finally.

"First, to say how sorry I am about Samar. I know you were close."

"Yes," Kai answered simply. "We were." She glanced over at him, her brown eyes full of mistrust. "Why are you really here, Joben?"

*Direct as always.*

It was one of the many things he admired about the younger commander, although it made him sad to think that Kai found his condolences disingenuous, just a means to an end, when the reality was very much the opposite. He knew how hard it was to lose soldiers, and he knew what Kai must be going through—after all, he'd been in the business of losing soldiers for nearly as long as she'd been alive.

But trying to convince her that he was genuinely reaching out, one commander to another, would be useless; he knew, no matter what he said, that Kai wouldn't believe him. It was just how she was.

So he moved on. "The vampire is being escorted from the fortress," he said. "It's going smoothly, despite the light guard retinue. I must admit I'm surprised you only ordered three soldiers to escort her out."

Kai's lips twisted. "For whatever reason, this vampire clearly isn't willing to jeopardize the others' safety by making a scene, so I didn't see the point in creating an unnecessary fanfare. Three guards will suffice."

Joben nodded. "She has been rather…amenable to our laws."

"So it would appear." Kai's mouth tightened with impatience. "Was there anything else, Joben?"

Joben repressed a sigh and offered the young woman a polite smile. "No," he said, rising to his feet. "I just wanted to keep you informed."

Kai eyed him in a way that said she was seeing through his bullshit. "Right. Because Brianne and my own soldiers clearly couldn't have relayed that message themselves."

Joben stared back at her, not intimidated by her biting sarcasm. Kai may have been able to see through his bullshit, but he could just as easily see through her caustic demeanor. She was hurting, and for reasons he wasn't entirely comfortable admitting to, that fact bothered him.

"Kai," he started, placing his hands on top of the chair he'd just vacated. "I admire what you did in the courtroom yesterday. You may not be happy with yourself right now, but you saved an innocent life."

Genuine surprise flitted across Kai's face. "I thought you of all people would have been disappointed by my vote," she admitted. "You voted for the vampire's amnesty, after all. I didn't."

"No, although I did amend my vote later to coincide with yours." He paused. "Why *did* you introduce the alternative vote?"

He half expected her to bristle and become defensive, but she didn't. Kai's shapely eyebrows drew together. "You probably think it was because I didn't want to share a roof with a creature I despise, but it…it wasn't that." She looked up at him. "It would have been unjust to execute her, knowing what we now know, but I truly believe that her presence here would have caused chaos. Even if she wasn't directly responsible, she could have easily become a scapegoat or catalyst for others to engage in violence or criminal activity. Or Mason would have instigated something, which could have driven her or the Easthaven survivors to violence." She leaned back in her chair. "I was thinking about what was best for our people," she said.

Joben gave her a half smile. "I thought as much," he answered quietly. "And while I may not agree with all of your reasoning, I think your decision was good for Ashland."

Kai's lower lip trembled for a second and then relaxed, a small but telling reaction that prompted Joben to say one further thing.

"Your sister would have been proud," he added softly.

Kai took a breath before meeting his eyes, and when she did, her mask was fully in place. "Have a good day, Joben," she said in a measured tone. Whether she was suppressing anger or pain wasn't obvious, but Joben suspected it was the latter.

In a lot of ways, she reminded him of Marcus: cold, hard, and distrustful of the world. And beneath all that, consumed with suffering mostly of her own making.

Joben hoped that one day Kai might come to realize that there were people worth trusting, people worth opening up to, as Marcus had, but until then, all he could do was respect her boundaries.

"Enjoy your drink, Commander Ramirez," he said as he turned away. "That's a very fine vintage."

When he left the archives room, Joben closed the door behind him.

· · · · ·

The guards escorted her from Ashland in the early hours of the chilly, damp morning. Her friends were there, too, following behind her like a somber entourage as the guards led her to the very edge of Ashland's perimeter. No one spoke, and there was no sound other than the occasional squelch of muddy earth underfoot until they reached the outer gate and one of the guards unbarred the heavy metal door. "All right," he said. His gaze traveled briefly over Aya. "You can take a few minutes to say your goodbyes. Let us know when you're ready."

Aya nodded, grateful, and then she watched as all three of her guards stepped away, giving her and her family a respectful few feet of privacy.

Everyone was there, except, of course, for the one person who counted most, but Aya didn't allow herself to think about him. Not now.

She said her goodbyes to Panko, Bird, and Ralph first, followed by the two women she hadn't really gotten to know and the twins, and then Ed and Jillian.

Savannah and Adam came next, and although Aya knew Olivia wasn't with them because the infant was still in intensive care, she felt a stab of disappointment that she wouldn't get to see the newborn one last time.

"Hey, Aya," Savannah said, her brown eyes already filled with tears.

Aya looked at the couple for a long moment. They were the first two humans she had ever saved, and the first two to accept her into the group, and as such, they both had a special place in her heart. "Olivia is a lucky girl," she said, smiling in spite of her teary eyes. "You're going to make great parents."

That was it for Savannah. She started crying and threw her arms around Aya's neck. "I wish you didn't have to go," she sobbed. "It's so unfair. And I need you. Olivia needs you."

Aya pulled Savannah away gently and brushed the tears from her cheeks. "Olivia has you, Savannah. You'll be just fine."

Savannah's brown eyes flooded with fresh tears. "But what if I can't protect her on my own? What if I'm not strong enough?"

"Olivia is safe here, Savannah. You all are."

Savannah's expression clouded. "No," came her hushed response. "We're not. Not for long. Not when people find out what Olivia is."

Aya frowned. "What Olivia is…?" She repeated, mystified.

Before Savannah could speak, Adam was there. He gently peeled Savannah away, drawing her into his side. "You're right, Aya. We will be fine," he said firmly. And then more quietly, against Savannah's hair, "Don't burden Aya – she has enough of those already." He caught Aya's gaze. "We will be fine," he repeated. "But we will miss you."

Curiosity bloomed in Aya's chest, but she kept it restrained. "And I you," she answered simply, turning away before her emotions could get the better of her.

"Wait!" A voice called out.

Aya turned towards the sound, her eyes widening as she saw the slight frame of Dr. Emmanuel Mason pushing his way through the Easthaven survivors. He stopped in front of her, breathing hard, beads of perspiration dotting his forehead.

"Aya," he said once he managed to catch his breath. "I was worried I was too late." He held out his hand. "I wanted to give this to you before you left."

Aya took the small item from him, her eyebrows drawing together as she studied the unexpected gift.

It resembled a rather large locket made entirely of what looked to be a fine, braided metal. There was a clasp on the side and a metal loop on top, where a chain could be threaded through.

Aya was baffled.

"Open it," the doctor instructed.

She did, her fingers working at the clasp until the two halves opened. Then she sucked in a breath, her finger tracing over the delicate leather lining the inside as she realized what it was. She looked up at the doctor. "Is this...is this for my heart?"

Emmanuel nodded. "It's made of a very fine, reinforced steel mesh," he said. "The next person who makes the mistake of shooting at you will have a very difficult time piercing through it, I'd imagine."

Speechless, Aya untied the leather strings from around her neck and removed them from her worn out, damaged leather pouch. Then she placed the pouch inside the locket Dr. Mason had given her.

It fit perfectly.

Filled with gratitude, Aya gently redid the clasp and slipped the leather straps through the metal ring at the top of the locket. "I don't know what to say," she admitted as she secured the straps around her neck and ran her fingers over the sturdy yet delicate form of the metal locket.

Dr. Mason tried for a smile. "It's the least I could do after what you were put through here at Ashland, by my father and by others," he said, his brown eyes filled with guilt. "On behalf of all the decent people within these walls, I am so very, very sorry."

Aya reached out and squeezed his hand. "It's your kindness that I will remember, Dr. Mason. Not other people's hatred." She let go of his hand and gave him a smile. "Thank you," she said. "For everything."

The doctor nodded. "Safe travels, Aya," he replied, and then he turned and headed back towards the inner gate.

The last to come forward were Enwezor, Sloane, Clio, and Cody. The little girl seemed to realize that the grownups would want to say their goodbyes separately, so she walked up first, hugging Aya around the waist. "I'm glad you were with us," she said, her words slightly muffled since she spoke them against Aya's stomach. Then she pulled back and looked up, her amber eyes full of a maturity that didn't match her age. "I'm sorry," she said. "I always thought vampires were the bad ones, but now I know that humans can be just as bad."

Aya crouched down and placed a hand on the little girl's shoulder. "These people aren't bad people, Cody. They're just scared of what they don't understand."

"They should *get* to understand you, then," the young Reade insisted. "Being afraid of something just because you don't understand it doesn't make any sense."

Aya gave her a gentle smile. "You're right; it doesn't. But just remember that we were all like that when we first met, too—afraid of each other because we didn't understand. Give these people a chance, okay? Maybe, if they have people like you to show them the way, they'll learn."

Cody pouted, but she didn't argue. "Okay. But if you change your mind and want to come back and fight these guys, I'll be there."

"Thank you, Cody," she said, touched and a bit awed by the little girl's fierceness. *She'll be a force to reckon with one day, no doubt about it,* Aya mused as the little girl stepped away.

"Last chance," Sloane said as she materialized at Aya's side. "You sure you don't want us to do something—to find a way for you to stay?"

Aya looked over at the redhead and saw the same resolve that had been present in Cody's six-year-old eyes in Sloane's green ones, and she knew that if she gave the word, her friends would defend her, no matter the cost.

Which was why, as tempting as it was, Aya had to leave. She didn't want anyone else to get turned out because of her.

"No," she answered firmly. "My mind is made up." She gave Sloane the bravest smile she could muster. "Try not to worry about me. I won't be alone like before. I'll be with my own kind again."

Sloane pursed her lips and then shrugged. "All right, then," she relented. She punched Aya lightly in the shoulder. "Take care, Fangs."

"You too," Aya replied. "All of you," she added, looking at Enwezor and Clio.

Enwezor stepped forward and drew her into a tight hug. "I'm really gonna miss you, Aya," he said into her hair. "You stay safe out there, okay?"

"I will." Aya squeezed him tightly. "Goodbye, Enwezor." She took a deep breath and released him, turning at last to Clio.

But the hybrid had moved off to the side and was talking to the guards. A few moments later, he caught her eye and jogged over.

"Clio…" Aya felt her resilience faltering as she looked into the familiar warmth of his hazel eye. "I…it's time. I have to go."

He gave her a solemn nod, his expression full of compassion. "I know. The guards said it would be okay for me to walk you out." He extended his arm. "Ready when you are."

Beyond grateful for the added strength, Aya slipped her arm into his and turned to face the others. She gave them a tearful smile and waved, knowing that if she tried to speak, the words would come out as a garbled mess. So instead, she just took one final moment to memorize their faces and hoped that they all knew how much she cared for them and how much she would miss them. Then she turned back to Clio. "Ready," she lied.

Clio brought his other hand up and laid it on top of hers, giving her a gentle squeeze. Then he nodded to the guards and they raised the heavy crossbar and opened the door.

Aya didn't look back as they passed through the gate and into the pale light of the early morning. She just clung to Clio and let him guide her forward, relying on him to help her take the first painful steps away from the people she cared about.

She flinched at the sound of the door being closed behind them.

Clio gave her a moment to compose herself, and then he slowly began walking them forward, towards the edge of the forest.

They passed by the place Aya had been shot, and continued on, neither saying a word until they reached the tree line. When they did, Aya slipped her arm from Clio's and turned to face him.

"Thank you," she said tremulously. "I don't think I could have made it without you." She meant the words in reference to leaving Ashland, but in many ways, she meant them on a much deeper level. If it hadn't been for Clio's support, trust, and friendship over the long, arduous months of their journey, Aya wasn't sure that everything would have unfolded the way it had.

The hybrid gave her a tender smile. "You're one in a million, Aya. And our group wouldn't be here without you. No matter how far apart we are, that will never change." He pulled her to him, then, and Aya buried her face against his chest and wept, finally allowing herself to grieve for the family she was losing.

Clio let her cry, stroking her hair soothingly and holding her, being a pillar of strength for her one last time, and Aya clung to him until she was spent. When she finally pulled back enough to glance up at him, she was astonished to see that Clio's human eye was full of tears.

Chuckling softly, Clio brushed them away. "What?" He said. "You're not the only one ruing this goodbye."

Aya placed a hand over the hybrid's heart, feeling the slow, steady beat of it. "I wish things could have been different," she said, her voice broken and earnest. "I never imagined it would be so hard to leave a group of humans."

Clio covered her hand with his, the tender smile reappearing on his face. "The harder the goodbye, the luckier we are," he replied. "Not everyone gets to experience the kind of love and friendship that makes it this difficult to walk away."

Aya returned his smile. "Wise words as always," she murmured.

Clio shrugged and dropped his hand. "Just speaking from experience." The expression on the human side of his face sobered up. "I know you didn't want to talk about it last night, but I have to ask. What about Marcus?"

Aya's fingers moved automatically to the leather strings around her neck, and for the first time that morning, she allowed herself to reach out through their bond. There was a faint, directional pull to the north – strangely enough – but nothing else. The bond was quiet.

Loneliness began to seep in. "I'm grateful for the time we had," she answered truthfully. "But I always knew that we didn't have a future. Not in a world like this." She looked up at Clio. "Will you keep an eye on him, though? Just…make sure he's okay?"

Clio nodded. "Of course, Aya," he promised.

Aya blinked back a fresh wave of tears and nodded. There was nothing else to say, really.

Except for the obvious thing that she'd put off for as long as she could.

"Goodbye, Clio."

Clio pulled her into one final embrace. "Goodbye, Aya," he murmured. "It's been a true privilege getting to know you."

"You too," Aya answered, meaning it. Exhaling, she pulled back and then stood there for a moment, rooted in place. She'd lost everyone else, and she wasn't sure she had the strength to watch Clio turn his back on her and return to Ashland. She wasn't sure her heart could take it.

As usual, though, Clio seemed to sense what she needed. "You go on," he said. "I'll stay here and make sure you're safe."

His words managed to lift some of the weight from her shoulders, and she gave him a nod in reply, feeling marginally more able to cope with her departure. *Thank you, Clio*, she thought. *For everything.* Then she took a deep, steadying breath and headed into the forest.

She glanced back once, just before the trees swallowed up the clearing, and sure enough, Clio was still standing there, the early morning sun warming the human side of his face as he watched her.

Comforted slightly, Aya once more started forward, and this time she didn't look back.

· · · · ·

Being back in the woods was liberating, in a way. She'd spent her whole life there; being able to breathe the fresh air and see the sky overhead and feel the rustle of the wind felt like home.

Well, almost, anyway.

Aya didn't let herself think too much about what she was leaving behind as she started out on her new journey, not wanting to feel the pain and the loneliness that were already creeping into her mind and bones. So instead she closed her eyes and focused all her senses on the earth and her surroundings, homing all her energy on the gift she'd inherited from her grandmother.

She hadn't used it in months, but it was like slipping into a shirt she'd worn countless times—effortless, natural, comfortable. And while it may not have been the wisest move since seeing without eyes often drained her energy, it was a blessed distraction from the emotions roiling within her.

The ground, the trees, the air, the tug...

All at once, Aya paused. She'd been concentrating so much on her senses that she hadn't even realized she'd been moving towards that faint pull in her awareness until it blossomed into something that wasn't faint at all. It was solid, grounded, and real.

Aya opened her eyes.

And there he was, standing in front of her.

*Marcus.*

"How...?" She managed after a moment. She knew that Governor Mason had kept Marcus under lock and key, purposely, to ensure that the two of them wouldn't be allowed to say goodbye.

"Joben," Marcus answered. "He let me out late last night during the guard change."

The blond commander. Marcus's friend. That made sense, though it still didn't explain why Marcus was here.

"I'm sorry," he continued when she failed to say anything. He looked miserable. "I should've kept my cool, should've—"

"It wouldn't have mattered," Aya interjected, stepping towards him. She gave him a sad smile. "You and I both know that this was the only real solution."

Marcus scowled. "It shouldn't be," he muttered darkly.

Aya sighed. "None of that matters now. I'm just..." Her eyes flickered over his muscular frame, moving from his downturned lips to the boomerang and other weapons once more secured to his belt, down to his clean, military boots, already feeling the ache of their impending separation. "I'm glad you found a way to come say goodbye."

Marcus's hooded eyes met hers. "I'm not here to say goodbye, Aya. Not this time."

Confusion and surprise overtook her. "What are you saying?" She asked, although she could sense his answer in their bond and in the way he was looking at her.

"You're heading north," he guessed, "to meet up with the vampires?"

Aya pressed her lips together. "That was my plan, yes."

Marcus nodded, pursing his lips. "If you want to do that, you can, but I wanted you to know that there's another option."

It was then that Aya saw the large knapsack resting on the ground by Marcus's feet. Her eyes widened as she realized the full implication of its presence. "You..." Her voice faltered. "You'd leave your people for me?"

His steel eyes softened. "I love you, Aya. Staying here without you..." He shook his head. "I don't want that. I've lost you twice. I don't think I can handle losing you a third time."

Aya choked back a sob of happiness. Marcus loved her. He *loved* her. She'd wanted to hear those words for so long, wanted to know it wasn't just the bond connecting them. And here was proof. He loved her, and he was willing to give up everything he knew so that they could have a chance at a future. Together.

Aya couldn't speak past the emotions choking her.

Marcus closed the distance between them and brushed the tears from her eyes. "But if you'd rather go and be with your own kind, I won't stop you," he said, voice heavy. "I just...I wanted you to know that this time, you have a choice."

Aya knew he meant it. And she also knew what her answer was. "Where will we go?" She asked, her voice still thick with emotion.

The way the tension eased from Marcus's brow and shoulders was enough to make Aya laugh out loud.

She reached up and tenderly stroked the side of his face. "I love you too, Marcus. Did you really think, given the choice, that I would choose to be with anyone else?"

The boyish smile she was beginning to grow very fond of appeared on his face. "The thought did cross my mind." He leaned down and kissed her, briefly, sweetly. "But I am sure as shit relieved that you didn't."

Aya stifled the urge to roll her eyes at his crassness. "So," she repeated. "Where will we go?"

Marcus was quiet for a moment. "There's this...well, I don't know if it's there anymore, but there was this town, west of here, on the ocean. It's where I was born, where my mother grew up..." His eyes clouded over for a moment. "Like I said," he went on, "I don't know if it's still there, but I've always wanted to go back. It was a—a good place. A peaceful place."

A pang went through Aya, a feeling that dimmed the rosiness she'd felt moments earlier. "Do you think it's even possible that we can find peace in this world?" She asked quietly.

Given everything they'd been through, given all of the omens that promised the worst wasn't over, peace seemed like something far, far from tangible.

"I think…" Marcus gave a slow, sad shrug. "I think things might get worse, that there might be awful times coming for all of us, but I still hope we can, yeah. And I'd rather try to find that peace with you than with anyone else."

Peace. With Marcus. Near the ocean. Aya had never seen an ocean before, but she'd heard others speak of it. Endless water stretching far out into the horizon, the sound of waves breaking on the shore, the smell of salt…it had always sounded a bit too calm and serene for Aya's tastes when she'd been a child, but now…

Now it sounded perfect.

"Let's go," she decided.

Marcus's expression brightened. "Really?"

Aya nodded. "Yes. It sounds like a beautiful place to make a home."

Marcus smiled then, really and truly smiled, and then he picked up the knapsack he'd brought and hoisted it onto his shoulders. Aya reached out her hand, and Marcus took it. "Okay, then," he said, gaze moving towards the distance they would now have to cover. "The ocean it is."

In answer, Aya threaded her fingers through his.

Marcus glanced over at her. "Ready?" He asked.

*I've been ready since long before you asked, Marcus,* she thought. She smiled. "Ready."

And hand in hand, with the morning sun at their backs, they headed west.

# THE END

# Acknowledgments

Many thanks to the team at Black Rose Writing for once again helping me complete and bring to life a project close to my heart, and many thanks to the friends and family members who read this and gave me feedback and motivation as I wrote and edited this story. Working on this book during the challenging times of 2020 was difficult, but also served as a much-needed escape for me during self-quarantine. While the other facets of my life were shutting down or put on hold, I was still able to travel with Aya, Marcus, Clio, and the TWP gang. It really drove home the idea that our imaginations are miraculous, limitless places, and that no matter what is going on in the physical world, no one can strip that from us. I hope that those of you who read this book can find an escape in the story and the characters the way that I have. Stay safe, stay healthy, and dream on. And as always, thank you for your support.

Interested in seeing sneak peeks of the TWP world and what's coming? Follow me on Instagram @gmdwrites to stay up to date!

# Note from the Author

Word-of-mouth is crucial for any author to succeed. If you enjoyed *The Western Passage: Arrival,* please leave a review online—anywhere you are able. Even if it's just a sentence or two. It would make all the difference and would be very much appreciated.

Thanks!
G. DiCarlo

# About the Author

Author G. DiCarlo is a musician who spends most of her time performing, teaching, and conducting. In addition to music and the violin, writing has become a great passion for her. *The Western Passage: Arrival* is her second published novel and a sequel to her debut novel, *The Western Passage: Exodus.*

Thank you so much for reading one of our **G. DiCarlo's** novels. If you enjoyed the experience, please check out Part One of *The Western Passage* series!

*The Western Passage: Exodus*

A thousand miles of wilderness. Innumerable dangers. Uneasy alliances. A bond forged in blood. The odds are great, and survival has never been more uncertain.

Vampires and humans have always been bitter enemies, destined to push each other to extinction. But when a group of scientists develops a genetic enhancement meant to boost the effectiveness of human hunters, tragic results threaten to bring about the destruction of vampires and humans alike.

After the fallout of Year Zero and rise of mutated hybrids known as morphs, the remaining humans retreat into five fortresses.

All seems well until Easthaven is attacked in an assault that leaves only thirty survivors. Enter Marcus Warren, one of the most powerful hunters in existence. Reluctantly, Marcus assumes leadership and decides that the group's only chance of survival is to cross a thousand miles of wilderness to Ashland.

Forced to trust a hybrid named Clio and a vampire called Aya, Marcus and the others set out. Dangers lurk everywhere, and enemies seem destined to destroy them...if they don't destroy each other first.

CPSIA information can be obtained
at www.ICGtesting.com
Printed in the USA
LVHW041030171120
671900LV00003B/125